MW00898742

THE DEMON'S APPRENTICE

BY BEN REEDER

The Demon's Apprentice

The Demon's Apprentice

Copyright © 2014 Ben Reeder

Cover art by Angela Gulick.

Model photo by Jetrel/Bigstock.com

Other books by Ben Reeder:

The Demon's Apprentice series:

The Demon's Apprentice

Page of Swords (February, 2015)

The Zompoc Survivor series:

Zompoc Survivor: Exodus

Zompoc Survivor: Inferno

Zompoc Survivor: Odyssey (January, 2015)

Dedication

Peter Paddon, may your journey through the Summerland be pleasant.

Musaba, wherever you are, may there always be plenty of food and a warm place to sleep.

You are both missed.

Acknowledgements (*new material in italics*)

Writing is a solitary craft, but writing a *book* is a process that requires help from a lot of other people. Without them, this story would still be languishing on my hard drive, and not be nearly as good.

As always, first thinks have to go to my girlfriend Randi, who put up with this process from beginning to end for this story and many others that never got told.

Musaba, my trusty writing partner. You grew up on this book, almost literally, from kitten to 10 pound orange furball, perched on my arm through many late nights trying to get it right. *I miss you, big guy.*

Greg Price, thank you for helping me find the starting point for this story, and all your input from the first chapter until the last.

Laura Davis, my editor, you did a thankless job that REALLY needed doing. You kept the colors straight, caught all the ripples, and helped make this book as good as it is.

Leah Walcott and Miranda Johnson, you were Chance's first true believers. You were my first fans, and you helped me believe when believing was hard.

Jason, Cherie and my friends in the Living Myth LARP, you guys are awesome. Thanks for your support and encouragement, and helping me blow off steam while I was trying to get this done.

My best friend Roanen Barron, I finally caught my own contrail. Thanks for helping me keep my eyes on the sky.

Finally, my publisher, Peter Paddon. Thanks for having faith in this story, and your patience with a first-time author's inexperience. *Peter, you have passed on from this world. Thank you once again for giving me a chance. You will be missed.*

Special thanks to Angela Gulick for breathing new life into the cover concept. You exceeded my expectations.

Chapter 1

~ Free will above all, this you shall not violate. ~ The First Rule of Magic.

Friday afternoons are always the worst when you work for a demon. My boss did a booming business in desperation measures before everyone's date night, or the official start of their weekend, or whatever it means to whoever it is. I looked over at him as he drove the borrowed school district van, his eyes bright with anticipation of the payoff he'd be getting at the end of the day. Right now, he looked like a plump, middle-aged geek in a pale green polyester shirt and black slacks. Glasses and a receding hairline completed the harmless teacher look. At least until you looked at his eyes. There was a gleam there that wasn't human, wasn't healthy. He could sense the desperation in the air even better than I could. The difference between us was, he enjoyed it, and it showed in those eyes.

I called him my boss, but in truth, he was my Master, and I hated him for that. So, in my own head, at least, I didn't give him the title. It'd been three years since he'd had any access to my mind, but he hadn't figured that out. I'd been letting him catch a steady drone of despair to make him think I was still his broken, beaten slave with occasional rebellious thoughts, and he let me keep them. He let me wish I could be free, but he didn't think I had any possibility of it, and that's what he liked: the sheer hopelessness of the situation. Yeah, the bastard dug that. He would. The boss stopped the van and turned to me.

"You have four deals at Lincoln Heights High School. Be quick about it. We have another four in the business district before six o'clock," he shoved me toward the door.

"Yes, Master," I answered meekly, and got out of the van. I caught a quick glimpse of myself in the reflection of the window as I closed the door. A teenager with unruly, greasy curls of black hair that hung down to his shoulders, a mouth that almost never smiled and dark, hateful eyes stared back at me. The boss hit the gas as soon as the door slammed shut, and I watched the beige minivan pull away. He'd be hidden nearby, where he could keep tabs on me without scaring off any of my marks. With its school district plates, it was the perfect cover for what we were doing. Who was going to question what a school vehicle was doing near a school? I checked the various amulets, talismans, and charms that I'd whipped up over the past week. All of them were ready, each pumped with just a little bit more essence than they needed to work. I stuck my hands in the pockets of my leather jacket and took off for the first meet at the nearby park.

In the world I lived in, I was what was known as a warlock: a person who used dark magick. It's not very far from the safe and sane world most people know. Pretty much right underneath it, really. Right around the corner, and just at the edge of your vision. My world had rules, just like a normal person's, and I broke most of them at my Master's command. I lied, I cheated, and I stole from people every day. And I was good at it. Since I was a human working for him, I could also get close to places he couldn't, like most schools. If you look, you can find some kind of holy ground, usually a church, less than a mile from most schools. Demons tended to get pretty toasty, pretty quick when they got closer than three miles from holy ground. That meant job security for me.

I'd done business with the girl I was about to meet before, and I knew the boss almost had her where he wanted her. A few more deals like this, and he would have controlling interest. Lucinda was a vain little blonde who figured out really quickly what she wanted in life: love. Not to *be* in love, but to have men fall in love with her. I had trolled her during one of my online crawls in a Wicca forum a couple of years ago when she'd asked for a love spell. The practicing Wiccans had nailed her from her opening line, when she'd asked if there were any "real" witches in the room, and when she asked for a love spell, they all turned her down. I offered her exactly what she wanted, and she didn't even think twice about saying yes.

Today made the fifth deal Lucinda had cut with me. I saw her sitting at the usual park bench, almost-wearing some sort of white plastic outfit that looked very expensive and seriously slutty, with matching knee-high boots perching on uncomfortably high, narrow-looking heels. Those boots weren't made for walkin'. I sat down beside her without asking.

"Hi, Chance," she purred.

6

"You have the money?"

"Yeah," she said, popping her gum and straightening.

I looked over at her and blinked in surprise when I got an eyeful of her profile. Lucinda had new boobs, probably courtesy of her latest mark, a wealthy friend of her dad's.

"Why's it so expensive now?" she whined. I had jacked the price up by a few hundred dollars on the sly, but the boss had been upping it, too. She had it to spare, so I didn't feel too bad about it.

"Takes more power to keep that many guys in love with you at the same time, even with the new tits," I lied. "If you can't afford it, I can always undo some of the other spells."

"I can handle the price!" she said with a sly smile. "Maybe we can work out a trade. I can make it worth your while." She pointed her breasts at me and gave me a sultry look.

I just gestured for the money. "I don't do casual sex," I growled as she slid a thick envelope across the space between us. I slipped it into my jacket pocket and pulled out her charm, a little gold locket she'd given me earlier in the week. I dropped it into her palm and wrapped her hand up in mine. She smiled and shivered a little at the contact, then looked at me with wide eyes, looking like an innocent little girl. I didn't buy it.

"*Amoricae insinadra voluptos*" I intoned in pseudo-Latin. I let the meaning I'd assigned the words in my head bring my mind into the right state to pour the energy into the charm. As the magick flowed, I also extracted the *real* price, a small portion of her soul, into the heavy black amulet I wore around my neck.

She jerked as she felt the small emptiness open up inside her. She could feel the wound I left on her spirit, but she didn't understand the loss. The more of her soul essence I took, the less joy she'd be able to feel, until she was completely drained of the spark of life that allowed her to feel *anything* good, including love. Even now, she wasn't truly happy with the fake love of four men; she wanted even more. A couple more deals, and she would belong to the boss.

While I was taking the piece of her soul, I felt the blackness creeping onto my own. What I was doing was wrong in so many ways, even if I didn't have much of a choice. I couldn't take a piece of someone's soul without polluting my own in the process. Meanwhile, the boss was technically off the hook for everything I did in his name. As the spiritual fee filled the amulet, I siphoned off a tiny sliver into another charm I wore etched into my skin, a Lemurian blood tattoo that I'd carved one into the soft skin along inside of my right biceps. I was already in for a spiritual ass kicking, so a little extra bad karma wasn't a real problem for me. Besides, if everything went the way I planned tonight, my mystical embezzling would pay off in spades.

"There," I said, as the last trickles of essence flowed into the two charms. "It's ready to go. Same as always, say the guy's name while the charm is touching his skin, and he's yours."

"Great, thanks! This time, I'm going to make Daddy's bank president fall in love with me!" she gushed, full of her own plans. "I'm going to be rich! I think I'm going to let him marry me, when I get old enough!" And there it was, the thing that ate at me the worst; Lucy was only sixteen. The boss liked his victims young. I nodded and gestured for her to leave, and she walked away unsteadily on her skyscraper heels.

The boss was a demon Count, name of Dulka. He made his living on people's misery, trading them a little bit of power for the low, low cost of their souls. Soul essence was the going currency in the Underrealms, and a whole soul was like a self-regenerating supply of power, at least as far as I understood. It had been about five hundred years or so since demons were able to just pop up and offer deals to humans. Something to do with some guy named Faust during the Middle Ages or Renaissance who screwed everything up for them. It was a touchy subject for demons. The boss didn't talk about it much.

Even though demons couldn't just show up to do the deal directly for a person's soul any more, they could still be summoned, and people could still offer them their souls in return for stuff. But demons didn't like waiting around for someone to find the right grimoire or summoning ritual. Patience was a virtue, and demons avoided that like drinking holy water. So, instead of waiting around, they used people like me. Me, I'm Chance Fortunato. I'm a familiar, which is just a fancy word for a slave. I pimp souls for him and do his dirty work.

I hated my job. I hated my whole life. I leaned back on the bench, and mentally kicked my own ass for a minute or two before I got up and headed to the next meet across from Lincoln Heights High School. After years of practice, I'm very good at temptation and self-flagellation.

A few minutes later, I was watching the front of the high school from across the street, waiting for my next mark. Riker McKane was a new kid in town. He was already into us for several charms, some minor glamours that made girls hot for him, and some heavier augmentations that gave him extra speed and strength. He'd contacted us wanting to beef up the physical augments even more, and out of professional habit, I was curious about that. With the augmentations he had requested, he would be hitting the top end of human limits. These charms had some serious punch to them. What could make him need that much power? Knowing that might give me some leverage on him.

The last bell rang, and kids started pouring out the front doors, backpacks slung over their shoulders, talking, laughing, and planning what they were going to do for the weekend. I let my eyes un-focus and opened my third eye, the source of most of my mystic senses, just a fraction. Dulka had forced it open when I was seven, so I could use magick for him. I didn't know exactly how it worked, but it let me feel magick, and use it. Most times, I kept it nailed shut to keep Dulka out of my head. But when I opened it up a little, I could also see peoples' auras: the energy fields around people. Moods, desires, big events, they all left their mark on the aura. I could tell a lot about a person from looking at one. My senses shifted a fraction, and I *Saw* them.

They were beautiful. Bright, shining, full of life, innocent in a way I would never be again. There were only tiny spots on some of their auras: little things like jealousy or minor greed. A lot of them were bright with lust, and that had a beauty all its own. I held my own hand up and looked at the red and black swirl of crap that oozed through my aura, the stain of eight years of doing Dulka's dirty work. I blinked and re-focused once I saw the dark blotch that covered McKane's aura. I recognized my own work when I saw it. Riker saw me and broke away from a gaggle of adoring girls to cut across the street. I faded back into the shadows and waited for him to come to me.

"You got my payment?" I asked as he stepped into the alleyway.

"Not till I see the goods," he countered with a sneer. "You lay it on me, and if it's up to par, then you get paid, punk. Do we have an understanding?"

I'd seen *this* before. The idiot was drunk on his own power, and he wasn't thinking. You'd figure people would learn. "No, we don't. Let me lay it down for you, McKane. You don't get buffed until I get paid, just like before."

"I'm changing the deal. I couldn't boot your ass into next week last time, and now I can. So you hand over the goods, and I'll decide what I pay you, if I pay you a damn thing!"

"Look, that wasn't the deal, man," I said, letting a little fake desperation creep into my voice. "I'm outta here!" I took a step back to make it look real.

Just like I'd hoped, he reached out and grabbed the collar of my leather jacket with both hands. He yanked me to him, and I let myself go with the pull so I could be in contact with him.

"It's the deal now, asshole. You fork over the damn charm right now, or I beat it out of you!" he hissed in my face.

"*Vox probrum, aufero quod transfero volo*" I whispered while he was threatening me. In a heartbeat, the counter-spell removed all of the charms I had already put on him, and transferred them to me. On impulse, I reached into my pocket and activated the charm I had ready for him today. Added together, all of those charms made me stronger and faster than the average steroidal ox. At least, for a while. They were designed to crap out eventually, so the client would have to fork over more of their soul for the next slice of brawn.

I reached up and grabbed his hands from my collar and bent his wrists backward until he cried out and fell to his knees in front of me. I gave him a wicked grin as I leaned over him. Now he was in the shoes of the people he'd probably been lording it over all week. I liked the irony.

"You are seriously stupid, McKane. I *laid* those charms on you. Did you think I couldn't turn the damn things off when I wanted to? You don't change the deal. You don't have any power except what *I* give you, and I can take it back whenever the hell I want. I can also *change* the deal whenever I want to, so here's how it's gonna go: the price is tripled, and until you come up with the cash, I keep all of the charms I laid on you. Do we have an understanding?" I pushed a little harder against his hands as I finished.

"Ow, shit, yeah! Ow! Ow!" He yelped, and I let him go. He hurried toward the mouth of the alley, cradling his hands close to his chest.

I waited until he was gone to shudder in revulsion. While I had him on his knees, the activated amulet had been draining his soul essence, the real payment Dulka wanted. The boss would be happy to get something for nothing. I still ended up with another stain on my soul, Dulka got paid in essence, and McKane was out all of his charms and glamours. Only the hijacked charms and the tiny bit of essence that I'd drained into my own blood charm had made this deal work for me.

The other two deals were new people, one a protection charm for a wanna-be sorcerer, and the other, a persuasion charm for a girl to make the cheerleading squad. Both took only a few minutes each, and then I was on my way toward the pickup point.

Chapter 2

~ The only sure way to avoid treachery is to do it first. ~ Infernal proverb

The sun had gone down a couple of hours ago, and I was sitting in the passenger seat of the van again, as Dulka drove us back from the business district.

Working New Essex's downtown was a lot easier on me than doing the schools in the suburbs. At least there, my marks were old enough to know better, and I could make myself feel better by thinking that they knew the risks. Sometimes, it even worked, and I came back feeling less slimy. Mostly, though, I just felt like crap at the end of the day.

My father's black Lincoln Town Car was waiting in the back parking lot when we pulled back into Truman High School. I slipped out of the van and headed for the doors as soon as the van stopped. My father was at Dulka's side before I even cleared the seat leather. He probably had business he needed some help with. In Stefanos "the Spartan" Fortunato's line of work, that usually meant he needed someone killed or maimed, and Dulka was his go-to guy for untraceable murders and mutilations. Since those didn't involve any deals or contracts, I was off the hook.

They muttered together for a couple of moments as we made our way down the dim hallways. I never liked the halls at Truman. The floor was a puke colored pattern, and the walls were a beige so bland it bordered on white. Lincoln Heights was also the only school in the city that didn't have a church, mosque or synagogue within three miles of it. My father had bought out the nearest church, registered another one on its property and left it empty. Then it had been a simple matter of going in and breaking the sanctification without desecrating it. With that protection gone, there was nothing to keep a demon out of the area. The low murmur of the conversation behind me and the dull slap of shoe leather against the stone floors made my skin crawl as I approached Dulka's wards. I slipped through them with a shudder of revulsion and waited for my Master and my father to cross them as well.

I looked back over my shoulder at the old man, and tried not to see myself in him. His hair was as dark and curly as mine, but had plenty of gray in it, and his nose had a bigger hook to it than mine. Of course, over the past few years, it had been easier and easier to stop seeing any resemblance. His cheeks had gotten fatter, and his lips reminded me of two dead fish, all pale and slimy. He'd started a collection of chins, too, each one weaker than the original, and not even the Armani suit could hide his gut. I was grateful to my mom for giving me more of her looks than his. They passed the wards, and the familiar pressure across the back of my neck settled back into place as Dulka reactivated them.

"Boy, go prepare the circle. You have a love spell to do tonight!" Dulka crowed as my father grimaced.

My father hated these visits, and so did I. He didn't like to see me work magick. I just hated my father. Not in the usual teenage "I hate you because it's trendy" way. I had a good reason; I was his first-born son…and his price for power.

I bowed my head and headed for the unused science lab that I had called home for the past four years. A few *neglenom* charms made sure people ignored the door to the lab, and over time, the charms' influence had even made them forget that room 113 ever existed. They were some of my earliest charms, and I'd been adding to them every year. By now, they even protected the room from divinations, so that the Conclave of the Magi couldn't sniff us out and send their Sentinels after us.

A fist-sized bag of bone ash mixed with dried blood sat between a bone knife and an iron rod on the teacher's desk: the basic tools for casting a sorcerer's circle. By themselves, they were useless to me. I could prepare Dulka's circle with them, but it was still his circle to do with as he pleased. He'd inscribed it into the floor himself; all I was doing was charging it. It wouldn't keep him out any more than a strong breeze could stop a charging minotaur. The tools felt cold and greasy in my hands as I walked the edge of the circle, dropping a fine stream of bone ash beside me as I muttered the protection curses in Infernal patois. As I completed the circle, I twisted my right foot and bore down with my toe. The piece of glass that I'd wedged into the soft rubber grated almost silently across the etched line of the circle's edge, and broke it.

With the circle done, I headed for the store room off the lab, supposedly to get the supplies for the love spell for my father. Not tonight, though. The old man was going to have to get laid without my help from now on.

I looked around the little room for a moment, and realized I might actually miss this place. This room was where Dulka kept me. I only had a pallet on the floor under one of the storage tables, and a few changes of clothes, but this was the one space that was even a little bit mine. At least, up to now it was. But, I really didn't have the time to be all gushy and sentimental. I still had work to do.

I reached up to one of the higher shelves and grabbed the jar hidden in the back. There was a pale glint to it as I brought it out into the half-light of the room and pulled the large glass dish up to set beside it. The jar held a golden amulet that I'd made months ago, hidden in a solution of aqua regia, the only acid I knew of that would dissolve gold. I dumped that into the glass dish, then added a reactant, and traced a symbol of Recollection in the air over it. In seconds, the amulet was re-forming, bubbling back into existence in reverse of the way it dissolved months ago when I first dropped it into the corrosive bath. I snatched it up with a pair of glass rods, and laid it on another dish before the suddenly potent aqua regia could start to work on it again. Carefully, I wiped the last residue of acid from it and slipped it onto a leather thong that I wrapped around my wrist. Next came a quick trip to Dulka's potion supply. The amulet was designed to negate Dulka's magick, and it went through the wards on the cabinet like butter. I snagged the last curative potion, and tucked the half-full bottle into my jacket pocket for later. What I had in mind was going to get violent.

"Boy!" Dulka bellowed. "Get your worthless ass out here!"

I stepped out into the room and into the middle of my own circle, which I had etched into the floor with a razor blade over several weeks. Inside it was an upright pentacle, with its primary point facing North. From my jacket pocket, I took two packets of salt I'd lifted from McDonald's that afternoon and tore them open, so that the coarse grains fell into the palm of my hand.

"My name is Chance Fortunato, asshole!" I growled by way of challenge, both fists clenched tight and held at my sides. "Hear me, oh Master."

"Insubordinate and submissive in the same breath," Dulka said with a wicked grin. "Have a seat, Stefan, this should be fun to watch." Dulka got up and stepped around his desk, letting his form shift from the high school science teacher into his true shell on this plane: a black-skinned demon with ram's horns on either side of his head, black eyes, and cloven hooves. Wicked talons stretched from his fingertips, and spikes stuck out from his elbows and knees.

"Let me remind you of something, slave. I own you, body and soul. You're property, *my* property. Daddy here sold you to me fair and square, and Mommy didn't even put up a fight for you." He laughed, a loud, harsh sound, and I knew he almost believed the crap he was spouting.

I opened my right hand, revealing the pile of salt.

"Oh, my!" he gasped melodramatically. "What's this? Salt? For a circle? Whatever will I do, Stefan?" he asked as he put the back of his right hand to his wrinkled black forehead. "The half trained familiar that I taught to use magick is going to cast a circle! I'm doomed!" My father joined in on the laughter then.

"*Circumvare!*" I chanted. The salt flew into a perfect circle with the quick-casting invocation.

Dulka laughed as he stepped up to the edge of the floating column of white crystals and ran his finger through them, seemingly unaffected by their border. I cringed back, and he laughed again.

"Hmmm, looks like somebody went and broke the circle you cut into the linoleum," he taunted. "Did you think I wouldn't notice the box knife missing every night? That I don't know every single thing you do?" He reached through the swirling cloud for me.

"No, I kinda counted on you noticing that one," I said, smiling as his hand got almost to my throat. I leaned back as I went on. "I made two." I held up the last of the razor blades and closed the inner circle with a flourish. Dulka barely had time to look surprised as the salt closed the inner ward with his hand still inside it. Energy filled the circle as the salt closed around his arm like piano wire. The over-pressure of energy slammed him away, but he left a lot of his skin sliding down the inside of the circle before he smashed into the chalkboard.

I had made the more noticeable circle with the box cutter, knowing Dulka would be watching me. At the same time, I'd used razor blades to inscribe a second, nearly invisible circle a foot inside it as I went along. He'd found the one I wanted him to, just like he'd found the four I'd made before.

Dulka picked himself up and stood facing me, disbelief plain on his face.

"Thrice three times has the sun set on the hour of my birth since you I crossed your threshold," I intoned. The first words of the rite hung in the air for a moment, and Dulka's brow wrinkled up a little more. My father stopped laughing and looked to Dulka.

"The Rite of Severing," Dulka snarled as he stalked toward me. "Who taught it to you?" I flipped him off by way of reply.

"That only applies to apprentices," he said, his confidence almost convincing. "Your soul belongs to me."

"My father gave me to you as part of his price," I said with a glare at the offending parent. "I never signed a contract." Dulka's face looked like he'd just eaten a Communion wafer for a moment, then he smiled.

"You think you're clever, slave, but you forgot that it's only been eight years," he said as he walked toward me.

"Eight years, nine birthdays," I said. "You took me on the morning on my seventh birthday. I was born at night."

Dulka's eyes narrowed as he saw the wide-eyed confirmation on my father's face. It was a technicality, but demons lived by them. Their magick was ruled by them. Dulka roared and slammed his fist into the edge of the circle hard enough to crack the windows behind me, but the barrier held. I smiled until he drew his left hand up and uttered a harsh-sounding syllable in Infernal.

"Kneel, slave, and know the agony I reserve for those who forget their place!" There was a pressure on my mental defenses, but by now, even his best effort wasn't much more than an annoyance. The smug grin on his face faltered when I cocked my head to one side.

"You done with the warm up? You haven't been in my head for years now. Try harder."

He stepped back and threw a solid lance of Hellfire that flickered against the shield before dying away. Two more followed it in quick succession, and I felt my defenses being pushed toward their limits. I bolstered them with my own energy, leaving myself drained when he finally let up. I brushed the sweat out of my eyes as I straightened, and Dulka smiled.

"You're not as strong as you think, boy."

"Strong enough. Three blows unanswered, and still I stand," I recited the next part of the Rite. "Thrice I claim my freedom, and state it clear. I am free." The words reverberated inside the circle and rang through the room as Dulka's controls over me strained against my will.

"I am free!" I said louder, and the glass in the windows behind me exploded into the room as the spell shattered under my will.

"I AM FREE!" I shouted at the top of my lungs. I stepped forward as the last words left my mouth, and the opened circle burst out in a wave of force. Desks flew across the room and the walls buckled when it hit. It knocked my former boss back against the chalkboard again, and I heard other things breaking elsewhere in the science wing. "Thrice I say, and with you…be done."

Now came the hardest part.

"Thrice three times, I smite thee. Once rebuked art thou for each year's passing lost to thee!" I yelled. Then, I unleashed the soul essence I had taken for Dulka that day. It flared around me like a living flame as I stepped toward him, drunk with the pure power I held in the palm of my hand.

Soul essence fueled a lot of Dulka's spells, and most of his defenses. I sent a ton of it at him, a blast of pure Soulfire that slammed into his chest and knocked him through the wall, across the hallway, through the next wall, and out into the courtyard. I sent another gout of it after him, pinning him to the ground while I walked toward him through the smoking hole I'd made. I reached down and pulled him to me by one horn. The skin on his chest was raw and blistered, and wisps of fetid smoke rose off his skin, but he was still alive. Not happy about it, maybe, but still alive.

"No!" he cried as I kicked him between the legs. He doubled over in agony, his hands cupping his crotch. Even demons had sensitive gonads. I grabbed the other horn and muscled him up to his knees. I drew on my will as I pulled my left arm back and drove my fist into his bovine nose, using every ounce of the strength I had taken from McKane. There was a crunching sound and a snap as he went flying. The curve of a horn was still clutched in my right hand, and a crumpled demon lay several feet away. My left fist throbbed as I walked over to my fallen former owner. With a toss, I moved the broken horn from my right hand to my left, and drew back again, using it to club him while I held him by the other horn. The horn broke again on the sixth blow, and I realized it on the eighth. I punched him one more time, to make the full nine. He hung limp in my grip, his physical form barely solid, his grasp on this realm weakening with each blow.

"Nine blows unanswered...for my freedom," I panted as I tucked the piece of his horn in my back pocket. "I have bested thee. Thou art my master no longer," I finished the ritual phrase while I dragged him back into the lab by his other horn. I was starting to feel sweat run down my back as I pulled him through the hole I'd made in the wall. My father moaned as he started to come to, but I ignored him. The Rite was almost done, but the last part was the most important and the hardest.

Once I had dragged my Master's limp form into the circle I had started out in, I took my place at the northern point and closed it again. Words that were never intended to be heard by human ears, much less uttered by a human tongue, fell from my lips like verbal bricks. Most of them hurt to pronounce, and it felt like I was going to choke on a few of them as I walked around the circle three times deosil, or clockwise in magickal speak. It felt good to finally be doing something the right way, though. When I completed the third circuit, I stopped at the northern point again.

"As once you bound me, I bind thee, self to self," I hissed at him. I coughed on smoke and went on. "Thou art beaten by thine own student, undone by thine own teachings, bound by thine own hand through me. Choke on it, you ugly son of a bitch!" The circle closed with a vile sound. I left Dulka's limp form in the circle and turned to face the old man. The rite was done, and I was almost free. But I still had business with my father.

"Son, wait!" he cried as I started toward him.

"You never get to call me that again!" I screamed at him, rage making my words raw, ripping them from my throat. The wall behind him cracked with the force of raw emotion given impact by the magick coursing through me. "You gave me to a demon, and beat the crap out of me whenever I didn't make things easy for you! Well, I am *done* being your price!" I reached for him as he stumbled against the wall, and I loved seeing the fear in his face. Someday, a tiny voice reminded me, I might regret enjoying his terror, but today sure as hell wasn't that day.

"Don't you see?" he asked, gesturing at Dulka with his outstretched hands. "Don't you see what an opportunity this presents for us?"

"Us?" I growled.

"Yes! If you kill him now, he'll be sent back into the Abyss! My contract will be null and void! I'll be in the clear!"

"Not everything is about you, you selfish son of a bitch," I growled, parroting the words he had said to me eight years ago on my birthday. I balled my fist up and punched him in the mouth to make my point. It had been all me: no borrowed strength or magick, just a pissed off teenager beating the crap out of his asshole of a father. Damn, it felt good. "You're not getting out of your contract, you son of a bitch. Dulka still gets your soul when you die, and you still go to Hell."

"Son, please!" he cried. I hit him again.

"Never again!" I yelled at him. My left hand was swollen and bruised, and I could barely make a fist, but with a little draw from the strength charm, it delivered one last punch across his jaw. He folded like a wet noodle and went down. I coughed again and went back to my pallet in the store room to grab my gym bag.

"Well, done, slave," Dulka's voice caught me up short as I walked past the circle.

"Fuck off," I said as I started walking again.

"You're still not free, boy. You haven't crossed the threshold yet, and I promise you, I won't let you make it to the door."

That made my gut clench. As much as I hated to admit it, he was right.

"Circle's too strong," I said as I walked to the hole in the wall.

"The fire will weaken it. I'll get out before you make it halfway down the hall."

Fire? I turned toward him, and saw what he was talking about. Scattered papers and desks were still flickering from the blasts I'd thrown around so casually a few minutes before. But they weren't that bad: just tiny fires, already guttering and dying. Then the smell of natural gas hit my nose. Somewhere, a line had busted. It was just a matter of time before it went up.

I hissed an Infernal curse and scrambled to my father. He was still out. Damn it! Limp as he was, "dead weight" didn't even begin to cover how hard it was to move him, but I finally managed to get him through the smoldering hole in the wall and out into the hallway.

Dulka's irritating laugh followed me into the hall. Then, the gas caught.

Chapter 3

~ A man is best repaid in his own coin. ~ Johann Faust 15ᵗʰ century Mage

I shook my head and tried to get to my feet. My legs turned traitor on me and I flopped back down on my side. The second time, they worked a little better and I staggered through the smoke to my unconscious father. My left hand was pretty much useless now, and my ears were ringing from the explosion that had knocked us both down the hallway. There was no way I was going to get us both out of there like that. And I wasn't going to leave him to die. With all the crap that was already on my soul, I wasn't going to add any more.

Without being able to use my left hand, it took a little extra fumbling to dig the curative out of my pocket, and I nearly dropped it on the floor before I got a good grip on it. The cork crumbled under my teeth as I pulled it out, and I spat flecks of it out before I upended the bottle. The pain in my left hand faded before I could so much as gag on the taste, and I heard the grating of bone on bone as it knit itself back together. Even the rib that Dulka had cracked that morning stopped hurting. It should have hurt like hell, but all it did was feel weird as my body did things it wasn't meant to do. Curatives were expensive for a reason. Now, I all I had to do was drag my father out of a burning building.

Mage duels tended to be hard on real estate. I should have thought of that, and made sure no one else was around when I challenged Dulka. If I had, maybe I wouldn't have been dragging my unconscious father by his shirt collar through a burning school building. In my defense, it hadn't been on fire when I knocked him out.

I could still hear Dulka screaming Infernal obscenities and pounding against the circle I'd trapped him in, even over the roar of flames. Another gas line went off in the science lab to my right. I stumbled under the shockwave as the lab door flew across the hall in front of me and stuck at an angle in the green painted lockers. Glass from the louvered windows near the ceiling pelted us, and crunched under my combat boots as I dragged my old man through it. Lincoln Heights High School was nearly a century old, and a lot of it was still made of wood. The science wing was going to be a total loss for sure.

Behind me, Dulka stopped screaming, and I felt the subtle shift of energy as he went to work on the summoning circle with magick instead of fists and curses. Damn, he'd calmed down fast. I'd never seen one of his tantrums go for less than twenty minutes. This time, he'd only ranted for about five minutes, and I'd counted on having at least twice that long to get to the school's main doors. Once I got to the exit, I'd be free. I leaned forward and tried to go faster, but with my father's weight dragging at my left hand, "faster" was still too damned slow. More magick pulsed behind me, and I felt the circle's barrier crack open. The door was still a minute away, but Dulka was only seconds from obliterating my hastily cast circle. At this rate, he'd catch me before I was halfway there.

"*Chance*," Dulka's voice grated through my thoughts, "*you can't escape, my slave. Making it to the door won't stop me. I will break free from this flimsy cage, and I will drag you back. Stop now, and I'll be merciful in my punishments.*"

Old compulsions kicked in as he sent his thoughts through mine, and I felt my muscles start to tighten up. In a few seconds, I'd be completely paralyzed and my muscles would seize up in a body-wide cramp. But I had at least one more surprise for the boss.

"*Compulsis negatis*," I hissed through my teeth. In my mind, I saw the glowing red compulsion glyphs on my aura covered with spheres of runes. The compulsions disintegrated under the counter spell as the focus, a set of runes tattooed under my left arm, burned away. They hurt more as they burned themselves out than they had when I'd inked them in.

He reacted just like I'd hoped he would. Another roar echoed through the hallways, and I heard his massive fists pounding against the circle again. He made more cracks in the barrier, but brute force couldn't break it as fast as a skilled magickal assault could. I leaned into my father's limp mass again and tried to weigh how long I needed to make it to the exit against how soon Dulka would break free. I still came up short; he'd still catch me a few feet from the door.

"Crap," I muttered. *"Crebresco minuta."* The smaller amulet around my neck warmed, and a tingle went through my arms and legs as I became a little stronger, a little faster. I didn't really want to use the strength amulet any more than I needed to. Buff charms had nasty side effects if you used them too much, and I'd already used it a lot tonight. It was also designed to crap out faster the more it was used. But it was either risk the charm, or get caught by a pissed-off demon. Yeah, no contest there. The thought of the daily beatings and broken bones goaded me to put my back into pulling my father to the doors. Smoke swirled around me, and I coughed hard as I dragged him forward.

Another gas line went somewhere down the hall, and the school's fire alarm finally went off. Klaxons warred with older bells, and I could see the bright strobes of the newer alarms on either side of the hallway. Dank water sprayed from overhead for a few seconds, but by the time I dragged my old man's fat ass to the doors, it had stopped. The water had evaporated in the heat, but it left its rancid stench behind on my ripped jeans and black leather jacket.

The pale rectangles of the windows in the doors loomed in front of me, and I dropped my father to push on the bars. They opened about an inch, but then I felt them jar against my hands. I looked down to see the security chains wrapped around the push bars, the padlock shining up at me like it was proud of how well it was locked. I shouted a few choice words at it in Infernal then went quiet as I felt my circle shatter. Dulka was free, and I was still inside.

"Boy!" he yelled. "I'm coming for you!"

Great, at least I had a warning. There was a crash from down the hall, and I heard heavy steps coming my way. I needed time: only a few more seconds. That meant using one of the few spells I could cast without a focus, one I hated to cast because of the taint it left on my soul. My eyes closed, and I pulled stolen soul essence from the Lemurian blood tattoo on the inside of my right biceps. I poured it into the mental construct I had created for the spell, and once the glowing image was complete in my head, I uttered the release phrase, *"Ignus Infernum!"* The whole process took less than a heartbeat.

24

A glowing sphere of Hellfire flew from my hands and sped down the hall toward the sound of demon hoof beats. There was a bright flash of impact, and I heard Dulka's outraged roar from way down the hall a few seconds later. Time to get out of here.

I turned and kicked the door. The shock of the impact sent jolts of pain up my leg, but I stepped back up and kicked again. The metal bar between the two doors popped free, but the chain looped through the push bars still held the doors closed. I ramped the strength charm up a little more.

"On your knees slave!" Dulka said as he charged back toward me. "Getting out that door won't save you! You're my property! Mine!"

"Not," I said as I kicked, "Any," I kicked again and the bar bent, "MORE!" The door gave on the next kick and flew open. I grabbed my father's ankle and stepped across the threshold. Inside my head, I felt something give, like a rope breaking, and I sensed the power of spells lashing back toward their caster. Another explosion ripped through the school, and I was treated to yet another bellow of pain from my old master. Music to my freaking ears.

Sirens added their mournful wail to the sounds of the night: fire trucks on their way to save the day. I dragged the old man down the steps, careful not to let his head bounce more than once on each step on the way down. Heavy steps just behind me made me turn back toward the door I'd just stepped through. Dulka emerged from the smoke, and I started to wonder if maybe he was right about crossing the threshold not being enough to free myself.

"Return to me, my slave," he said in my head, *"and I will be merciful. My hold on you is still intact."*

The doubt was hard to fight, but there was only one way to be sure he was lying.

"Then come out and get me, asshole!"

He smiled and took a step forward, then bounced back as a sheet of blue energy flashed in front of him. The threshold had stopped him! I put my arms up and let out a whoop of joy.

"Your freedom is temporary. I will come and reclaim you, slave."

"We both know you can't," I said through clenched teeth. My voice was raspy from all the smoke I'd breathed. "Now, get the Hell out of my head!" I exerted my will and closed my mind to him completely.

He responded with more Infernal swearing.

Higher-pitched sirens sounded behind me, the oscillating wail of police cars, and I heard the screech of tires. Bright red and blue lights flashed against the front of the school, then a brilliant beam hit me. Dulka scowled and stepped back into the smoke, and I heard the cops behind me yell at me to put my hands up and turn around. My hands went up as I turned to face the two New Essex police cruisers that had their spotlights on me. Two uniformed cops came out from behind the cars, Tasers out. I was looking down the laser sight of one, and the other one was dancing across my father's back. The one on me never wavered. Figured that I'd get the one cop with nerves of freaking steel aiming at me.

"Take the bag off, kid," he told me. He didn't sound like he'd grown up in Missouri. Maybe L. A.

I used my right hand to reach up to my right shoulder and pulled the strap of the blue and yellow duffel bag over my head. It hit the ground at my side, and the cop took a step up.

"Awright, face down on the ground, kid. Arms out to your side, feet spread."

The other cop had already holstered his Taser and had rolled my father over. His hands were sliding over his clothes in a quick and dirty pat down as I slowly got down on my stomach and tried not to cough much.

"Holy crap, Collins," the other cop said as I heard the sound of a Taser being holstered, "you know who we got here?"

Hands ran up my right leg, then up my left, and moved to my back pockets. My fake school ID came out, and the folded stack of bills I'd collected that day for the boss. I must have forgotten to give him his money in all of the confusion. An accident, I swear.

"I dunno, but this kid's ID says he's Chance Fortunato, so I'm gonna take a big leap and say that's his dad," Collins said as he kept frisking me.

"None other than Stavros 'the Spartan' Fortunato. At a fire in a school. Whaddya think, meth lab explosion or a drug deal that went bad?" his buddy asked. Funny how he didn't go for the popular "fight with a demon that got out of hand" angle. Cops: no imagination.

"Can it, Franklin," Collins said as he finished patting me down. "You okay, kid?" I answered him with a wracking cough and a nod. He pulled me to my feet and led me over to the lead patrol car.

"Get a damn paramedic over here. Kid needs some oxygen," Collins said.

Moments later, I was sitting on the back bumper of an ambulance with a clear plastic mask over my nose and mouth. Collins had my bag on the hood of his cruiser, and I watched as he methodically pulled out everything I owned in the world and laid it next to the bag. A few t-shirts, two extra pairs of jeans, four balled-up pairs of socks, and a few pairs of underwear were laid out before he got to the one thing that made me tense up. He held a business card for Spirit Garden, the little herb and sundry shop where my mom worked, with Mom's name listed on it as their master herbalist. It wasn't much, but it was more important than anything else I had. My stomach sank as he slipped the card into his breast pocket and started to put the rest of my stuff back in the bag. Finally, he headed over to me.

"Awright, kid. You wanna tell me what's goin' on?"

"Sure. We were here on some kind of business for my father. He left me outside the room, and next thing I know, he's out cold and the place is burning down around me. So I dragged him out." It was a good lie, and it came out as smooth as silk. Simple, vague, and hard to disprove, since most of it was true. Now, all it needed was the personal touch. "Wish I could tell you more, sir, but truth is, my um, dad doesn't like to let me see much of his, you know, business."

I'd only stumbled over the word "dad" because I usually refused to call the old bastard that. I didn't even like calling him my father, but biology was biology, and father was easier to say than "the lousy son of a bitch who got my mother pregnant." It also didn't give me disturbing images of my mother sleeping with him. I had enough nightmares without adding that to them.

Collins just nodded and scribbled on his notepad. "Your dad's telling a different story, kid," he finally said, "and he ain't painting you as the model citizen, either. You got a rap sheet of your own, so this ain't looking good for either one of you."

I shrugged and spread my hands. "Hey, I dragged his sorry ass out of there," I said. "I coulda just left him."

"Maybe so, but we're gonna bring you both in, until we can sort this all out." Collins turned to talk to the paramedic, and I let out a tired sigh.

Over by the steps of the school, I could see another team of paramedics working on my father. He was sitting up now, and hopefully, in a lot of pain. The worst he was likely to have, though, was a black eye where I'd punched him, and a ton of little cuts from the broken glass I'd dragged him though. I'd only used the strength charm a little when I'd hit him, honest. If I was lucky, the cops would place me in the foster system by the end of the night, and I'd never have to see my father again.

That thought made a warm place in my head for a while, until the EMTs led the old man over and sat him down beside me. My glare didn't stop him, so I settled in for a good long scowl as they slipped the oxygen mask over his face. He waited for the paramedic to get a few feet away before he lifted the mask.

"Listen, son, you need to get me out of this," he said quietly. His tone was stern, and left no room for argument. My frown broke as my left eyebrow tried to climb into my scalp in sheer disbelief.

"First off, you *never* get to call me that again," I said. "Second, no. No way, hell no, never gonna happen, and let me just throw in a 'screw you' while I'm at it. I don't have to do a damn thing for you ever again, you slimy son of a bitch, and even if I wanted to, I couldn't. All of my foci got torched. I can't cast a spell without one. Never thought *that* would come back to bite your fat ass, did ya?"

"That attitude is what made us resort to using foci to maintain control," he said. "This is your fault, and I expect you to clean up the mess you made. You're already in enough trouble with me. You don't even want to think about how angry Dulka is going to be with you."

"I'm free, old man. I couldn't care less how mad Dulka is, and the more I piss *you* off, the happier I am. And," I raised my voice, "no, I'm not gonna lie for you!" Heads turned toward us as I stood up and ripped the plastic mask off.

My father went pale as he understood what had just happened. "What are you...you can't!" he gaped.

"I did. I am *done* being your price. From now on, you deal with him on your own, asshole." Cops ushered me to one of the cruisers, and, best of all, away from my father.

By the time I got to the police station, I had the better part of a new plan worked out. While I sat in a bare interrogation room, I worked on the finer points. I figured the cops really only had a couple options: either juvie, or the foster program. It all depended on whether they thought I'd committed a crime tonight.

The bored cop who'd been standing in the corner got me a cup of crappy coffee while I waited, and I toyed with how much leverage to put on my old man as the clock edged up on one a.m. On a Friday night, I figured one fifteen year old with a record, even if his father was a suspected criminal, wouldn't be big enough to pull someone from the usual rush of nuisance calls the NEPD had to deal with until the bars closed. I settled in for a long wait. At least they hadn't handcuffed me to the chair this time. That meant the odds were good I'd end up placed in a foster home before the night was out. A foster family would be a *lot* easier to escape from. Well, in cop-speak, they'd call it running away. Not that I couldn't get out of juvie; it just took longer. With a foster home, I could be lost in New Essex's mystical Underworld before Sunday morning. Getting out of juvenile detention would take about a week.

The door opened, and all of my plans went out the window when Officer Collins led my Mom in. My world just stopped as she crossed the threshold, and I think my heart took a moment before it restarted. Between heartbeats, my brain registered about a million things. The black skirt with red roses embroidered along the hem, the white blouse, and her hair caught up under a red headband. I noticed strands of gray in the thick curls, but her face was still the same. Except for her eyes. They were dark, and sad.

I came to my feet, my eyes still catching details. The thick silver rings on her hands. Then her hands went past my face, and she had me caught up in a fierce hug. I closed my eyes and gave as good as I got. She still smelled like vanilla and sandalwood, but I was taller than she was now.

"Oh, son, I missed you so much!" she said into my shoulder.

I opened my eyes and looked over her shoulder at the image in the room's two-way mirror. I'd gotten my color from her, hair and skin both, but I had a little of the classic Greek curl to my hair as well.

"Missed you, too, Mom," I said quietly. It wasn't anywhere near the whole truth, but it was all I could handle at the moment. All I'd known of family for the past eight years was a father who had traded my freedom to a demon so he could get rich and laid, and who saw me as nothing more than a tool for keeping the money and babes rolling through his life. Now, here was my Mom, genuinely happy to see me, and pulling back from me with damp eyes and a broad, beautiful smile on her face. It was either typical fifteen-year-old surliness, or total meltdown. And I figured the meltdown would mean a medicated haze in a soft, comfy room somewhere, in a nice white coat with extra long sleeves.

Mom pulled back and held me at arm's length with one hand while she wiped at her eyes with the other hand. "You've grown up so much." Her voice was tight with emotion, and all I could manage was a stupid shrug.

"It's been a while, Mom," I offered. "Don't take this the wrong way, but what are you doing here?" She smiled, and some of the sadness seemed to leave her eyes.

"Officer Collins called me. And…" she paused for a second and looked down before she went on. "I've been trying to find a way to get custody of you for years, son. Ever since the divorce. My lawyer thinks he can get me full custody after what happened tonight. If that's what you want."

"Oh, HELL yeah!" I blurted out.

"I can see we're going to have to work on your language, young man," Mom said with mock seriousness. "Especially around your sister."

"I have a sister? How did that happen?"

"The same way you happened, son, just later," Mom said with a wicked smile.

Collins choked on a laugh, and I fought down the flush I felt creeping up my neck.

"So, I'll call Mister Vor…" she started to say, but the door slamming open cut her off.

Mike Cassavetes, my father's lawyer, stormed into the room and slammed his fist down on the table. My mother jumped, but Collins had his Taser out and trained on the pudgy shyster's ample gut before he could get his trademarked dramatic entrance line out. His chins wobbled as he gulped, and his comb-over went damp as he broke out in a sweat, then he recovered a little. He looked down at the red dot on his tan suit jacket and back up at Collins with his eyes a little wide.

"I *do* need a new car, officer…Collins is it? So by all means pull the trigger."

"And I need an excuse to charge your client with assault by proxy and tampering with a witness, so by all means, keep shootin' your damn mouth off," Collins shot back.

"This is a clear violation of the custody decision, Miss Murathy. I'm going to have you leave now, and I'm sure Mr. Fortunato can be persuaded not to have charges filed against you."

"She stays, and you get to go back and tell your client I'm adding child endangerment to the list of charges," Collins stepped forward. "Then I'm calling in Family Services to have the kid placed with his nearest relative, and your client's parental rights revoked completely."

"My client has yet to hear a single charge against him."

"It keeps gettin' longer every time you open your mouth."

"It's okay," I said. Three pairs of eyes turned to me, none of them looking like they were believing what their ears were telling them. "I'll talk to him." Cassavetes turned and gave them a smug look, and made a dismissive gesture. Mom looked back over her shoulder at me, and I gave her a reassuring smile and a nod.

"Good boy," Cassavetes said as the door closed. "Here's what you're going to tell them happened. You and your father…"

"Shut up." The words felt good coming from my mouth. Mike looked at me like I'd just turned into someone else. "Right now, my memory is kinda hazy about what happened tonight. Tell the old man to back the fuck off, or I start making shit up. If he *really* pisses me off…I'll just start telling the truth."

"They'll never believe the truth," Mike sneered.

"Didn't say I'd tell them all of it. Just enough to give them an excuse to start looking in all the right places. Either he goes away and leaves me alone, or I make sure someone else does it for him. And I ain't too picky about who makes him gone." That made his pasty face a couple of shades lighter. Cheap aftershave and sweat assaulted my nose as he stood there slack-jawed for a moment.

"You…you wouldn't dare!" he sputtered.

"Try me." We matched glares for a moment, then he flinched. I got the impression of desperate bluffing, and a contempt for everyone who had all the things he wanted. What did he see in my eyes, I wondered?

"You have no idea what I'm capable of," he said. It was supposed to sound like a threat, I was pretty sure, but all I heard was injured pride trying to make a comeback.

"You've got a good idea what I can do, though. And if you ever want to find out first hand, just cop an attitude with my Mom again." I copied the gesture he'd used earlier to let him know I was done talking to him, and weathered a glare for it. But, since pissing him off was almost as much fun as pissing my father off, it lost a lot of the intimidation factor.

Mom and Officer Collins came back in as soon as the door opened, and neither of them looked happy. Both of them eyed me, like they were looking for some kind of damage. I smiled, partly to reassure Mom, but mostly because, for the first time in a long time, I just felt like it.

"What did he want, son?" Mom asked as she came over to me.

"To make sure I told the cops what he wanted them to hear. I told him that wasn't happening."

"He didn't look happy to hear that," Collins remarked. "I'm gonna go talk to my captain, see if we can't at least get temporary custody for you, Miss Murathy. With your husband's rep, I think we can find a judge who'll do that, at least for a few days. Especially after what happened tonight. But I can't promise nothin' beyond that."

"I understand, officer. I think my lawyer can handle it from there. I've been waiting for this night for too long to waste this chance." Her eyes never left my face as she spoke, and she brushed the back of two fingers across my cheek. My gruff teen act broke under that touch, and I was all kid again, with a goofy smile for my mom. I got up and wrapped her in a hug to make sure she was still real.

"Okay, then," Collins said. "Let's go fill out some paperwork."

Chapter 4

~ No place in the world is so safe as a place one of the Roma calls home. ~

Friedrich Horst, 17th century mage

"Let's go home, son."

Mom's words kept playing through my head as she drove. Home. I liked the sound of that. I didn't even know where home was, and I didn't really care. Almost anything would be better than sleeping on the floor in an abandoned high school science lab and living with a demon.

The neon and concrete skin of New Essex blurred by my window as Mom navigated her battered beige VW van out of the Old Joplin District without a word. Off to my right, the sparkling towers of downtown pointed into the night sky. Mom was heading through the edge of downtown, where the industrial parks of the Joplin district gave way to the convenience stores and strip malls that catered to the financial section of town. Even at three a.m., the streets weren't empty. New Essex was called Night City for more than one reason. Brightly painted high-performance racers prowled through the parking lot of a strip mall on mobile pools of neon off to my right. Further down on the opposite side, heavy bass beats thumped out competing rhythms from the trunks and back seats of chromed-out Caddies and Lincolns. Sodium streetlights turned blues to black on the bandanas and left-skewed baseball caps of a group of men and women standing outside a liquor store in baggy jeans and hoodies.

These were familiar faces. Not that I knew them personally. It was their eyes. It was the combination of resignation and desperation that made these people familiar to me. Unexpected tears made hot trails down my face as we drove by. Up until tonight, I had helped my former master prey on these people's dreams and fears. Now I was going to a home I didn't deserve. If I thought anyone would have listened, I would have prayed for some kind of forgiveness.

"What's wrong, honey?" Mom broke the silence when I sniffed.

"Nothin'," I said with a thick voice. "Nothin' at all." In spite of myself, I smiled.

"Tears of joy?" she asked. I could see the glistening wet lines down her face.

"Big time." It was even a little true. In spite of the sudden guilt attack, I was as happy as I could ever remember being. Maybe that was where the guilt came in. It wasn't like I didn't have plenty of scars to show for the past few years, and I sure as Hell hadn't been willing, but I'd still done a lot of really bad things. I leaned my head against the cool glass and looked up at the overcast October sky.

"Give me a chance to make this right somehow," I whispered to the night. "I'll do whatever it takes. I swear I will."

Something…some*one* must have heard me. I felt a subtle pressure for a moment, and an ethereal wind blew through my hair. For just a moment, I got the feeling that I'd just made a bargain with something that was vastly amused, and that I'd get the chance I'd asked for. Then the pressure went away, and I felt like I was just catching up to the world again.

"Did you feel something?" Mom asked.

I shook my head, but I saw several loose strands of her hair falling back into place. Note to self: no magick while Mom was nearby. She shrugged and went back to watching the road. As she turned left at a stoplight and headed down a smaller street, the smaller brick businesses started to give way to cheap houses with vinyl siding, and stunted trees in postage stamp sized front yards.

"We'll have to clear out the guest bedroom for you," she said after a moment, like she was picking up in the middle of a list. "I've been using it for storage, but I can move that stuff into the garage. What you have with you will be okay for the weekend, but it won't do for school. I know it's probably not as nice as what you're used to with your father but you'll have to put up with shopping for school clothes at Wal-Mart."

"I'm good with Wal-Mart," I said, and added a shrug to make it seem more casual than I felt. New clothes of my own would be so cool. I didn't give a crap if they were from Wal-Mart or Macy's. They would be mine. I'd get to pick them out. That alone made it as cool to me as any expensive boutique shop or high-end, name-brand store.

The homes sliding by my window were getting bigger and nicer, with bigger yards and older trees to match. Mom pulled onto a side street, and into the driveway of a compact two-story house. Flowers lined the walk to the front door, and I could see a tall tree looming behind the house on the right. Mom came around the front of the van as I climbed out and grabbed my bag. My stomach flip-flopped as I followed her to the front door. She unlocked it and turned on the light, then turned back to me.

"Welcome home son," she said, as I stepped past her.

The front room was carpeted in a dark brown, and Mom had laid down a big red rug in the middle. There was a familiar easy chair against the wall to my right, almost in line with the door. On my left, under the broad front window, there was a worn and comfortable-looking beige sofa. The side table with its built-in reading lamp sat on the right side of Mom's chair, just where I remembered she used to have it...before.

Bookshelves took up the far wall, each shelf stacked two rows high, and it looked like two books deep. To my left, a beat-up television set squatted on a low stand, with a double handful of DVD cases stacked neatly below it. Flanking it were two more sets of shelves. More DVDs in bright cases filled the bottom two shelves of the one on the right. A set of candles and candle lanterns shared space on the third shelf with a collection of amethysts, citrines, and quartz crystals. The top shelf and the top of the case were devoted to pictures of a dark-haired girl with my Mom's eyes and nose, and an impish grin in every shot. That could only be my unknown sister. They ran in order: shots of her as a baby with a full head of dark curls and a toothless grin on her chubby little face, through her toddler years, and into grade school. I felt a burn in my stomach as I followed my sister's life in pictures, instead of memories. I added it to the list of things I owed my father, and looked at the shelves on the left. More DVDs occupied the bottom shelf. Above them, I saw myself. Baby pictures, my kindergarten and first grade pictures, shots of family vacations, and a few candid shots. At the top, standing by itself, was a framed picture of Mom and me on the carousel at Worlds of Fun. I remembered the moment, a cool March afternoon, just before my seventh birthday. In the photograph, I was on the horse as it was on the downswing, laughing as I threw my hands in the air. Mom was standing beside me, holding one hand behind my back, waiting to catch me if I fell. It was one of the last times I remembered seeing her happy. It was also the first time I had seen that picture.

"I found the film in my camera after the divorce," Mom said softly, from just over my shoulder. I'd crossed the room and picked up the frame without thinking. "It's the only picture I have where we're all three together." Her eyes went to the pictures of my sister, and I suddenly understood who she was talking about. She took the frame from me and her eyes got a distant look as she held it for a moment.

"You were…you know…then?"

"It's called being pregnant, son, and yes, your mother was in a family way in that picture." I heard a little bit of laughter in her voice as she put the picture back.

I shook my head at the images that threatened my teenage sanity, then went to the bookshelves and stared in awe at all of the titles. Mysteries, craft, and gardening books dominated, but there were a lot of other topics covered, both in fiction and non-fiction. I felt my jaw slowly fall open, and I think my eyes glazed a little.

"You still like to read?" she asked. I gave an absent nod. "Bookshelves, then. We'll have to get some bookshelves for your room as soon as we can work them into the budget. But that room's not getting any cleaner on its own. Let's get to work on it."

The room, *my* room, was about ten feet on a side, maybe a little bigger, with a little closet just left of the door as I came in. The bed was on the left wall, a little desk was opposite the door, and there was a dresser on the right. There was a boxy little machine on the desk, and a dozen spools of thread. The dresser looked like it was supplying the desk's thread habit, and also like it was pimping out yarn and cloth on the side, too.

"This shouldn't be too hard," I told myself. Three hours later, my back was calling my brain a rat bastard for lying to it about how easy this looked. Every drawer in the dresser was full of crap, and the closet had cardboard boxes stacked to the hanging bar, all of them marked "Fragile!" in big red block letters. None of it could just be carted out and thrown somewhere. It all had to be stacked neatly, and with other stuff that fit some pattern that only Mom seemed to be able to make sense of.

We talked as we worked. Well, mostly, Mom talked and I grunted. She'd covered a lot of conversational turf over the past three hours, most of it to do with my sister, Deirdre, and her own work at Spirit Garden. I'd mostly tried not to lie about what the last few years had been like.

"Well, Kennedy probably won't compare to the private schools you've been to, but it has a great arts program, and one of the best advanced placement science programs in the state," she told me as we put sheets on the bed. "But you always were smart. You'll do just fine."

"Thanks, Mom." I took a look around the room. It didn't look much different, but it was really mine now. My gym bag sat on the dresser: a shot glass full of stuff in a fifty-five gallon drum of a room.

It hit me then that nothing had gone the way I'd planned after I escaped. By now, I'd expected to be good and lost in the city's mystic underground. I had expected to see this sunrise from an alleyway in the Hive, not through venetian blinds in a bedroom of my own in the suburbs of New Essex.

"Damn," Mom muttered. "it's after six. It'll be almost seven by the time I get over to the Romanov's to pick your sister up. This must be the worst homecoming ever."

"Huh?" I managed to grunt. Did I have the snappy comebacks or what?

"I get you home, make you stay up all night, put you to work as soon as you walk in the door, then abandon you at sunrise with no breakfast."

"Well, there was that fire and the trip to the police station last night, though," I said. "You were the last person I expected to see come through that door last night at the station."

"Well, if officer Collins hadn't called me, you wouldn't have seen me until later on today. But you *would* have seen me, son. I promise you that." She stepped up and wrapped me in a fierce hug. "I'm so glad you're home, honey."

"So'm I," I mumbled through a mouthful of her hair.

She stepped back and gave me a long look, like she was trying to memorize my face. "I hate to leave you alone, but I do need to go get your sister, and frankly, sweetie, you look like someone pulled you out of a fire and put you to work at hard labor all night."

"Feels like it, too."

"The bathroom's across the hall, and there are clean towels and washcloths in the linen closet at the end of the hall. Get cleaned up, and I'll make breakfast when I get back." She kissed me on the cheek and left me standing in my room.

I said it a couple more times to enjoy the sound of it: my room. Mom's voice floated through the hallway outside as she hummed an old tune I vaguely remembered. Before long, I heard her call out a goodbye, and the sound of the front door closing.

I grabbed fresh clothes from my smoke-stained gym bag and tossed them on the newly made bed, then dug into the bottom. After a moment, I pried the thick cardboard liner away from the second, original bottom of the bag to reveal my few pieces of magickal and mundane working gear. A black folding knife, a slim flashlight and a set of *very* illegal lock picks were nestled in wadded up newspaper padding, next to two battered Altoids tins: one blue, the other red. The red one held the sharpened piano wire and tiny vials of blood ink I'd used to give myself the blood tats that had helped me in my escape last night. I left that one be, and opened the blue one. A single, thin quartz crystal lay inside, its cheap gold chain caught on the thin layer of scavenged foam that was duct taped to the lid. A silver ring with skulls and crossbones etched around the band lay next to it. But it was what lay beneath the cheap trinkets that I needed to see. Several sheets of translucent onionskin paper were folded up beneath the crystal and the ring, the few magickal notes I'd managed to keep hidden from my master over the past few months. The cut-down stick pen I used was wrapped in the folds of the thin sheets, still intact. I breathed a sigh of relief. I'd been afraid that the ink had boiled out in the heat of the fire and ruined my notes. *That* would have sucked. I carefully pulled the pages out and unfolded them. Line after line of tiny words marched across the page, with larger glyphs and sigils around the edge of each page, done bigger to keep the details right. Just glancing over them gave me a sense of relief. At least I had a little magick to work with. I had stuff for two foci, I had my basic notes, and more importantly, I had privacy. What I needed now was a safe place to stash my stuff.

Fortunately, my new room had lots of good places to hide things, and no one poking through it regularly to find my gear. Even though the need to hide it wasn't as bad, I still wanted a safe place for what little I had. I opened my pocket knife and pulled the closet door open, then stepped in, turned around, and sat on the floor. The spot I picked was low, on the wall facing away from anyone looking into the closet, and on the left as well. Hidden below eye level, on most people's off-hand side, and with the wall itself acting as a sort of barrier, no casual observer would ever notice it. I cut an almost-neat rectangle about the size of my foot in the drywall, and pulled it away to reveal the wooden framing of the wall, and stuck my gear inside. A quick run of the vacuum from the hall closet later, there was almost no sign of my work.

Five minutes later, I was in the bathroom with the door locked, under a scalding hot shower. The steaming spray and lots of soap made the stench of smoke, sweat, and black magick run off my skin in black streams. Even though the last wasn't purely physical, the running water grounded it and broke the bonds between it and my body's aura. I stayed under the shower until the hot water turned frigid, then let the cold water run over me for a minute because I could. Mom's thick towels were a lot softer and bigger than the scratchy white ones I was used to using in the boys' gym, and they didn't have "Property of…" stamped on them. For the first time in a long time, I felt clean. At least, on the outside.

My eyes went out of focus, and I cracked my Third Eye open just a little, enough to see my aura reassert itself over my skin. Running water would disrupt an aura temporarily just like it would most energy. While most mages wrote about how vulnerable that left a practitioner, I didn't mind. My aura swirled blood-red and black down my forearm as it re-formed, but just at the leading edge of it, I could see the deep blue of what it would look like without seven years of black-magickal crap smeared all over it. It covered my fingertips, and I let go of my aura sight and got dressed as quickly as I could without getting in front of the mirror. Even fogged up, it could still serve as a window that went both ways, so I preferred not to be naked in front of one. There were things I didn't want anyone to see. Not even me.

Once I was dressed, though, there was no avoiding it. I was behind a threshold, and Mom had made one very strong hearth-hold. I doubted Dulka could see in here, since he didn't know where I was and he didn't have a familiar to do his dirty work for him. For the moment, I figured I'd be safe enough. I wiped a circle clear and ran one of Mom's brushes through my hair to get the tangles out. My hair fell down past my shoulders in lazy half-curls that framed my face. Where the rest of my face was a mix of Romany and Greek features, my eyes were all Rom. There was a darkness in them that had nothing to do with my blood, but, like my mother's eyes, there were secrets behind them that even I didn't dare to delve into sometimes: mysteries held for thousands of years within the soul of my mother's people. After a moment, I looked away and stepped back from the mirror. Soul-searching wasn't something I needed to be doing. I already knew what I'd find there, and I already knew I didn't much like it.

If the slam of the front door didn't tell me Mom and Deirdre had just gotten home, my little sister's voice made up for it.

"Chance!" she called out from somewhere downstairs.

I barely had time to unlock the bathroom door before she was pounding up the stairs. She caught me in a flying tackle as soon as I opened the door,

41

though I think it was supposed to be a hug. If Mom's hugs were fierce, Deirdre's were more like a vice.

"Hi, sis," I groaned. "A little air here? Please?"

She relaxed her affectionate chokehold on my ribs and stepped back. "Sorry, Mom just told me on the way home that you were here and how happy she was that you were home and I finally got to meet you and ..." She talked faster and faster as she went until I could barely tell one word from the next until she had to stop for air.

"I'm glad to meet you, too," I said quickly.

The sound of Mom's footsteps came from the stairwell, and Deirdre looked back over her shoulder, then back at me.

"I had dreams about you sometimes. Don't tell Mom. They made her sad because you were so sad in them. And don't tell me they were just dreams. I mean they *were* dreams, but they were real dreams. Promise not to tell!" she said, and raised her crooked pinky. The words had tumbled out almost as fast as her first barrage, but there was an urgency to this that caught me off guard. I didn't know what the bent pinky meant, but it seemed important to her, so I copied the gesture and raised my own little finger. She snagged it with her own and pulled my hand to her. "Pinky swear!" I couldn't tell if it was a question or a demand.

"Uh, yeah, pinky swear," I repeated. I felt a small surge, and saw her rock back as her hair fluttered.

"Whoa!" she said softly. "That almost never happens!"

I stared at my little finger in shock. I really needed to be more careful about making binding promises, maybe set a limit or something. No more than two a day.

"You two seem to be getting along," Mom said from the door. "Get cleaned up, Dee, and I'll make us all some breakfast." She turned away, and I circled past Dee, tossed my dirty clothes on the bed and headed for the stairs.

"Moooom!" Dee's voice called from the bathroom, "Chance used all the hot water!"

"Oh, dear," Mom called back from the stairs, "and they're not making any more! I guess it's cold showers for everyone from now on. We'll flog your brother daily for his sins. Just get cleaned up the best you can, honey." She gestured for me to follow her to the kitchen as she went.

The kitchen felt like what Mom used to describe as The Old Country. Mom had re-painted it, and redone the cabinets, and it just sang of her presence. A rich green paint covered the wall, with leaves and grapes around the doors and windows. The cabinets were stained a dark brown that I figured Mom had worked over for days to get right. One wall held a wire shelving unit that was covered in recipe and herb books, with a potted plant centered on the top-most shelf. The grayish-green, fuzzy leaves and the slightly peppery smell that hit my nose when I crushed a leaf between my fingers told me it was sage. There was a little nook with a table near the back door, and with the sun in the back windows, it was the brightest spot in the room.

I helped with fixing breakfast, if you can call chopping up a few potatoes and watching bacon sizzle in a pan helping. More importantly, I checked Mom's spice rack for possible ingredients. Some of the potions I knew required herbs like sage and basil. If I'd been thinking, I wouldn't have even worried. Mom was a master herbalist; her spice rack looked like an apothecary's wet dream.

When she dished up plates for Dee and me, I forced myself to let Dee go first. It had been a long time since I'd eaten a real meal, and even longer since I'd had Mom's cooking, and it was pure torture to wait. Once I got to the table, I forced myself to eat like I was determined to finish last in an eating contest. I savored each bite, trying to make the moment last and fought the urge to wolf it all down as fast as I could. The bacon's smoky flavor, the spices on the crispy potatoes and how soft and starchy they were on the inside, the slightly salty taste of the egg yolk next to the taste of the egg white. Nothing in the world could have tasted better just then. This was Mom food. It could have tasted like dried crap on asphalt, and I'd have still loved it.

Mom and Dee talked about going to Wal-Mart while I slowly made my way through a second helping. Dee had a collage on her favorite female hero due next week, so today's trip would serve a double purpose. While they talked about who she would do her collage and project on, I took my plate to the sink and started on the dishes. By the time I was done, the kitchen was silent. I folded the washcloth over the partition in the middle of the sink and stepped back to make sure everything was spotless, so...I stopped the line of thought. Beatings for the tiniest things were a thing of the past. I had to remember that. I turned to see Mom looking at me from the doorway.

"Wow, honey. Thank you. You know, you didn't have to wash all the dishes all by yourself," she said.

I shrugged. "It's no big deal. You cooked, I figured this was the least I could do to help."

"Chance, honey, sit down." She led me over to the table and waved a hand at the chair across from her.

I felt my heart start to race, and I could barely breathe. I'd done something wrong, I could tell from the way her voice had gone different. My mind raced, trying to figure out what I'd screwed up. Her eyes went to the dishes drying by the sink.

"I don't know how your father did things at his house, or what it was like there," she said softly, "but you're not there anymore, son. You don't have to try so hard."

"I'm not...it's nothing, really, just some...I'm trying Mom," I said, trying to keep my voice even.

"Honey, this is your home now. You're not a guest here, and you're not a servant," she said gently. "I know your father was all about order and detail, and he had control issues. But I'm not. Don't worry about doing everything yourself, or how to make me happy. Just bringing you back home made me the happiest mother in the world."

My shoulders unclenched a little, but I still didn't dare to hope too much yet.

"So, I didn't f...uh, screw up?" I asked, my eyes threatening to water up.

"No, honey, you're doing fine, more than fine," Mom smiled at me. She took my hand in hers and patted it. "Just relax a little, don't worry so much about doing everything right. You can even be a little messy sometimes. I sort of expect it."

"You do?" That was a surprise!

"It's a mom thing. If I don't clean up behind you sometimes, I don't have anything to nag you about."

"So, I should leave my socks on the floor sometimes?" She laughed at that, and I guess my face showed something of how confused I was.

"I guess I forget sometimes how different things can be outside my own little world," she said gently. "I'll make a deal with you..."

"No, Mom," I interrupted. "No deals. I don't make deals, not with you or Dee, at least. Just tell me what you want; there doesn't have to be any trade." I was through trading favors. I'd do anything for Mom or Dee, and I wouldn't ask for anything in return. I'd done too much of that for Dulka.

"Okay. No deals. You can leave your socks on the floor sometimes if you want. And no more doing everything on your own. We share the chores, okay?"

"Okay," I agreed.

Chapter 5

~ To know, to will, to dare, to keep silent. ~

Eliphas Levi, 19th century mage

I woke up to the touch of Daddy's hand on my shoulder. The house was quiet and dark. Batman crouched over blue numbers on the clock showing it was 12:01. Dad put a finger to his lips and smiled.

"What's going on, Daddy?" One fist scrubbed sleep out of my eye, and I yawned wide and long.

"Happy birthday sport!" he whispered. "I've got a surprise for you."

"But...my birthday's tomorrow. We're going to Chuck E. Cheese, 'member?" I sat up in the bed and looked at Dad in confusion.

He put his hand out, and I took it without thinking. With a gentle tug, he pulled me out of my bed and to my feet. He handed me a robe to put on, and it looked like the one he had on. "I know, son. But this is a special surprise. Just between you and me. You're a big boy now, and there's something special that we have to do to commemorate your coming of age."

My little hand was so small in his, and I felt safe as he led me out of my room toward his office, which he'd converted from the garage last year. It was the only part of the house I wasn't allowed into. Even Mom stayed out of it.

His business partner, Konstantin Suliakos, was standing beside the door in a long robe. He gave me a weak smile before he spoke to my father in Greek. "It's to be the boy, then?" He gave me another look, then turned away.

"You've already given him yours," my dad replied with a laugh in his voice. "I'd hate to do the same thing you did. Besides, it does go a little deeper, yes?"

"Is this like one of Mom's Romany things?" I asked him. He made a little noise that sounded rude.

"This is a Greek ceremony," Dad said, and nodded to Konstantin. They both put their hoods up to cover their faces before Konstnatin turned and opened the door.

Dad crouched beside me and put my hood up, too. "You have to be very brave, son, and very quiet. This might seem a little scary, but I promise you, everything will be just fine. It's just part of growing up, is all." I nodded and tried to be as serious and grown up as I could. We walked through the door together, and into darkness.

"Ignus!" Konstantin said, and suddenly, candles lit all by themselves in a circle. Strange designs were laid out on the floor, and my Dad led me to one small circle and let go of my hand once I was inside it. He handed me a stick of burning incense. The purple smoke was sickly sweet in my nose.

"Hold this, son, and don't leave this circle, no matter what you think you see," he told me. "It's all part of your ceremony." I looked up at him and nodded with every drop of seven-year-old dignity I could muster. He stepped away from me, and a moment, later, I heard his voice nearby. He chanted in some language I didn't understand. Truthfully, I didn't want to understand it. It sounded ugly, and it hurt my ears just to listen to it. But this was part of being a big boy, so I stood still and listened as my dad and his partner chanted. The skin on my arms rose in goose bumps as a cold tingle washed over me, and I suppressed a shudder as the world went a little blurry around me. The chant started to repeat, and then, out of the corner of my eye, I saw something flicker in the middle of the big circle. Whatever was there, it felt very wrong. *My first urge was to run like hell. The best I could manage, though, was to not look.*

The smoke from the incense stick seemed to be thicker, now, and I was starting to feel a little dizzy. Another flicker in the center of the circle distracted me, even as I tried hard to look away from it. Then, it flickered rapidly and suddenly, there was something standing in the middle of the big circle. Terror swelled up inside me, and it was all I could do to keep from screaming. But Dad had said it would be all right, no matter what I

47

*thought I saw. Whatever it was...wasn't real. My brain clung to that
thought desperately. It wasn't real. It wasn't real. It became a chant of its
own.*

Then the thing inside the circle spoke.

*"You summon me at your peril, mortals," it said in a voice that
reminded me of car wrecks and people screaming. "I am Dulka, Baron of
the four hundred twenty second ring of the Abyss, commander of six
legions of the Damned. For five thousand years have I dwelt in comfort in
my palaces. Who dares violate my person, and summon me to this putrid
dung heap of a world?"*

*"I am Stavros Fortunato, demon, and we two have an accord," my dad
said boldly.*

*"I am Konstantin Suliakos, demon, and we two have an accord," his
partner said.*

"Neglect your duties to us at your peril," Dad said.

*"Ah, forgive me, my mortal co-conspirators," the thing in the circle
said. Its voice became less harsh, and sounded almost sincere. "I did not
recognize you. There is a new soul here tonight, and I was confused. To
what end have you allowed me the pleasure of once again basking in your
presence?"*

*"We call you here to complete our compact, and make permanent our
agreement," Konstantin said.*

*"Our agreement has already been finalized, Konstantin," Dulka said. I
forced my eyes to look at the creature, and saw twelve feet of black-
skinned, ram-horned demon in all its naked glory. How could something so
ugly sound so...polite? I saw it turn red eyes from Konstantin to my father.*

*"But your agreement with me has yet to become so consummated," my
father said.*

*"Yes, you speak correctly, Stavros Fortunato. There was the matter of a
betrayal. But you wished to keep your soul until your death. And as I*

recall, you offered me another in its place." The demon looked from my father to his friend, who was giving him a wide-eyed look of his own.

"My son," my father said, and gestured to me. "I offer him to you as my price, until death claims my body." The demon turned and looked at me. Its eyes bored into me, and I found myself taking a step back.

"You offer me his soul, as your act of betrayal, and as a boon to keep your own soul intact," it said thoughtfully. It took two steps on cloven hooves, and stared down at me.

For all that I wanted to run, my legs felt like they weighed a thousand pounds. This had to be a test, I thought. My Dad would never give me to a demon. He loved me more than anything in the world. He told me that every day.

"I do," Dad said, and something in me started to break.

"Dad, please, it's a test, right? You're not really gonna give me to it, are you?" I turned to look at Dad, to find someone I could trust here: someone, anyone that wasn't Dulka.

Konstantin was grinning beside my father, and my father's eyes were on the demon, hopeful and expectant. He wasn't even listening to me.

"An apprentice would be useful," Dulka said thoughtfully. "I have a counter-proposal, Stavros Fortunato. I will allow you your soul until you die if you give me the boy, alive, for my own use. I will accept in his stead as your blood betrayal...the blood of Konstantin Suliakos." My eyes went wide and my stomach dropped to my toes as my father grinned.

"Done!" he cried.

Konstantin turned to face him, and flinched. Then, my father stepped forward, and I saw something sticking out of Konstantin's back. Something dark and wet glistened in the candlelight, and Konstantin slumped to his knees. He raised one hand, and I saw something dark and red drip from his fingers. My father stepped back as his partner gasped something, then fell forward. Then his eyes fell on me.

"Our agreement is complete, then. I'll take possession of the boy now," the demon said.

"Be a good boy, and go with your new owner," Dad told me.

"Daddy, no!" I screamed and tried to run to him. I hit some invisible wall and bounced off to fall on my backside.

"He's all yours," the man I once called Dad said.

I felt a shift of some kind, and I knew that the barrier was gone. I heard the heavy thump of a cloven hoof hitting the floor, and turned to look at the demon. It was reaching for me as it came closer. I ran to one side, screaming for my father. The demon's leg kicked my feet out from under me, and I hit the ground face first. I went to get up, and something slammed into the back of my left calf. There was a cracking sound, and I couldn't feel my leg for a moment. Then the pain slammed into me, and I screamed. A heavy weight landed on my right leg, and this time, I felt the bones break as the demon put all his weight on it.

"Daddy, please! Help me! Please, don't let it get me!" I tried to crawl to him.

He looked down at me. "Not everything is about you, you selfish little brat," he sneered, then he smiled and turned his back. "I'll be back in the morning," he said over his shoulder. "I expect the divorce to go my way."

"Oh, it will, never fear," the demon said as I felt it wrap its hand around my neck and pick me up. Its other hand grabbed my right arm and slowly began to squeeze. "Now, it's time you learned to behave yourself. Oh, stop your squealing, boy, it's just a few broken bones and damaged muscle tissue. By morning, I'll have your arms and legs working like new again. On second thought, scream all you like. I might as well have a little fun before I start training you. Now, the bones you're about to hear break are called the radius and the ulna. Let's see which one goes first..."

I hit the floor to the sounds of my own cries. It was dark, and I didn't know where I was. My first thought was that Dulka had somehow caught me. My right arm flung the heavy blanket off me and came to my feet as I heard the door open. The sound gave me a target, and I drew my fist back as I took a step toward it. Light hit my eyes, and I stopped my punch as Mom's startled face registered on my brain.

"Oh God!" she shrieked. My eyes focused against the light, and I saw her with her arm raised to cover her face.

I took a step back and lowered my hand. "Sorry, Mom," I said, panting.

"Chance, honey, are you all right? You were screaming. What's wrong?" Mom's gentle hands fell on one shoulder and on my cheek.

"Bad dream. That's all. New bed, I got confused." The words were coming out all jumbled.

She guided me back to the bed and sat me down, and I was too confused to do anything else. The pain I remembered in the nightmare was still fresh in my head, and I was having a hard time holding off a panic attack. Dulka had used illusions before to trick me into giving things away, and some part of my head wasn't convinced this was real. Every illusion had flaws, though: minor details that didn't fit, because our two minds weren't in perfect sync. I looked at the wastebasket by my desk. The plastic bags from our shopping trip were there. It was a little detail: small enough that Dulka would probably have forgotten about it. The little divot in the carpet where I'd dropped my pocket knife when I was cutting tags was still there. Again, a tiny detail, something I remembered that the boss might have forgotten. My pulse started to slow, and I realized Mom had just asked me something.

"What?" I asked her.

"Is there anything you need?"

"He can have my old night light," Dee said from the door. She looked almost as scared as I did. "I'm not scared of the dark anymore." She didn't sound as confident as she was trying to.

"I'm good," I told them. "Just a bad dream, really."

"I'll make you a dream sachet. Some lavender, vervain, lemon grass, and St John's wort, for restful sleep." She left and shooed Dee out with her. A couple of minutes later, she came back in with a little bundle of cloth in her hand. She tucked it under my pillow and kissed me on the cheek. "Sweet dreams, honey."

When I lay back down, the panic started all over again. Sweet dreams. I wished. I felt like I was being smothered. The bed sucked me in, the pillow wrapped up around my face, and the blanket was like a lead weight on my shoulders as I lay there trying to sleep. Everything was too…*soft*. The pillow tilted my neck to a weird angle, and I was sweating from the bedclothes that draped over me like a shroud. I turned on my side, and it helped my neck, but my arm kept flopping off the bed, and I felt like I was falling then. I tried the other way, but with my back to the door, I was too exposed, and I kept looking over my shoulder, waiting for Dulka to slip in and kick me from behind. The blanket ended up on the floor first, then the pillow, but the mattress still felt like it was trying to swallow me. Was I going to have to go for two days at a time without sleep? That had to have been the reason I'd been able to fall asleep the first time.

Meditation seemed to help me get drowsy, but I jerked awake when I heard a noise in the hallway. My heart was thumping like a drum in my chest, and I couldn't breathe. This wasn't working.

Quietly, with my gut feeling like I had just eaten a bowl full of hot coals, I slipped out of bed, grabbed my sheet and crawled under my desk. As I lay on the floor, the silent sobs welled up, and I hated myself for my weakness. For eight years, I had slept on the floor, and I didn't know how to sleep in a bed any more. Even after I was free, Dulka was still screwing my life up. He was invading my mom's home like a plague, and I hated myself for letting him win. I kicked my own ass over it for what seemed like forever, but then, somewhere along the way, the familiar took over, and I fell asleep.

By the time ten o'clock rolled around on Sunday night, I figured I was tired enough to at least try sleeping *next* to the bed. My arms and legs were still carrying a grudge from Friday night, and helping Mom in her garden hadn't made them any happier with me. She'd called it dirt therapy, and it had felt pretty good, but now my body hated me for it. I snagged the sheet and curled up with my back to the bed, and waited for the panic attack to come. After a few minutes, I figured I'd either out-waited it, or it was laying in ambush for me once I nodded off.

The rumble of thunder woke me up. My eyes opened to a still-dark room, with only the red glow of my boxy alarm clock to focus on. It read 5:50. White light flashed at the windows, and thunder rumbled again. The thin hiss of rain followed it, and I sat up. Mom was supposed to enroll me in school today. Visions of walking down the halls of a high school flitted across my thoughts as I tossed the sheet on the bed and grabbed some fresh clothes. In the shower, I imagined sitting in a classroom and taking notes on fascinating subjects, enthralled with the mysteries of algebra, or, for me, the equally strange subject of Home Economics.

The clock showed only three minutes after six by the time I made it back to my room, and I could hear Mom and Dee just starting to move around in their rooms. The morning was going to take forever to go by at this rate. A little less than an eternity later, Mom and I had dropped Dee off at her school, and Mom finally turned her van toward…home.

"Where are we going? Don't we have to go to the school to enroll me?" I asked as we headed down rain-slick streets.

"I need to get your immunization records and your birth certificate transferred over. My lawyer is having them sent by courier to the house. In the meantime, I need to stop by the courthouse and sign the temporary custody papers, and we need to file the motion for…well, it's pretty boring stuff. Do you mind staying at the house to sign for your records?" Mom looked over at me hopefully, and, so help me, I couldn't make myself disappoint her.

"So, I'm not going to go to school today?" I tried to hide my disappointment, but my voice wasn't in the mood to help me out.

"It would probably be tomorrow in any case, sweetie. The school would still have to look your records over and get you scheduled for the right classes and everything. Think of it as…an unexpected three-day weekend. Though, I should be counting my blessings, having a son who *wants* to go to school. Your sister practically has to be forced out the door some days."

I shrugged. "School's not so bad. I'll deny it totally if you tell anyone I said that, though."

"Your secret's safe with me. But, more seriously, I'm afraid your father or his lawyer will be there, and I don't want to tempt fate any more than I have to." I nodded, and my mood went from disappointed to dark. Missing a day of school didn't seem so bad suddenly, when I thought about seeing my father again.

Mom pulled into the driveway and handed me a key. "I'll be back in a little while, and hopefully by then, we can get you transferred over to Kennedy, and maybe grab lunch afterward to celebrate," she said as I popped the door open. After I grunted a yes and hopped out, she pulled out of the driveway and puttered off, leaving me with a whole morning to myself, nothing urgent that needed doing, and a whole shelf full of books to read.

The knock at the front door came less than half an hour later, just when I was starting the third chapter in the mystery I'd chosen. I memorized the page number and closed the book. Old habits kicked in, and I ducked down beside the couch and bent one of the blind's slats to peer out at the front porch. A cold chill ran down my back when I recognized my father's butler, Jeremy. What in the Nine Hells was he doing here? If my father was going to send someone to bring me back, he'd use a guy with a thicker neck and a smaller brain. Someone who opened doors with his foot instead of knocking politely.

"You're not taking me back," I said, when I opened the door.

He gave the same neutral smile I was used to seeing from him, but this time, I could see it in his eyes, too. "Of course not, Master Chance. I'd hardly dream of it. I am merely doing my part to maintain the illusion that you actually resided with your father," he said, his accent still the proper English butler. He sounded like a man who was resigned to his fate, and it made my stomach twist.

54

"Whether you want to or not," I said bitterly. I closed my eyes, took a slow breath and opened my Third Eye just enough to see his aura. It was mostly a deep blue, with ugly gray streaks that surfaced in places. Around his neck, though, I could see a band of dark red laced with black tendrils that reached up along his face to hover in front of his mouth like poisonous little vines. It was my own handiwork: one of the first compulsion spells I ever cast. Crude, sloppy as hell, but it worked.

"I wouldn't be able to speak to that, sir," Jeremy said, still prim. Guilt settled on me like a lead blanket. Jeremy was one of the few guys who worked for my father who'd ever been nice to me, and he was still under the bastard's thumb, while I was walking free. My own promise from Friday night came back to me, and I felt my lips peel back from my teeth in a wolfish grin.

"You should be able to. This is for your own good. Don't move," I commanded him. The compulsion kicked in with the trigger phrase and he went still. Dulka had made sure that every spell I cast had a counter-hex built into it, in case someone tried to screw him over. I reached up and put my hand into the compulsion's stain on his aura, and felt the greasy, chill touch close around my fingers. It tried to creep onto my aura, and I suppressed a shudder as I uttered the counter hex, *Adactio spretum.*" The smear dissipated into a fine gray haze on the edge of his aura.

His eyes went a little wide, and I saw his jaw go slack for the first time. He could talk and act freely now, but until I destroyed the focus, the spell could be reactivated. "Oh, I say!" he said.

"Yeah, say whatever you want."

He blinked a few times, and his lips went thin as he stood up straighter, which for him was almost impossible. "Your father...is an absolute...wanker!" he finally blurted. "Master Chance, whatever you just did, thank you! You can't imagine what it's been like all the...well, perhaps you can. Even better than I can," he went quiet as he finished.

I shook my head. "I just undid some of my own work. And, I'm sorry for doing it to you in the first place."

"No, sir. You needn't apologize. It was all him, and that…thing he called up. Don't you ever think otherwise. I'm relieved you were finally able to do something about it. Which brings me to the purpose of my visit. Your things are in the car."

"My things? Jeremy, all of my stuff didn't even fill up a gym bag."

"Indeed, sir. All of which gives lie to the appearance your poor, much-maligned father was attempting to maintain. Hence, my excursions to such exclusive establishments as American Eagle and…Hot Topic. Shall I bring it in?" He gestured to the tan Cadillac that lurked in the driveway. I followed him to the rear of the car. Bags filled the trunk, and a pair of suitcases sat in the backseat. I grabbed the bags and took them to my room before he could protest. Jeremy took the suitcases without a word, but his expression told me how dismayed her was. All that was left in the trunk when we went back out was a big shoebox and a black backpack. Those we just brought to the living room.

"That should be all, sir. You'll find a laptop computer and other school supplies in your backpack. Here is your last month's allowance, and an advance on next month's, as well. I…should be going." He pressed a roll of bills into my hand as he turned to go.

"Jeremy, wait!" I said quickly as he turned away. He looked back over his shoulder at me and raised his eyebrows, as if to encourage me to continue.

"What I just did…it's temporary. If my father figures it out, he can get Dulka to activate the spell again."

"Then I shall be discreet, sir, and make the best use of my freedom while I have it." His smile resurfaced as he came over to me and put one hand on my shoulder. "It is a gift beyond measure, Master Chance. I assure you, I will not squander it."

"I'll try to…make it permanent, somehow," the words tumbled out of my mouth in a rush. "If I can find the focus, I can break the spell for good. I want to fix this."

"Chance, you have done more than enough." There was a warmth to his voice that didn't sound like my father's butler was just speaking to his young charge. "You need not take responsibility for the wrongs of others. If you are asking for my forgiveness, you've long had it."

Part of the weight on my heart lifted, and I felt the corners of my mouth try to stretch into a smile, but it was still weak. "Thanks, Jeremy."

"Think nothing of it, sir. Nothing to forgive." He gave my shoulder a squeeze and stepped back, then gave me a "Good day, sir," before he left. Even though I felt better, something still bothered me. The nagging guilt was still there, and seeing Jeremy had just made it worse. In spite of what he'd said, I still felt responsible for all the things I'd done for Dulka and my old man. I paced back and forth as I wrestled with my thoughts, and made absolutely no progress in getting them pinned down by the time my records were delivered. When Mom showed up around two o'clock, my psyche and I decided to call it a draw, but I promised it I wasn't finished with it. I imagined it like some Saturday morning cartoon villain, twirling its mustache and chuckling threateningly as it retreated into the dark parts of my mind.

Mom and I swapped stories about our morning over cheeseburgers and fries. For once, I lost the "Sucks to Be Me" contest. I got new stuff, while Mom had to sit in uncomfortable chairs and deal with assholes all morning.

I practically dragged her to the van, though, because the best part of the day was still to come. I bounced in the seat all the way to the parking lot of Kennedy High School, and it was all I could do to wait until she stopped the van to jump out. The red brick building loomed in front of me, three stories of normal teenage life just waiting to be experienced.

Half an hour later, I was elbow-deep in enrollment forms, while Mom filled out other paperwork. I'd just decided on French for my foreign language credit when a thick file folder with my name on the front of it plopped down in front of me. I looked up to my right to see Mom standing in front of a dark-haired woman in a blue business skirt and matching blazer. The dark-haired woman was glaring at me over the narrow lenses of her glasses. Mom looked down at the folder, then at me, so I opened it with shaky, sweaty hands.

Detention for fighting. Suspended for assault. Suspended for trespassing. Expelled for carrying a weapon. Expelled for possession. Expelled for fighting. My school record read like the rap sheet for a thug in training. I'd never actually seen what my old boss had been putting in my academic file, but none of it came as a surprise. Most of it was watered down for public consumption. I looked back up at Mom, but I couldn't meet her gaze for more than a few seconds.

"I'm sorry, Mom," I said to the floor. I could still feel Mom's eyes on me, and my gut churned at the thought that I'd let her down already. Bad karma *really* sucked.

Mom's gentle hand on my face was the last thing I expected. She lifted my chin up until I could see her face, and she laid her other hand on my file. "This isn't the boy I see in front of me. It's not the young man I think you want to be, either. But it *is* who Principal Ravenhearst, here, thinks you are, and she doesn't think this young man," she patted the damning file, "should be in her school. She's only willing to give you one chance. If you step out of line even once, she'll expel you." Mom's voice was sharp as she spoke, and I couldn't tell if she was angry with me, Miss Ravenhearst, or both of us. Miss Ravenhearst gave us a cold smile, and I figured this was playing out the way she wanted it to. The conditions were almost impossible to meet, and I was betting she knew it.

"If you don't want to deal with this crap, say the word and we'll figure something else out," Mom offered. Ravenhearst's smile get a little broader, a little colder, and I made my decision.

"I'll take it." I narrowed my eyes at Ravenhearst, and her smile flipped.

"Chance, you don't have to…"

"I'll take it, Mom. If she's going to give me just one shot, I'll take it."

It was Mom's turn to smile, and I could see the gleam in her eyes as she turned to face the principal. "Well, then, you heard my son. Get him enrolled."

I was about to start high school.

Chapter 6

~ Among the cowan, be mysterious. They'll come to far more useful conclusions on their own than you could suggest. ~ Myrddin Wyltt, 6th century Master

Tuesday morning took its sweet time to show up. My breakfast was sharing space in my stomach with a bunch of butterflies as Mom pulled into the school parking lot again. We passed kids milling around near the front doors and along the narrow strip of grass in front of the school. The groups were easy to sort by their wardrobes. Polo shirts and ass-hugging designer jeans didn't mingle with the baggy, strap-laden pants and dark t-shirts; and the sports jerseys and angled ball caps didn't mix often with the dress shirts and earth-tone pants and fedoras.

I took a quick look down at my clothes, and tried to see where I might fit. Black cargo pants tucked into my new black, mid-calf combat boots, and a gray t-shirt with black sleeves under a black leather jacket. The only groups that even looked remotely like me were the pale and tragic goths, and the equally pale group of pimple-faced guys in black trench coats and combat boots. I wasn't sure I wanted to hang out with anyone who dressed like I did.

The van came to a stop. "I'll pick you up here around four-thirty," Mom said. I nodded, too excited to talk, and I tried for surly acceptance when she kissed my cheek.

"See you this afternoon," I managed as I hopped out and slung my backpack on my right shoulder. Mom's van sputtered away, and I looked at the school. My brain tried to register everything, lock it away as vividly as possible. For anyone else, this looked like me transferring in from another school. But for me, this was another first. My first day of high school. I wanted to remember this.

I closed my eyes and opened my aura sight. Like any public building, the school wasn't warded. No one claimed any place with a flag in front of it. Flags marked *cowan* territory as well as any glyphs or sigils. Lusty reds and passionate oranges shone in auras all over the place, with an occasional unconventional mauve flash moving through them. The group of trench-coated guys was a spiky, angry gray, and some of the goths had mournful, muddy yellow streaks running through their auras. They were bright, beautiful…untainted. I held my own hand up. Murky red and black taint swirled over my skin: the anger and the corruption of black magick all over my aura. Maybe some of the pretty would rub off on me, and not the other way around.

With a shake of my head, I cleared my aura sight and started for the front doors. Scraps of conversations reached my ears, only a few words making sense at a time.

"…believe she bought the same dress…"

"…kicked his ass on the ghetto level, with my new…"

"…think he'd go out with me? I'd just…"

"… a condensed copy of the *Necronomicon* last week. Only…"

I stopped as I heard the last and tilted my head to hear more.

"… spells. None of the weak crap." The guy who was talking was one of the trench coat crowd, with a narrow face and shoulder length brown hair.

"That would be so cool," one of his friends said.

"Yeah, I figure I'm going to be the most powerful warlock in the city by next week," the first guy said. "Check it out." He pulled a thin book from his coat pocket, and I almost choked on a laugh. It looked like a pulp paperback, with a black cover and white lettering and designs, one of the hoax versions of the *Necronomicon* anyone could buy in a mainstream bookstore. If he was a warlock, I was a televangelist.

I turned and headed through the main doors. My locker lurked somewhere in this maze of people and stone, and I didn't have a lot of time to find it. In theory, I knew where it was; I'd even been to it and dumped my books in it yesterday afternoon. Finding it again, though, that was going to be a real trick with so many people in the halls, and I didn't have time to waste on wanna-be sorcerers trying to do mail-order magic.

The Demon's Apprentice

With people leaning on the lockers, it was almost impossible to figure out where mine was. The halls cleared some when the first bell rang, and I figured out I'd passed mine about a halfway down the hallway, so I had to backtrack. Like most things I needed to remember, I'd gotten my locker combination down pretty quickly. But getting the numbers to line up and open the lock? Whole different story.

The tardy bell rang just as I coaxed the lock open, and I ran for my first class after I grabbed my American History textbook. Room numbers counted down in my head as my feet pounded on the linoleum. The heavy sound of my boots echoed off the empty hall like doom in my ears. Late for my first class. This day wasn't starting off well at all.

My luck held true when I overshot the room and nearly slipped on the slick tiles as I tried to stop myself. The doorknob only jiggled a little when I tried to turn it, and the little balding man behind the desk gave me a glare through the narrow rectangle of safety glass. He raised a warning finger at me when I knocked. I could see him look back down at his roll-sheet and hear him drone off another name in a nasal voice. I pulled my crumpled schedule out of my front pocket and read the name by American History. Strickland. I didn't like him already.

I sighed and slumped against the door. Great. If Principal Ravenhearst really wanted to get rid of me, I was giving her plenty to work with, right off the bat. Strickland's droning tone kept going behind me, reciting the names of people who knew where his class was and could get there on time. While I was contemplating a suitable Infernal torment for the little man, another sound danced across my thoughts: a girl's giggle.

"Bra-ad!" I heard her voice rise and fall from around the corner to my right. "We're late as it is! Stop that!" I heard another giggle, and a long-legged redhead came around the corner with one hand swiping behind her blue skirt. Blue straps from her backpack pulled her white button-down blouse tight against her, and showed every curve between her shoulders and hips.

A tall blond guy in a purple jacket with gold sleeves swooped in behind her and caught her up with one arm. He spun her to face him, and his other arm reached behind her to grab a handful of her ass. I could see patches on his jacket sleeve for pretty much any sport with a ball. She gave a little cry and pushed him away, and he gave way with a laugh.

"Mr. Abrams wouldn't dare give us detention," he said as he pulled her under his arm and turned them toward me. More patches and medals decorated the right side of his jacket, and I could see the big "K" on the left side of his chest. If there was a Kennedy team he *didn't* play on, it was the chess team. "Coach would have his ass if I couldn't make it to practice."

The girl saw me first, and her face went red, even as Brad ducked his head down to nuzzle at her neck. She slapped his free hand down. "Brad!" she hissed.

He looked up and finally saw me.

The next thing I knew, I was up against the lockers, looking eye to eye with Brad. He had a double handful of my jacket and shirt, and was holding me at eye level, which left my feet not touching floor.

"Getting a good eyeful, you little pervert?" he growled at me.

My brain clamped down on my body's instinct to fight back, but my mouth didn't seem to be in the loop. "Isn't that what a trophy girlfriend's for? So people will look?"Behind him, the girl gave a little gasp, and I saw her gray eyes get wide. Brad just looked at me with a slack expression on his face. "Does she match your car?" Finally, he seemed to get it. One hand left my jacket, and slammed into my stomach. Pain exploded into nausea as I hit the floor.

"My girl isn't a trophy!" Brad said in my ear as I gasped for breath on my hands and knees. I leaned back on my knees and took a shuddering breath as my diaphragm tried to relax.

"Oh, sorry, do you prefer the term accessory?" I asked the girl when I could breathe again.

Her jaw dropped, but her eyes went to Brad, and I saw pain there instead of wounded pride. She turned and ran down the hallway, and Brad grabbed my jacket again. His right fist went back to his ear.

"I'm gonna beat you six ways from Sunday, asshole!" he said.

Movement to my left caught my eye, and I saw the teacher come around the corner before Brad did. He was a pudgy man with wiry, salt-and-pepper hair that didn't seem to want to hang out next to his head, and a pair of rectangular glasses that rode low on his nose, letting him peer over them at us with intense green eyes. He had a yellow shirt under a brown sweater vest and brown pants, and somehow he made that look more comfortable than dorky.

"One for every other day of the week, I take it?" the teacher said. A thin smile creased his round face, and I could hear steel in his voice.

Brad flinched and turned to face the man. "Huh?" And I thought I had the snappy comebacks.

"Six ways from Sunday, Mister Duncan. It means once for every other day of the week, which is to say, you will do it many times, or frequently. Not quite the context you had in mind, I'm sure, but I understand that you were threatening violence to this young man. Am I correct?" This guy was smart. I liked him already.

"I dunno what you're talking about Mister Chomsky," Brad said as he pulled me to my feet. The name sounded familiar.

"Don't try to lie to me, Brad. To your credit, you're not very good at it. Coach Brenner may have most of the other teachers toeing his little line, but I will remind you that you enjoy no special protection where I am concerned. If you are not elsewhere with extreme haste, you will learn first-hand the definition of the term 'sidelined.' Do I make myself abundantly clear, Mr. Duncan?"

"Yeah." He leaned in closer to me and put his index finger in the middle of my chest. "This ain't over, asshole," he whispered.

I looked down at his hand, then back up at him and tried to keep any expression off my face. "Are you left handed?" I asked him. He gave me a blank look. "Are. You. Left. Handed?"

"No."

"Then, the next time you touch me, don't use your good hand." I stepped back and let the threat hang in the air between us. I probably shouldn't have tried to be a smart ass about it, because it looked like he was going to have to go rough up a smart kid to find out what I meant.

He gave me a sneer and stalked off.

"I don't condone violence as a solution to conflicts, Mr. Fortunato," Mr. Chomsky said. "Even where people like Mr. Duncan are concerned."

"How did you know my name?"

"Oh, simple deduction, really. Principal Ravenhearst has informed us of a new student arriving today. Said new student, Chance Fortunato, is in my Physical Science class for fifth period, and Mr. Strickland has him in his first period class. Seeing as you are outside Mr. Strickland's classroom during first period, and you are still carrying your class schedule in hand, I can deduce that you are a new student, and as Chance Fortunato is the only new student we have today, I deduce that you are he."

"Okay. Um…thanks for…you know," I stammered.

"You're welcome. And Mr. Fortunato?"

"Yes, sir?"

"While violence is not an optimal solution, I do understand that it can be an excellent deterrent. However, I still cannot condone the implied threat of violence, no matter how well-put." He smiled and walked past me. "Don't use your good hand," he chuckled as he headed down the hall.

I revised my first impression of Mr. Chomsky. This guy was really, *really* smart. Still, the way the girl had reacted bugged me. I'd expected her to insult me back or something. Instead, I felt like something I should have been scraping off the bottom of my shoe.

American History wasn't so bad after Strickland let me in, and Algebra was a lot easier than spell theory, even if Mrs. Meyers seemed to teach by hypnosis. Everything about her, from her flat, bored tone, to her old-lady dress in the most boring shade of pastel blue I'd ever seen, seemed designed to numb the brain into a trance. At least in algebra, the formulas stayed the same all the time, and didn't change with the stars.

English was more interesting. Mr. Abrams had the desks in his room set up in a big circle. The man himself was slim and energetic, with a pair of thick glasses that made his watery eyes seem huge on his face. The class was reading *The Scarlet Letter*, and even by my standards, it seemed boring at first glance. Mr. Abrams asked questions about why the characters did things, and explained about the way people did things back then. Maybe I started to like it because it was about sin and redemption; I had a deeply personal understanding of that.

Fourth period was P.E. with Coach Connors. As long as we at least tried to be active, he seemed happy. It was only at the end of the period that I started to worry. Everyone around me stripped out of their t-shirts and gym shorts and headed for the showers. I was hot and sweaty from class, and there was no way I was going to go to lunch smelling like I did.

I grabbed a towel and waited for most of the guys around me to head for the shower, then put my back to the lockers and took my shirt off, and draped the towel across my shoulders so it covered most of my back. The scars on my chest and legs still showed, but there weren't as many of those. I headed for the showers, and felt a wash of relief as I stepped past the partition. The shower heads were on four round pillars with semi-partitioned sections set around them, so I figured I could get in, shower, and get out without anyone seeing the scars on my back. Still, I made quick work of getting myself cleaned up. The locker room was mostly empty by the time I got out, so getting dressed wasn't too bad, and I was headed for my locker to grab my lunch only a couple of minutes after the bell rang.

My heart sank as I stepped into the cafeteria and looked at the sea of people in front of me. The buzz of a hundred conversations washed over me like an invisible wave, and the energy of a room full of people pressed in on my mystic senses. The subtle pressure made me feel like my ears wanted to pop as I walked through the subtle ebb and flow of mystic currents toward an unoccupied table in the corner.

Suddenly, I felt very alone. The sense of isolation caught me off guard. Only three days back with people I loved, and I couldn't go for more than four hours away from them without getting lonely. I shook my head as I opened the insulated lunch sack Mom had given me that morning. I'd gone for years on my own; I could handle another few hours. When I pulled out the two sandwiches Mom had made, I smiled and felt a little of the loneliness vanish. Mom had made them with bread she'd baked on Sunday. She'd packed some chips, and a thick piece of baklava. It was like having a little piece of home there with me.

I caught myself closing up the chips before I was finished, and forced myself to eat all of them. Mom wasn't going to let me go hungry, I reminded myself. I didn't need to stash food for later. Thoughts of stale pizza and flat soda surfaced for a moment, and I forced them into the big box in my head marked "The Past – Don't Open. Ever." Besides, I told myself, the future was looking a lot brighter now; Mr. Chomsky's class was right after lunch, and I still had French and Wood Shop to look forward to.

I took my time with the baklava, and still had a few minutes to enjoy my soda. I'd forgotten how good cold, still-fizzy soda could taste until Saturday, and I decided I liked orange soda, but not as much as root beer. I crossed orange off my mental list. Clear citrus drinks were next, though I had no idea what the difference could be between any of them, I was looking forward to finding out.

The taste of my soda was just starting to fade on my tongue when the bell rang. People started heading for the doors across the cafeteria from me. Crap. If just being in the same room with so many people pushed on my mystic senses, I didn't want to find out what getting caught up in the bottleneck a door would cause.

Two guys ducked past me, both a little chubby, both wearing t-shirts with slogans on them, both moving like they didn't want to be seen. They slipped out of a set of doors that were half-hidden by stacks of chairs, and I followed. It opened out into an almost-empty hallway next to the auditorium. It put me on the far side of the cafeteria from my locker, but I preferred having to hustle a little to the headache a mystic overload would cause.

I ducked into a narrow hallway that looked like it went where I needed to go, and hoped I wasn't getting myself lost. When I got close to the end, though, I heard Brad's voice, and saw a flash of purple and gold. More letter jackets gathered near the end of the hall, and I heard another voice. The hall came to a T a few yards in front of me, and people were passing between Brad's group and me, so I couldn't see the other guy.

"Brad, look, I'm gonna be late for class, man," the unseen guy said.

"We wouldn't want that, would we?" Brad mocked. "This ain't gonna take long."

A door opened across the hallway, and Brad's buddies chuckled as they all followed him in. As tempting as it was to leave the guy to his fate, it wasn't tempting enough. I hit the intersection of the hallway at a jog and wove my way through the other students toward what I could see was a boys' bathroom. The door hadn't quite closed, and I pushed it open just far enough to slip inside. The privacy wall hid me from view, and I slid along it until I was near the edge. I was out of direct sight, but I could see the end mirror on the line of sinks. In the reflection, I could see Brad's victim pinned against the stalls, a dark-haired kid wearing a denim trench coat that was covered in ink drawings.

"Look, Brad," the kid was saying, "I told you I'm not going to say anything. No one would believe me!"

"Mr. Chomsky might," Brad countered. "He likes you, Lucas, and he has it in for me. So if you run and tell him you saw me in his classroom during lunch, he might think I was up to something."

"Dude, you were in his briefcase!" Lucas said.

"See, that's the kind of attitude that'll get you in trouble. We need to fix that. We're gonna give you a taste of what'll happen if you open your big mouth. What did Coach call that again, Bryce?"

"Negative reinforcement," one of the other jocks said.

"Guys, I promise, I won't say anything!" Lucas' voice came out almost as a squeak.

"We just want to be sure, see," one of the jocks said from Brad's left.

"If you tell anyone what you saw, you're gonna hurt a lot worse than this." Brad drew his fist back and gut-punched Lucas. He went down to his hands and knees and retched.

The rest of the jocks moved in on him and my heart sped up. Lucas gave a moan that sounded like a kid who'd been through this before, and I stepped around the corner. The part of my brain that had probably never evolved was screaming at me like a monkey to go the other way, but the seven-year-old kid in me could only see himself there on the floor. I slapped the hairy monkey part of my brain down and kept going. All I had was a desperate bluff that one of my marks had tried on me once.

"He doesn't have to say anything." I looked down at my empty right hand and slipped it into my pocket. "All I have to do is hit the send button, and you guys are all over my home page."

Eight jocks gave me slack-jawed looks, while Lucas just seemed relieved. It looked like they were buying my bluff. Their eyes kept moving back and forth between my face and my jacket pocket. All I had was the suggestion of a cell phone in my pocket and a credible-sounding threat. Hell, smoke and mirrors were more real than what I was trying to pull off.

"You. What do you want?" Brad asked.

"Let the skinny dude walk," I said.

Lucas started to scramble to his feet, and Brad grabbed him by the back of his jacket. "Erase the video first," he demanded.

"Don't try to negotiate with me, Duncan. You don't have the leverage here. I do. Cut him loose, or you're an instant Internet sensation."

Brad tried to look unconcerned, but his friends were sweating. "Brad, the big dog would kill us if something like that got out," one of them said softly. Brad let go of Lucas like his jacket had just caught on fire. He scrambled across the bathroom toward me and I heard him turn around behind me.

The Demon's Apprentice

"Awright, he's cut loose," Brad said. "Now erase the video, damn it."

"Oh, I figure this is good at least till the end of football season. Call it a little negative reinforcement," I said as I stepped back and slipped out the door. Lucas was right beside me as I headed for my locker. The halls were almost empty around us.

"Dude, that was awesome!" he crowed as he bounced beside me. "You ought to post it anyway. Brad will just try to kick your ass."

"Leverage is only good 'til you use it," I said. The fact that I didn't actually *have* any leverage didn't help. But as long as everyone believed it was real, the bluff would keep working.

"This is going to be the best year ever. Hey, I'm Lucas Kale." He stuck a hand out.

"Chance Fortunato." I felt the faint tingle of potential talent as I shook his hand. "You're gonna be late for class."

He looked at his watch and cursed. "Dude, you're right. See you later?" He turned and jogged off, and I broke into a trot, too. I barely made it to Physical Science before the tardy bell rang. There was only one seat left, near the front of the lab, to the left of the teacher's desk. My heart started thumping in my chest at the too-familiar sight of a lab room. This one was a lot like the one at Truman High School where I'd spent the last four years. Except for the students. The difference was enough to help me get my feet going, and I slid into the open seat.

The girl next to me was dressed in a lot of black, with fingerless lace gloves, a fishnet top under a black t-shirt, and a lace-over-satin skirt. Her hair was a bright red bob with black streaks through it, and she wore thick, dark eyeliner and a nose ring. The rest of her face was as pale as cosmetics could make it, except for black lipstick.

Two guys sat across from us, both wearing t-shirts with superheroes on the front.

"You must be the new guy everyone's talking about," the girl said cheerfully.

"New guy, I'll cop to. I didn't know anyone was talking about me, though. I'm Chance."

"I'm Wanda. Yeah, word is Brad Duncan already hates you, good going there, and Strickland's doing his best to help the principal kick you out. Gina Morales' brother, Sammy, said you had a bunch of scars and some tattoos; were you in a gang or something?" she blurted in one breath.

I replayed the whole thing in my head to make sure I didn't miss anything before I answered.

"Okay, in order: nice to meet you; yes, he does, the feeling's mutual; it figures, the guy's a jerk; yes, I do; and no, I wasn't." I waited for a moment while she sorted that all out.

"Wanda's like the CIA," the guy on the left said with a smirk.

"Only with boobs," the one on the right added. They both snickered as Wanda flipped them off.

"Any time, babe," Left said.

There was a chorus of giggles behind us, and a square of colored paper landed on the lab table between us. Wanda and I both looked over our shoulders for the source. Two lab tables back, we saw a trio of blonde heads turned our way with a fashion magazine open on the desk in front of them.

"Try some, it'll cover the smell of bitch," one of them said sweetly.

Wanda's face turned red, and she picked up the little perfume sample from the table. "I'll take bitch over skank any day, Leda," she hissed and threw it back. Whatever Leda was about to say back was cut short as the door opened. The room went quiet for a second then the murmur of conversations started back up again as a familiar-looking redhead walked into the room.

"Speaking of skanks," Wanda said, "all hail the Queen Skank. I heard you *really* pissed her off before first period. Shanté said she was crying all through Algebra. What did you say to her?"

"I called her…an accessory," I said quietly. "Asked Brad if she matched his car."

She turned her head to face me as she passed, and I could see fresh hurt in her eyes when they met mine. There was no way she could have heard me from halfway across the room, but she was acting like she had.

"Oh, wow!" Wanda gasped. "His truck is bright red, she totally matches it!" Was that all it was, I wondered? Brad's girlfriend made her way to the Blonde Table and was instantly surrounded by designer tops and perfect hair.

"All right, class, let's begin," Mr. Chomsky's voice came from the front of the room. He was standing behind his desk with a blue ice chest in his hands.

"I hate it when he does that!" Right whispered, as Chomsky pulled the attendance book out of his desk.

I sat back to wait for him to call out names, and tried to think of a cool way to say, "Here." However, Mr. Chomsky didn't seem to do anything the normal way. He looked out over the room, down at his roll sheet, then grabbed a pen.

"Here; here; here; absent; here; here; here; Brianna et al., here; here; Mr. Fortunato, barely here on time; and Miss Cooper, technically tardy. And, there's me, also technically tardy, so I can't hold it against you." He set the attendance book down, then smiled before he spoke again. "Very well, class, let's get some learning done! First of all, we have a new student today, Mr. Fortunato. Make him feel welcome. Now, let's review briefly what we went over yesterday in chapter seven on thermal energy, then we'll be breaking out the Bunsen burners and playing with fire to demonstrate some of water's more interesting properties. Who remembers the boiling point of water?"

"Two hundred twelve degrees Fahrenheit, or one hundred degrees Celsius," I said quickly.

"Excellent, Mister Fortunato. Next time, though, raise the hand, please. Now, can water in an open container get any hotter?" I started to raise my hand, but Chomsky pointed to one of the blondes behind me.

"Total no-brainer there!" she said. "Of course it can! My mom's stove goes up to like four hundred, and she puts it up to the highest setting when she boils water all the time."

"Thank you, Miss Case. An interesting observation. Anyone disagree?"

My hand went up slowly, and I was the lone holdout against her opinion.

"All right, Mister Fortunato. Why?" he asked, as a few chuckles went around the room.

"Okay," I started, "um, so, yeah, a stove goes higher than two-twelve, and yeah, her mom uses higher temperatures when she cooks, but that doesn't mean the water gets any hotter, it just means it boils faster. When water boils, it turns into steam, and that can get as hot as it wants." I stopped for a moment to try to find the right way to describe what I'd seen hundreds of times while making potions and elixirs for the boss.

"Dork," Leda said.

"Thank you, Miss Carson, for volunteering to defend Mister Fortunato's theory," Chomsky said with a smile. "Now, stand up and explain to the class why he's right."

"But…he's not, Mister Chomsky!" Leda said.

"Care to bet an A on that?" Chomsky said, as he carried the ice chest to the middle of the room.

Leda's face went slack as the wheels seemed to click in her brain.

"Sure, Mister Chomsky!" the first girl who had spoken up said. "I'll bet an A on it, if the loser gets an F!" Chomsky turned a knowing eye on her before he answered. "Ah, interesting stakes. So, the age-old question comes back to the fore: how does the universe work? Even more importantly, it would seem, whose version of the truth does the cosmos favor?" He turned slowly as he spoke, clearly enjoying his topic.

"Well, class, the universe favors only its own truth. All we have are hypotheses that we test. If we can neither prove nor disprove them, they evolve into theories. But, if we can prove them, they grow up to be Laws. Thus, today's experiment. Mister Fortunato's table will be testing to prove his hypothesis that water does not get hotter than its boiling point. Miss Carson's table will be testing to prove that it does. Everyone else will be the control groups, repeating the experiment to see if they can get the same data. Hence, we are the scientific community in microcosm. So, Bunsen burners, everyone, and safety glasses. Remember the safety rules for using gas; we don't want to duplicate Friday night's destruction of Truman High School's science wing." He slipped his own pair of safety glasses on, then opened the ice chest and had half of us add three ice cubes to our water, to test the theory that cold water boiled faster.

"So, Kelly says you transferred in from Truman, and you've got a file like a foot thick. Did you have anything to do with, you know…" Wanda asked as we set up our experiment.

"It's a good theory," I said as people around us complained about the safety goggles messing up their hair. "Can't be proven or disproven. The cops haven't charged me with anything yet."

Wanda smiled and nodded, but the two guys on the far side of the table traded wide-eyed looks.

We stared at the thermometers in our beakers of water as they stayed at thirty two degrees until the ice was all gone. I got another thermometer and double checked that ours wasn't broken or something, but it showed the same temperature. The mercury slowly climbed until it hit two-twelve…and didn't boil. And kept right on not-boiling for another three minutes.

"Proving that a watched pot never boils, Mister Fortunato?" Chomsky said from over my right shoulder.

"Maybe," I growled. "The temperature's right. Why doesn't it just boil?"

"Excellent question, my boy. The energy required to actually make water boil is five times that required to simply heat it to two hundred twelve degrees."

"So, what is all that extra energy doing?"

"As you know, water is composed of an oxygen atom and two hydrogen atoms. A very sentimental element, hydrogen. It forms relatively strong bonds when it attaches to another atom. The extra energy is required to break those bonds. Ah, your water is boiling. Please make a note of your temperature, Miss Romanov."

"Still two hundred twelve Fahrenheit," Wanda whispered to me.

Chomsky's face broke into a grin. "Really? Imagine that. Ladies, I see your water is boiling, as well. Mark your temperatures down, class, and check again in five minutes, then place your cards face down on the corner of your tables so I can collect them."

"We are so getting an A," Wanda said as he left. I shrugged.

"So, what's her name?" I asked as I looked over my shoulder at the spot of red in the sea of blonde, two tables back.

"Brad's girlfriend? Hang on a second. I have to take a second to enjoy this. A guy who didn't know Alexis Cooper's name."

"Until now."

"Good things never last."

"I knew your name first."

"Yeah, you did." She smiled and glanced at the thermometer for a moment, then wrote down the temperature. I added my card to the pile at the corner of the table, and waited for Mr. Chomsky to come by. I didn't hear him come up behind me, but somehow, I felt him there. I looked over my shoulder at him to catch him blinking and shaking his head.

"Chance," he said thoughtfully, "I'd like you to stop by after school today. I think we need to discuss better placement for you."

"Better placement?" I asked warily. This was already the most basic science class I could be in without dropping back a grade.

"Yes. The questions you ask demonstrate a certain type of critical thinking. Which leads me to wonder if your true aptitude can't be measured by a standardized test. I believe that you might do better with a more challenging curriculum. One better suited to your...talents."

"Really?" The right side of my mouth quirked up on its own.

"Stop by after school, and we will discuss it further."

"Well, that was the kiss of death to your social life," Wanda said under her breath as he walked away.

"What do you mean?"

"He's talking advanced placement classes, dude. Might as well buy yourself a pocket protector and glasses now and avoid the Yuletide rush."

"I don't have much of a social life now. It can't be any worse than sharing class space with half the cheerleading squad." I nodded back at the blonde table.

"Uh-oh," Wanda muttered.

I followed her gaze, and saw one of the blondes, Leda, grab Mr. Chomsky's arm.

"So, do we get the A?" she asked, loud enough for the whole room to hear.

"Interesting supposition," Chomsky said. "You assume that there was a competition for the grade. You should know better by now, Miss Carson. When I asked if you cared to bet an A on the outcome, I was testing how certain you were of your hypothesis, seeing as it flew in the face of facts that are in your text book. Your grade, as always, will be based on the academic quality of your work, and the effort you put into it. It helped that you and Mister Fortunato had the courage to speak out in defense of your separate hypotheses."

He turned a little to address the whole class. "In science, courage can be as important as knowledge. True innovation, original thinking, and most of all, change, are not always well received. However, in the end, the truth will always be known. Very well, lecture over. Let's clean up." There was a rush of noise as everyone started working at once. Our table was done first, mostly because the other two guys went out of their way to outdo each other, but I also knew my way around a lab. The other tables weren't so fast, though, and it looked like the blondes were going to be cutting it close.

"You should come hang out with us tonight at Dante's," Wanda said as we waited for the bell to ring. "I think you'd like my friends. I'm sure they'd love you."

"I'll see if I can make it." I tried not to sound too eager.

"Let me know if you need a ride." She handed me a scrap of paper with a number scribbled on it.

That got me glares from Left and Right, but the bell cut those short before they could do any permanent damage to my ego. Wanda was out of her chair and halfway to the door before the bell stopped ringing, and our two tablemates weren't far behind her. I grabbed my backpack and fought the urge to clean up the rest of the lab. Some part of me was still afraid I was going to get a beating for leaving it this way.

"That's over now," I told myself as I tried to slip in behind the kids from the table behind us. A moment later, I was on the floor, buried beneath three blondes. For a moment, my hairy monkey brain had a field day. Then even that primitive part of me went shrieking back to its mental cave when I realized who I was buried under.

"Watch where you're going, reject!" Leda hissed at me as we untangled ourselves. "This is a two hundred dollar jacket. You're gonna pay for the cleaning!"

"Actually, Miss Carson, he's not. He's going to go to his next class, while you three come back to your table and finish cleaning up." Chomsky said. He put an emphasis on the last three words, pausing for a heartbeat between them. He stood over us, and for a moment, he looked like some ancient, angry god in a sweater.

Leda and her cronies got up and sulked back toward the lab table. Alexis was still there, struggling to disassemble the ring stand. She gave them a lethal look as they came back, but they didn't fall over and die right away. She snapped orders at them, and they started moving a little faster. Me, I was just happy I wasn't on the receiving end of that look.

"Away with you, Mister Fortunato," Chomsky said with a warm smile. "You've a great deal more to learn today, I'm sure. And we have an appointment this afternoon, don't forget." I was good at something other than sorcery and corruption. There was no way in all the Nine Hells was I going to forget.

Chapter 7

~ Make no pact with the Infernal Powers ~ Third Rule of Magick.

French and Wood Shop took way too long. If it wasn't such a beautiful sounding language, French would have been a snoozer of a class. Mrs. Solier was a nervous little woman with a soft voice, kind of like a mouse with self-esteem problems. Until she spoke French. Then she sounded like a completely different woman. I did my best, but I mangled the words at first. As I went along, it got easier, and I liked having something with a little beauty to it running around in my head.

Wood shop was my last class. Mr. Gonzalez was a round little man with brown skin and coal black hair that had gray at the temples. He barely came up to my shoulder, but he might as well have been a giant for the respect he got in the shop. The man was all business, but he went about it in the way a father with two dozen sons might. My first day was spent on safety and learning how to use *every* tool he could get my hands on. When the last bell rang, he told me that I would be able to start on a project next Monday, after I finished the safety lessons and showed him I knew how to use the tools.

My first day of school was done. All in all, it hadn't been too bad. I headed back to my locker and picked up my French, Algebra and American History books, then headed to Mr. Chomsky's classroom with a little extra spring in my step. I was hoping Wanda was right about advanced classes. All afternoon, I'd been imagining what Mom would say if I told her I was going to be in an advanced class. It took the edge off the memory of seeing her face when she laid my file in front of me.

My daydream crumbled when I heard Alexis Cooper's subdued voice. I froze in place as she came around the corner with her head down. I had just a moment to catch that she was putting her phone away before she bumped into me. Her head came up and her expression turned to ice.

"You," she hissed.

"Yeah, me," I said.

We stared at each other for a moment, and I could feel the pressure of her glare against my own gape-mouthed stare. She had pretty eyes, gray like storm clouds about to unleash a storm on me, and I felt myself start to be drawn into them. There was a weight to her stare that I could literally feel against my Third Eye. I focused hastily on the tip of her upturned nose, and felt the pressure fade from my senses. Locking eyes usually didn't create that kind of connection. Dulka had forced his way into my mind that way the first morning after he'd acquired me, so he could pry my Third Eye open and make me more useful to him. It was one of my least favorite memories ever. There was still pain in her eyes, though, pain I was pretty sure I'd caused.

"Hey, um, Alexis," I blurted, "about this morning. I, um…I'm sorry about that."

"For what? Perving on me and Brad? Being an asshole to me? Or pissing Brad off so I get to put up with his crappy mood all day?" Me-freaking-ow!

"The middle one. It was mean, and you didn't deserve it. The other two, well, you guys were pretty much putting on a free show in the middle of the hall, and as far as his mood goes…he's your boyfriend, so you kind of chose that on your own."

"Oh, so now I'm stupid?"

"If you were stupid, being called a trophy wouldn't have hurt you. But with Brad…like I said, he's your boyfriend, your choice. If he takes being in a shitty mood out on you…make a different choice."

"It's not that easy." Her eyes dropped away from mine, and she wrapped her arms around her middle. "Make both of our lives a lot easier and watch your ass with Brad, okay? You can't win with him." She shoved her way past me, and hurried down the hall.

I watched her go, then shook myself when I realized what part I was watching leave. Yeah, watch *my* ass. How was I supposed to do that when I couldn't keep my eyes off of hers? I resolved to take that secret to my grave and turned my feet back toward the science lab.

Mr. Chomsky's door was open, so I stepped in, and barely noticed a slight tingle as I crossed the threshold. The room was empty, but the storage room door was open at the back of the room.

"Mr. Chomsky?" I called out.

"Back here, my boy," his voice emerged from the store room door. "Do me a favor and close the door."

I set my backpack down and pushed the door closed. There was another, stronger tingle against my hand as it clicked closed, and I felt a pressure in the back of my head as something *else* closed. I looked down at my hand, then over my shoulder toward the store room. What the Hell was going on here? The light threshold presence wasn't too weird in a public room that someone had worked in for years. But the other two felt like…magick. I reached for my backpack with one hand, and the doorknob with the other as I heard movement from behind me.

"Excipio!" Chomsky bellowed from the back of the room.

A brief image of him with a green stole across his shoulders and a thick black rod in his outstretched right hand was burned onto my mind's eye before I was turned around in midair and slammed against the blackboard behind his desk. My wrists burned as some kind of ward clamped around them, and a lead weight seemed to fall on my chest. It forced my head to my left, until my neck was held at a painful angle. Two concentric circles were drawn beneath my left wrist on the chalkboard, with mystic sigils glowing between the inner and outer circle. I'd have bet that it had a twin beneath my right hand. Mr. Chomsky walked toward me slowly, the rod still held out in front of him. Mystic symbols of gold blazed on the green satin of the stole, and the tip of his wand blazed with a blue light.

"Mr. Chomsky, please! Wait!" I wheezed out. The lead weight feeling on my chest turned into an anvil.

"Silence, warlock!" his voice boomed. "I am Wizard Chomsky, of the Conclave of Magi. You face the judgment of the High Council for your crimes. Surrender peacefully and renounce your dark Master, and the council will be lenient." The last part came out in a bored-sounding monotone, and I didn't think he believed it.

"I already...did!" I managed to gasp out.

He frowned and his hand faltered. "Pardon me?"

The pressure on my chest let up, and I could turn my head enough to look almost right at him. "I already renounced him. Friday night. I serve no power of Hell, no demon, no Infernal lord. I am free," I said formally. I felt the pressure ease off of me almost entirely.

"If you still served as his apprentice, you would not be able to utter those words so readily," Mr. Chomsky said thoughtfully. "Your oath and contract would prevent it."

"Apprentice? Slave is more like it. I never signed any damn contract or swore any oaths."

"Your former Master tells a different story, of releasing an apprentice for incompetence."

"Yeah, let's believe the demon, because they're all so fucking honest!" I snarled.

"Their apprentices are not known for their sincerity either. And the only way to come to a demon's care is by choice."

"Choice! Choice? You think I had a fucking choice? My father *sold* me to that piece of Hell spawn when I was seven! I was his down payment for Dulka's services. Don't you dare tell me I went to him by *choice*!" I was practically screaming now, leaning away from the chalkboard as my wrists pulled against the mystic bonds that pinned me to the wall. For all that I was angry, I felt tears streaming down my face, too. Just as suddenly as I had been pinned to the wall, I found myself on the floor. Instinct kicked in, and I scrambled for the nearest corner and put my back to it.

Chomsky came slowly around the side of his desk and laid his rod on it. With exaggerated care, he took the stole off and laid it aside, too. He took a couple of slow steps forward, then went to one knee, so he was almost eye level with me. "Your father offered you, his first-born son, as his price for power. I'm so sorry, my boy. We let you down when you needed us the most." The thought hit some hidden nerve in my heart, and I found my lip trembling as I realized, for the first time, that the people Dulka had trained me to fear were *supposed* to be there to help me.

"Where were you?" I asked. I felt like the same scared kid who'd screamed his lungs out on the floor eight years ago. "Why did you let that happen to me?" Pain and anger were almost the same feeling just then. Some bone-deep part of me hurt so bad I could barely even think straight. I couldn't even be embarrassed about crying in front of a stranger.

"Because I didn't know, Chance," he said with a sincerity that I'd never heard from anyone but my mom. "I have no excuse for failing you then. I can only try to make amends for it now. Will you let me help you?" My throat seemed to close up, and I could only nod. I'd been beaten and whipped, had bones broken and skin torn by Dulka, and I'd screamed bloody murder, but I hadn't cried. But just a few kind words had ripped away every defense I had, and I choked out a short sob before I could get myself under control.

"What are you going to tell the Council?" I asked, once I could trust my voice again.

"For the moment, nothing. They're searching for an incompetent but somehow dangerous warlock. I believe you are neither. What you are, my boy, is unique. No apprentice, willing or otherwise, has ever been able to renounce his or her master voluntarily before. How you managed it is beyond me."

"It wasn't easy."

"Of that, I have no doubt. If it was, others before you would have done so, and the Council would be more likely to believe you. But you are the first in living memory, and the memories of the Magi are long indeed. Change doesn't come easily to the Conclave. I will, of course, vouch for you, which will help, but the High Council will need more convincing."

"Why did you believe me?"

"Rage is common enough in warlocks, and they can cry for you at the drop of a hat, if it serves their ends, but I have never seen both anger and tears at the same time. And, your story held no hidden praise for your Master couched as a warning." He held out his hand, and after a couple of seconds, I took it. If contact with Lucas gave me a little tingle, touching Mr. Chomsky was like shaking hands with a light socket. I let him pull me to my feet and we stood facing each other for a few seconds.

"So, what now?" I asked finally.

Mr. Chomsky sighed and shrugged. "For tonight, you return to your life as a normal teenager. Lay low, as it were. Tomorrow, your training begins."

"Training?" Boy, did I sound brilliant, or what?

"Yes, my boy, training. It's what apprentices do. They train. Vouching for you before the High Council won't be enough, Chance. The Council won't allow you to go about unsupervised, not with your past. However, as my apprentice, your disposition will have been decided *a priori*."

"Before the fact," I translated. "Kinda."

"Admittedly, something of an abuse of the Latin. But true, nevertheless."

"I'd get to learn the Ways? I'd really like that. Sorcery's...rough."

"Oh, yes, I quite understand. All that blood and pain, stealing of life force. Very unpleasant business. Not to worry, we'll fill your head with a much better sort of magick. I imagine you're well versed in spell theory and alchemy? Excellent. And circle lore, wards and ritual?"

"He made me learn about hexes and focus craft, too. Plus, I know the names of a few demons."

Chomsky smiled like a cat with a bowl full of cream. "You were an apt pupil, indeed. You should be able to handle the advanced science courses adequately."

"That was for real then?"

"It most certainly is now, my boy. If you've grasped the basics of spell theory, you can certainly comprehend the *cowan* sciences. We'll undoubtedly have to fill in some blanks here and there, but I'm sure you'll do well. You're a bright boy, with a gem of a mind under that rough exterior. Now, go. You have a mother to share some good news with, and I have a Council to shock." His eyes took on a mischievous twinkle as he finished, and he gestured toward his door. I practically danced past him to grab my backpack.

"Chance, one more thing," he said as I reached for the doorknob. I looked back over my left shoulder at him.

"Start writing down what you were taught. It will help."

I blinked through the curtain of hair that slid in front of my eyes, then nodded and hustled into the hallway. The hall clock showed twenty-five after four. My feet took me toward the stairs, but my mind was already a million miles ahead of me, telling my mom about advanced classes. My brain took a quick side trip to where I'd have been if I followed my own plan, and conjured up a miserable squat in the Hive, the ghetto of the Veiled world in New Essex. My brain left the image of me huddling in a ramshackle lean-to, and headed back to the warmer climes of the present, real world as I hit the front doors.   From the top of the steps, every side street and alley was visible. The front parking lot, nothing more than a big blur in my memory from that morning, formed a triangle bordered by the road angling past the front of the school. It stretched off to my right, with a cutout near the point for cars to turn in.

I gave the parking lot a quick glance again, and found Brad's big, cherry red pick-up truck. Brad was leaning with his back against it, with Alexis leaning on him. She looked up at him for a second, but he looked away, and her head bowed again, and I watched her put her hands on his chest, then turn her head and lay it against his letter jacket. Even from where I was, it looked like she was upset. Brad put one meaty paw around her waist without looking, and lifted his cell phone to his ear with the other. Alexis' shoulders rose then fell, and she seemed to deflate in his arms.

I scowled. Why I gave a crap about a stuck-up cheerleader was beyond me, but I could see she wasn't happy. Even from across the parking lot, I could see that. Brad had her in his arms, and he was Mister Oblivious. Some of the spells I'd done for people started to make a lot more sense to me now, and I wondered idly if Brad had used any charms on his girlfriend.

"...and then he says 'Cut him loose, asshole, or you're an Internet sensation,' and Brad's all like 'Awright, me let go now. You erase video.'"

My own words caught my attention, mostly because the person repeating them had mimicked my voice almost perfectly. He'd also made Brad sound like a brain-damaged ape, and there was only one other person who had been there for that part of my day.

"He did not!" Wanda's voice came to my ears before I could turn to find Lucas.

"Well, not exactly, but it's my story, I get to make Brad sound like a moron if I want to. So, this guy Chance is like, 'I figure this is good till I graduate. Call it...negative reinforcement.' And then, he slips the phone into his pocket and turns his back on them." They passed by without seeing me, so I sidestepped behind them and followed them down the steps.

"On the whole varsity squad?" Wanda asked.

"Eight of them, at least," I said over her shoulder.

They both jumped and swiveled their heads toward me.

"Dude, you're worse than Mr. Chomsky!" Lucas said with a grin. "You gonna come hang with us tonight at Dante's?"

"I'll have to check with my mom real quick, but I think she'll be cool with it. I'd need a ride, too."

"I have that covered. Where do you live?"

The question was simple enough, but I still had to think about it for a second before I could give him my address.

"Great. Why don't we come pick you up around seven?"

"Sure. There's my mom," I said as I saw her van turn into the lot. My feet barely touched the ground between the steps and the curb.

Dee looked at me from the passenger seat as I leaned into the window. "I already called shotgun!" she said quickly.

"Yeah, fine, whatever. Mom, a couple of kids invited me to hang out with them tonight at Dante's. Can I go?" The words couldn't seem to come out of my mouth fast enough.

"Which kids?" Mom asked as her eyes narrowed. I pointed to Lucas and Wanda, and her face relaxed into a smile.

"Oh, sure, honey! That's Missy Romanoff's daughter. I don't think she'll be a bad influence on you." She waved at Wanda, and I gave them a thumbs-up before I opened the sliding door and hopped into the rear seat in the van. Mom didn't even have to ask how my first day went. My mouth went into overdrive all by itself on the trip home.

"Mr. Chomsky said he didn't think my true aptitude showed up on a test. He wants to see about getting me into the advanced placement classes for science," I said as we pulled into the driveway.

"Honey, that's wonderful!" Mom said as she got out of the van. I slid out the side door and got caught up in a hug.

"I knew you'd do well, son. I'm so proud of you." The world was pretty damn close to perfect, just then.

"Brown-noser," Dee said *sotto voice* as she walked past me.

"Slacker," I tossed back at her.

"All right, you two, homework first, and Chance, I want your chores done before you go out with your friends," Mom said as she unlocked the door.

Dee and I moaned our disappointment, but mine was mostly imitating Dee's. After cleaning up animal sacrifices, or, for that matter, making them, taking out the trash was easy. But, try telling that to your Mom. I was done by six thirty, and out on the front steps at ten till with *The Scarlet Letter* to keep me company. I had until ten o'clock to be out with my new friends.

A couple of minutes after seven, a pale green Honda Accord pulled up to the curb, and I saw Wanda's bright red hair in the passenger window. The car looked ancient, with dents and red patches over rough areas, like primer over rust. All I could hear as I crossed the yard toward it was a faint hum of its engine. I'd half expected to hear it sputter and cough or backfire every now and then. Wanda opened her door and got out to let me in the cramped back seat.

"Welcome aboard the *Falcon*. No smart-ass comments, or you're gonna find yourself floating home," Lucas recited. Wanda rolled her eyes as she got back in, like it was a joke she'd heard before. We were moving before her seatbelt clicked, and the *Falcon* proved it could get up and go, though it wasn't going to break any speed records.

"Seriously, though," Wanda said, like she was picking up a conversation, "do you think he might consider doing special orders? Just at first, to try it out?" She turned in her seat and laid her cheek against the headrest.

"He might. I think he's worried about getting a lot of customers like Julian and his crowd, coming in and asking after the *Dark Evil Grimoire of Sho-Hogloth* or something stupid like that." Lucas looked back at me in the rearview mirror as I gave out a snort.

"Sorry," I said. "It sounds like this guy's read too much Lovecraft. So, what are you guys talking about?"

"Lucas works in the coolest bookstore in town, and he's trying to get his grandfather to start ordering some books on Wicca for me."

"The religion, right?"

"Yeah!" Wanda's face lit up. "My mom's Wiccan, and when I turn sixteen, I'm going to do my year and a day with one of her coven sisters. She won't let me do it until I've checked out all of the other paths, though.

But I've always just felt like that was who I was, you know?" Like all true believers I'd ever run into, Wanda seemed to like having an understanding audience.

"Yeah, every Wiccan I've talked to, well, the ones who weren't in it just for the magic, said it felt like they'd come home when they learned about Wicca," I told her.

"So, what about you, dude?" Lucas asked. "What's your path?"

"Undecided," I said after a few seconds. Religion hadn't really been on my mind for a while. What most people took on faith, I *knew* was real. At least on the dark side of things, but I'd always figured that if demons were real, then their counterparts were, too. Either way, I figured there was no way I was going to see anything in my afterlife *but* demons, with my soul as screwed up as it was.

"I'm thinking about majoring in undecided when I go to college," Lucas said. I gave him a courtesy smile and tried to get my mind off the hereafter. It was depressing enough without dwelling on it.

"You said you were majoring in women's studies," Wanda said with a knowing smile.

"That's part of the course curriculum for a major in undecided. Studying women, biology, anatomy in particular, and chemistry, especially fermentation and distillation of spirits."

"You wouldn't touch alcohol if I paid you," she said back.

"Hey, I'm an AP geek during the day. Let me at least *pretend* to be cool after school," Lucas shot back.

"He wants to write," Wanda told me confidentially. "What about you?"

"I don't know. I haven't really thought about anything past graduating. I'm not sure if I'm going to college." Was an apprenticeship to a mage like trade school, I wondered?

Lucas pulled into the parking lot of Dante's a few seconds later. I unfolded myself from the back seat and looked around before I followed Wanda and him in. There was a strip mall across the street, and I spotted a nail salon, two insurance agencies, and an ice cream parlor with just a quick glance. Dante's was housed in a two-story metal building, and if the empty neon sign's shape was any clue, it had been a skating rink in another life. A newer sign proclaimed Wednesdays were Karaoke Night, and that Suicidal Jester was playing on Halloween. Two metal buildings flanked it, and an even taller one loomed up behind it. Alleyways yawned on either side of it, and if gambling was one of my weaknesses, I would have bet that Dante's had a dark chasm between it and the rear building too.

"*Ego sum inter illustrator*," I whispered as I followed my friends toward the door. *I am among the enlightened.*

Three warding sigils flared to life above the door in response, only visible to those who could see beyond the Veil. One was a vampiric glyph that warned this was another's territory. The second was an Infernal symbol that meant "stay away," and the third was a sign in the ominous flowing script of the *Unseleighe* Courts, marking the place as dangerous. Three warnings from people who didn't necessarily get along, all of them pretty much saying, "don't hunt here." That screamed Conclave to me. Subtle, quick to anger, and always ready to lay down a little extra crispy justice, hold the mercy.

There were a few little knots of people in the lot. A group of skaters were doing flips and grinds at the edge of the lot, near an iron handrail, while a trio of goths was huddled around someone's phone. Off to the right, Brad and his cronies hung out by his red monster of a truck laughing about something, and I spotted Alexis walking away from them with her cell phone to her ear. She had her head down, and her barely visible eyebrows were furrowed as she stalked away from them.

"No," she said into the phone as she got closer. "We're already at Dante's...Are you stoned, Mitchell? Alone? With you? Yes, Brad *does* have to know. Well, fine, if you have the balls to show up, *you* tell him that to his face...Yeah, I thought so." She closed the phone up and looked at it for a moment, then muttered, "Asshole," at it before she slipped it into her pocket. She stepped out from behind a car, and pulled up before she ran into me. Blue jeans and a red tank top never looked so good. Her eyes went from me to Lucas's car behind me, and I could hear her sniff.

"You came in *that*?" she said with a chilly smile. Behind her, Lucas turned and stopped.

"Yeah," I answered.

"You're braver than I thought," she said. I expected Lucas to protest, but both he and Wanda broke into broad grins instead.

I shrugged, so it wasn't so obvious that I didn't get the joke. "I'm full of surprises."

"That's not all you're full of," she shot back. She took a quick look over her shoulder before she leaned close to me. "I meant what I said this afternoon. Stay away from Brad, and stay away from me, if you know what's good for you," she said softly. If she was going to say more, it was lost when Brad called her name from across the parking lot. Her shoulders slumped and she started in his direction.

"Way to go, Romeo," Wanda said as she took me by the arm.

While she was dragging me to the entrance, I craned my neck to sneak a look over my shoulder, just in time to see Alexis slide into Brad's arms. Her hand went to his chest and she looked up at him. He was busy talking to one of the other jocks, so he didn't see the resigned look on her face as she closed her eyes and laid her head against his chest.

Brad didn't deserve her. The thought was like a spike through my chest. He didn't deserve her loyalty, and what was worse, he didn't even seem to know he had it. I shook myself free of the funk my thoughts were stuck in. Alexis was a cheerleader, dating the varsity quarterback. They deserved each other. By the time I reached the door, I almost believed it.

Once we were inside, I was lost in a flood of sound and energy. Dozens of people in the same place, dancing, talking, making out, all generated a low-level power buzz that left my skin tingling as it washed over me.

Compared to what I'd felt at lunch, this was a lot softer, less focused. The atmosphere in here was a lot more relaxed, and the energy felt less intense.

Inside, Dante's wasn't much different from outside. The sheet metal siding was exposed in some places, and the floor was hard concrete. It had two levels, with a big cut-out over the dance floor so you could look down on it from upstairs. The main counter and juice bar were next to the dance floor, and there were tables and some alcoves off to the right as you came in, past the six pool tables in the center of the floor. There were a few tables around the dance floor, and a stage on the left end of the building from the main door. A DJ was running a techno-heavy mix from the booth on the left side of the stage, and there were a few couples out on the floor.

Brad and his crew of jocks muscled their way in behind us in a herd of purple and gold, and shoved a couple of guys off one of the pool tables. Lucas and Wanda led me to a trio of couches set in a u-shape around a low, black cube table that was littered with drinks and empty plastic baskets overflowing with food-stained wax paper. Pales faces turned to us as we approached, and there was a ripple of movement as Lucas and Wanda were greeted with somber nods and lifted hands.

I was admitted to the circle of goths with a round of raised eyebrows and dark-eyed stares. Lucas and Wanda said I was cool, so butts slid, and a spot opened up at the end of the left side of the U. I sat and listened to them talk about music and gossip, and before long, everyone was pitching in on an order of cheesy fries. I was clueless for most of the conversation. That was cool, though. It wasn't about magick, and the worst it got was petty jealousies. There was plenty of laughter and smiles, in spite of the somber rep goths tended to have. Even if I wasn't a part of it, I was happy to be on the edge of it. I relaxed and let myself enjoy the energy in the place, especially right around me, feeling it with my mystic senses. A pleasant tingle crawled up my arms and across my chest as I slipped into a semi-trance, and let the energy of the room wash over me.

My eyes snapped open when a cold spot brushed against the edge of my senses for a fraction of a heartbeat. I scanned the room, but the feeling was gone, and part of my mind was starting to doubt I'd even felt it. There were half a dozen perfectly rational explanations for what I'd felt. I was just about to chalk it up to paranoia when I saw Brad straighten up from the pool table and hand his cue stick to one of his letter-jacketed clones, then head for a door on the far side of the dance floor. Half way there, he turned his head and stared down at the empty space beside him, and I saw his lips move. Something slippery slid across the surface of my memory, the image of someone walking beside him, someone who'd been walking beside him from the moment he left the table. Someone vague, hard to describe…

"Son of a…" I bit down on the curse and clamped my mental defenses down as I got to my feet. The flickering memory faded, and I still couldn't see who was walking beside Brad. At least part of whatever spell they were using was still working on me, but the influence on my memory dissipated. I was better than this. I'd kept a demon out of my head for three years, there was no way I should have been caught in a simple *neglenom* charm. Except that I was. My mind was already ignoring the person beside Brad. Even as the thought occurred to me, I found it hard to hold on to.

Neglenom spells were illegal, because they used a form of mind control. They made the subject simply not want to think about the person or thing at the center of them. The eye would see them, but the mind would dismiss what it saw, ignore it as not worth worrying about. On most people, that was all it took. Ignoring the out-of-place was second nature to the *cowan* mind. They chose to disbelieve most of what they saw. A strong enough will could resist a *neglenom* spell by simple brute force, refusing to ignore what it was told to. Most of my defenses were like that. The rest were simple visualizations, like the iron wall I erected in my thoughts. It became easier to think about the person walking next to Brad, the person I still couldn't see. I kept the mental wall in place as I followed them across the dance floor.

Brad opened a metal door behind the DJ's booth and headed into the alley, and I had to hustle to catch it before it latched. I stopped for a few seconds, waiting for the sound of Brad's footsteps to get farther away before I pushed it open and slipped out behind him. Combat boots on concrete weren't a good combo for stealth, but any sound I made was covered between Brad talking and the muted thump of the music from inside.

They headed deeper into the alley, toward the lone circle of light by the back door to another building. I ducked behind a dumpster and watched as they crossed the trickle of water that ran down the middle of the alleyway. Two pairs of wet footprints appeared as Brad crossed it, and the other guy shimmered into view, his presence too obvious to be ignored now that I could see his footprints, and probably grounded out at least temporarily by walking through running water. I couldn't make out many details in the dim light except dark clothes, stringy black hair, and cowboy boots. They stopped just before the well-lit spot, and I saw Brad hold up what looked like a stack of bills. I crept closer, and caught part of their conversation.

"…this better work better than the last one."

"You got my word on it," the dark man said. His voice was thin and reedy, and there was a wheeze to it. "This'll do what you need. It's stronger than the crap you been buyin'." He held up a necklace, and Brad handed over the cash in exchange.

This was worse than I thought. Whoever the guy was, he was selling charms at my new school. Selling to *cowans* was illegal to start with, and I was willing to bet that the charms in his repertoire weren't the warm and fuzzy kind, either. And if he was working for a demon as a familiar, this was an even bigger problem. A surge of unexpected anger brought me up short, and I wondered why I was so pissed off all of the sudden. Maybe it was the thought of a demon sending a familiar to work my school. To do the things I had been taught to do, to my classmates. Whatever the reason, now wasn't the time to do any navel-gazing. I'd made a promise, and it was time to start making good on it. The dark man reached for the amulet, and suddenly, I was out of options.

"There's more than one price for that kind of thing," I said, as I took a couple of steps forward.

The dark man turned to face me with a wide-eyed look of terror, while Brad snarled and started toward me. The dark man's grip on the amulet pulled him up short, and I saw his lips move, then felt the brush of magick on the edge of my senses, that tingle down that the spine makes the hair on the back of most people's necks stand up. I frowned as I came forward another step, and hoped Brad's soul wasn't too damaged as the dark man ran into the darkness.

"I'll give you a price, you little prick," he said as he came forward, his fist already on its way up.

I shook my head and whispered, "*Crebresco minuta.*" The strength amulet kicked in fractionally. He was in for a big surprise if he thought he was going to get a shot in on me. Even at low power, I was still a match for most guys my age.

The stars spun in my vision, and I wondered how I ended up on my back. A throbbing pain was exploding across the right side of my face, and I remembered Brad's left hook connecting with my cheek, then a bright flash of white. Brad's face floated into my view, and I felt him grab me by the jacket, then the world swam again.

When my vision stopped spinning and tilting, I was up against the wall, and Brad was giving me a feral grin, with his right fist cocked back behind his ear. My left foot snapped up more by reflex than anything, into the soft spot between his legs, and he just sort of folded up in the middle. He let me go and staggered back a couple of steps before he fell on his ass. I just slid down the wall as my legs went out from under me.

On the second try, I got to my feet and staggered over to where Brad was still doubled over and clutching at his groin. I put a boot to the side of his face to even things out from the first punch, and he sprawled onto his back. Without a second's hesitation, I drew my leg up and brought my boot down on his outstretched right hand as hard as my augmented strength could manage. There was a sickening crack as bone gave way under my boot heel, and I twisted my foot back and forth just to make sure I got the job done right.

"I told you," I said through bloody lips, as I squatted down beside him, "not to use your good hand the next time you touched me."

He drew his mangled hand to his chest and curled up on his right side, facing me. "Screw you," he hissed, then his leg snapped forward and caught me in the ribs. It was like being hit by a car, and I ended up bouncing off the metal back wall of Dante's. I hit almost upside down, and landed on my shoulder, with my ribs and back a solid screaming mass of agony.

Brad was on his feet by the time I rolled onto my side, shaking, then flexing his right hand slowly. My brain froze up for a second in total revolt. There was no way he should have been able to move his fingers, much less clench and unclench them into a fist. But there it was, and I was warlock enough to know that if I was seeing it, it was damn sure possible. Un-freaking-likely, but possible.

"*Crebresco*," I whispered as he walked toward me. The strength charm activated at full power, and I felt my bones and muscles get denser to make up for the strain I was about to put on them. Something in my face and ribcage shifted, bones grated against each other as the spell pulled everything into place and held it there.

Brad came at me with his right hand back, and I came to my feet. He moved in slow motion to my spell-enhanced senses, and I had all the time in the world to get my hand up to catch his fist. He only looked like he was moving slow, though. When his fist hit my palm, my arm went numb almost to the elbow, with a promise to bring a ton of hurt back when feeling returned to it. The punch nearly drove me to my knees, but I held my ground, and looked Brad full in the face.

"How the hell…?" he asked with wide eyes. He looked from his fist to my face, and I gave him a grin.

"You ain't the only one with upgrades, asshole," I growled, right before I drove my fist into his gut. He doubled over and staggered back, and I drove my knee into his face. That knocked him back further, but before I could cross the few steps between us, he shook his head and swung a haymaker left at me. I ducked under it and bobbed back up, then put my left fist into the side of his face. It didn't seem to faze him so much as surprise him. His backhand surprised *me*, and I didn't quite manage to get out of the way in time. Stars exploded behind my eyes, and I tasted fresh blood on my tongue as I hit the concrete. For a few seconds, all I could do was lay there and wish I'd had a better idea, like not getting up this morning. Then he hit me again, and the fist he put in my gut made me think being born wasn't a very good idea, either. It was my turn to hit the pavement on my hands and knees, but I added retching to the routine, too, for added difficulty. But I'd been beaten by pros, and this chump wasn't even close to my former master when it came to handing out a beat-down. Instead of kicking me while I was down, he grabbed me by the jacket…again. Kicking me would have been safe, and it would have kept me on the ground.

When he got me to my feet, I drove my hand forward, fingers rigid like a knife, and caught him under the chin, right in the throat. His eyes went wide for a moment, and he gave a startled, choked gasp, and I followed up with a punch to the middle of his chest. I heard and felt bone crack under my knuckles, and felt a spike of pain even through the numbness in my arm. That knocked him back across the alley, and his hand went to his chest as he looked up at me with uncertain eyes. I drew myself up as straight as I could, which ended up being more of a slouch, and tried to face him down across the ten feet of dirty concrete that separated us. My left arm felt like it was on fire, and my ribs and stomach sent sharp jolts of pain through me with every breath.

"That all you got, asshole?" I growled slowly. He hesitated, then took a step toward me. I clenched my fists to match him, and a new feeling rose in my chest: anger. If he was going to try to kick my ass, I wasn't going to make it easy for him. "C'mon!" I yelled. "Bring it!"

Brad took a step back, then turned and took off at a run for the mouth of the alley. I slumped against the dumpster once he turned the corner. This was one gift horse I wasn't going to look in the mouth. With a handful of broken ribs, yelling had been a lot like swallowing broken glass, and my hands weren't happy with being clenched into fists, either. For that matter, my body wasn't happy with me in general, and it seemed to think that now was as good a time as any to let the numb feeling in my left arm fade, so I could feel the damage blocking Brad's punch had done in excruciating detail.

With Brad and the dark man gone, all I was left with were a few guesses and a lot of questions that I didn't really want the answers to. The dark man was selling charms; that much I knew. It was a toss-up whether he worked for a demon or not. Brad must have been into him for some serious strength charms. I was pushing the upper limits of human strength with the charm I had, but Brad's strength left things like human limits in the dust. And he could heal fast. No wonder he was the varsity quarterback his freshman year. If the dark man's strength charms were turning him into Super-Brad without aging him a year for every ten seconds he used it or something nasty like that, then he was a better warlock than I was. A *lot* better.

"In over my head much?" I asked myself as I leaned against the wall of Dante's. My ribs ached but I could feel them grating together as the strength charm's reinforcement enchantment pulled them back into place. My left hand felt like it was being pounded back into shape with a dozen ball-peen hammers. My stomach growled as my body began the process of healing. The strength charm made me stronger by ramping up my metabolism, so it was like my body was on a constant adrenaline rush. It drained the body, and using the charm for too long would kill me. Not of old age, like most people thought. No, I'd die of starvation or dehydration way before my body had a chance to age too much. By putting the body in overdrive, it made the *whole* body work faster, and that included healing. I should have deactivated it. What I was doing was dangerous. It was stupid, but it was important. If Mom saw me looking like I probably did, she'd freak. How could I explain that I'd gotten into a fight with a guy who could probably bench press our house? And I couldn't walk around school with busted ribs and a broken wrist, either. So I was about to sit through about a week's worth of healing in the next half hour or so.

The back door to Dante's swung open and spilled my two friends into the alleyway before I could get back on my own two feet.

"Chance!" Wanda called out when she saw me.

"Dude! Brad came in looking all busted up! You don't look so hot either." Lucas pulled up short when he caught sight of me. In the distance, the high-pitched whine of sport bikes rose.

"You hear that? We better get him inside, Lucas," Wanda said. She cast a nervous eye toward the opening of the alleyway then at Lucas.

He nodded, and came over to my left side. "Can you walk on your own?"

"Yeah." I stood up, didn't like it, but I started for the door anyway. Walking hurt in places that I didn't think had anything to do with the fight, and my pace turned into this shambling limp. My left arm curled up against my side, and every step made pain cascade down my sides.

Wanda held the door open and Lucas stayed beside me as I stepped back inside Dante's. I felt the thump of the bass from the speakers through every bruise and broken bone as we walked across the floor. I leaned in the direction of the counter, and dug my wallet out as I went. The sandy haired guy behind the counter came up out of his bored slouch when he spotted us.

"What'll it be?" he asked.

I took one of the plastic menus from the rack and opened it. "Burger…no, double cheeseburger…four of 'em." I answered through swollen lips. He turned to relay the order through the opening in the back wall, and I went on. "Four orders of potato skins…load 'em up with everything. Fries, onion rings and four strawberry shakes…biggest you make."

He turned back and looked at me with a wary eye until I laid cash on the table. The bills disappeared, and he shoved the order slip though the opening in the wall. The fry cook did a double take when he saw it, then he shrugged and went to work.

"You guys want anything?" I asked. Lucas gave me a look, but Wanda added another order of cheesy fries and a Diet Coke to the order. Lucas and I gave her a stare of our own.

"It's not like you're not going to mooch half my fries, Lucas," she said off our look. Her head tilted to one side, and she put a hand on her hip, challenging him to contradict her. He gave her a shrug and a nod and slumped onto the stool next to me.

The guy behind the counter planted a pitcher full of pink goo in front of me and handed me a straw and a spoon. "Dig in," he said, and I did.

As fast as the food appeared, I made it disappear. The strength charm had to get its power from somewhere, and in the case of Dulka's, and, for that matter, most demons' charms, it came from the user's body. If I fed my body fast enough, my accelerated metabolism would digest it almost as fast as it hit my stomach, and I wouldn't burn my body out while it healed itself. As I downed the first pitcher of milkshake, I felt my temperature start to climb, and my heart started pumping faster.

Even as I wolfed down the food, I hated having to rush through it. I wanted to take my time to enjoy the new tastes I was experiencing, but my stomach had different ideas about things. Wanda and Lucas talked while I shoveled it in as fast as I could, trying to enjoy each gulp for a few seconds, at least.

"The jocks cleared out of here just in time," Lucas said as he reached over my plate to snag one of Wanda's cheese covered fries.

"No doubt," Wanda agreed. "I wouldn't want to be on the road when the Wolf Pack was around. Monique's brother said they ran him off the road a couple of months ago."

"I figure we'll just wait for a little bit before we take off," he said around a mouthful of fried potato and cheese. "You good with that, Chance?" I managed a nod that didn't interrupt my eating, grateful that they hadn't asked me what had happened, yet. Between eating and whatever they were talking about, I'd dodged that bullet for now. Most of the bruises had healed, but bones took a little bit longer to mend. Midway through my forced feast, I laid another bill on the counter. I could already feel my body getting hungry again as it digested almost three days' worth of food, nearly as fast as I could eat it. The sandy-haired guy was in front of me in a heartbeat.

"Do it again," I mumbled through a mouthful of food.

"All of it?"

I nodded. "And a pitcher of water, too."

He nodded and relayed the order to the guy in the kitchen, and I settled down to some more serious eating. The water showed up, and I swear nothing ever tasted that good to me. I drained half the pitcher in a single, long pull, and relished the icy pure liquid nirvana that coursed down my throat. I finished the last of the second round, and took a careful breath. My ribs still hurt, but it was bearable. My face had almost stopped hurting completely, and my back just felt stiff and sore, instead of like I'd just been body-slammed by a building. I was going to be sore for a few days, but at least I didn't look I'd just gone toe-to-toe with a golem.

I whispered the charm's deactivation command, "*Cessare*," and felt a week's worth of tired fall on my shoulders like a dead horse. It wasn't even nine, and I was ready to go to bed. Lucas and Wanda were just as ready to get out of there, and my fuzzy brain kept trying to tell me that there was something important about that, but it was too tired to tell me what it was. I promised myself I'd figure it out later, and took myself at my word for the moment.

Chapter 8

~ When faced with the unexpected, keep your wits about you. Fear profits a man nothing. ~

Halfdan the Grim, 7th century mage

Morning stole up on padded feet and dropped an anvil on my head. I woke up beside my bed, sore from head to toe, which was about the way I'd gone to sleep. For a few seconds, I fooled myself into thinking that things hadn't gotten any worse. That delusion went away as soon as I tried to move anything but my eyelids. Sleeping on the floor hadn't helped the stiffness in my muscles, either.

A hot shower sounded *really* good just then, so I crawled to my feet and shuffled across the hall to the bathroom in my bare feet. The sweat pants and t-shirt hit the floor, and I groaned as I bent over to start the water. All I managed to get out of the faucet was a lukewarm spray, and that only lasted for about a minute and a half before it went straight to frigid. I knew a spell that would heat the water, but I didn't have the focus for it. And while I could get my hands on a thimble full of salt, I didn't want to explain to Mom *why* I needed it. "My little sister is gonna have to die," I thought as I shivered under the water. Muscles screamed in protest as I tried to rush my shower, and there were parts of me that weren't gonna be reached with a washcloth no matter how slow I went. By the time I finished and shuffled back across the hall, I knew no amount of cuteness was going to save Dee from cruel and unusual revenge.

I managed to make it through breakfast without killing my little sister or letting on how much I hurt, but the last part was harder than I thought it would be. Mom kept stopping to just look at me with a distracted smile on her face. It wasn't any different from the moments I spent just looking around at Mom's place and marveling that I wasn't back in Dulka's lair, but it sure made it hard to hide the aches and pains from the beating I'd survived last night. But the bowl full of hot oatmeal went a long way toward making me feel human again, especially with the tangy little bits of apple and the zing of cinnamon that Mom had put in it.

As I slouched in the seat on the way to school, I got a few things worked out, but the list didn't seem much more encouraging than it had been last night. Alexis had to know that there was more to Brad than met the eye. She was his girlfriend; there was almost no way she *couldn't*. Plus, she'd been trying to warn me about him both times we'd talked after school. Somehow, it cast her in a different light. It made me wonder what she put up with, being with him. Guys my age aren't famous for our self-discipline, and if he got pissed, he could snap her neck, easy. If he lost his temper, a slap from him might break bones.

To make matters worse, I was pretty damn sure there was another warlock working my school, trading on people's misery for little bits of their souls. That meant another demon. I sure as all Nine Hells didn't want that. And, as much as I hated to admit it, he was better than I was, if Brad's strength was anything to go by. If I tried to take him on myself, I was going to be in way over my head. I needed help. I needed a full-fledged wizard. Fortunately, I knew where to find one.

As Mom pulled away from the curb, I saw Brad drive up in his cherry red truck. Like I expected, he didn't have a scratch on him. No cast or splint on a broken hand, no limp or stiffness from broken ribs, no bruises from being kicked in the face. Nothing. Our eyes met as he crossed the lot toward the group of jocks clustered near the door. He glared at me as he went, and stabbed a finger at me from across the lot. Oh, yeah, this was going to make today, and probably the rest of my life, interesting. Alexis went to him and he wrapped an arm around her and kissed her. Her whole body seemed to melt into his as he reached down and grabbed her ass.

My lip curled at that, if for no other reason than it felt like he was marking his territory, and that bothered me. Less than a week ago, I'd been someone else's property. It shouldn't have surprised me how much I hated to see anyone, even Alexis Cooper, treated like someone owned them. And if I wanted to be the one doing the kissing, well I was taking that particular dirty secret to Hell with me. Maybe it would have bugged me less if she didn't seem to be enjoying the way he was manhandling her.

"Yo, Chance!" Lucas voice cut across the background chatter, and I scanned the front of the school for him. He and Wanda were surrounded by the Goth crowd, standing under a tired-looking tree that was in the middle of shedding red leaves. Something in my head said "maple tree," and the uses for its wood came to mind as I wove through the other kids.

"Hey, guys," I said when I got to them.

"Hey!" Wanda said. She was almost bouncing up and down, and if she got much more excited, she was likely to vibrate right out of her clothes. "Did you hear?"

"Not yet," I told her slowly.

It was like the floodgates opened. "The Wolf Pack hit three convenience stores last night. Half the cops in the city were trying to chase them down! It was all over the news this morning! Stacy Pettijohn said she saw them on her way home from Dante's, she stayed later than we did, and Melanie said they ran her brother off the road and made him crash out by the lake!" The words tumbled out of her mouth like they were late for dinner.

I interrupted her as she took a breath, "You'll have to tell me about it at lunch. I need to find Mr. Chomsky before school starts." I tried not to chuckle at Wanda's look as the thought of waiting four more hours to tell someone else what she knew flashed across her face.

"Dude, you're in luck. First period is his conference time, and he writes tardy excuses if you're gonna be late," Lucas volunteered. "He's usually in the teacher's lounge about now." I grunted my thanks and headed for the doors.

"Nerd much?" Wanda snorted.

"The term is geek," I heard Lucas say.

Then I was out of earshot and threading my way through the other kids clustered by the front doors. Brad gave me a glare as I got close to his spot on the front steps, but that was as far he seemed willing to go. Each of us knew the other had more going on than met the eye, and he didn't seem any more willing for a rematch this morning than I was.

Alexis had draped herself along his left side, with her arms folded over his shoulder and her head laid on her hands. Pink sweat bottoms covered her legs, and I could see an inch of pale skin between the low-slung waist of the sweats and the white tank top that pasted itself to her curves under the light blue hoodie she wore. Her hair was pulled up behind her head in a loose bun, and her lips were shiny with some pale gloss. The thought of kissing them to see how they tasted came to mind, right before my eyes found hers.

It felt like her eyes were trying to bore their way into me. With her head cocked to one side like it was, I got the feeling of intense curiosity, like she was studying me. There was a trace of desperation in that look, and just a hint of pain. I wondered what she saw when she looked at me, and forced myself to keep going. If there was any chance of making things better for her, it was with Mr. Chomsky. I pushed the fantasies of Alexis and me together to the back of my head and pushed the doors open. It was a stupid thought, anyway, I told myself, as I went from the overcast October gloom outside to the warm, quiet space of the front hall. My blue jeans, black t-shirt, and beat-up leather jacket all together probably didn't cost as much as any single thing she had on today. And there was no way I was playing football.

The teachers' lounge was right off the front hall, marked by a single plain wooden door on my left. I rapped on the varnished wood a couple of times, and the door opened to reveal Mr. Strickland's pinched little weasel face.

"What do *you* want?" Strickland asked. If I had offered to give him a disfiguring disease, I don't think he could have looked less happy to see me.

"Need to talk to Mr. Chomsky," I growled.

"Not here. Check his classroom." The door clicked shut in my face before I could say anything else.

"Thanks," I said to the door.

Chomsky's classroom was on the second floor toward the end of the middle of the school's three main wings. I was going to have to hustle if I was going to make it to his class and talk to him before the bell rang. The halls were pretty much empty, so it was just the sound of my boots on the stone floor accompanying me down the hallway. The only person I saw was a girl near Mr. Chomsky's door, with a black hoodie and jeans on. She caught sight of me as I came up and offered me a tentative smile.

"You trying to find Mr. Chomsky, too?" she asked softly.

"Yeah, figured I'd catch him before first period."

"Me, too. The whole physics class is rough from start to finish, but especially...I'm sorry, I'm geeking out. Anyway, first period is his conference period, but he wasn't in the teachers' lounge. Mr. Strickland said he might be here." I got to the door first and put my hand on the knob.

"He told me the same thing." I opened the door for her to go in first, since what I had to talk to Mr. Chomsky about wasn't something I wanted someone else in the room for. She smiled and stepped past me, then stopped. Her face went pale as she staggered back from the doorway, one hand over her mouth, the other dropping her books to clutch at her stomach. That put her right next to me when she screamed.

There is something about a girl's scream that can paralyze some people. Me, especially. Maybe it was the way the inside of my eardrums seemed to reverberate with it, or how it felt like there was a spike going from my ears to the center of my skull. I could only stare at her for a second while she gave a shrill, high-pitched screech that told the world a girl being horrifically murdered in the science wing. After a few seconds, she stopped, and I watched her face go green. Then, she went to her knees and threw up on the floor.

Belatedly, the same barbaric reflexes that inspired things like chivalry and other noble-sounding words kicked in, and I got myself in front of the door. The deep, hairy monkey part of my brain was saying things like "Woman in danger. Must protect woman. Ugh"; while the smarter, more civilized part of my brain was looking at it and saying "Are you stupid? We should be telling the feet to run like hell!" Of course, my feet were listening to the monkey brain, because I was getting hyped up on adrenaline to face whatever it was that could make a girl scream so hard she puked.

I looked into the room for a threat, and the next thought through my mind was, *"But it's only an arm."* Monkey brain isn't too bright. The other half, however, figured out that it was an arm that wasn't attached to all the things that you usually see them connected to. Like, shoulders, or anything else that resembles a whole, living human being. I took a step into the room, because I was wondering where the rest of Mr. Chomsky was, and I found him. Not the whole him in one place, just parts of him spread all over the room. His head was on his desk, looking out at the classroom, and one of his legs was over by the windows. His other arm was on the lab table where I had been sitting yesterday. His torso was in the center of the room, taking up a lot more space than a torso ought to because his insides were now outsides, and they were spread around on the floor. I barely registered the tingle of residual magick in the room through the numb feeling my brain was spreading liberally along the inside of my skull. Mr. Chomsky wasn't the first dead guy I'd ever seen, but he was the first one I had met and talked to while he was a living, breathing person. And, he was the first dead person that I'd ever seen that came disassembled.

I looked around, searching for details, and my memory, well trained at picking things up quickly from serving a bad tempered demon, was cataloging the moment for later review. Bloodstains covered the wall: some splatters, some smears. There were deep, body-sized imprints in the drywall, and one of the windows was missing. Not shattered with pieces of glass pointing toward the center: the window *frame* was gone, wood and all. Desks were scattered all over the room, and I saw several burn marks on the walls. And slash marks. Most of them were on Mr. Chomsky's body, but there were also four deep furrows in the concrete column by the missing window. Shards of glass lay below the window opening. I swallowed and tried hard not to join the girl outside in heaving up breakfast and a few less recent meals. If I stayed much longer in here, I was going to hurl, but I needed to do something before other people brought their energies into the room and made a mess of things.

I closed my eyes, and touched the place in my mind where magick lived. Like many practitioners, I could open my third eye all the way if I needed to. I just hated to do it. It made peeping at someone's aura seem like a casual look in a window. Nothing could be hidden from a fully opened third eye, and a lot of magi had lost themselves to the wonders and horrors they *Saw*. Illusions, masks, lies: all of those were ripped aside, and you were able to see the world as it truly was. People were revealed as their true selves; secrets and lies all revealed at the same time. But more importantly, the past and future were no barrier to it, either. Given what had happened in this room, I was pretty damned sure I didn't want to see what the past held in here.

I did it anyway.

When I opened my eyes, I felt my mystic eye open completely, and I Saw. The auras of a thousand students flowed into and through the room, then faded as my Sight went deeper, and the series of wards on the walls and ceiling were revealed. They were beautiful in their symmetry and grace, masterpieces of harmony between wielder and the Magick he had used to create them. All of them had the red glow of activation, and loose strands of energy floating toward the center of the room, and I willed my Eye to seek who or what they had been tethered to. A ghostly figure of Mr. Chomsky appeared at the center of the energy strands, and I could see several others that stretched out of the room as well, and those were glowing red, too.

Mr. Chomsky's aura permeated the whole room, a vibrant yellow color that felt like sunshine and campfires and the scent of baking bread. After a moment, I saw the aura footprint of whoever had come into this room the night before. It was ugly, a dark brown, murky thing, and I smelled wet fur, moldy forest gloom, and dead things through it. It wasn't human, and it wasn't anything I had ever run into before. Then, my Eye began revealing bits of the past, a clawed hand slashing, flinging blood in its wake, and loving the way the pain lanced through its prey. The undeniable feel of a mage invoking enough power to flip a car, yet focusing it so tightly that it didn't even disturb the papers on the desk. And then came the response, and I found myself closing my third eye reflexively. Sorcery, as black as it came, was about to blast through the memory of that room, and it wasn't all that focused. Even an after-flash of that kind of raw, untamed malevolence could send me into a brainless oblivion. I closed my eyes in a sympathetic response and took a step backwards blindly, and caught the doorjamb before I fell. Then, there was a hand on my shoulder, and soothing words came to my ears. I let my brain sort of shut down then, and let the world kind of fade into a haze for a while.

After that, it was mostly impressions. There were sirens and people in uniforms. Someone was asking me questions, and I said, "I don't know," a lot. The girl who had been with me cried, and threw up a couple more times. Somewhere in the whole thing, Mom showed up, looking worried and relieved at the same time. She asked me a lot of questions, and I said, "I'm fine, Mom," a lot.

I knew my head was getting clearer when someone finally brought up counseling and therapy, and I instantly wanted to tell them where they could stick *that* idea.

"No, thanks," I said instead.

"But, son, what you've seen today was pretty terrible, and you have no idea what kind of impact that can have on the human psyche," the chubby guy in a sweater and glasses was telling me. "You have to process the deathing experience and work through the trauma, so that you can go on to work through the grieving process in a healthy and positive way."

"Look, it sucked," I said, "and all the psychobabble bullshit in the world isn't going to erase it from the inside of my head. There's nothing positive about someone getting killed. It just sucks, and you go on. I don't need to lay on a couch to know how to do that." I stood up, and Mom got to her feet with me.

She gave me a serious, searching look. "You're sure you're okay, then?" I nodded.

"Miss Fortunato, please," the analyst started, missing Mom's last name. He didn't get any further.

"My son has said no," Mom said icily. "You should stop talking." With that said, she led the way back out of the little conference room into the main office.

Principal Ravenhearst was waiting for us. "Miss Murathy, I'm sorry Chance had to see this," she said with a little warmth. Coming from her, I figured this was what passed for gushing sympathy. "We have no idea who would want to do something like this. Mr. Chomsky was a favorite with almost all of the students. The police are doing everything they can to find the…person responsible. We're canceling classes for today, but the police have some questions for your son before you go."

"He's already told them everything he saw. Haven't they made him relive that enough?" Mom demanded.

"It's not about the body, Miss Murathy," another voice cut into the conversation.

Mom and I turned to look at the newcomer, a tall woman with medium-brown skin, in gray slacks and a matching jacket with a white blouse. She wore a badge on her belt, and the butt of a pistol was visible at her right hip. Even without the badge, everything about this woman screamed "cop," right down to the reddish hair pulled back into a severe bun at the back of her head.

"It seems that your son was the last person to see Mr. Chomsky alive yesterday afternoon."

Mom started at the woman's claim, and I frowned. I had seen him right after school, and he'd made no secret of it, but I doubted he'd penciled in "4:30, ambush demonic apprentice; 5:00, turn over to Conclave for judgment; 6:00, dinner at Olive Garden." I was pretty sure it wasn't common knowledge.

"He was still in one piece when I left him," I said defensively.

"Let's take this into Principal Ravenhurst's office, shall we?" the detective said with a gesture toward the door.

We followed her into Miss Ravenhurst's office, and she closed the door behind us before she slid in behind the principal's desk. Miss Ravenhearst looked like she'd just eaten a lemon whole, but I didn't think she was going to argue with a woman carrying a badge and a gun.

"Chance, I'm Detective Holly Roberts, with the eighth precinct homicide division," she began, after we had all sat down. She took out a bent and battered notepad and a cheap ballpoint pen, and flipped through a few pages before she went on. "To answer your mother's question, Mr. Chomsky had your name in his appointment book yesterday afternoon. What did you two discuss?"

"He'd asked me to come by his classroom to discuss, um, more appropriate placement for me," I told her. It seemed to satisfy her, because she smiled and wrote something down. I wasn't sure if that was good thing or not. "He wanted me to test for his um, his AP science class." Just saying the words made me feel something heavy and painful in my chest, a sadness I'd been able to ward off up until then.

"So, you didn't argue with him?" Detective Roberts asked.

"No," I growled, "Mr. Chomsky was really cool to me yesterday. He even got Brad Duncan off my back before first period."

"Did he now?" Her pen scratched on her trusty notepad. "Can you account for your whereabouts between four thirty and about eleven thirty?"

"Is my son a suspect in this, detective?" Mom asked before I could answer, her voice hard.

"That's what I'm tying to determine right now, Miss Murathy," Detective Roberts said. "If your son can establish an alibi, then we can eliminate him as a potential suspect."

"I was home with my mom and my sister until about seven, and I was at Dante's from seven thirty until I got home around ten."

"Why are you focusing on *my* son, detective? Chance only started here yesterday," Mom pressed on.

"Your son's name has come up several times in the opening hours of our investigation, and given his recent connection to the fire at Truman High school, we couldn't discount the possibility of his involvement in this. But if his story checks out, you won't hear any more from us." Roberts stood up and offered her hand across the desk.

I stood up when Detectives Roberts did, but Mom stayed in her seat for a heartbeat longer.

"I understand that you're just doing your job, detective," Mom said calmly as she stood slowly and reached across the desk to take the other woman's hand, "but that doesn't mean I like the way my son is being treated." You could have chipped ice off my mom's words, her voice was so cold.

"I'm sorry, Miss Murathy, I truly am," Roberts said without a trace of remorse in her voice. Mom all but dragged me out of the office. The halls were empty. Nothing like a murder to clear a place out.

"What happened between you and this Brad Duncan?" Mom demanded as soon as we were out the door.

"Turned out to be nothing, Mom. He was in my face, and Mr. Chomsky came along and took care of it. You would've been proud of me, I didn't start a fight, and I so could have."

"Then why didn't you say anything about it?"

I shrugged. "Forgot about it after fifth period. I had better stuff on my mind. Besides, I figured you'd make a big deal out of it."

"If you'd told me yesterday, I wouldn't be!"

"I told you, it was no big deal! Can't you just be okay with me doing the right thing, Mom? I didn't fu...I didn't screw up! That's the best I can do!" The tight feeling in my chest was getting worse, and Mom looked at me with a shocked expression on her face.

"Oh, son...you did fine," she said after a moment. She put a hand on my shoulder and pulled me to her. I was too messed up to give even a token protest, though I was probably breaking about a dozen rules of being a teenager by letting my mom hug me in public. "I forgot…what you saw this morning. I'm sorry."

"It's okay, Mom," I said into her shoulder before she let me go.

"Why don't we drop your books off at your locker, son, and I'll take you home. The last thing you should be thinking about is this place for the rest of the day." We headed down the halls, both silent until we reached my locker, and I tossed my books inside.

"He said I had a gem of a mind," I told her as we passed the teachers' lounge.

"He was right, son. He sounds like a wonderful man, and I'm sorry you lost him so soon after you met him. Are you sure you don't want to go to the grief counseling the school offered?"

I shook my head. "I'll be fine, Mom. I just miss him. Grief therapy won't bring him back."

The tight ache in my chest was fading, replaced by a cold certainty. The cops were going to be looking for a normal human as their killer, but anything tough enough to kill a mage as powerful as Mr. Chomsky was as *not*-normal as you were likely to get, and certainly not human. There was no way the cops were going to even find Mr. Chomsky's killer, and they sure as all Nine Hells weren't prepared to stop them.

There was only one person that I knew of who could do both.

Me.

Chapter 9

~ You will never find a more wretched hive of scum and villainy. We must be cautious. ~

Obi Wan Kenobi, Star Wars Episode IV: A New Hope

I had a paranormal murder to solve, and a supernatural killer to bring to justice. If only I could get my mother to leave the house so I could get started. The detectives in her novels didn't have these problems. I was beginning to see why people didn't always enjoy normal life as much as I did. It took an hour of reassuring Mom that I wasn't going to have a nervous breakdown on the spot before she convinced herself it was okay to leave me alone at home.

"There's *sarma* left in the fridge if you get hungry, and you have my number at Spirit Garden if you need me. Are you sure you don't want to come with me to the store? Elaine would love to meet you, and she wouldn't mind if you hung out with us." She stood at the door, keys in hand, but her stance made it look more like she was coming in than getting ready to head out.

"I really don't want to be around people right now, Mom. I just need to sort stuff out in my head, ya know?" Mom just nodded, and her eyes looked kind of sad for a moment. She came back in and put her arms around me. It was the tenth hug she'd given me in the past hour, and I was beginning to think they were as much for her as for me.

"I understand, sweetheart. If you need to talk or anything, just call me, okay? I hate leaving you at home like this, but..." Her face scrunched up in a pained look.

"You have to make a living, Mom, I know. I'll be fine, really." I stepped back and gave her a smile, but it wasn't very convincing.

"All right, son. You're so strong, sometimes. Okay, I'm going! If you need anything..." she said as she made for the door.

"I'll call. I'm fine, Mom. Don't worry!" I waited until I heard her van pull away, then I took the stairs two at a time up to my room. It was just now coming up on eleven, and I knew Dee got out of school at three thirty, then stayed at a friend's house until Mom got off work at four. I had about five hours to myself, and I had a list as long as my arm of things I needed. Some of it, I knew I could get at a hardware store, but the really important stuff meant going behind the Veil, back into the world I had just left. That was a trip I wasn't really looking forward to.

I grabbed my meager supply of magickal gear and my knife, then headed back down to the garage. When Mom and I had been cleaning her stuff out of my room, I'd seen her bike hanging up on hooks on one wall. I had a lot of ground to cover today, and I couldn't do it on foot with the time I had. Mom's Schwinn would have to be my wheels today, and no matter how dorky it seemed, twelve speeds beat two feet any day of the week.

The first few moments were dicey as I coasted out of the driveway, but you really don't ever forget how to ride a bike. I wobbled into the street for a few yards before I got the hang of pedaling and steering at the same time again, and it was all good. The feel of the cool, damp October wind on my face and flowing through my hair was the most wonderful thing I had felt in a long time. For a little while I forgot about what I had to do, and just went where the front wheel pointed me. I took turns randomly, and went through all twelve speeds to see just how fast I could go. Somewhere along the way, I started laughing.

I was free, really free, to go wherever I wanted, even if that was just…nowhere. I never wanted to lose that, and I was sure as the Nine Hells *not* going to let Dulka get me back. It was a sobering reminder that there were things I had to do. If I was going to stay free, I needed more spell materials than I had access to. Divinations and invocations took more juice than I could scrounge from my mom's spice rack. I needed the real stuff, the esoteric items that could fuel some serious magick. I turned the bike southeast, and leaned into the corner.

My first stop was a hardware store I'd seen during our shopping trip on Sunday. For a seeking spell, I needed copper filings, a magnet, and chalk: all things I could get with a little smart shopping at the local Hammer'N'Post. I grabbed a few pieces of copper tubing, a few magnets, a coil of copper wire, and a large chunk of purple chalk to start with, and some copper connectors and caps for another project I wanted to work on. The last thing I picked up was a heavy file. The clerk gave me a look as she rang my order up.

"Science project," I said flatly, as she took my money and looked skeptical. Her mouth made a silent "o" as she suddenly filed everything away as not needing to make sense anymore and made change. She never did ask me why I wasn't in school in the middle of the day. I stepped out of the hardware store and took a deep breath. The next part was what I was really dreading.

There were three places in New Essex that existed completely behind the barrier of illusion and disbelief that the mystical community called the Veil. The biggest was the Underground, a place below downtown where most of the legitimate folks lived and did their otherworldly business. A person could live a full and happy life without setting foot, tentacle, or other locomotive appendage outside the Underground, and there were a lot of beings who did just that. It was also the center of the Conclave's power, so it was off-limits to me, thanks to my father and Dulka. Warlocks were considered "kill on sight" there.

The second place, the Bazaar, was kind of the mixing place between the mystical and *cowan* worlds. Merchants in-the-know from the normal world made serious bank selling ordinary crap to magickals at prices that would have been considered extortion on the mundane side but were completely fair behind the Veil. The convenience was worth it for a lot of the magickals. Mystic merchants did the same thing for folks in-the-know from the *cowan* side.

The place I needed to go was the sleaziest of the three: a maze of back alleys and dark corners in the old Joplin district called the Hive. I had to take a bus to the nearest El-train station, and pay extra to stash Mom's bike in one of the special lockers. On the up side, I had it for the whole week if I needed it.

The train was mostly empty, except for a few guys in Night City Kings' colors at the back of the car. They gave me the eye as I got on, and one of them made to move. I flashed a sign that said I was a warlock "walking,"

116

or on my way somewhere important, and I wasn't in a mood to be asked to whip up a number nine potion for a horny gangbanger. Most gang members believed in the mystical, mostly because they spent too much time on the wrong side of a threshold after dark. The Kings even had their own shaman, and they weren't willing to cross a warlock or a mage. After I flashed the sign at them, they sat back and gave me their own walking sign. We kept a wary distance from each other until they got off on K Street.

The entrance to the Hive was only a few blocks from the Q Street station, and I didn't waste any time getting there. Joplin might have been a bustling industrial town back when New Essex first annexed it, but it was a slum now, and not everyone on the streets respected magick workers.

The entrance looked like the brick wall of an old warehouse. But to someone who could See, like yours truly, there was an iron gate set in a jagged hole in the wall behind the illusion. The gate was mostly to keep the High Fae out, since they were deathly allergic to the touch of iron. It was easy to open, but you had to know it was there, first. I lifted the latch and let myself in, and the sounds and sights of the normal world faded behind me. Not that the Hive was much better.

People milled about, many with hoods and cowls up, or elaborate masks that demonstrated wealth or power without giving their names away. The sides of the main alleyway were crammed with makeshift stalls, carpets, and cubbies with wares laid out on display. Tables, shelves, carpets, racks, and hanging baskets held anything a budding young sorcerer could want for casting most spells: from basic herbs to ground gems to wands and staves. The crowd was quiet, but it was still a crowd, so there was still a little chatter going on as people went from stall to stall. In the Hive, you could find pretty much anything if you knew who to bribe. Forbidden tomes of Infernal lore, illegal ingredients from endangered creatures, or reality-warping devices were all here, for a price. If you knew where to look and who to ask, you could buy people here, mostly by the hour, and oblivion, usually by the gram.

Located on a conjunction of ley lines, New Essex had more magi and hedge witches than some entire states did. Humans made up about half of the mystic population in New Essex, though. The other half was very *not* human. It felt like most of the non-humans in New Essex were trying to walk through the Hive as I threaded my way through the noise and smell of too many species packed into too little space. Some of them were just as nasty as my former employer, but most were okay folks just trying to make a dishonest living. It was one of the second that I was looking for.

I threaded my way through the press of beings, occasionally stopping to ask for directions. Things tended to move around in the Hive, so it was anyone's guess where a particular merchant was going to be from one day to the next. Finally, I found a sprite who knew where Billy the Gnome's new place was. It ended up being not too far from where it had been in September. He'd moved it to a more secluded location, this one in the corner of two buildings, so that two of his walls were brick or wood and the third was at an angle between them. The front of his squat was a mix of aluminum, wood, and cloth: an old frame of some sort that he had fitted up against the wall to make a triangular affair. He'd covered the frame with a heavy white cloth, and painted his name in several languages across the front. Billy himself was nowhere to be seen, but judging from the throaty giggling from his tent, he was definitely around, and not alone. I stopped at the line of runes painted on the brick cobblestones, the edge of his wards.

"Hey, Billy!" I called out. "You there?"

Billy didn't answer, but the noises from inside his squat stopped, and an image shimmered into existence in front of me. The ghostly figure of a troll in what looked like a decent knockoff of a Brooks Brothers suit was standing in front of me, translucent and slightly out of focus.

"The proprietor is not in at the moment. Protective wards of a lethal nature are currently active for your protection, and that of your accounts," the troll's image said in a tinny radio voice. "To leave a message for the proprietor, please speak your full name, or the alias your account is held under, and the proper name of the person for whom the message is intended. This simulacrum will not ask for your account's password or access item under any circumstances. Have a nice day!" Then, it froze in place, with a smile plastered on its face.

Trolls don't have pretty smiles. Eight feet tall, broad as a building, hairy, and ugly, they made great bodyguards or thugs. They don't have a neck to speak of, but what they lack in neck, they more than make up for in teeth. This one had never met a dentist he didn't eat, with fangs that pointed every which way, some of them broken and jagged, all of them some shade of brown or yellow. On him, a smile made a good threat, which is what I figured Billy was going for.

I sighed and leaned forward, where I could be heard by anyone in the tent, but not by everyone else. "It's Dulka's servant Chance, here to see Biladon Garnet, gnome, loan shark and all around degenerate."

"Hey!" Billy's high-pitched voice came from inside the tented squat, "Who're you calling a loan shark?" The cloth moved aside, revealing an indignant looking, half-dressed gnome sitting between a pair of long, shapely red legs. The top half of the woman attached to the legs, slightly less-dressed, leaned into view a heartbeat later, revealing dark black hair, deep black eyes, and a pair of stubby black horns that protruded from her bangs. Even under the thick furs she was covering herself with, I could tell she had some pretty dangerous curves. With red skin and mostly human lower legs, she had to be a cambion: a half demon, with incubus or succubus blood on one side, and human on the other.

Billy wasn't much to look at beside the woman. All of three feet tall if he jumped, he had the bald dome that all gnome men shared, a ring of brown hair, and an elaborate mustache and mutton chops. His mustache drew attention to his nose, a feature all of his kind were inordinately proud of. Among gnomes, the size of the nose was a sign of virility, and Billy's shnoz must have made him a real sex symbol.

"Did I interrupt something?" I asked innocently.

"Pillow talk, nothing important," Billy said quickly as he stepped out of his squat and pulled the cloth in place behind him. That left him outside with his pants undone, but in the Hive, that was better than letting anyone see how expensive a whore you could afford. And if he could afford an hour of a cambion's time, Billy was pretty well off.

"I could come back later," I teased him.

"Nah, we were done," he said as he laced his trousers up. "Her owner isn't expecting to see her back on her feet for a little while," he explained quietly. "I figure she's better off here than there, ya know?"

My fists curled up at my side at his remark. It was a reminder to me that freedom in the Hive was a relative thing. Half-breeds, especially demon half-breeds, had very few rights, since neither side of their heritage was usually willing to claim them. Odds were good that she was a slave, being tricked out to make a tidy profit for her owner. I wondered if the girl in his squat had a life as crappy as mine used to be, and something in me went cold and angry.

Billy went to the gnome-sized desk he kept out front and sat down behind it: his version of an open sign. The desk was essentially a board he'd laid across two wood crates and covered with a threadbare piece of blue velvet.

"What do you need?" he asked in his best business tone.

I ignored the anger for the moment, and tried to remember that aside from using a sex slave, Billy was a pretty decent guy. He probably hadn't even hit her.

"How much is left in the account?" I shot back.

"Quite a bit. Without consulting the books, my best guess would be about twelve thousand six hundred ninety five trade points: mostly in gems, gold and silver ounces, and some in trade bars. Roughly." For Billy, "roughly" meant he didn't get into fractions of grams.

I stifled a gasp of surprise at the number he rattled off. I knew I'd been working hard for Dulka, but I had never dreamed I'd earned him that much in trade. It was enough to buy everything I needed, and outfit my own lab if I had the space.

"He needs about…" I stopped, and put on my best thoughtful look, "half of that. Six thousand five hundred trade points' worth. In as small a package as you can manage."

"So, this wouldn't have anything to do with you busting your master's chops the other night, would it?" Billy asked as he dug his books out from under the makeshift desk. He sounded just too casual to be serious, but I was more concerned that he already knew.

"Technically, let's just say I'm still making a legit claim to an open account," I answered him, hoping he'd take that.

"Hey, I got no beef with that," he smiled, hands up. "Seems to me you did most of the work there anyway, so half is the least you deserve. I haven't heard anything official yet, so for all I know, you still work for the Count. And it ain't like he's ever gonna see the inside of this place, is it?"

"Or any other place with a ward or a threshold," I agreed. Like most summoned beings, demons weren't really welcome on the physical plane. A simple threshold would hold them out of a personal home, at least in most places, or a well-constructed ward.

As we were talking, he had been scratching away in his thick ledger with a pen, and I saw a flutter of movement from inside his squat. Black-within-black eyes stared out at me from inside the folds of cloth for a moment before the woman slid the fabric aside and strode out into full view: six and a half feet of red skin and black leather. If she had been dangerously built when she was mostly covered with loose, baggy furs, she was damn near lethal when she was dressed. A black corset hugged her figure into a serious hourglass shape, while black leather gloves covered her from upper arm to her knuckles. She barely wore a black leather mini-skirt, but what it didn't cover of her thighs, it left to a pair of boots that came up to a few of inches from the bottom of the skirt's hem. I stared. I think I drooled. Until I looked at her eyes, and saw the black iron collar around her throat.

While I was ogling the demoness, Billy got up from his stool and went back into the depths of his squat. A few moments later, he came back out, a leather satchel in his right hand, and a canvas sack in his left. "Without sending a runner, I can only give you part of it in actual hard currency, mostly in gems, with a little gold and silver thrown in. There's a hundred and fifty in here," he told me, holding up the bag. "The rest is in here, in bearer chits from Bjerning Depository," he held up the satchel to make his point.

"Bjerning?" I asked, incredulous. "Billy, they're dwarves! The only thing greedier than a dwarf is a demon!" The demoness snickered at the comment, but I knew better than to try to apologize. To most demons, an apology was a sign of weakness. No self-respecting demon could let a weakness go unexploited.

"They may love their gold, kid, but they're also the most honorable folk you could hope to deal with. A dwarf might squeeze you for every last penny he can get, but you'll get what you bargained for. No better folk to watch your money than the dwarves. If you want my advice, and trust me, kid, you *do,* you'll head over there right now, and open up a strong room of your own with what you got. They won't deal with *any* demon, much less the Count. The fact that you escaped from him will sit pretty with them, too. Especially now."

"I don't have time to go to the Underground today, Billy. I just need some stuff for some charms, and maybe a wand blank. Besides, the Conclave pretty much runs that place. I've broken about a thousand of their stupid Laws of Magick."

"Believe me kid, now is the time to go. Somethin's brewing out there, and the Sentinels are thin on the ground right about now. You do what you gotta do today, and you get to Bjerning's as soon as you can."

As Billy was talking, the half-demon hooker sashayed up to me on improbably high boot heels, laid one hand on my shoulder, and moved around behind me, so that her arm ended up draped over my shoulder, and some of her softer curves were pressed up against me. From up close, I could see that she was making the corset work overtime to keep her breasts covered, and as tall as she was, they were pretty much at eye level for me. But none of that was as hard to resist as her voice.

"I suggest you make time, young mage," she said softly in my ear, her voice like a touch by itself, "as soon as you may. You will want to be prepared for the times that are to come." Her full, black lips brushed my hair as she bent down over me, and I shivered at how good it felt. "Biladon does not give advice lightly, and never for free."

"Even Synreah knows I'm right," Billy said as he backed toward his squat. "But you better get outta here. No one knows you're here, and right about now, you got a rep about as big as a dragon's ego. Oh, and I'd take it as a favor if you wouldn't mention the free advice thing," he said from the flap to his squat. "If word of that gets out, people will think I've gone soft. Then *everybody* will start asking for a handout."

"If it helps, I'll complain about how much you charged me, and bitch about your fees," I said with a smile.

"Your kindness is killing me," he groused. "But seriously, you need to get the hell out of here, before it gets too crowded." With that, he slipped back into his squat and closed the flap, and I felt the static in my head a few seconds later as his wards came back up.

"Movement is the best camouflage," Synreah purred from beside me. "For both of us. If time is an issue, I can guide you to the places you need, for a fee. And, if you've the time afterward, and the currency, we can add to your list of sins."

"Yes to the guide services, but no to the other," I told her as I pulled a pair of topazes out of the bag. Her eyes gleamed at sight of the yellow gems, and I held the smaller one up in my fingers. "This one now, and the other if you can get me where I need to go, with everything I came for, before an hour and a half passes. Have we an accord between us?"

She smiled as she reached for the gem. "Between us? Aye," she said, and tucked the gem down the front of her corset. "I trust your discretion is assured?"

"It is," I said. My assurance of discretion meant that she wouldn't have to tell her owner about our deal, because he hadn't brokered it. Slaves could sometimes buy their way out of their contract, and deals like this helped them pay it off sooner because their owners didn't take the dragon's share of the profits. I shouldered the satchel and tucked the bag of hard currency inside, then headed for the mouth of the little side alley.

"How close are you to meeting your owner's price?" I asked as we stepped back out into the busier throughway.

"He hasn't set one," she said with a grim smile. It was hard to suppress a shudder at the sudden cold tone in her voice. Without a price set for her freedom in her contract, my guess was that she was saving up to purchase the kind of contract that her owner wouldn't survive.

"So, where do you need to go?" Her voice shifted back to a sultry purr without a breath of hesitation, and I reminded myself that for all that she was enslaved, she was still half-demon. I took it as a warning not to underestimate her, and told her the name of the place I had in mind.

Shopping with six and a half feet of Infernal wet dream at my side was a new experience. I tried not to stare but I'm a guy, and Synreah was all kinds of woman. She bounced, she jiggled, and she shimmied in all the right places as she took me to the first place I asked about. The wizened little geomancer I was hoping to barter an amethyst from could barely keep his eyes out of her cleavage when she knelt at the edge of his blanket and cooed over his selection of gems. When I squatted down beside her, she reached for an oval piece of onyx and placed it over her bosom.

"What do you think, baby? Wouldn't that look nice?" she simpered.

"It already does," I said. "How much for the onyx, Mr. Krishnamurti?" He looked at me for all of a microsecond before muttering something that sounded like fifteen sterling. Then his eyes went back to Synreah's body as she leaned forward and reached for a rough point of amethyst about an inch around. Leather creaked as her top strained to contain ample curves, and her cleavage deepened to the point where I was pretty sure it had its own gravity. She laid it in the same spot and gave Krishnamurti a broad smile, and I knew he was pretty much lost.

"Twenty sterling for both pieces," he said in his clipped accent. "No less."

"Is that a *firm* price?" Synreah asked. Her mouth quirked up a little on one side, and she tilted her head a little like she was sharing a subtle joke with him.

124

"Very," he said with a little squeak.

I laid the twenty silver ounces down, and reached for a bowl full of crushed quartz pieces. "I need three ounces of these, too," I added.

After he poured a pile of them onto his scale, carefully measuring out the three ounces, he added another two sterling ounces to the price, but threw in a silver chain. A quartz generator crystal and a half dozen pieces of magnetite only added another ounce sterling to the price. We walked away from the blanket, out only twenty-four sterling, when I had expected my pouch to be lighter by thirty or more. Well, I walked, what Synreah did was more of a strut.

"Are you sure you want to be dealing with Ashkhabad?" she asked me softly as we waited in a side alley for a gang of redcaps to stalk past us with their iron pikes carried against their shoulders. While they didn't look like they were on the hunt, their caps were still glistening wet with blood, and I didn't want to get their attention if I could avoid it.

"Not really, but I can afford his stuff," I told her, once the sound of their iron-clad boots started to fade away around the corner.

She muttered something as we stepped into the larger alley, and Ashkhabad's latest squat came into view. It looked like he'd taken over the front room of a burnt-out building. Boards were nailed across the two doorways on either side of the front room, and a canvas tarp served as his roof, with a pole in the center giving it a broad point at the top. Most of the front wall was missing above waist height, and the doorway was just an empty rectangle, with no actual door to fill it.

Synreah led the way inside, where a pair of gossamer-winged fairies were fluttering over a pair of four inch wands on the makeshift counter, and a man in brown robes with a girl in off-white robes were sorting through cubit-long pieces of plain wood. Both of them had their hoods up, so that only the lower halves of their faces were visible. A blue-green rune glowed into existence in the air at the back of the shop as Synreah stepped across the shop's threshold, and a red one flared to life beside it as my feet crossed the invisible line across the shop's doorway. Heads turned my way, and I heard footsteps from the back of the shop. A second later, a dark-haired, olive-skinned man in baggy black pants, long-sleeved white shirt, and a patched brown vest came out of the doorway to the back of the shop with a wooden crate in his hands. He took a look at the runes as he came out, then turned to face us with narrowed eyes.

"You...leave my shop this instant!" he hissed as he hurried to set the box down on the cloth covered counter. "I'll have nothing to do with you!"

"Huh? Hey, I just wanted to buy stuff for a rod, that's all, dude," I raised my hands to show open palms.

He pulled a black wand out of his vest and pointed it at me, and I could feel the soft static against my aura as the spell focused on me. Red runes blazed along its surface, and the soft static turned into a cold buzz.

"You can't fool me, boy. You're the apprentice Count Dulka cast out. You cast your lot when you took up service with the powers of Hell, and you'll get no sympathy from me."

"He didn't cast me out, I kicked his ass and left on my own!" I said hotly. "I'm trying to..."

Whatever I intended to tell Ashkhabad, it went away when the spell hit me in the center of the chest and threw me over the wall and across the alleyway. I came up hard against the wall on the far side and shook my head. My vision cleared to the sight of him manhandling Synreah out the door with his hand wrapped in the hair at the nape of her neck, and I scrambled to my feet with an Infernal oath on my lips. Tossing me around was one thing, but getting physical with a girl, even a half-demon prostitute, pushed the wrong damn buttons with me. He shoved her to her knees outside his shop, and backhanded her across the face when she protested.

"Silence, whore!" he snarled and drew his hand back again.

"Back off, asshole," I said as I came across the alley at him.

He recoiled as he saw me, and I saw the glimmer of black flames reflected in his eyes. I raised my left fist to find it engulfed in Hellfire. Somewhere along the way, I must have uttered the activation words for the spell. Just using it tainted my soul, but at the moment, it was worth it to see the look on Ashkhabad's face as I drew up in front of Synreah.

"Touch her again, and I'll burn you so bad there won't even be a stench left." My teeth ground together as I snarled the words at him, and he backed over the threshold of his shop. Depending on how strong his door wards were, he could probably shrug off most of what I could throw.

"Take your filthy bitch and leave," he ordered from the safety of his shop. The Hellfire flickered and went out as I lost the anger I needed to sustain it, and I offered Synreah my other hand. She got to her feet on her own, and I tried not to let the hurt show on my face at having her refuse my help.

"From where I'm standing, the only bitch I see, Ashkhabad," Synreah said, "is the sniveling wand-crafter who isn't man enough to take two steps out of his shop and put a woman in her place." She turned her back on him to add to the insult, and took my hand. My laugh was loud and long as she led me away from his shop.

"Are you okay?" I asked as she led me toward one of the broader alleys.

"We both made an enemy of him," she said softly. "You'd better lay low if you come back to the Hive any time soon."

"What about you?"

"I'll manage. And...thank you for what you did back there. No one...ever helped me before." The words came out slowly, like she wasn't used to saying them.

I gave her a shrug and a half smile. If she was anything like me, it had cost her a lot to say that. The best thing I figured I could do was just let it go and press on. But...it felt good to hear it.   The next place Synreah led me to was Arianh-Rod's. It was one of the few permanent shops in the Hive, in the middle of a fork in the lane, a full two-story stone building, shaped like a wedge. The door faced straight into the lane. A round turret rose above the doorway, and the shop's sign hung beneath it: a plain black plank with the shop's name and the silver wheel of seven spokes that was her maker's mark below it. Windows showcased the front of the shop, where she displayed an assortment of wands in velvet-lined cases.

It was one place Dulka never wanted me to go. He had a thing about not letting me get my hands on a focus, especially a wand. The spells I had thrown at him during my escape had been potent, but sloppy. Magickally, I was the equivalent of a blunt object. A *very* blunt object. Say, a Mack truck, or a car, if you were feeling generous. I made a heavy club seem like a precision instrument by comparison. Dulka's training had concentrated on stamina, strength, and knowledge, but he'd left me painfully short on things like fine control and theory. I could memorize an incantation, cast it from a circle perfectly and repeatedly, but I had to pour a ton of energy into it each and every time. To cast spells outside of a circle, I needed to have a focus and barring another eight years of training at the feet of a real mage, wands were the best tools for the job.

I held the door open for Synreah, who gave me a bemused smile as she ducked her head under the lintel and slipped inside. The threshold here was strong enough to leave goose bumps across my skin as I crossed it, and the sounds from outside faded to almost nothing as the door creaked shut. A half-circle display case held some of the more expensive wands, and served as a barrier between the front half of the shop and the back. A selection of staves lined the walls on either side, and the back wall held drawers and cabinets with labels on them that I couldn't read in the soft light. A curtained doorway was set in the middle of the back wall, and from behind it, I could hear a rhythmic hissing sound. The smell of sawdust was a pleasant tang in my nose, and Synreah's boot heels made a sharp counterpoint to the hissing sound as she crossed the floor. There was no one else in the shop but us, and I wondered if we were going to get the same reception we'd gotten at Ashkhabad's.

The hissing sound stopped, and I heard movement in the back. Then the curtain parted, and I found myself face to face with the glowing crystal tip of a power rod.

"Ye'd best turn about and leave," the woman behind the rod hissed at me in a soft brogue. She was a little taller than me, maybe five foot ten, and slender, with pale blonde hair and almond-shaped violet eyes that suggested fae blood. I wondered what would fall out of her family tree if I gave it a good shake, as I concentrated on standing verrrrry still. The power in the length of silver metal she was pointing at me was strong enough that I could feel it pressing against me without it being truly focused on me. If she cast the spell that I could feel pointed at me, I was pretty sure I was going to end up splattered across a good-sized chunk of the Hive. Of course, the whole front of her shop would be equally obliterated, as well.

"Okay," I said, "I'm going." I turned and opened the door for Synreah, who hadn't moved an inch.

"What?" Synreah sputtered after a moment. "You're not even going to try to defend yourself?"

I sighed, already tired of being treated like this. "She's no different than Ashkhabad. She's gonna believe what she wants to believe, and I can't change that. No point arguing with her about it over a charged weapon. Let's go. I don't feel like getting blasted out of another shop." Synreah shrugged and started across the floor toward the door.

"You stop right there, ye little strumpet! And yew! Close that fecking door and get yer arse back in here!"

I looked at Arianh-Rod with a frown. "You made your point; we're leaving."

"Ye'll be doin' nae such thing! I'll not be treated like I'm a fecking idiot. Believe what I want to believe, indeed. D'ye think I dinnae know when a body is after calling me stupid? And I'll be thrice damned if *any* man can say I treated him the same as that wrong-headed bastard, Ashkhabad." The silver rod came down, and she nodded toward Synreah. "Besides, it's the first time I've heard a whore speak up for a man. Says a lot about ye, it does."

"Don't call her that again, Arianh-Rod," I said.

Arianh-Rod gave out a bark of laughter and smiled at me. "That says a lot about ye too. Best ye call me Ari, if we're ta be talkin' much more, lad. Ye'd be the apprentice the Red Count says he let go then, wouldn't ye?"

"I wasn't his apprentice, I was his slave. I escaped. End of story." I managed to keep my cool when she looked to Synreah and raised an eyebrow.

"Biladon Garnet believes he's a good kid, Ari" Synreah said. "And so do I."

The wand-wright gave me an appraising look, then nodded. "I'm willing ta take a bit on faith. What were ye needin' today, anyroad?" she asked. The rod had disappeared, and she leaned on the glass of her display case.

I blinked at the sudden change while my brain tried to catch up with things. "Uh…a stylus for a copper force rod, and sigils. And…" I hesitated, but there was no way to avoid looking like a total wanna-be with the time I had. "I need a charging spell for it."

"Needin' it quick, then are ye?" she asked with a smile that made the pride I'd just swallowed go down a little easier. "I can do ye for all of that, but ye'll also be needin' some garnet and carnelian powder and a *chrism* of hawthorn to anoint it with."

The knot between my shoulders loosened when she didn't call me out as a fake. Most magi could charge their own tools, but warlocks had a well-deserved reputation for taking shortcuts. Most of the time, it was why they chose to serve a demon. And the last thing I wanted people to think of me was that I'd *chosen* to serve Dulka.

"I can get the gems and the hawthorn oil," I told her. "I just need the spell and the stylus quickly."

"Aye, I have both ta hand, to be sure. The stylus will be twenty sterling, and the sigils forty. The charging spell, that's another sixty on its own."

I pulled the pouch out of my satchel, and ended up with only a handful left to buy the oils and powdered gems. But, one good thing about the Hive, the art of haggling was still alive and well. After about twenty minutes of wrangling, I worked her down to a hundred ten sterling, and figured I got a good bargain. With a show of grumbling over how I was cheating her, she went back into the back and started rummaging around.

"Ari meant no disrespect," Synreah said from over my right shoulder.

"I know, it's all part of the deal," I said. "This isn't the first time I haggled a price down."

"When she called me a whore. It's what I am…what I do. From her, it was no insult."

"Oh," I said slowly. I didn't know how to put what went through my head into the right words, and years of being slapped down if I said something the wrong way paralyzed my voice while I struggled with my thoughts. "It makes you…less," I finally managed to get out. "It maybe what you do, but it isn't who you are."

"That's sweet, but it *is* who I am. I enjoy what I do. Sex is power for me; it's in my blood." She shrugged and leaned toward me. One full breast brushed my arm as she gave me a knowing smile. "But I like that you treat me nice."

Ari came out of the back room with a wooden box that was stained a dark red, and laid it down on the display case. The lid opened with a slight creak, and she turned it to face us. Inside was a scroll wrapped around a slim stylus. I could see the pale tan butt of the wooden handle and the bronze point of the stylus sticking out of the scroll.

"Here it all is, then," she said proudly. "Sigils, charging spell, and stylus. One hundred ten sterling, as agreed." I laid a couple of trade bars and the last of my gems on the countertop, and she closed the lid on the box and slid it across to me. With my money pouch a lot lighter, there was plenty of room in the satchel for the case, and I gave Ari a nod before we made for the door.

"Good luck, then, Chance Fortunato," she said, as I opened to door for Synreah. I muttered thanks to her and slipped out into the street.

Synreah led me to an apothecary's squat a couple of turns down the way from Ari's shop, and I ended up walking away from the little man's trailer setup with almost all of the rest of my trade silver gone, and a glass vial of hawthorn oil and two paper envelopes with a couple of grams of carnelian and garnet chips in each of them. Enough to do the job right the first time.

"Here's the rest of what I owe you," I told Synreah after we made it back to the main alleyway.

The topaz sparkled between my fingertips, but her eyes didn't seem to shine as bright as they had earlier. Still, she took the yellow gem with slender, black-taloned fingers, and it disappeared into the chasm behind the top of her corset.

"Don't go getting any ideas about getting your money back," she joked, then turned hot eyes on me. "Then again, I wouldn't mind it if you tried." She leaned forward and squeezed her arms together and leather creaked as she displayed another few inches of barely contained bosom. I took in the view that she was offering, but I shook my head at the other offer.

"Here's a bonus," I told her, and put the onyx pendant over her head. "You earned it, and a lot more. Thanks for sticking up for me at Ari's shop."

She shrugged as she touched the pendant as it lay in the cleft between her breasts. "If it weren't for this, I'd be almost disappointed that you didn't try anything. A girl might think she was losing her touch. Other than that, you're all right."

"I'm on a tight schedule," I told her as I closed the satchel up. "Maybe next time."

"Promises, promises," she said with a half-smile.

I headed for the gate. I had a tracking spell to cast and a force rod to craft, all the while having to dodge the Conclave, and keep my Mom from finding out I was a warlock. And if that wasn't enough, I had to get it all done before my mom got home from work.

Yeah, that was me, livin' the glamorous life of a teenage warlock.

Chapter 10

~ Justice is cold and swift, and often leaves both parties unsatisfied with the outcome. Vengeance however, finds favor only in the hearts of the aggrieved. ~ John Dee, 17th century Wizard

The school's parking lot was mostly empty by the time I made it back there on Mom's bike. There was only one news van left, and only two police cruisers near the entrance. Another, unmarked police car was parked behind them. The news crew was filming the reporter's wrap-up as I slipped around the edge of the building and headed for the back of the school to play junior psychic detective. I passed the first two wings of classrooms and turned to my right between the second and the third when I saw the yellow strip of crime scene tape fluttering in the light wind. The cops had strung it across the end of the breezeway between the second and third wing, under the still-gaping hole of the lab's missing window. The cloudy, gray sky did a pretty good job of mirroring my mood as I eyed the black square that marred the building like a missing tooth. The hole in my life seemed a lot bigger.

I left Mom's bike leaning against the building and headed across the damp grass on foot. My boots clomped against the covered concrete walkway that ran between the wings, then I was out from under the beige-painted breezeway, and standing at the yellow line of tape, suddenly not sure of what to do. How was I supposed to do this? I looked back at where I'd walked across the grass and wondered if I'd trampled on anything important. But the whole area looked pretty much stomped flat, so I figured I wasn't making things much worse. Now what? My gaze went back to the area inside the tape.

The window, frame and all, was still on the ground outside the science lab, about fifteen feet from the wall. I looked up at the hole it used to occupy, and blinked. The window wasn't right beneath the opening. It hadn't been knocked out; it had been torn out and tossed aside. I slipped under the tape and went over to the frame. Four parallel furrows ran across the pale wood sill, and I remembered the gray lines scored in the concrete column in the lab. There was no blood on the wood or the glass. I looked up at the concrete pillar that ran up the outside of the building, and saw

133

another set of claw marks in the pillar, level with the window, but this set had something the others didn't: a fifth claw mark on the adjacent side of the pillar. The killer had an opposable thumb. It ruled out a lot of things, but still left a pretty long list of possible species for the perp. Hence, my spell.

I moved back into the breezeway and pulled some of my new purchases out of the satchel Billy had given me. As I held them in my hands, they looked pretty innocuous. Copper tubing, a few sandwich bags from Mom's kitchen, a file, a piece of purple chalk, and a piece of amethyst on a chain. In anyone else's hands, they were harmless: completely unconnected. In mine, they were tools that would cast a finding spell.

I looked back up at the gray gap where the window used to be and wondered if I was ready for what I was about to step into. Right now, I was almost where I wanted to be, just a normal kid, going to high school. If I wanted to, I could turn around and leave this to the cops. If I wanted to, I could be done with this. I didn't have to get involved, and my life could go on being almost normal. The question running around in my head was, "Could I really?"

My teeth ground together as my heart answered the question in my head. The cops would never find the killer. The Conclave might be able to find them, and if they did, they'd exact their own brand of justice. I'd seen their retribution before, when a warlock got careless. Conclave vengeance was cold, calculated, and almost always done from a distance. Mr. Chomsky deserved better than that. He deserved better from me. I couldn't walk away.

A cold stillness spread from my center, shutting down any thought that wasn't about finding the killer, and I knelt there in the middle of the sidewalk. First, I inscribed a rough circle on the ground, making the ends touch but not overlap, then broke out the file and a short length of copper tubing, and went to work. After a few minutes effort, I had a small pile of copper filings on the ground in front of me. I drew the sigils for divination around the inside edge of the circle before muttering *Circumvare,* to close the circle.

The world went ripply for a second as I felt the circle close around me, then the normal feeling of static in the back of my head faded, and I was left with a pure, clear focus on the spell. *"Velle potestatem quaero, videtur tacta, soluta tenere,"* I chanted as I concentrated on my goal.

The words were in Latin, like most of my spells. Latin gave my words power because it was the language I used only for magick. It helped my brain get into the place it needed to be to shape my will into reality, because I didn't have any association with the words other than magick. I sat with my legs crossed, back straight, and put my hands on my knees. My eyelids lowered as I started the next step.

The words and symbols of the circle had created the start of a seeking spell. Now all I needed to do was give it something to seek. Magick was shaped by the will, and the will, as much as most magi hated to admit it, was fueled by emotion. I'd seen rage drive people to impossible acts of stupidity, and love drive them to superhuman acts of courage and strength. I focused on my few memories of Mr. Chomsky. He'd only known me for a few hours, but he'd believed in me, seen things in me that no one else had. He'd offered to teach me. Me: a warlock, a demon's slave. In his eyes, a demon's apprentice. And he'd been willing to risk his life for me to do it. He didn't know me, but he believed in me. My breath caught at that thought, and it felt like someone had poured a pound of sand down my throat as my eyes stung. After years of being a slave, having someone see me for something other than an Infernal plaything had felt really, really good.

And someone had taken that away from me. Hurt and anger boiled over in my head as I concentrated on the loss, and on my hunger for vengeance on the person who'd killed Mr. Chomsky. The first person who'd seen who I really was and offered me a hand in friendship had been taken from me, and I wanted to find the thing who had done that in the worst way. All my thoughts focused in on that one goal, and I uttered the spell again. The words forced their way through my teeth as I scooped up the pile of copper filings and held them in my left palm. I held the amethyst pendant in my right hand as I focused my will on the copper filings. They started to glow as I repeated it a second time, and started to float and swirl over my palm as I chanted the third time, letting the pendant drop to dangle from its chain as they spun. When the pendant started to rotate in the same direction, I stood with the little metal slivers spinning like a miniature tornado over my palm and moved the toe of my boot to the purple ring of chalk.

"*Invenio!*" I hissed, as I broke the circle with my boot. The whirlwind of metal scattered in two directions: some going toward the school, and the rest flying the opposite way. My pendulum started swinging back and forth. I took a couple of steps to one side, and the pendant's swing changed, one half of its arc pointing toward the window frame on the grass. When I moved in the direction of the swing, it got faster and faster, until I had it suspended right over a spot where it spun in place. Bingo.

I dropped to one knee and looked down at the grass, but I couldn't see anything worth picking up. Whatever the spell had homed in on was small; I had to practically lie on the ground before I saw it. A single hair, thick, coarse, and brown, was sticking up among the blades of grass with bits of copper filings sticking to it. I kind of doubted that the cops would have seen it, or even given it much attention. Only my fine-tuned little spell had led me to it. I plucked the lone hair from the grass and slipped it one of the baggies, then stood up and swung the pendulum in a circle to reset it.

It started swinging back and forth again right away, only this time, it barely moved when I took a few steps to zero it in. I stood there for a few moments trying to figure that out. If it had been here, even one step would have made it change direction a lot. Then I remembered that some of the filings had gone flying the other way, and I looked the other way. Past the end of the wings of the school was an open field, backed by a neat line of wood privacy fences. I chuckled as I started following the pendulum toward the fence line.

New Essex cops were good at dealing with normal crimes. I'd been lucky to catch a single fiber outside the actual crime scene. I figured they'd probably scoured the lab pretty thoroughly, and had all kinds of things they couldn't identify. But whatever had ripped the window out of its frame to come in had left the same way, courtesy of Mr. Chomsky. The cops had searched the area for thirty feet or so outside the building, but anything that a full-fledged wizard had hit was probably going to fly a lot further than that before it hit the ground. I almost didn't need the pendulum to find where it had landed. A five-foot wide section of fence was simply obliterated, and it had taken out a good-sized section of someone's tool shed, too.

The last thing I needed was a trespassing charge, so I snuck a quick look in before I slipped in through the gap in the fence. The pendulum led me to the crumpled remains of a riding lawnmower. An inch-long sliver of something horn-like was glistening with copper filings, stuck on the edge of the mower's bent blade. There was even a little blood on it. I snagged the sliver, then turned one of the baggies inside out to use as a kind of a glove to scrape some of it off, then pulled it back right-side out when I was done.

I reset the pendulum again, but it just hung there after that. And here I'd been hoping for something vague, like a wallet with an ID in it, or perhaps a taped confession. It probably wasn't nearly as much as the cops had, but the things I could do with what I had were a lot more effective. Talon, fur, and blood, I mused as I jogged back across the field. More than enough for a dozen curses I knew.

It took only a few seconds to collect Mom's bike and head for the back of the school through the breezeway that ran through the middle of the wing. The sound of a door opening and closing made me pull up short, then I heard a voice I recognized.

"Damn, sergeant, this is wrong!" I heard the familiar tenor of Officer Collins.

"Collins, I know you don't like it, but it's not our call," came a familiar woman's voice.

I nosed the bike forward and hoped they weren't looking my way. Luck was with me. Detective Roberts stood just behind and to the left of the tall, lean form of Collins. He turned away from her for a moment, and I heard the rasp of a lighter and smelled tobacco smoke a moment later. When he turned back, I could see his eyes were ablaze with anger. He paused long enough to blow smoke away from Roberts before he spoke again.

"It may not be our call, but it's still the *wrong* call, Sergeant. We both know that," Collins growled.

"Look, I know you don't agree with Captain Sloan, but…"

"This is no animal attack, Holly," Collins interrupted her. "This is a murder. At a *high school*. Sloan is just trying to cover his ass."

"What would you suggest he tell the press, Collins?" Roberts demanded. "We think a creature with four inch claws tore a teacher apart and *ate* part of him?"

"It'd sure make good copy," he said.

"For the *World Post,* maybe!" she shot back. I stifled a snicker at the irony in that, because most of the time, the *World Post* was partly accurate. Most of what they wrote about actually did happen, but the reporters' understanding of what they saw or heard were usually a long way from right. But no one took a tabloid seriously.

"What if he just said something brilliant like, 'No comment,' or that line about not commenting on an active investigation, or some shit like that? Like he does when it's something he can get the big, believable headlines for later on."

"Collins, you can't make waves on this. The only reason you're here is because of the Fortunato kid. If you buck the captain on this, he'll bust you down to traffic in a heartbeat, if he doesn't fire you just to get your ass off the force. You're too good a cop to let that happen."

"I'm too good a cop to let *this* happen, Holly. Whoev…*whatever* the hell did this, it did it at a school. What if the next time we come out here, it's to mop up some kid off the gymnasium floor?" Collins hissed. Roberts gasped, and I even found my nose wrinkling at the thought. But, to her credit, she didn't have a good answer to his question.

"Point," she said, holding up one hand in surrender. "Look, let me talk to my father. The Gang Task Force is usually short-handed for things like school presence and Drug Awareness presenters. I'll see if we can get you assigned to them for the next week or so, okay?"

"Aw, hell," Collins spat.

"It'll keep you here, at least for a little while, and out from under Sloan's thumb," Roberts said quickly. "I know you don't think he had anything to do with it, but keep an eye on the Fortunato kid. His story checked out, but I know he's hiding something."

For a moment, Collins glared at her, then gave a nod and shrug. "The Spartan's kid? Hell, yeah he's hiding something." I stifled a curse. Being on the cops' radar was going to make this a lot tougher.

"Damn straight. But, what? Now get your ass back down to precinct and get your report done. If it's on the chief's desk before Sloan shoots his mouth off to the press, we might be able to at least keep the case open, even if it's put on the back burner."

At Roberts' order, Collins headed for the other side of the building: away from me, thankfully. Once he was away, she reached into her jacket and pulled out a cigarette of her own and lit it, taking a deep drag with her eyes closed. She exhaled the plume of smoke, and I could see her trying to relax. Today, I didn't envy her for her job.

I turned the bike around and was silently grateful that there were cops like her and Collins working this case. Mr. Chomsky deserved better than a lame-ass lie about his death. Even if no one else ever knew, I wanted his killer. And even if they didn't catch the son of a bitch, at least they were really trying. I rode home with a sense of accomplishment growing in me. In the satchel at my side were the beginnings of my spell arsenal, and I had put a dent in Dulka's resources in the process. I ran the math in my head as the city streets flew beneath my wheels. Between the physical and mystical beat-down I'd laid on him, Dulka would be at least two months in recovering to the point where he could get another apprentice and at least another six after that to get them trained. And I didn't envy his new familiar when the poor idiot had to come back with the news that he had only half the money he thought he had.

The clock in the living room showed a few minutes past one when I got home. Only a couple of hours left before my time wasn't my own again, and I needed a weapon if I was going to handle Mr. Chomsky's killer on my own.

Magick is mostly done in the practitioner's head. The caster has to be in the right frame of mind to channel mystic energy through his or her body and create the desired effect out in the world. That takes years and years to get good at. Eventually, you get to the point where you can simply *will* something to happen without saying a word or moving a muscle. Usually, by that time, you're older than dirt, and you can do more with your mind than with your body, anyway.

For everyone who's not a Master, there are foci and rituals. Tools act as a physical focus for the energy you're trying to channel, like a magnifying glass turning a sunbeam into a pinpoint of heat that can start a fire. That's why the materials and shapes and squiggly marks on them are so damn important. Foci are also symbols that help the mind to get in magick making mode. Ritual helps the mind tune itself like a radio to the right station for magick. The words themselves are important, but not the language, because you only need to understand what they were supposed to mean. The big thing was, it had to be something outside of your normal everyday language. The more often you used a word for normal things, the more it became tuned to the mundane station in your head. Even without the Gift, if you had enough tools and toys, and followed the ritual just right, you could get some halfway decent results every now and then.

Tools, because they're symbols, and they're usually made with stuff that is naturally sympathetic to magickal energy anyway, take spells very easily. That was going to be important today. I pulled out the copper tubing and caps, and grabbed some of the red leather strips I'd picked up at the craft store. The quartz chips and lodestone from the Hive joined the rest of the stuff on my desk, and I started constructing a power rod.

A power rod isn't really a "rod" so much as a copper wand filled with lodestone and quartz fragments, since lodestone acts as a terrific amplifier for magickal energy, and quartz is a good focusing element for it. Copper is a great conductor, and all it takes then is a decent-sized quartz crystal on the end to act as the focuser. Putting the materials together only took a few minutes. Etching the power runes on the copper rod was the time-consuming part. They were like the circuitry that guided the flow of magickal power that the lodestone and quartz created, and turned it from unfocused energy into a bolt of pure kinetic energy that would hit like a minotaur.

The sigil sheet Ari had sold me was the best I'd ever seen, and she hadn't stopped with just marking the sigils down. Ratios for placement, angles of relationship, and order of inscription lined the margin, making it worth every single ounce of silver I'd paid for it. It took me over an hour to etch the sigils into the copper tube. My eyes stung and my hands ached from holding the stylus when I finally straightened up from my work and stretched.

My shoulders weren't too happy with me, and I still had several steps to go. The packets of carnelian and garnet chips I'd bought had to be ground into a powder and mixed with the hawthorn oil, then worked into the sigils I'd just etched. Mom's marble mortar and pestle were perfect for the job, but crushing gems wasn't easy work, even with the right tool. I could almost hear Mr. Gonzalez's voice in my ear, telling me there was a tool for every job, and a job for every tool, as I twisted the marble pestle to grind the gemstones into a powder. My forearms were burning by the time I got them to the right consistency and added half of the hawthorn oil to the mix. The oil made it a sort of conduit, and made it stick better in the etched grooves of the sigils.

Once the oil was mixed in, I dug the point of my knife into the soft flesh of my thumb, and added three drops of my blood to link the magick to me. I slowly followed the lines I'd carefully carved into the copper, and made sure each one was properly filled in. I wrapped it gently with strips of red leather to hold the powdered gemstones in place, and pulled out the charging spell.

Spelling scrolls always fascinated me because they were so complex. The activation phrases were scattered among the symbols that covered the page, in colored and metallic inks to store the energy. I closed my eyes and picked up the rod in my left hand, with the scroll in my right. I was left-handed, so my left was my projecting hand, and my right was my receiving hand, opposite of most people. As I uttered each phrase, the corresponding symbol on the page flared to life, its magickal power contained by the border until I said the last phrase, when it erupted into flame, and the power flowed up my right arm, down my left, and into the rod. I could feel the power slide through the sigils I'd carved into the copper with the stylus as the spell took hold and turned it from a collection of random parts into a potent weapon.

The sweet scents of hay and clover filled the room as the spell finished, and I could feel the now-complete TK rod hum under my fingertips, ready to be charged. I had a lead on Mr. Chomsky's killer, and a weapon to use against him when I found him. For my first day as a sleuth, I figured I was doing okay. I wondered if he would have been proud of me.

Evidently, my little sister didn't do pink. She came storming into the house with a purple backpack held by the straps in one little fist, and a bag from Bangles And Beads dangling from the other. Her feet thumped on the stairs as she ran up them, and Mom came in a few seconds behind her.

"Hey, Mom," I said from behind my book. "You're late, young lady," I looked over it at her with a mock frown. Being flat on my back robbed me of every bit of seriousness I had.

"Feet off the couch, Chance," she said without missing a beat.

My boots hit the floor and I sat up at her tone. "Is everything okay?" Her head tilted toward me and one eyebrow went up. "I mean, aside from one of my teachers getting killed in his classroom, and me being a suspect," I clarified.

"No, I think that pretty much covers it, son," she said as she sat down beside me. "Are you all right?"

I shrugged. "I guess so. It doesn't seem like it's real, ya know? I mean, I only knew him the one day and all, but…" My thoughts went back to the bloody room, and I fought back a shudder.

"What you saw today was really terrible," Mom said. Her hand was warm on my arm, and the contact helped me anchor myself as my head started to spin a little.

"Big time," I said with a little nod.

"Listen, son. By tomorrow morning, everyone at school is going to know you were one of the people who found Mr. Chomsky. Your friends are going to have a lot of questions, and you're going to need to be able to either answer them, or put them off. Whichever you do, think it out tonight, so you can deal with it tomorrow without thinking too hard about it. It won't be easy, but that's the way people are."

"Why can't you tell me everything is going to be all right and let me be surprised tomorrow?"

"Because you know better, so you wouldn't believe me," she said sagely. She was right, I had to give her that. "Besides, I'd rather you be prepared than painfully surprised. It's one of those enigmatic Mom Things. It's unpleasant, so it has to be good for you." She smiled sadly as she kissed me on the forehead. "I wish you didn't have to be dealing with this, son, but it's what's in front of you. All you can choose is how you deal with it." I couldn't help the quirk at the corner of my mouth as I thought of the little copper rod I had hidden in my closet. My version of dealing with it wasn't going to be fun for the guy who did this, that was certain.

"Can we work on my backpack Mom?" Dee yelled from upstairs. The heavy sound of an elephant sprinting down the stairs reached us, and Dee came back into the room with her backpack and craft booty still in hand, only now she was dressed in jeans and a t-shirt with an orange-haired girl on it.

"Yes, honey, we will, but chores and dinner come first." Mom's words fell on deaf ears while Dee upended the plastic bag and dumped a pile of bright and shiny things out onto the couch beside me. Like Mom, she had the Roma love of color, glitter, and jingle, and, to hear her talk, a plain backpack, even a cool purple one, was just too boring to even take to school.

"I'm gonna put a star here, in beads, and see, I got a unicorn for this zipper, and they had these little gargoyle charms, they can watch over my backpack for me, I'm gonna put this one here, see?" she held an ugly little bauble near the zipper for the main compartment. I nodded like I understood.

"Dee," Mom said, drawing out the "e" sound into a warning tone. My little sister turned wide, innocent eyes to Mom. "Chores, young lady. Now. Then dinner, *then* we work on your project."

"But Mo-oooommmm," Dee protested.

"Don't 'Mom' me, young lady."

"Come on, munchkin," I said. "She Who Must Be Obeyed has spoken, and her word is Law. It's no use arguing." Dee followed me as I got up off the couch, and I caught a glimpse of Mom giving me an approving smile as we left the room. Something in my chest went tight at that.

"Moms can be a pain sometimes," Dee said from in front of me. She grabbed the broom from the narrow opening between the refrigerator and the wall and looked at me from across the kitchen.

My shoulders rose and fell in a quick shrug. "Beats not having one." Dee stopped and gave me a look while I grabbed the recycling bin and headed for the door.

"I guess so," she answered. "Was it…really bad, not having a mom?"

"Worse than you can imagine," I told her, not sure of what else I could say. Dee had a wide-eyed innocence most of the time, and I didn't want to screw that up. Her frown scrunched into something more thoughtful before she turned to sweeping the kitchen.

Mom started dinner while we took care of business, and Dee carefully marked each of her chores off on the chart on the refrigerator as she finished it. Everything seemed to float past while Mom made dinner, and even while I tried to savor each bite of Mom's stew, none of what was happening seemed to fit with what I'd seen at the start of the day.

Finally, it felt too weird, and I had to get up and leave the table. Being able to just leave a place felt strange all on its own, and I didn't really know where I wanted to go, I just needed to be somewhere else. I ended up near the top of the stairs. Mom came up a few minutes later with a steaming cup in her hand. She handed it to me as she sat on the step above me, and I took a sip of the black brew. Peppermint, chamomile, and strawberry hit my nose before they coursed across my tongue, with an herbal aftertaste that was softened with honey. Mom laid a hand on my shoulder, and didn't say a word.

"Doesn't seem right," I said after a couple of sips of Mom's tea. "Mr. Chomsky's dead, and we're just sitting here eating dinner like nothing happened."

"No, it *isn't* right, son," Mom said after a couple of moments. "But, life always moves forward, and you still have to live it. You can't honor his memory properly if you neglect your own life, and I don't think a teacher would want one of his students to do that."

"Guess not." Mom was right, in more ways than one. I couldn't find his killer if I let this screw me up too bad. The normal things in my new life, the things I wasn't used to, those were the things that I owed Mr. Chomsky. He could have turned me in. If he had, I would have been locked in a cell tonight, instead of sitting on the stairs at home.

"Translating that from teen-speak to English, that must have been you agreeing with your tragically out-of-touch mother. I'll take it as the compliment, and leave you to brood in peace," Mom said. She stood and walked down the stairs past me, her bare feet quiet on the brown carpet.

I went down to help clean up after dinner, then hung out in the living room with Mom and Dee while they decorated her new backpack. As much as I wanted to sit on the steps and brood all night, being with them was the gift my favorite teacher had given me. I wasn't going to waste it.

If someone had asked me six days ago what I would be doing tonight, I wouldn't have thought to tell them that I'd be sitting in my mom's living room, reading and watching my mom and my sister sitting in the middle of the floor, decorating a backpack. The image of me huddled in a makeshift squat somewhere in the depths of the Hive came to mind again, and I felt the corner of my mouth pull up a little. My luck had been a lot better than my planning. I tried to keep my mind on the mystery I was reading, but when I wasn't wrapped up in the simple pleasure of this moment, my thoughts kept wandering back to my real-life whodunit.

The cold, nauseating feel of demon magick hammered my mystic senses, and I felt my spine go weak in fear. All I could think of was that Dulka had found me, and the sound of my pulse hammered in my ears as I fought to catch a breath. I wasn't ready to face him again; I hadn't even gotten a decent ward on the house yet! Some part of my brain tried to remind me I was behind a threshold, that he couldn't possibly be ready to come after me himself, but the screaming, gibbering monkey part of my brain wasn't having any of that crap. It was all for getting me out of the house even if I had to make a new exit to do it.

The knock at the door stopped my thoughts for a moment, and damn near did the same to my heart. Mom looked at the door with a curious look in her eyes. I tried not to run screaming.

"Were you expecting one of your friends, honey?" she asked me as she got to her feet. I managed a fairly calm headshake, but I kept my tongue still. If I opened my mouth, all that was likely to come out was a squeak. My body was paralyzed, and so was my voice; I couldn't decide whether to scream at her to stay away from the door, or run for the back door, but I couldn't do either one.

"It's okay," Dee said from beside me. "You're safe at home." Her little hands fell on my shoulder and forearm, and I tore my eyes from Mom to look at her.

"What?" I managed. My instincts got jumbled, and the part of my head that could actually think clawed its way up to the top of the swirl of thoughts and impulses that I was drowning in.

"It's what Mom always says when I have my dreams and I'm afraid," she said softly.

"I'm not afraid," I said reflexively.

"Liar, liar pants on fire," she taunted. "You're shaking." I looked down to see the book trembling in my hands. I put it down, then looked over at her.

"Am not."

"Are too."

"Not anymore." I tried to pass it off with a grin, and she stuck her tongue out at me. I stuck mine out at her, then frowned as I realized that there was no screaming or fire, like I'd expect during a demon assault. Not even a gasp or a raised voice. No, I was hearing…mom giggle.

I'd only been doing the normal teenager thing for a few days, but I knew even from my zero to seven days that moms…Did. Not. Giggle. Especially not when a demon was at the door. My head turned at the same time Dee's did. A tall man was standing next to Mom, with one hand on her shoulder, and a thick yellow envelope in the other.

"I doubt very seriously that it will come to it, Mara," he said with a honeyed smoothness, "but I would be happy to act as defense counsel for your son if any charges are filed in this matter. Provided, of course, he is also amenable to the arrangement." He turned dark eyes to me, and I felt a shiver go down my spine again. The narrow smile that creased his angular face made me feel like a bird under a snake's gaze. The tight weave of a black braid looped over the shoulder of his gray suit jacket. He had matching gray slacks and a black shirt with a red silk tie on, and shoes that had to be more expensive than mom's van.

"Mom, who is this guy?" I asked. Now that he was in the house, the urge to run had been replaced with the urge to throw myself between my mother and the demon dressed like a lawyer. My feet went to the floor and I slid my butt to the edge of the couch.

"This is Kyle Vortigern, honey. He's my lawyer. *Our* lawyer." She gave him a grateful smile and came over to me. The name of Kyle Vortigern set alarm bells off in my head and sent chills down my spine.

"Of Sammael and Berith?" I asked. "Mom, they're the most expensive law firm in the city!" Vortigern's eyes narrowed a little at my use of the firm's real name, but he didn't have any other reaction I could see.

"In three states, actually," Vortigern corrected me. "But *Samuels and Barrett* does encourage its partners to engage in the occasional pro bono case. And after hearing of your mother's plight…well, it tugged at my heart strings, you might say."

He would have had to have a heart to have heart strings, but I let the comment slide. "So, what's the deal? Why is he here?"

"Chance, mind your manners," Mom said. The iron in her tone stopped the next remark off my tongue. "Mr. Vortigern is here to offer his help, and you'd be wise to at least listen to him. He's the reason you're here tonight, instead of in a foster home or back at your father's."

"Sorry," I managed.

"Not at all, my boy," Vortigern said with an oily smile. "A healthy dose of caution is never amiss. Perhaps you and I should talk this over in the other room." He tilted his head toward Dee and raised his eyebrows, and I gave him a glare that should have taken years off his life.

"Sure," I said, and hoped there was no growl in my tone.

"Only with your consent, Mara," he said with a little nod at my mom. She gave him a nod and gestured toward the kitchen. I followed him into the kitchen and slid into the seat that had become mine at meal times while Mom led Dee upstairs.

"What's your angle, Vortigern?" I growled as soon as we were alone. "S&B doesn't do anything without an agenda, and they *never* do something for free."

"First, I will thank you never to use the firm's true name on this side of the Veil. As to my angle...to be frank, you are my angle." He smiled at my dumbfounded frown. "Allow me a moment to explain, and I assure you, all will be made clear, my boy."

"You got it. I'll even give you two moments, seeing as how I'm feeling generous."

"Thank you ever so much. I'll contact the Vatican straight away to extoll your virtues and petition for sainthood."

"Skip to the part about my mom," I demanded. "What are you trying to get out of her?"

"Your mother? Nothing! In fact, I already have what I want, and you are the one who delivered it to me last Friday night. Your mother was simply a rather novel means to accomplish my ends, to wit, to deprive the Red Count of his apprentice, one Chance Fortunato."

"I wasn't his apprentice."

"Not willingly, no, but that is little more than a variation on a theme. The most important thing was, through your efforts, he had become far more powerful than certain parties were comfortable with."

"Too powerful to move against directly," I supplied.

"Quite so. Hence, my involvement. The Count himself was not only powerful behind the Veil, but he had also secured himself a bastion in the *cowan* world, safe from many of the machinations of his plentiful rivals. The logical solution was to cripple him by removing you from the picture."

"News flash: I did that myself."

149

"Not entirely. Who do you think arranged for you to find the Rite of Severing?" His grin soured my stomach, and I felt my freedom start to slip through my fingers. "The desired outcome was to weaken Dulka by depriving him of his slave, to wit, you," he went on. "Certain of the more traditional partners favored a more…fatal solution. However, convincing accidents are so passé, and reliable assassins are very expensive. My more subtle solution was simply the most cost effective."

"Either way, you won."

"Precisely. Your freedom was an unlikely, but acceptable outcome. The odds against you were astronomical. The betting was very…spirited." Demons would gamble on anything, but most seemed to lean toward the sure thing. Why do you think they own so much of Vegas? The house always wins. Something clicked in my head; thought processes I'd been able to avoid for the past few days woke up suddenly.

"I don't owe you squat, Vortigern. There was no deal between us."

"Oh, too true, there is no formal debt between us, which the firm is not at all pleased with. This is not a contract, boy. It's a matter of honor. Yours, to be precise. You owe me a favor. A big one. Some day…I'll collect."

"Asshole," I growled at him. "I hope you lost a bundle betting on Dulka."

"Oh, no, my young friend. I bet on *you*. More than you can imagine," he finished thoughtfully. "Now, to the matter at hand, the custody issue. I have some papers for you to sign…oh, do calm yourself. If you fear for your soul, don't. It's virtually useless to the firm, given the abuse the Red Count put it through. The firm has what it wants, as long as you remain free of your former Master. This is just part of the formalities required to keep you out of his control. It is merely an affidavit." He slid some pages toward me.

Despite his reassurance, I made sure to read them all carefully...twice. It wasn't until I was sure I wasn't signing my soul or someone else's freedom away that I put my signature on the pages. He read it over, then tapped the pages to straighten them and tucked them into his leather briefcase.

"Hey, Vortigern," I called. He stopped at the entrance to the living room and turned back to face me. "Thanks, man."

His face contorted into a grimace, and he stood there for a few seconds before he shook his head, and the calm mask of the lawyer fell back into place. He called out a goodbye to my mom and strode out the front door like the house was on fire. I watched him slip into the back of the gray limo parked in front of the house, and didn't move until it turned the corner.

"He just feels wrong," Dee said from beside me. Mom was behind her, her eyes deep and thoughtful.

"What do you expect, he's a lawyer," I joked.

"I pray we don't need his services any more than we already do," Mom said softly.

"I don't like him." Dee turned and went back to her project, and I silently agreed with her as my eyes went back to the deepening gloom that was settling over the street. I was in debt to a demon, and it scared me more than I thought anything could. For a moment, I wondered who Mom was praying to, and whether they took requests.

I'm in the science lab, and it's still liberally covered in Mr. Chomsky, but his head is still alive and talking, telling his arms to get the rest of him put back together.

"There's something I've still got to finish," he says. "You're not done yet," he tells me when he notices me.

"What do you mean?" I ask his head.

"I just started on you, and now I'm all in pieces. How am I supposed to finish up with you if I'm all over the room like this? Hell of a way to run a lab, if you ask me." His arms spread themselves wide as if they're still attached to his shoulders.

"Finish up with me?"

"Of course. I hate to leave a project unfinished. But don't worry; you'll get done one way or the other. I just hope you turn out well."

"What were you going to do with me?"

"I wasn't really sure. You have some potential, but you're broken in a few places. I really wanted to see if I could help fix you. But, now I've got this to deal with, and who knows when I'll be able to help you." He sounds a little sad, and I find myself wanting to help somehow, wanting to put him back together. His head turns to me with a sad smile.

"You can't fix me, Chance. All you can do is find out who broke me. Who knows, it might fix something in you, too." A disembodied hand shoos me out of the room...

I woke up with the window getting lighter, before I could ask Mr. Chomsky who'd broken him. Of course, I knew he was right, too. I *was* broken, in a lot of ways. What normal, healthy person would dream of a room full of blood and gore, and hold a conversation with a severed head? That went straight past broken and took the express train to seriously screwed up. Especially since, as dreams went...this one was pretty tame.

Chapter 11

~ Assume nothing. ~ Wizard's proverb.

When Mom dropped me off at school, I found Wanda and Lucas waiting under a tree to the left of the front steps, while Brad and his cronies held court by the flagpole. The jock herd gave me a group of glares, which I smiled back at, then promptly ignored, and went to join my two friends. I sat down with my back against the tree. Wanda was wearing all black today, and not going for Goth style in the slightest. Her eyes looked dark and tragic with runny mascara beneath them, but they weren't red like she'd been crying.

Lucas wore a black armband on his left sleeve, and a plain black t-shirt and blue jeans. "You doing okay?" he asked somberly.

"Yeah," I answered, "thanks." It was macho boy-code for a deep, emotional outburst and gratitude for being there, minus the tears and chocolate.

"Did you really see him?" Wanda asked hesitantly. "I mean, did you really find his...body?" I just nodded. "That must have been terrible. Louise Harding said you were as pale as a sheet, and she said Stacy Pinkett, the girl that was with you, had a nervous breakdown and her parents had her admitted to the psych unit last night." Even though she was still talking like the girl I had met in fifth period, it was a subdued version: slower, quieter and less bubbly.

"The cops are trying to say it was an animal attack," Lucas offered softly. "Like a lion or something that some rich guy had bought and couldn't take care of. I don't buy it."

"Me, either," Wanda put in. Both of their voices took on an edge like iron, and I wondered where they were going with this. "No animal jumps through a second story window and dismembers a person like that. Not without leaving tracks or something. But the cops don't have anything." I fought to keep my face composed. Of course the cops didn't have squat; I had it all.

"And if it was an animal attack, it's the second one this year, and there was another one last year, too. But they never catch anything. And all of them were just as weird."

"So, what do you think it is?" I asked. If this was part of a pattern, I needed to hear more, even if I didn't want them to go in the right direction.

"That's the thing, I don't know. It's just not a wild animal." Lucas' face lost the look of certainty it had before, and I let myself relax a little. A little bit of doubt was all it took to keep them on the wrong track, and hopefully keep them safe. The bell for first period rang, and we got to our feet and headed for class.

"You need something to wipe your eyes with?" I asked Wanda as we headed for the doors.

She smiled at me. "It's a look, Chance. I want to show that I'm grieving, so..." she pointed at her eyes, "the mask of tragedy. Besides...it makes it easier when I really do cry."

I nodded and put an arm around her. It was a thing I'd seen people do when they were trying to offer comfort, and in spite of how awkward I felt, Wanda put her head on my shoulder for a second.

I looked up to see a wall of purple and gold in front of me. I was standing face to face with Brad and the varsity football team, with a reluctant-looking Alexis held against his left side. Wanda and Lucas took a step back, and a testosterone-soaked semi-circle formed around me.

"Hey, freak boy," Duncan sneered. Up close, he looked as bad as I thought he should have the other night, minus the freaky fast healing. His right hand was purple and swollen again, and his face was bruised worse than I remembered.

"Did you come for some more of what I gave you Tuesday night, Brad?" I asked casually.

He glowered at me for a moment before he pressed on. "I tried being nice to you, and you had to go and jump me. Now it's your ass, freak. I'm gonna catch you alone in a dark alley and beat the crap out of you!" He poked his left hand at me, but pulled up short before he actually touched me.

I looked down at it, then shifted my eyes back up to his slowly and gave him a grim, I'm-going-to-eat-you smile. I leaned in close: close enough that I could smell his cologne.

"You *had* me alone in a dark alley," I said softly enough that only he could hear me clearly, "and all your extra strength and speed wasn't enough to take me. I know the source of your strength, Brad, and I know how to take it away from you."

I was bluffing big time, but I knew that if it *was* just a matter of beating me up, he really *would* wait to catch me alone and off-guard to jump me. I wasn't sure he'd stop at a beating. If he thought I could do more than beat him up, maybe he'd steer clear of me for good and all. Besides, if his injuries had reappeared, I was betting that whatever he'd used to fix them was something temporary, like a poorly done potion or charm. Those, I really *could* undo, and from a distance.

"Mess with me again, and I'll leave you weak as a kitten."

His eyes narrowed and he stepped back a little, almost leaving Alexis behind. She went with him, but her eyes were on me for the first few steps as she followed him.

"What did you say to him?" Lucas asked from behind me as I headed inside. I didn't answer. I was almost late to class already. He caught up to me and leaned against the locker next to mine. "Seriously, Chance, what did you say?"

"Nothing important."

"Come on, man. Brad Duncan has been the bane of my existence for years, and nothing I do seems to get him off my back. You're here for three *days* and you made him run like a little girl just by whispering to him. I gotta know what you said!" He was practically hopping up and down in his eagerness, and I looked at him with a grim smile.

155

"It wouldn't work for you like it did for me. It's all about the leverage, Lucas. I've got plenty on him." I closed my locker door and turned to go to history.

"Oh," he only paused a beat before he spoke again. "Hey, see you at lunch! We're over in the corner by the back door. Just look for all the Goths!" I smiled as I hurried to class, inordinately pleased to be invited to the Goth table.

No one talked to me all morning. Mr. Strickland took great pains to avoid looking at me, aside from an initial glare when I walked into class. There were whispers and the occasional snicker behind my back, but no one got in my way between classes, and I got chosen last for softball in PE. I didn't mind that, I hated swinging a bat at a ball, and since I was at the end of the batting lineup, I didn't have to. I didn't even sweat, so I didn't bother with showering. By the time I got to the Goth table with something that was loosely based on food on my tray, I was feeling pretty lonely.

The double row of pale and tragically pretty faces that looked up at me when I stopped at the end of the table had the same mix of fear and apprehension I'd seen all day. I was just about to give up and go find an empty spot somewhere else when Lucas stood up at the far end of the table and waved at me, calling me over. Dead silence reigned on my left as I walked beside the table to the seat he pulled out for me. When my butt hit the plastic, a buzz of relieved whispers erupted from my left, as the whole table started talking again.

"You know, word is going around about you like wildfire," Lucas said conspiratorially.

"Yeah, everybody knows you kicked Brad Duncan's ass," Wanda chimed in with a vengeful glee. "Chrissy Barlowe's brother is on the junior varsity team, and he told her that Duncan is out until at least the end of the week. He says Coach Brenner is pissed. He wants your butt in a sling, Chance."

"Great," I muttered. "Now I have the head coach after my ass, too."

"Well, he can't make too big of a deal out of it, unless he wants to admit that you beat the crap out of his starting quarterback. Brenner's not one to let something like that get out," Lucas said.

"Never underestimate how bad an adult can screw up your life," I replied.

"Spoken like a Jedi Master," Lucas laughed.

"A what-I master?"

"A Jedi, you know, from *Star Wars*?" Lucas asked off my blank look. I shook my head.

"Still," Wanda said through a mouthful of something that looked like meatloaf, "you're getting a reputation as something of a bad boy around here. Word is, two of the unattached cheerleaders are looking to score with you at least once. For that matter, one of the attached cheerleaders is gunning for you, too."

"Well, you can spread the word early and beat the Christmas rush. I don't dig polyester skirts and pom-poms. Besides, I thought they all hated me. Why would they want to date me all of a sudden?"

"They don't want to date you, dummy, they just want to screw you! You know, get a little danger between their legs."

"Well, I don't want to screw a cheerleader, either. Just because a girl can do sideways splits doesn't mean she's good in bed. Besides," I said, thinking back to some of the things Dulka had subjected me to, "I don't do casual sex." That pretty much killed that line of conversation, and Lucas leaned closer.

"Dude, don't look now, but Officer Friendly over there has been eyeballing you since you walked in," he said quietly. I followed his glance to see Collins standing near the teacher's table, with Strickland bending his ear.

"Kelly Logan says he's been asking around about you all day, and Sarah said he was reading your file this morning when she got to second period! Mr. Strickland's been bugging him all day, trying to tell him what an 'unsavory type' you are." Wanda stopped as she noticed Lucas and I staring at her. "What?"

"Where do you get this stuff? You're better than the FBI, girl! Where were you when JFK was shot? Or when Jimmy Hoffa disappeared?" Lucas asked.

"I just listen, that's all."

"When?" I asked, and barely blocked a chunk of meat product covered in mystery sauce. The bell for fifth period was like a kick to the stomach for me, and I saw Wanda's face go tight, too. Before yesterday, it meant class with Mr. Chomsky. Today, it meant meeting the person who was his replacement, at least temporarily. That, more than anything, would be what killed him for me. We trudged to the classroom with heavy hearts, only to find a sign on the door saying class was moved to the botany lab downstairs. We exchanged looks, and I could see in Wanda's eyes that she was at least as grateful as I was not to have to spend an hour in the room Mr. Chomsky had been dismembered in.

We headed downstairs to the botany lab, which was just a big greenhouse that had been built next to the school building. We stepped inside to find a wooded wonderland. Deep greens laid themselves out as a backdrop for an explosion of color in the form of flower petals in every shade under the rainbow. On either wall, tiers of plants ran up at an angle to well over the head of the tallest person in the room. A long work bench ran along the bottom of either row, with a similar setup in the middle of the room, though there, the plants were laid flat on the table four or five pots across. There were stools set up at the workbenches, and they were almost all filled. By the time Wanda and I came in, only the two closest to the front were open. Our butts had barely hit the seats when a man in dark robes strode into the room, and headed to the front of the class.

"There will be no inane flailing about with wands in this class, no arcane muttering of silly incantations," he said with a bad English accent.

I recognized the line from one of the books Dee had given me, and I didn't catch the laugh in time. A few snickers came from behind me, though I didn't know if they were at my expense or at the new guy's performance. I looked, and almost everyone was smiling, and a few people were hiding laughter.

"I'm glad to see that at least one of you reads something other than *Cosmopolitan* or *Auto Weekly*," the new guy said with a smile and a more Midwestern accent. He shrugged his way out of the robe to reveal a dark green polo shirt and tan slacks. Brown hair hung down to his shoulders, and a neat goatee hid his chin. He scanned the room with intense hazel eyes.

"I'm Dr. Corwin, your replacement science teacher. I'll be teaching Mr. Chomsky's classes until the end of the semester. Sydney Chomsky was twice the teacher I could ever hope to be. That being said, don't get the idea that I don't know what I'm talking about. The "Doctor" in front of my name is not just for decoration. And, don't make the mistake of thinking that because I'm new, I don't know that you're texting to one of your friends in another classroom, young lady. The phone, please?" He gestured to one of Alexis' friends with one hand and stepped up to her. The girl handed the phone over with ill grace.

"Thank you. You will get this back at the end of the day."

"Legally, you have to give that back to me before I leave your class," the girl said in a superior tone.

"According to the school district's attorney, I don't have to give it back at all," Dr. Corwin said as he dropped it into his briefcase, "and until you get *your* degree in jurisprudence, I would hesitate to give out legal advice." Wanda and I shared a laugh at her expense as he turned back to the class.

He started taking roll, and when he came to my name, he stopped. "Mr. Fortunato, sometime this semester, I would like to have you test for advanced placement classes. Mr. Chomsky had noted a certain aptitude after your first day. You would honor his memory if you made the attempt."

I nodded, my throat suddenly too tight to speak.

"Now, given the recent events, I thought it would be rather therapeutic to begin with the introduction to botany a little early. A little life to balance the scales a bit." I had to admit, I liked this guy. He understood dirt therapy.

The bell for sixth period came too early for me. Wanda looked like she was having more fun getting her hands dirty than I would have thought. We put our seedlings on the shelf with our table's number on it and headed for the door.

I stopped when a gentle touch fell on my shoulder. I knew who it was before I turned around. I found myself staring into a pair of searching, green eyes: eyes that drew me in and tried to see into my soul. There was a jarring moment as my mental barriers kicked in, as if she was trying to get inside my mind with her gaze, but then I blinked, and she was just a girl staring into my eyes.

"Can I talk to you?" Alexis asked. She asked it like she was asking for more than a minute of my time. I just didn't have a clue what it was. So, I did what any fifteen-year-old warlock would do when the girl who was dating his magickally augmented rival came up and asked if she could bare her soul to him.

"Yeah. Sure. I'll catch up to you after school, Wanda."

"Suuuure you will," Wanda drawled over her shoulder. Alexis took me by the arm and pulled me behind a wall of ferns. I could feel her touch tingling on my skin, and the scent of cinnamon hit my nose like a velvet sledgehammer. When we got behind the ferns, she looked around for a second, then turned to me with her head down.

"Did you mean what you said this morning? About what gives Brad his...strength?" She looked up at me through her bangs, her green eyes soft with an expression I couldn't fight.

I'd give her any answer, just so I could keep seeing that look. "What do you mean?" I managed.

"Can you really take it away?" Her voice was almost timid, hopeful, like the battered girls who used make deals with Dulka to get rid of abusive boyfriends or parents. She kept her arms crossed in front of her. Her scent was driving me crazy with her so close. She tilted her head and intensified the look, and I felt my resolve weaken a little more.

"Yeah, but, why do you want to know?" Instead of answering me, she smiled and ducked her head as she hurried past me. Before I could catch up to her, she was lost in the swirl of students in the hallway, and I was running late to French.

Through sixth and seventh period, only one thing was on my mind. *Alexis knew.* She knew where Brad's strength came from, and she thought I could do something about it. She *believed* that I could do something about it. She was subject to that strength, and that gave me more than a moment's pause. It seemed that we had more than a little in common, if the way she was acting was any clue. I sure as hell had to find out if I was right about that. By the time the bell rang for the end of seventh period, my head was pounding, and I was ready to go home. After I grabbed my homework books from my locker, I headed to the front doors, and came up on Wanda and Lucas already deep in conversation.

"I'm just saying it's weird, that's all," Lucas was saying as he shook his head. "I mean, it hasn't even been two days since Mr. Chomsky was killed, and they already have someone in for the rest of the semester. That's a little too quick, if you ask me."

"Sarah told me this guy flew in from Houston yesterday, said he went to the same college as Mr. Chomsky or something. He's got like six degrees!" Wanda's voice dropped into the singsong rhythm I was starting to recognize as her gossip voice. It made her sound about half as smart as she did the rest of the time.

"So, he's more than a little qualified?" I asked from behind them.

Lucas jumped. "Gods, man," he exclaimed in a bad British accent, "I hate it when you do that!"

"Sorry," I lied.

"Yeah, right. Dude, we were just waiting for you. We're heading over to Dante's. You want to come and hang out for a while?"

"My mom's expecting me home. I'd have to call her or something," I said, feeling like I was seven again. It didn't bug me as much as I figured it should, but I still felt a little dorky saying it out loud, especially with my bad boy image.

Like magic, Wanda's cell phone was out and open. I gave her my number, and she handed it to me with the phone already ringing. A minute later, Mom had my promise to be home by seven and get my homework done, and fifteen minutes after that, we were piled into the *Falcon* with my bike stuffed into the hatchback, on our way to Dante's.

"So, Chance," Lucas asked as we turned onto the road, "are you going to go über-geek on us and take the advanced placement te...HOLY SHIT!" The car lurched as Lucas swerved and hit the brakes, throwing me up against the window on the passenger side. Tires squealed along with Wanda, as she splayed her hands across the dash. I caught a glimpse of a shiny black blur as it streaked by my window with a howling sound. More high-pitched howls followed six more black sport bikes as they swerved around us with uncanny precision.

I levered myself up to look out the back window at the bikes and their riders, and saw a pair of green eyes and a red ponytail on one of the passengers as she looked me in the eye. I could almost feel the distance from her gaze growing, then it felt like a connection broke between us. Her eyes closed, and she slowly turned her head and laid her helmet against the rider's back. The movement reminded me of someone and I struggled to recall who it was, as I realized that what had taken a split second felt like an hour. In a flash, my memory filled in the blanks.

In the front seat, Lucas was busy asking Wanda if she was okay and cursing at the motorcycles with every other word. I reached out and grabbed his shoulder, realizing that this was my chance to find out if I was right about my suspicions about Alexis, Brad and their whole clique.

"Dude, we have to follow them!" I exclaimed. Lucas gave me a blank look, and I shook his shoulder quickly. "That was Alexis Cooper and Brad Duncan on the lead bike!"

He gave Wanda a quick look, and she gave him a nod. He reached for the stick shift, and suddenly, I was almost in the front seat. This time, the squealing tires were intentional. The *Falcon* jumped backward, then whipped around as he hit the brakes and shifted gears on the fly, and we were facing the right way on the other side of the road. I got slammed back into the seat as he stomped on the gas and burned rubber after them.

We saw them make a left turn, and Lucas slammed on the brakes again as the light changed ahead of us, and the intersection filled with cars. By the time the light changed again, they were nowhere in sight, though we could hear the scream of their engines in the distance as they sped away.

Lucas shook his head resignedly as he pulled into the parking lot of a convenience store and turned to face Wanda and me. "Sorry, dude, they had too much of a head start."

"It's okay," I reassured him. "That was some awesome driving."

"Thanks. YouTube driving tutorials."

"He still can't parallel park," Wanda offered.

"So, what do you think they're up to? And why do you think that was Brad and Alexis?" Lucas asked.

"I know that was Alexis on that bike, and where she goes…" I let it hang for a moment.

"Brad takes her," Wanda finished.

"Right. I don't know what they're up to, but why are they on crotch rockets when Brad has a truck?" I asked.

"And a convertible," Wanda supplied. Lucas and I gave her a look. "Well, he does, and it's pretty nice. But, you're right. Why go somewhere on a bike no one knows you have? I mean, Brad's not one to keep something like that a secret. They're up to something." Lucas and I shrugged, sharing a moment of understanding. It wasn't *all* about the car, but it helped.

"Point," Lucas said, "but how do we find out where they're going?"

"We don't, not tonight. But I have a hunch; let's go back by the school." Lucas took another left turn that took us through some side streets, and a few minutes later, we emerged behind the school. He drove around toward the student parking lot, where Wanda pointed out Brad's monster of a truck, and Alexis' shiny gray Mustang.

"They must keep the bikes somewhere near here, then," Lucas suggested as we pulled out of the parking lot and headed for Dante's. I nodded.

"Okay, then we see if they do the same thing tomorrow night. We hang out after school, and when they take off, we follow them."

"You're enjoying this, aren't you?" I asked.

"Hell, yeah! The chance to catch Brad Duncan, All-American Asshole, in something fishy? You bet I am!" he crowed. "Besides, life is dull unless you put some adventure into it."

"Tell me about it," Wanda said. "This is the most excitement we've had since the American Idol season finale," she said dryly.

By the time they dropped me off from Dante's, we had a pretty good plan. I would stay after school to talk to Dr. Corwin, and they'd come back after half an hour or so to pick me up, with the grownups given the excuse that we were going to Dante's after school. We'd probably even end up there, so it was mostly true. We'd just leave out the part where we followed the popular kids to find out what the Wolf Pack was all about.

Chapter 12

~ Question everything. ~ Wizard proverb

Fridays during football season were on a different schedule. The teachers called it an assembly schedule, but the kids called it the pep rally schedule. All the classes were about ten minutes shorter than usual, and no one's mind was really on schoolwork. Maybe it was because the varsity and junior varsity players wore their game jerseys, or, more likely, it was because the cheerleaders wore those little skirts.

I'd said I wasn't interested in cheerleaders, but by the start of second period on Friday, I knew I was a liar. I was in heaven. Cute girls wandered the halls in short skirts, showing off miles and miles of leg. The whole school was in a sort of testosterone-fueled frenzy. Under it all, though, was a sort of desperation to forget, at least for a little while, that Mr. Chomsky had been killed only a couple of days before.

When I walked into the locker room for P.E., I saw my chance to learn a little more about Brad and the boys when I saw a big man beside Coach Stanley, in blue shorts and a white polo shirt that was the uniform for all coaches in the school, and a baseball cap that had the school's howling wolf mascot on the front. When I read the name Brenner on his shirt, I knew that he wouldn't be able to pass up the shot to get me on the field for a little payback. After I resigned myself to a painful and messy fourth period, I went over to the pair of coaches.

"Chance," Coach Stanley called out with a smile. I went over to him, dreading the next forty minutes of my life.

"This is Coach Brenner. The football team is holding open tryouts today. Would you like to give it a shot?"

"Sure," I said with my best fake smile. This was too easy, I thought.

"Great. Today's an automatic A for anyone who tries out!" Coach Stanley announced, but no one else seemed ready to put himself in harm's way.

"That's gonna depend entirely on how Chance participates, Doug," Coach Brenner boomed. "But I'm sure he'll give it his best effort, won't you, son?"

"Sure," I growled.

"Good! C'mon, we'll get you suited up and put you through your paces. Brad says you might be quarterback material." He led me out of the gym and out one of the side doors, and across a grassy field to the football field house. It butted up on the school's stadium. "Seeing as how you cost me a quarterback this week, it seems only fair to do your part, doesn't it, son?" he added while we were alone. The menace in his voice gave me a moment of fear, but fear has always been a good friend of anger for me.

"I didn't cost you a player, Coach," I growled softly. "He came looking for a fight. I just defended myself."

Brenner stopped me and spun me to face him with a hand on my shoulder. "No one, and I mean *no one*, hurts one of my players!" he hissed, sticking a finger in my face. "Those boys represent this school on the field! You'll show them the respect they deserve, you little snot-nosed punk, or you'll be a tackling dummy for the rest of the year!"

Ten minutes later, I was decked out in what felt like twenty pounds of plastic, with shoulder pads that felt like they were too big, padded pants that felt way too tight, and a helmet that seemed to squeeze down on my head. I stood under one of the goal posts while the coach introduced me.

Brad stood on the sidelines with his arm in a sling, looking smug and dashing. Off on one sideline, I could see the cheerleaders going through their paces, and I felt my face going red. Alexis was probably going to see me getting my butt stomped, and for some reason, that really bothered me.

"All right, men, I know you're used to a light practice on Fridays, but I had you all get dressed out in full pads so we could hold open tryouts today. Some of you already know Chance. He's made something of a name for himself already as being a scrapper. Today, we're going to find out if he can live up to it. He's going to be trying out for quarterback, but I think you can rest easy about starting tomorrow night, Jimmy!"

The rest of the team laughed before forming up on opposite sides of the football.

Coach Brenner came up to me and spoke quietly, "Greg there, number eighty seven, is going to run a post pattern; that means he's gonna go out about ten yards, then turn and run toward the goal posts. You try to throw the ball to him."

He backed up and handed me a football, then called out, "On one! Down, set, HIKE!"

On the last word, everyone began to move. The guy he pointed out started running down the field. The guys in front of me just stood up and stepped aside, and I had about a second to see the nine guys coming to tackle me. Then I was buried under an avalanche of pain and noise. After a few seconds, they got off me, except for one guy I recognized as one of Brad's cronies.

"Your ass is grass, freak!" he said as he squatted over me with his finger in my face.

I got up slowly as the front line came back and got into the semi-circle around me, and Coach came up to me with a smile.

"What happened out there, Fortunato?" he asked.

"Your boys showed me why our team sucks," I shot back.

"A good quarterback can motivate his linemen to block for him. Not their fault you haven't earned their respect. Okay, now we're gonna try the same thing again, see how quick you learn. Break!" The front line clapped and headed back up to the same place, and coach called out the same drill again.

This time, when the wall of pain came my way, I had a plan. As they made it past the linemen, I drew my arm back and threw the football as hard as I could at the blocker on the left of the center man. I got to see the ball slam into the back of his helmet and knock him off his feet before I went down this time. My magick-enhanced strength had made that throw hit him like a brick, and he was shaking his head when I came back up from under the pile of bodies.

"Not so tough now, are you asshole?" another one of Brad's boys sneered as he got off of me. I ignored him as the lineman came up to me and grabbed my facemask.

"What the hell are you doing?" he asked.

"Throwing the ball. Block for me, and my aim might get better."

"Screw you, punk," another guy said. He was the one who lined up two men right of the center.

"Hey, he's got a point, man," the guy who was in the middle of the line said. He was a huge kid with coffee-colored skin, and a gentle face. "This ain't cool. We're supposed to block for the QB. Brad's using us to do his fightin' for him. If he ain't bad enough to do it on his own, I ain't helping him do it. Y'all be his bitches if you want, but I'm gonna do my job."

"Thanks, man," I said as they broke. He just nodded and went to his spot on the line.

Coach Brenner had the receiver do a pattern where he ran across the middle of the field from his spot, calling it a slant route. I nodded and waited for the call to come. Again, there was a rush of guys coming for me, and I drilled the ball into the back of the guy who had called me a punk. This time, instead of letting them hit me and knock me down, I chose the first guy coming at me, ducked my shoulder and charged into him. We went down as the rest of the guys intent on tackling me went past us. As luck had it, we also landed on the guy I'd nailed with the ball. Then a ton of pain came down on me again.

This time, I got to listen to the groans of the two guys beneath me. It was music to my ears. This time, there wasn't any trash talk. The tackler I'd charged rolled off my lineman and stumbled away, and my lineman limped slowly back to the huddle after me. I looked over to the sidelines to see Brad scowling, and I touched my fingers to the front of my helmet in a mock salute.

"What the hell is wrong with you, son?" Coach Brenner yelled at me as he came up. "Can't you throw a football?"

"Just making a point, sir. If I can't earn their respect, then fear and pain will have to do. Besides, I figure they're just doing what you told them to do. Not their fault I'm a vicious bastard. Name your play, coach, let's get on with this. I'm starting to have fun!"

"Okay, fly pattern, on two!" he yelled.

I stepped up to the huddle. "Guys, all I'm asking for is three seconds. Keep them off me for that long, and I'll put the ball somewhere else. Okay?"

"Man, you do that again, and I'll kick your ass!" the guy I'd beaned the second time snarled.

"If I do that again, you'll be pissing blood for a week. I don't like doing this, but if you're gonna play for the other side, I'm gonna treat you like one of them."

"Gabe, shut up and do your damn job," the center man drawled. "Just block for the guy for a few seconds."

"Piss off, T," Gabe spat.

"Hey, you didn't see me on my ass just now. Ain't none of them worth taking those kinda lumps for. Brad's an asshole. You gonna be his bitch?"

"C'mon, guys, three seconds. Let's go!" We broke up the huddle and headed for the line, and the coach called the cadence again. This time, T led the line, and I had a lot more time. The receiver ran for the end zone, but after three seconds, Gabe let his guy through, and I found myself facing a raging tackler while my receiver was still too close to the guy covering him for me to throw the ball. So I turned and drilled the ball into the helmet of the guy running at me. His feet flew up into the air as he fell, and then another half dozen guys were headed my way. The next guy jumped at me, and I ducked under him, only to come up when he was right over top of me. He flipped onto his back and skidded for a few feet, and then I was down again, face first into the turf this time, with a line of fire

169

down my forearms as I skidded across the turf. I got up slowly, aching and winded, and made my way back to the huddle.

"Aren't they supposed to stop trying to tackle me once I get rid of the ball?" I asked wearily.

"Yeah," T answered with a smile, "if this was a game. Coach Brenner, he's just trying to get some back for you hurtin' his boy Brad."

"Shut it, T!" one of the other players whispered.

"Man, you shut it. Y'all the ones doing all the work for him."

"Hey, it's all good. You guys gave me my three seconds, I'm good with that. Let's do it again, okay?" I looked at the circle of faces, and saw a change in their eyes.

"You sure?" another one asked.

"Yeah. I'm not gonna let the Coach win. So we run the fly pattern again. This time, I'll actually try to throw it down field, okay?" There was a chorus of assent, and we broke the huddle.

When the call went, I stepped back, and the line held. I took a couple more steps back and found my guy, just getting past the man covering him with his arms up. I drew my arm back and let fly, hoping I'd got it right. The ball wobbled a little, then settled into an almost-smooth spin that Greg ran under and snatched out of the air. He tucked it under his arm and sprinted for the end zone.

Just as I was about to give a victory cry, I caught movement out of the corner of my eye, and saw one of Brad's boys sprinting at me from the end of the line with his head down like a bull. I took a step back and saw T move to try to block him. He shoved the big center aside like a toy and kept coming, and all I could think to do was set myself to take the hit. I hunkered down with my feet planted and waited for him to get close enough, then I lunged forward with a yell. The world disappeared in a white flash, then I was standing over the other guy, my facemask cracked, my head spinning and hurting, but still up. I staggered over to find T. The big guy was picking himself up as I stumbled up.

"Sorry about that, man," he said as I offered him a hand.

"Hey, you tried to stop him. It's more than I asked. Thanks."

"Don't worry about it." We watched as a skinny guy with a blue bag ran out to check on the guy who'd rushed me. He was still on the ground, and he was barely moving. While he tended to him, Coach Brenner stormed up to me.

"Get off my damn field, boy," he said venomously. "I'm not gonna let you hurt any more of my boys."

"He came after me, Coach," I told him as I took off the busted helmet. "You're the one who brought me out here to get pummeled. Not my fault it didn't work." I tossed him the helmet and limped off the field feeling pain in places even Dulka hadn't been able to reach. I'd had enough of the macho bullshit. The sudden silence made its way past the fog in my aching head, and I noticed the cheerleaders looking at me as I made my slow, painful way toward the field house.

It took me a couple of minutes to figure out how to get the shoulder pads off. The pants were pretty easy, once I figured out the belt. For a minute, I just sat there on the wooden bench, hurting. My arms looked like hamburger, and felt like someone had poured hot coals over them. My ribs felt like someone was hitting them with a stick, and my head felt like someone else was using a hammer to pound their way out of my skull.

The door opened, and I watched the rest of the football team come trooping in. My heart started pounding as I realized I was deep in their turf, on my own, and there were no witnesses. And I was in a lot of pain. T was one of the first guys in, and he went over to the canvas-covered cart that said "Linen" on the side of it, and grabbed a handful of white fabric. One of the towels came flying across the room at me, and landed in my lap.

"Man, you need a shower. You smell somethin' awful," he joked.

A few of the other jocks laughed as they went to their own lockers and began stripping out of their gear with an efficiency born of long practice.

Most of them carried bruises or scrapes somewhere, and a couple had ankles or wrists covered in tape.

I took the towel T threw me and looked over at him, then shrugged out of my t-shirt and headed over to the showers. Midway across the open room, it got quiet.

"Holy shit," someone whispered as I walked past.

A quiet buzz started behind me as people got a look at the road map of scars on my shoulders and back. I turned on the shower, and the hiss of hot water drowned them out. For a few minutes, I could pretend I was ignoring the comments and stares. I winced as the water hit a set of scrapes on my lower back I didn't know I had. Muscles began to loosen up under the spray of warmth, and I began to feel a little closer to human again.

"Man, what happened to you?" T asked from beside me.

"A lot of stuff," I said. "I got into a lot of fights."

"Yeah," he agreed. Surprisingly, he let it drop at that.

I finished showering and went to get dressed, and noticed the rest of Brad's little group eying me from across the locker room. There was hostility there, like before, but now it was laced with something new. Fear. I kept my back to them while I put on my clothes, and I made sure my shirt went over my head quickly.

"You did pretty good out there today," Gabe said quietly from the locker next to where I was.

"Thanks," I replied. "Sorry about beaning you."

"Forget it. T was right; Brad was just trying to get us to do his fighting for him. But you were cool about it. No hard feelings, man?" He held out a hand, and I took it without having to think about it.

"Forget about it." We shook hands, and he got up and left.

The rest of the players were at least decent when they walked past. It was like I'd just passed some secret jock initiation, and even though I

172

wasn't one of them, I was a person to them now. Except for Brad and his little group of boot-lickers. I glanced across the room at them, all huddled together. Yesterday, they'd been the ones walking around like predators. Maybe having me lay them out on their butts had taught them not to mess with me.

As I walked out, I had to go past them, and I noticed something that made them stand out from all the other jocks. Of eight football players, including the one that I'd just knocked on his ass, not a one of them had a bruise, scrape or an inch of tape on them. Even T had some scrapes on his forearms, and he was bigger than two of me. I walked across the field to the rest of the school, and my brain began to piece together something else. When I had taken that last hit, he had hit me so hard that my facemask broke, and he had shoved T aside like a guy half his size. Brad wasn't the only jock into someone for special upgrades. The whole first string had them. Damn. My life just kept getting better and better.

I limped into the cafeteria as the bell rang, and made my way over to the Goth table after I piled enough food on my puke-patterned tray to feed an army. It was time to pay the price for being strong and healing fast. As I stuffed my face with hot dogs and cheeseburgers, Lucas and Wanda joined me.

"Dude, your arms!!" Lucas cried in alarm, noticing the angry red scrapes that ran from my wrists to my elbows as I reached for my third carton of milk. "What the hell happened to you?" he demanded.

"A football team tackled me. Hard. A lot."

"That must have hurt!"

"Yeah." What else could I say to something that obvious? I changed the subject. "Is everything ready to go for this afternoon?"

"Yeah, the *Falcon* is fueled up and ready, and she'll be waiting at docking bay 94." Lucas laughed at my puzzled look. "From *Star Wars*?" he said hopefully.

"Still not getting it," I muttered.

"You've never seen *Star Wars*?" he asked incredulously.

"Um, no. My dad was pretty strict about some things."

"Oh, no," Wanda moaned. "He's about to witness to you, Chance. Run, while you still have a social life."

"Dude, no witnessing needed. You just have to experience *Star Wars* in all its glory. We can watch it this weekend, so you can catch up with the civilized world, and get more of my jokes."

"Actually," I said, wincing inwardly at Wanda's inevitable reaction, "I'd like that." Wanda only rolled her eyes good-naturedly. That crisis averted, I went back to the serious business of eating.

When the bell rang, Wanda and I headed for the greenhouse, ready to take the next step in our plan. As we took our seats, I was even more aware of the girls in cheerleading skirts across the aisle from us, and I could have sworn I felt their eyes on my back all through class. I saw my chance as Dr. Corwin walked down the rows, handing out botany study sheets.

"Uh, Dr. Corwin?" I asked, as he laid the sheet down in front of me.

"Yes, Chance?"

"Could I drop by after school today and talk to you about the placement test?" I tried to keep my voice pitched as low as possible, but he had evidently never heard the word "subtle."

"Certainly, Chance!" he said with obvious pleasure. His voice carried across the room. "I'll be here for a little bit after the pep rally!"

"Thanks," I muttered over the giggles that came from the other side of the room.

"Oh, man, you are getting the major booty check, Chance," Wanda whispered, as Dr. Corwin moved on. I rolled my eyes and tried to go back to my worksheet, drawing a cross section of a leaf, but it wasn't an easy job. "You wear a pair of tight pants *one* time, and suddenly you're a piece of ass," I growled.

Wanda's smile surprised me as she leaned back and gave my seated bottom a mock appraisal. "It's not bad. Now you know how we girls feel when guys stare at our ass or tits all the time," she offered smugly.

"I'll keep that in mind next time I ogle your boobs," I told her before I turned back to my work.

She chuckled and bent to her own work before Dr. Corwin could make it back by. The bell, of course, took its own sweet time in ringing. French and shop class were mostly goof-off sessions, and then it was time for the pep rally.

My first pep rally. I was excited, since this time, I would be experiencing it from the bleachers instead of waiting outside to make a deal with a cheerleader, geek, or jock for whatever dream they wanted me to make come true. Just walking in to the gym, I could feel the raw power coming from the place. Pack five hundred kids from fourteen to eighteen into a big room on a Friday afternoon and play some marching music real loud. Even if it's badly played, you'll get five hundred pulses jumping a little quicker, and five hundred sets of hormones working overtime, especially when you add a dozen or so athletic, attractive girls in short skirts jumping around. It's a little like a hormonally enhanced version of a nuclear reactor, energy wise.

The marching band was already going, playing some song I'd never heard before, or maybe playing one I did know so badly I didn't recognize it in its clever new disguise. Either way, the drummers were doing their thing well enough, and working the ancient magick of rhythm on the whole crowd. Add to that the candy the cheerleaders were throwing to the people in the bleachers, and I figured the gymnasium would be pretty much orbital by the time everything was done. I found a spot next to Lucas and Wanda, or I should say, one opened up when I got close enough for the kid in it to see me coming. Having rep as a badass helped sometimes. They were both grinning like loons as I sat down, and I could see the pile of candy wrappers at their feet.

"Looks like you've been busy already!" I had to yell over the crowd.

Lucas nodded and dumped a handful of sugary delight into my hands. "We got here early!" he yelled back.

From where we were, high in the bleachers, I could see all the banners the cheerleaders had made, with "Go Howlers!" and "We're #1!" painted on them. Pictures of battered pirates were mixed in with the fierce wolf-looking things representing the Howlers and the Northview Pirates. It was barbarism reduced to ink and paper.

It was also a great place to pick up a *ton* of free-floating aggressive energy. The air was charged with it, practically crackling to my mystic senses, it was so thick. With that thought, I dug into my book bag, flipped open my pocket knife with my thumb, and let the point of the blade dig into the still-fresh cut I had made Wednesday. When I felt the slickness of blood on my fingertip, I let the blade slip closed and felt around until I found my telekinesis power rod. There was a tingle against my fingertips, and I felt the hair on my arms stand up as a cool wash of magick pulsed from the center of my being, down my arms and into the TK rod. With the connection between my blood and the rod, I could channel magickal power into it. I needed to have it next to my skin, so I palmed it and pulled it from the bag.

Suddenly, the band started up, and I felt the first wave of insistent, martial power slap against me like a hot wave of static. The song brought everyone to their feet, and I certainly couldn't resist the urge to get up myself. I felt the rod sucking up the energy I was pumping into it, as the lodestones and quartz did what came naturally: drawing and storing power for use later. The cheerleaders got everyone chanting, which drew even more potential into the air, and the rod drew it all in as fast as I could channel it.

Between the cheerleaders, the music, and the speeches by the coach and Brad, who turned out to be pretty charming when it suited him, the whole school was in a frenzy before it was all said and done. Brad and the coach dedicated this game's win to Mr. Chomsky, which only hyped everyone up even further, in spite of the somber tone of the speech. I was beginning to wonder if my little rod could hold any more juice. Then, as if the whole pep rally had been written just for me, it ended with the school song, which acted as a damper and a focus, keying more to pride and loyalty than to raw force and aggression. It had a feeling of solidity and endurance to it, so it served as a good point of closure. I wove the threads of my will through the song and directed it around the TK power rod, sealing the stored energy inside it for use when I might need it. Both the rod and I were pumped as full of energy as we could be, and I found myself grinning. This wasn't so different from what I was used to...just less grim. More innocent.

"Man, that is a weird look for you," Lucas said from beside me. Wanda's head was bobbing in an emphatic nod.

"What?"

"You, smiling like that," Wanda said.

"It's a little scary," Lucas said as he raised his hands with his fingers making a crude cross.

"I'll get right back to scowling, then," I joked. "This was fun!"

"You've never been to a pep rally before?" Wanda asked.

"They didn't have them at the boarding schools I went to," I lied smoothly. "I'm gonna go talk to Dr. C. You guys go get ready to follow Brad and his crew, okay? I'll catch up with you as soon as I'm done." I grabbed my bag and headed down the bleachers toward the door.

As I went, I caught sight of Brad and Alexis by the other set of doors. Alexis was in his arms, looking up at him, looking like she was trapped. Brad's face was set in hard, angry lines, but there was a hollow look in his eyes that told me he had just lost something, too. All was not right for Princess Pop Star and Prince Not-So-Charming, it seemed.

The halls were empty. You didn't have to give students a reason to clear out on a Friday afternoon. I jogged toward the botany lab, which was even further back, and even less likely to have anyone in it, hurrying for my own reasons. Though talking to Dr. C had been mainly an excuse, I found myself really wanting to make it into the advanced science classes. That much, at least, Mr. Chomsky had been honest about. It beat the Nine Hells out of being just another juvenile delinquent. As I jogged along, though, my shoulder blades began to tighten up, and I started to get the feeling that I wasn't alone in the halls.

The sound of a padlock slamming down against a locker stopped me in my tracks, and I spun in place, while my left hand dug in my book bag for my freshly charged TK wand. After a few seconds, I found it and palmed it, drawing my hand out slowly. Soft laughter mocked me from the suddenly dim hallway, and I realized that the lights had been turned off behind me. My eyes narrowed. I was being hunted, stalked. Of course, the hunters had no idea how dangerous their prey really was. If it was Brad and his buddies, thinking that numbers and a little mystical mojo was going to give them an unfair advantage over me, they were in for a huge surprise. I turned my back on the darkened hallway and continued back down the hall toward the greenhouse.

The first attack caught me flat-footed. The only warning I had of something coming was a dry scratching sound, then I was flying through the air with the memory of a heavy weight slamming into my back. I hit the ground with my hands out, and dropped the TK rod with a clatter and a curse. It landed a few feet further down: as good as a couple of miles, if I didn't get to it fast. I rolled onto my ass first, though, trying to see who or what had attacked me. My brain was dimly aware that I hadn't heard sneakers hitting the ground, or even hard-soled shoes. Rolling to one side was all that saved me from the second pounce. Even so, I felt it hit the ground beside me, and found myself looking into the blue eyes of a huge gray wolf. I remembered the eyes because they were over rows of about a million big teeth, separated by a gray muzzle and a black wolf nose. And there were teeth, in case I didn't mention that. My roll had put me closer to the rod, but the wolf's landing had put it closer to me than I was to the rod. Bad odds for me: better than great for the wolf.

Desperate, I backhanded it across the muzzle, letting my knuckles slam into the soft tissue of its nose, and cried out, "Bad dog!" It yelped, probably mostly in surprise, and recoiled. Before it could recover, I pulled my feet up and pushed myself along the slick tiles toward my rod, the only weapon I had. The push wasn't quite strong enough to get me to it, so I laid myself back out and stretched for it, just barely grasping it in my fingers. I heard a snarl and the scratching of claws as the wolf tried to get some purchase on the tiles himself, and turned back to him in time to see him gather himself and leap into the air at me. I thrust the rod at it and yelled *"Ictus!"*

A column of solid force exploded from the slender tip of the rod, caught the wolf between his forelegs mid-leap, and flung him up. Straight up. I wondered for a brief second how far I would have sent him if the damned concrete ceiling hadn't stopped him, but just the sound of the impact was pretty impressive. I shook my head as the muffled sound of air being displaced echoed down the hallway, and dust fell from the ceiling. Then two hundred pounds of fur, teeth and muscle hit the ground a foot away from me with a muted yelp.

"Bad dog!" I said again, shaking the rod at it for emphasis "BAD! DOG! No biscuit!" Of course, even as I was cracking wise, I was scrambling to my feet and backing away. As hard as I had hit it the first time, and after hitting the ground like a bag of wet cement, it was *still* scrambling to its feet. It shook its head and looked at me with curiously intelligent, human-looking eyes. It circled to my left, and I kept the rod pointed at it. After it made it as far to the left as it could, it turned and paced back toward the right until it reached the middle of the hall. I struggled to keep my rational mind in the moment, trying to guess what the wolf was going to do next and plan against whatever that was going to be. The challenge was that my hairy monkey brain was gibbering about how the walking, glaring wolf should have been a doggie-shaped splat mark on the ceiling, instead of still trying to eat me, just like in the stories.

I gaped as it arched its back and *changed*, becoming more human shaped, without losing its fur or any of those big damned teeth. It straightened to face me, and towered over me by a good two feet, with long claws extending from its fingertips. Long claws and opposable thumbs. My lips pulled back from my teeth, which were not even close to as dangerous looking as the wolf's, but then, I was armed with something far more dangerous than tooth and claw.

Evidently, it noticed my confidence, because it turned its head and barked. I stepped into the middle of the hall as two more half-wolves emerged from the shadows behind him. I heard a heavy claw scrape on the

179

tile behind me, and ducked instinctively when I heard the half bark of a wolf from behind me. The gray wolf stepped aside in time to avoid getting hit by the one that had tried to jump me from behind. The new one was black all over, sleek and lean with corded muscle; it landed gracefully and turned to face me. The other two, darker gray and dark brown, came up to flank the gray one, and I found myself faced with even more teeth than before.

"Crap," I muttered as I realized just how deep in the shit I was. If I waited for them to attack, I was a lupine Happy Meal. If I attacked, I might get one or two of them, three if I was lucky, and I would have a few more seconds before I ended up as a buffet for the four-legged and furry. Still, a few seconds was better than none.

"*Ictus! Ictus latior!*" I yelled, sending as wide a wave of force as I could manage crashing down the hallway. It took the two on the left and bowed them over the leading edge of the wave, throwing them into the darkness. The black one caught the edge of the strike, and got sent skidding down the hall. It worked better than I had hoped, but the darker gray one was still there, and it gathered itself and leaped before I could bring the rod back to bear on it.

We went down in a heap of fur and limbs, and I felt its teeth close on the collar of my leather jacket, just below my right ear. It drew its massive head back for another try, and I slammed my left fist into its ear, pouring every bit of the augmented strength I could muster from my stolen charm into the punch. It lunged again after the second punch, and I barely managed to wedge my right forearm under its jaw, barely keeping its teeth from closing on my throat. I smelled fetid doggie breath and held my arm up as it tried to rip my face off.

Only leverage was keeping me in one piece just then, since the wolf was depending on nothing more than his weight to bring his jaws to my flesh. He still had friends, though, and I didn't know how long they were going to be out of the fight. As he clawed at me and snapped his jaws together, I tucked my legs up between us and pushed as hard as I could, hoping to bounce him off the ceiling again with my borrowed strength. He sailed up and away from me in a slow, gentle arc, and landed on his feet maybe four feet away. I felt my arms and legs suddenly get heavier as the strength augment worked exactly the way it was designed to, giving out after a certain threshold had been reached. It had been made to keep its user dependent on the supplier, and it worked like…well, a charm. Suddenly, I was just plain Chance again, not ÜberChance.

Chance 1.0 was still not a guy to mess with lightly. I still had the TK rod, and I was still the most vicious bastard I knew. I just wasn't ready to go hand to hand with two hundred pounds of wolfman. The trick was to keep this fight on my terms instead letting it happen on his. I started off by pointing the rod at him and crying out "*Ictus!*" again before he could get his feet completely under him. He managed to duck under most of the blast, only taking part of it across one shoulder, but it was still enough to knock him spinning and off his feet. He hit the ground and rolled, coming up on all fours with fangs bared and a snarl rumbling from his throat as he turned his head to face me. I could see all seven feet of his left side as he gathered himself to spring again. I knew he was waiting for me to try to throw another blast at him, and I was waiting for him to jump. If he managed to twist in mid leap, or if I misjudged my shot, though, this fight was over. For a moment, the tableau held, then the wolf's eyes flicked to something behind and above me. I didn't dare take my eyes off of him, but I couldn't be sure of who or even what was behind me, either.

As I debated on how to get out from between the wolf and whoever was behind me (I was being optimistic, and assuming it was at least person-ish), I heard a soft coughing sound as something hit my furry foe in the shoulder. There was a little puff of fur flying, and I could see a rough circle of pale flesh where whatever it was had hit him. He let out a yelp of pain and recoiled. Another soft cough of air sounded from behind me, and another circle of bare skin appeared on his flank, then two more in rapid succession. I heard steps from behind me, and a tall figure in a black plastic mask and a leather jacket came up beside me as the big gray wolfman took a couple of steps back. The brown wolf came forward snarling and stepped between the newcomer and the gray.

The man beside me dropped the huge handgun he'd been using in my lap as he drew another pistol from a holster under his right arm. "Hang on to that for me, will ya?" he said casually as the long-barreled gun came up.

A red dot appeared on the brown wolf man's body and he pulled the trigger. This gun made a louder bark and spat a thin tongue of flame from the end of its smooth barrel. The wolfman yelped even louder than his gray friend and turned tail. All four scampered into the darkness with a scratching of claws. I took the heavy gun in my lap and pointed it down the hall, like it would help somehow. I got to my feet as I scanned the hallway, and even looked behind my masked rescuer, since I had been caught from behind both by him and the black wolf. After a few seconds, the sound of claws on tile faded into silence, and I turned to the masked man in front of me.

"Thanks," I panted, "whoever you are."

He pulled the mask up to reveal intense hazel eyes and a familiar, bearded face. "You were late," Dr. Corwin said casually as he pulled the magazine from the butt of his pistol. He tucked it away and slid a fresh one into place as he spoke. "I figured I'd better come check on you. And here I find you rolling around with a bunch of werewolves." He slid the gun back into its holster and held out his left hand for the gun he'd handed me. I found myself staring at him blankly as I handed it over. "I'm sure at some schools that would mean automatic detention or something, but I think we can overlook it this time."

"What kind of gun is that?" I asked as he worked a catch on the top of the massive weapon and pulled a piece of it off. It went into a pouch on the front of the oversized holster that rode on his left thigh. It had a stripe of green tape on the long edge. Next to it were two other pieces that looked almost exactly like it. One had a white piece of tape on it, and the other was marked with blue tape.

"It's a paintball gun. Very versatile weapon, perfect for what I do."

"You're like a monster hunter, right? What was that part on the top? Why are they colored differently?" I asked, my curiosity getting the better of me. Dr. C had cool toys, and I wanted one.

He pulled the blue marked piece and began to fit it to the top of the gun. "Paintball hopper, kind of like the magazine in a regular gun. I fill the paintballs with different things; the tape is so I can tell them apart easily.

The green one is loaded with a mixture of wolfsbane and silver nitrate, good against werewolves. The white one's holy water and garlic. Vampires hate it."

"What's in that blue one?" I asked enthusiastically. This was cool stuff.

Dr. C smiled as he looked at me and pressed a little red button on the side of the gun then gave it a quick look. "Chloroform," he said nonchalantly, then he shot me with it.

Aw, crap.

Chapter 13
~ If you can avoid a fight, do so. If you can't, then fight to win. ~ T.S. Cross, The Left Hand of Death.

It was dark when I came to. I opened my eyes, but all I could see was a faint light through the weave of a thick cloth. I blinked, and felt fabric against my eyelids. A blindfold, then. My head was still a little fuzzy from the chloroform, but I could hear movement nearby. I tried to move my hands, but they were bound behind me with some sort of thin metal strip. I reached for the minor magicks I could do without a focus, and felt a ring of fire blaze around my wrists. I managed to bite off the cry of pain before it could be more than a quick grunt, but my captor had to have heard it.

"Sorry about the blindfold and spell binders," I heard Dr. Corwin's voice say from behind me and to my left. I turned my head to hear better, and I caught the sound of fabric rustling. "But I can't take any risks, given what you are."

"You forgot to gag me," I growled back. "Aren't you afraid I might still manage to get a curse off?"

"No," came his voice from my right. "You can't see me, you can't get your hands up to direct a spell or make any gestures, and the binders won't let you draw any magick without creating so much feedback that you'll overload your brain if you try to fight it too hard. Besides, if I gagged you, we couldn't talk."

"Talk? You knocked me out, tied me up and blindfolded me and you want to *talk*?" I said, my voice rising with every word.

"Well, I was going to kill you. This is what you might call…Plan B."

"Sorry if I'm not just gushing with gratitude. Getting knocked out and tied up makes me a little cranky."

"Standing orders from the High Council are that you're to be terminated on sight. I think a little rough treatment is small price to pay for that kind of reprieve." I heard him move around behind me, until he was on my right, just a little way in front of me.

"Okay, yeah. Thanks for not killing me," I said dryly. "Mind if I ask why?"

"Two reasons. First, my friend Sidney didn't kill you when he had the chance to. Secondly…you're trying to find his killer, which does tend to raise my opinion of you somewhat. The copper wand was well done, by the way. I recognize the design. Arianh-Rod's work?"

"Bought the sigil layout and charging spell from her, yeah. So, what are you? A bounty hunter? A mage-slayer?"

He made a harsh noise like a buzzer, "Nope, try again."

"You're a mage?"

"Wizard, actually. But yes, I'm a member of the Conclave."

"Wizard, mage, what's the diff?" I asked sullenly. "You're still gonna kill me."

"It's the difference between a Jedi Knight and a Jedi Master."

"No idea what that is."

"A Jedi. You know, defenders of peace and justice throughout the galaxy for thousands of years?" The blindfold came off, and I found myself blinking at the sudden change in the light. I looked around, and found myself in the science lab, tied to one of the chairs. Dr. Corwin was standing in front of me with a puzzled look on his face. Beside him, my bag was open, and everything in it was laid out in his desk.

"You've never seen *Star Wars*?"

"No. Lucas was going to have me over this weekend to watch it." It was never going to happen now.

"Well, Sidney must have had a good reason for defying the Council's order. So unless you give me cause, I'm not going to kill you."

"What are you gonna tell the Council?"

"Nothing. Sidney was my mentor and oldest friend. I trusted his judgment more than most people's, and he saw something in you. I want to believe Sydney was right about you. He wrote in his journal that he wanted to take you on as an apprentice, and he hadn't done that for nearly twenty years. I was his last, and the Council practically had to force me on him. But you have to understand something, Chance. He was planning to defy the Council to do that, and he would have been taking a huge risk. I'm taking the same risk. If we're caught, we're both dead, unless I have a very, *very* good reason for ignoring their command. Are you with me so far?"

"This is the part where you tell me what I have to do to stay in your good graces and stay alive, right?" I asked. I wanted to tell him I was through making deals, I wanted to spit in his face and tell him to take his deal and shove it, but I couldn't. I had a lot of reasons to live, and I knew I would do pretty much anything he asked me to. I hated myself for it, but I couldn't see any other way out.

"No," he said sadly. "I'm only going to ask you to let me See you, to open your mind to me. If you say yes, good. If you say no, I let you go, and I wait for a few days to tell the Council I found you and you got away. I don't want you to do this because you feel like you're under duress. I want you to do this so I can help you. So if it comes down to it, I can tell the Council that I know you're not as bad as they think, and you have a fighting chance to walk away if they find you before you're ready to face them."

I looked at him, trying to see something in his face that would tell me what to do. I wasn't used to being given a choice. I wasn't used to trusting people. But, like it or not, he was asking me to trust him, and he was giving me a choice.

"Okay," I finally said. It was the hardest thing I had ever said; I felt like I was stepping off a cliff.

"Thank you, Chance. Have you ever experienced the *Udjat*, or Horus Gaze, before? It can be a rather disorienting process. I'm going to step into your mind, and you're going to step into mine. We'll see each other in all our glory and shame. There will be nothing in your head that is a secret from me, and nothing in my head that is a secret from you. I promise I will keep your secrets for you, and I can only ask that you keep mine for me." His voice took on a rhythm that spoke of a formula, an oath. He looked me in the eyes, and his voice grew solemn. "Look into my eyes, Chance. See me, and let me See you." His eyes bored into mine, and I felt the weight of his thoughts behind them, pressing against mine like against some rubbery barrier. After a moment, he shook his head and straightened up.

"Was that it?"

"No, nothing happened. Which is a little unusual, but not alarming. I haven't seen it in someone as young as you before, though."

"Is that...bad?"

"No, just odd. I need you to open yourself a little. Can you see auras?" I nodded. He continued, "Okay, look at my aura." I blinked a few times as I shifted my senses just slightly and relaxed my focus, so that I was seeing the soft amber glow of his aura, with a silvery green running through it. I looked into his eyes then, and felt myself falling.

For a brief second, I was standing face to face with him, then it felt like we passed through each other, and I was in the mind of Dr. Trevor James

Corwin, T.J. to his friends. It was a dizzy-making place. The man was smart: smarter than any three people I could name, and a LOT smarter than I was.

There was a strength to him, a will that could bend iron with a thought, tempered by sadness, by love lost. I saw the face of a beautiful Japanese woman with pale, almost silver eyes. In his thoughts, I knew she was also a mage: a *wu jen*, one of the Japanese wizards. I could feel the pang of loss, and knew that he still loved her, even after eight years had gone by since he'd seen her last. He still wore the ring he had planned to give her on a chain around his neck. For an instant, I loved her with the same intensity he did.

I saw a rash of split-second images from his apprenticeship under Sydney Chomsky, and understood in a heartbeat why he had idolized the man. The grief of his loss hit me, then the anger at whoever had done it ripped through me all over again like a firestorm. I felt the beauty of magick when it was wielded right, in harmony with the will of the mage, and with its own will. There was a Zen quality to it when he worked a spell just right, and somehow, things just flowed.

Then I was sailing back into my own mind. My head snapped back, and I blinked in surprise. Tears ran down my face as I experienced the loss of the woman he loved again in a whole new way, as his love for her became something separate from me, and I was once again Chance, a boy who had never felt what he had felt, or experienced what he had, a home where both parents were there, and could be trusted.

I knew then what it was like to be…pure, whole of body and spirit, and never to have known pain so intense that it made me hallucinate. I knew what it felt like to be free. Not only to be free, but to have always *been* free, never to have bowed my head to someone I didn't trust or respect. To have had my dignity intact my entire life. To see all that, and end up back in my own head made me feel even worse. The fleeting moment came when I understood, in the half of a heartbeat when Dr. C's awareness and mine had passed each other on their respective ways back to their own resting places, that he had seen everything I had endured, and would never see his own freedom so casually again. I heard the anguished cry from Dr. C, and saw him stagger up from his chair, hands over his eyes as he stumbled against the corner of his desk. He fell back against the chalkboard and pulled his hands down, staring at me with tears of his own streaming down his face.

After walking around in his brain, I almost couldn't avoid knowing what he was thinking. He had seen the eight years of Hell on earth that I had suffered under Dulka, felt the betrayal of my father and casual cruelty of the demon and my father as they had used me and treated me as something sub-human, a tool for their own ends. I got to see myself through his eyes: a young man standing between darkness and light; a young man with potential…touched by evil, tainted by it, but not ruled by it. He also saw the boy who had been abandoned by the Conclave, and then condemned for the results of that neglect.

"I'm sorry," he said. I shrugged. The people who *should* have been apologizing probably never would. He slumped forward a little and began to take measured breaths: in through his nose, out through his mouth. I leaned into the backrest on the chair, trying to sift through the complicated mess I'd seen while he did the same thing. Dr. C had seen some pretty crappy stuff in his life, but I figured I won the "Sucks to be you!" award hands down. It was going to take him a little while to get a grip on what he'd just seen. After a couple of minutes, I was able to think clearly enough to get past the fading memory of TJ…no…Dr. C's mind. I looked over at him and cleared my throat.

"Uh, Dr Corwin?" I asked. "Could you take these manacles off?" He looked up at me with distant eyes, then around the room. I saw his pupils dilate, and he started trembling, as he flinched back and brought his arms up. "*Crap*," I thought. He must have been sifting through all the memories I had of a science lab. Seeing…*feeling* all the times Dulka had beaten me on the floor. Of course, I was remembering spending an afternoon in a hot tub with a beautiful Asian babe with silvery eyes, and wondering why he had even *left* that room. I was definitely getting the better end of the experience.

Suddenly, in the whole jumbled mass of his past that was floating around in my head, I found one of his memories that I wanted to latch on to: of sleeping in his own bed again after a long trip, and being glad to be there. It ripped a sob from my throat. I wanted that, I wanted to be able to sleep in a bed so badly. Dr. Corwin had memories of nights like that all through his life. Getting in a bed and sleeping the whole night through was nothing to him. I could barely sleep the whole night through without night terrors waking me up, much less lie down on a bed and close my eyes for eight hours. I envied him that, and I wanted to hate him for it. I blinked the tears from my eyes and held on to the memory, tried to burn it across the inside of my brain, so that maybe, I could feel *that* tonight when I went to sleep, instead of huddling on the floor under my blanket.

When I heard the knob of the classroom door turning, I realized I'd had my eyes squeezed shut in concentration, or maybe I was still crying like a baby. I wasn't sure, but if anyone asked, I was going to go with the more manly and dignified version. I blinked my bleary eyes at the doorway, and found Lucas's worried face peering in at me through the narrow glass set in the door. He pulled open the door and rushed into the room brandishing a tire iron. Wanda was right on his heels with a baseball bat in her white-knuckled grip; her hands seemed so small around the bat's handle. Lucas was like a little dog; his whole body was clearly ready for violence, despite his size and lack of natural aggression, trusting tenacity and ferocity to carry him through.

They took in the scene, their eyes bouncing between Dr. C huddled on the floor and me manacled to the chair. After a heartbeat, Wanda moved to me while Lucas stepped between Dr C and me. I heard the manacles rattle behind me as Wanda tried to get them off me.

"Where's the key?" she demanded sternly of Dr. Corwin. "Where the hell is the lock?" she added.

His eyes barely focused on us, and a slight smile spread across his face. He probably recognized them through my memories, but that was about it. He blinked rapidly, then his eyes glazed again as I watched him go back into his head.

"Dude, what the hell's going on?" Lucas asked as Wanda went to Dr. C. "Are you okay?"

"Hard to explain without a program, but yeah, I'm fine, just a little disoriented. What are you guys doing here?"

"We saw lights on in here, and we heard you yelling at Dr. Corwin about knocking you out, so I went and lifted the spare set of keys from the janitor's closet. We figured he kidnapped you or something, but man, whatever you did to him, you messed him up good."

"That's not a good thing. Look, guys, it's not like...he wasn't trying to hurt me, or anything. I don't have time to explain everything, but he was trying to help me out."

"You're kidding, right?" Wanda said skeptically. "In case you didn't

189

notice, you're chained to a chair, Chance. We need to be calling the cops or something!"

"No, no cops. Believe me, it could have been a *lot* worse! Wanda, you said there wasn't a lock on the manacles?"

"I couldn't see one."

"Are there a bunch of symbols around the cuffs?" She came back and looked.

"Yeah, they're all silver." Her words made my stomach clench. There was no way I could get the binders off without exposing them to the truth and potentially screwing up their heads.

"Crap. Dr. C! Dr. Corwin!" I had to yell to get his attention, but after a few seconds, he managed to focus on me. "The cuffs, what is their key?" I spoke slowly, and as clearly as I could.

He blinked a few times, then he answered, "Knowledge is freedom." He leaned toward me and reached his hand out; I got the idea. He had to touch the binders when he said the key phrase. I looked at my new friends and weighed my options. A couple of weird things, they could rationalize away. Too many, and they would have to see their whole world in a different way. But I had to get them out of here, away from this situation, and back to something normal, before they saw too much.

"Lucas," I said, turning in the chair to get my hands forward. "Get him over to me. He has to touch the manacles." Lucas tucked the tire iron through his belt and grabbed Dr. Corwin under the arms. It took a few pulls and a little grunting to drag him across the few feet, but he managed. Dr. C said the key phrase again with his fingertips touching the manacles, and they fell from my wrists with a dull clank, sounding heavier than they felt.

"Shouldn't it be 'knowledge is power' instead?" Lucas asked as he eyed the binders cautiously.

"Probably. Kinda like a password on a computer. Easy for him to remember, hard for other people to guess," I told him as I gathered my stuff up and shoved it into my book bag before they could get a good look at the rod.

"Bad idea, Chance," Dr. C whispered. "Can't show them too much. Hear that grinding sound? That's a paradigm trying to shift without a clutch. Bad for the brain."

"This is weird," Lucas said speculatively, like he was trying the idea out to see if he really believed it. Wanda nodded slowly, mostly out of reflex.

"It just gets worse from here, if you hang out with me too much longer, man," I said as I turned to face them. "But, I'm glad you guys came after me. I'll explain everything a little later on. I guess we'll catch Brad and his crew Monday?" I went to Dr. C and helped him sit up, then we levered him into a chair.

"Only if you want to wait that long. They took off like the hounds of Hell were after them, and since you weren't out yet, we decided to follow them and come back for you. They went out to the old Boy Scout Camp on the north side of Diamond Lake."

"It's been abandoned for years, ever since they had that guy escape from Twisted Oaks and kill like a hundred kids or something one summer," Wanda offered. "Is he, uh, gonna be okay?"

I understood why she was asking, because Dr. C had started muttering under his breath. I listened closely, then nodded. He was reciting a list of dates and events. My peek into his soul had shown me that he never forgot anything, and I figured he was busy sorting out the memories that were trampling roughshod across his brain. My experience hadn't been so bad, I figured, because he'd had a pretty decent life. If anything, experiencing his memories might have helped me out some, even while mine traumatized him. I grimaced at the thought of my memories being hazardous to someone's mental health.

"He'll be fine," I told her. "But I don't think we should leave him here alone."

"Chance," he said softly. I looked at him. His eyes were still glazed, but he was trying to focus. "Do what you need to do. I'll be okay." I debated trying to argue the point that tailing Brad and his crew was just a schoolboy rivalry, but the thought of the Brad and all of his friends carrying mystical augmentations stopped me cold. They had access to a halfway-decent sorcerer, and there was no telling what else he might be capable of. I couldn't take that risk; what if they decided to hit Wanda or Lucas instead of me, or worse, Mom or Dee? Only one thing stopped me.

"What about the four we ran into earlier?" I asked, carefully avoiding the word "werewolf."

He pulled his jacket far enough aside that only I could see the silenced pistol still resting under his right arm, and gave me a grim smile. It would go far worse for any werewolf who came after him a second time. He reached down and found the catch for the buckle on the paintball gun's belt. There was a *click* as it came unfastened. Wanda and Lucas reached for their weapons as they saw the holster come into view, then relaxed as I stepped forward and grabbed it.

"Take the paintball gun," he managed to say. "They may still be out there. I'll be okay here." I sure as Hell wasn't going to argue with him. I fumbled with the straps holding the bulky toy gun to his left thigh, and after a moment, it came loose. The spare clip things–no, Dr. C's memories corrected me, hoppers, they were called hoppers–still rode in the pouch on the front, and I pulled the holy water one out.

"Got any spares of the blue or green ones?" I asked. He nodded, pointing to his briefcase. I went over to it and flipped the catches open, not thinking until after I raised the lid to check for any sorts of magickal surprises. I winced for a second, then relaxed after nothing happened. He probably didn't set traps like that in a school. As I rummaged around in it, I wondered if he shouldn't. A well-made wand was held snugly in a spot made for a pen, and amulets lay scattered across the bottom of the case. At least one potion bottle was slipped into the partition in the top, and a thin, leather-bound volume lay beneath the papers and amulets. Resting along the side were three more hoppers for the paintball gun, one each of the wolfsbane, holy water, and chloroform. I tossed the holy water hopper into the case and pulled out the spare wolfsbane and chloroform hoppers in its place. I wrapped the belt around the bulky holster and tucked it into my book bag, then turned to Lucas and Wanda.

"So, we've gone from him knocking you out and tying you up to him giving you toy guns and sage advice?" Wanda asked incredulously. "Does this strike anyone else as way weird?"

Lucas raised his hand slowly. Mine followed a heartbeat later, and I heard Lucas chuckle. I followed his eyes to see Dr. C raising a wavering hand as well. I laughed at the sight and turned to Wanda.

"I'm not sure I can explain it very well, Wanda, at least not in the time we have right now, but I *can* explain it. Short version…" I paused to think for a second. "No, that would still take too long. Super-short, back of the book version: Dr. C really is one of the good guys, he thought I was one of the bad guys, he wasn't really certain, so he had to make sure. It was kind of hard on him. He'll be okay, no hard feelings, we'll talk later."

"Okay, I'm good with that," Lucas said after a moment's pause. He looked over at Wanda, who was still blinking. It looked to me like she was replaying what I'd said in her head again. After a moment, she frowned and nodded.

"I am, too, and that's a little freaky. This is going to require lots of chocolate and more than a little groveling from someone before it's all over, though." Her response was a little surprising, but I was hoping the human mind's tendency to erase anything that was too weird would kick in for them both by the end of the night, and we'd do our best never to mention this again.

"I'm sure we'll find a volunteer," I told her as I went back to squat down in front of Dr. C again. "Are you sure you're going to be okay, sir?" I asked quietly. I was surprised that I meant it when I called him "sir." I really respected this man.

"I'll be fine, Chance. Just got to clear my head. Can't do that with you asking after my health every two minutes. Now get the hell out of here."

"All right, sir. But I'll be back in a little while." I turned to Wanda and Lucas. "Let's go see what Brad and the boys are up to."

We strode through the halls, three stupid kids feeling like big damned heroes in a TV show or a movie, until we came to the stairs. There's almost no dignified or heroic way to walk down a staircase. Thus humbled, we made it out of the school and to the *Falcon*. I sat in the back seat, trying to figure out how to buckle the holster for the paintball gun on and how to take the hoppers off and put them back on in a hurry. Dr. C's memories made it easier to figure out, but they were beginning to fade.

"So, what's with the toy gun?" Wanda asked as I fiddled with it quietly in the back seat. "Are you going to stop Duncan from beating the crap out of you by holding his wardrobe hostage or something?"

"No. The balls aren't filled with paint. The ones in here now have a contact version of chloroform in them. The other ones have an irritant that works on some people."

"You're kidding!" Lucas exclaimed from his seat. I saw his eyes go wide in the rearview mirror. "Dr Corwin let you *borrow* that? Where did he even *get* paintballs like that?"

"He's a scientist, man," I said, wincing inwardly at the white little lie. Well, he *was* a scientist, but that didn't have anything to do with the paintballs "I think he made them himself."

"That makes sense. I mean, if you have the school science lab, you could pretty much make…Hey, there they are!" He pointed excitedly as a trio of black motorcycles turned onto the road in front of us, accelerating incredibly fast until they were almost out of sight. Lucas slouched back into his seat and began the dance I had seen him do with the pedals and stick shift, and the *Falcon* sped up, her engine taking on a deeper hum as we began to pass cars. He managed to keep up with them, even had to slow down a little a couple of times to stay out of sight. He was surprisingly good at this, and the *Falcon* was damned fast for a little car. Soon, we were out of city traffic, and he fell back, letting the gloom of sunset do the work of hiding us. Besides, it wasn't like we didn't know where they were going. Soon enough, we were pulling up beside a faded sign.

"Shades of *Nightmare on Blood Lake,*" Wanda whispered.

"Thank the gods we're not in that flick. Still, we'd be okay," Lucas said confidently. "None of us have had sex, none of us are naked, and none of us are going to go get a beer. We're outside the formula!"

"What formula? What in the hell are you talking about?" I asked.

"It's a slasher flick," Lucas answered. "You could always tell who the psycho killer was going to get next. Anyone who'd just had sex, was naked, or said 'I'm going to go get a beer' inevitably died right after."

"That's the victim profile, idiot," Wanda said acidly. "We're still in the basic plot set up! The whole movie took place at an abandoned campground. We're doomed!"

"Guys, right now, the most dangerous thing out here is the pissed-off sophomore in the back seat with a loaded paintball gun!" I said, voice rising until I was almost yelling. "Now, let me out!"

Wanda leaned forward and pulled her seat back up so I could slide out behind her. By the glow of the *Falcon's* headlights, I buckled the paintball gun's belt around my hips and strapped the holster to my left thigh. When I had it in place, I went back to Lucas's window and tapped on the glass. He cranked it down and looked at me seriously.

"Dude, just do me a favor okay? Don't tell me you'll be right back. That's another way to make sure the killer gets you."

I sighed. "Look, I'm just going to go in, take a quick look, and come back out. I'll only be gone for a few minutes, maybe twenty at the outside. If I'm not back in thirty minutes, you know what to do, right?"

"Right," he answered confidently. "We follow you and get captured, instead of going to get help like you told us to. Got it."

"Lucas, so help me if you don't take this seriously, I will break your nose!" I growled. The smile took a little of the threat out of it, though.

"You're the one who changed genres on us, man. It's not my fault if the sidekicks never listen in action movies."

"Half an hour, no longer. If I pull a no-show, get the hell outta here fast, and call the cops. Got it?"

"Got it!" Wanda answered for Lucas, holding up her cell phone. I nodded and gave them a thumbs-up before I jumped the gate and started down the winding dirt road. The darkness got deeper as I went, the sun finally sliding down below the horizon just before I saw the lights from a long, wooden building. As night fell, I felt a rising wind come out of the north, bringing with it a chill and the promise of rain. The cold wind lashed across my left cheek as I slowed down. Beside the wood structure, I could see seven bikes parked, three of them still pinging as their engines cooled. I crouched and came up on the place slowly, just able to make out the words "Arrowhead Lodge" carved in burnt letters over the big side door. As I passed the ticking bikes, I heard the thump of music over the hiss of wind in the autumn leaves, and whoops of people celebrating.

Jimmy Two-Tone, one of my father's men, had taught me how to case a house a couple of years ago, and I silently thanked him for it. I'd hoped never to use those skills again, but tonight, they would come in handy. I crept up to the dirt-smeared window and looked inside from just below one corner. Most of the time, people really only looked at the center of windows, so they were a lot less likely to catch sight of my face if I was down and to one side.

Inside, the room looked like a war had been waged between country sensibilities and heavy metal chaos. Liquor and beer bottles littered the floors, tables, and any other flat surface, including the window sills, while pinups of scantily clad (or completely *un*-clad) women were tacked anywhere that could be reached without a ladder. Old scoutmasters in black and white photos looked out from behind the T&A posters, and I got the feeling that they really didn't approve of what they saw. At the far right side of my field of vision was a big screen TV, with almost any device you could stretch a wire from attached to it like cybernetic children to a digital mother. Beside it, a sleek CD player perched between a pair of large speakers, all mounted on an old-style entertainment center, with a green television screen in the middle of its dusty wooden case. Aside from the double door, off to my right, I saw two more doors: one on the far right wall, which was closed, and another heavy door that was ajar. Beyond it was a dark room, but I couldn't make out anything through it.

Three guys were in the middle of the room facing away from me, the center one holding a long black case covered with red symbols. Four more faced them, all eyes on the case. Another sat on a wooden couch that was covered in a cracked green vinyl, his right arm in a makeshift sling. Even he was eyeballing the case. All of them were in black leather, like they had been when we saw them last time, except the guy on the couch, who had his jacket beside him. A white bandage across his shoulder was all that he had on his upper body aside from the sling, and it was marred by a red stain near its center. He held a bottle of what looked like Johnny Walker in his good hand. I recognized him as the guy whose bell I'd rung that afternoon during my disastrous football tryout.

"Gimme some of that," the guy holding the case demanded, and I recognized Brad's voice. "I'm gonna need it." The guy across from him handed him the bottle, and he took a deep pull from it. I caught a familiar flash of red in my peripheral vision and switched my gaze back toward the couch as Alexis moved in from my left and bent over the wounded jock. I barely tore my eyes from the way the leather stretched tight across her ass in time to catch her pulling the bloody bandage from his shoulder. Beneath it was an almost unremarkable, slightly puckered hole that was distinctive of a gunshot wound. I blinked, wondering how they could have ended up catching bullets so early on a Friday night. A chill ran through me as I remembered at least one shot being fired today, back at the school. My mind rebelled at the thought, even as I put the pieces together.

If Duncan and his buddies were werewolves, they'd be a lot stronger than normal humans. They would heal from injuries much faster, and most minor cuts and bruises would be gone almost instantly. Another realization slammed into my head: one I didn't want to think about. The claw sliver and hair were probably from a Were. Duncan or one of his friends had probably killed Mr. Chomsky. The big question now was, which one?

The door on the right side of the room opened, and all eyes went to the tall man who stepped into the room through it. He was dressed in black leather, had greasy, dark hair, and his face resembled a thundercloud that was about to unleash a storm. As one, each of the kids in the room fell to one knee, even Alexis and the wounded pack member.

196

"My Lord," Brad said, as he extended the box toward the man. "We got it, sir. We got the case."

The man took the box from Brad and tucked it under one arm. He looked relieved for a moment, then backhanded Brad clear across the room, bowling over the two guys behind him. "It's about god-damned time!" he bellowed, and everyone in the room cowered in fear. "You were supposed to have this for me days ago! I just got off the phone with the buyer, and I damn near had to give it away! Do you know how much your fuck-ups cost me?"

Brad clambered back to his knees then laid himself flat on the floor as the older man walked up to him. He picked Brad up by the scruff of the neck and shook him as he yelled in his face. "I got a reputation to keep, and if you keep fucking up this bad, no one will say the name of Dominic King with the respect I deserve! You sure as HELL don't want to pay the price for that, boy!"

"No, sir," Brad stammered. "We did our best, sir! The place was protected! You never told us it had magic spells protecting it!"

King flung him back down to the floor and put a foot on his swollen right hand. "Too fucking bad! I gave you a job to do, and I do NOT accept excuses! I told our buyer we'd have it by Monday, and it took you almost a whole week to come up with the goods. You're lucky I was able to get them to take it after that." As he spoke, Dominic ground his boot into the back of Brad's injured hand. I could hear the whimper coming from Brad, even through the window.

"We got it, though. No one else could have!" Brad protested.

"Don't give me that 'we' bullshit!" King bent down as he bellowed at Brad. "*You* didn't get it. You had to have your bitch get you in!" he pointed at Alexis. "If you can't do a man's job without getting a woman to do the real work, I got no use for you!"

"I'm sorry, sir!" he yelped. "It'll never happen again!"

"It better not," Dominic growled. Up close, I could see that his beard covered a face that was ravaged by a hard life. His eyes were black little beads behind puffy lids, and his face was lined and pitted. When he spoke, I could see yellowed and broken teeth, and the gray in his wiry beard was threatening to win in its battle with the black. What could work a werewolf over so badly that he wasn't able to heal from it?

"This just ain't been your week, boy," he said with a final twist of his heel into Brad's hand. "You screw up a simple snatch, get your ass handed to you by some punk who stumbles onto you making a buy, then you get one of your buddies shot trying to take him out, and you want to blame your mistakes on me. Get outta my sight. Hell, go party a little, celebrate fixing your screw-up. Me and Shade, we're gonna have a party of our own."

Brad pulled his hand back as Dominic went over to Alexis and wrapped one arm around her waist. Brad managed to get to his knees, with his injured arm cradled against his chest.

Dominic smiled as he pulled Alexis to him and groped inside her jacket. Her hands came up and pressed against his chest, trying to keep herself away.

"Please, sir, no," I could hear her protest. For a moment, she held herself, arms rigid against King's chest, his face darkening with the effort. She looked to Brad, and I could see her eyes pleading for help. Brad's brows furrowed as he turned his face away from her, and I saw her arms slowly start to bend as her face fell.

It took everything I had to keep from going through the window at King as he tried to force himself on her. I watched anger creep across his face as she resisted, and he looked to Brad, then back to Alexis. As he drew in a ragged breath, I could feel some dark power gathering around him, and when he let it out, the word that followed was laced with a dank, corrupt magick that made me feel dirty all the way down to my boots. From me, that was saying something. I couldn't understand it, and I didn't want to.

"Obey!" he snarled.

Silence followed for a moment after he uttered it. As one, everyone in the room ducked their heads and went submissive. Alexis laid her head on his shoulder and molded her body against his. She murmured something into his chest, and the boys said in unison, "Yes, Master."

Even I felt the force of that slimy will trying to push my spirit back into itself and force me to submit to Dominic King. It wasn't in my nature to submit to him, and somehow, the magick felt…off. Like it was a command spoken in a language I didn't quite understand. This was a dark sorcery like nothing I had ever wielded, an evil power and a slithering, oily distortion of what it was made for. This magick was originally supposed to do something beautiful, but King had subverted it to mind control and to feed his own lust.

"That's better," he sneered. "There's not a one of you can take me, so don't even think of trying to challenge me. You do as I say, and you don't ask questions. That is the Law of the Wolf. The strong rule, the weak obey, or suffer." He pulled Alexis to him and covered her mouth with his. I shuddered as she went limp in his arms. She turned away when he let her go, her face pinched in revulsion and pain that I could almost feel in my own chest. He dragged her toward the door in the back of the room, and I could see Brad's head turning to follow them as they made their way through the rest of the pack of teenaged werewolves.

While they were down and focused on Alexis and King, I started moving along the side of the building toward the back. I crept as quietly past the door as I could and hoped no one opened it before I got past it, then headed for the corner of the lodge. I crept around the side and peered into the first window I came to as the wind moaned through the trees and along the sides of the building. Here, the lodge provided me with some shelter from the wind, and the tall trees that grew along the south side shielded me from most of the light, so I was essentially invisible in the darkness. I got to the window in time to see Alexis picking herself up off the bed, and Dominic starting to undo his belt.

"You know the drill, bitch. Strip," he commanded her. She sat up on her knees on the bed and pulled her black t-shirt off, revealing a satiny white bra and a perfect back. Smooth white skin that flowed into seductive, but somehow still wholesome, curves dipped into the black leather pants she had on. Her arms came up behind her back to unhook the clasp, and her hands went to opposite shoulders, trying to keep herself covered for as long as possible. Dominic smiled as the bra fell away completely, and I found myself shaking with suppressed anger.

I had to do the smart thing and get the hell out of there. I was outnumbered ten to one by werewolves, one of them a potent sorcerer. If I got caught peeping, Alexis would never forgive me, and that was more upsetting than the thought of facing nine other pissed-off lycanthropes. Still, I didn't move, trembling with stifled anger as she got up off the bed and slipped out of her leather pants. As the top of her pants slid down, I got a peek at what most of the guys in my class would have traded limbs and other body parts to see. Alexis wore matching white bikini panties that covered just enough to be modest, but left enough bare skin that she didn't look like she'd borrowed her grandmother's underwear. There was some sort of pattern, but I couldn't make it out, and I was trying not to look all that hard. I tried not to let my eyes stay for too long on any one part. She was revealing the long, trim legs that I had seen earlier that day, but seeing them like this was much different. Once her pants were down, she kicked them to the side and straightened with her arms crossed over her breasts again.

Dominic stepped up to her and grabbed the panties by the waistband, ripping them away with a quick motion, then he shoved her back onto the bed. He opened his pants and fell on top of her, struggling for a moment to get things started. As he worked his hand in between their bodies, Alexis turned her head to one side, and I could see her eyes squeezed shut. Her body convulsed once in an unheard sob, and I saw the first tears slide down the side of her face, leaving glistening trails on her cheek.

My anger turned into barely controlled rage. It might as well have been me on that bed, for all I was concerned. No one was helping her, not her boyfriend or her classmates, and her parents didn't even know. The man on top of her was using her for his own ends, and she was just a kid. Just like me.

Some part of my head tried to tell me not to do something stupid. The hairy monkey brain was alternating between wanting to beat the ugly bastard paw the hot babe on the bed and wanting to grab her for its own. There was a white-hot fury burning in my head that suddenly became a cold, calculating wrath. All that Alexis knew was that she was alone. She didn't have any hope of rescue, no glimmering light at the end of the tunnel. All she could do was endure the pain and humiliation and try not to cry too loudly later on. She had no knight in shining armor to come to her rescue, no dashing prince to sweep her off her feet to a fairy tale ending. She only had one person who could help her.

She had me.

Not much in the shining armor department, and nowhere near being a prince, charming or otherwise. I should have done the smart thing. I should have left.

I did the right thing, instead.

Hairy monkey brain shut down, rational thinking mind shut up, and the pure, cold intelligence that had planned Dulka's defeat kicked into gear. I stood up and whispered dark, angry words into the night.

"*Ignus Infernum!*" I hissed, and called up pure Hellfire. It slid up my legs and over my body until it settled on my arms and hands. There's no way to miss being lit up by it, but King managed. Alexis, however, opened her red-rimmed eyes and looked directly at me. Maybe it was her gasp that caught Dominic's attention, maybe it was the sickly black light that was flickering across the ceiling and walls, but whichever it was, it made him turn to face me. He rose up to look at me, and that put him right where I wanted him. Off of Alexis.

"Dominic King!" I yelled. The Hellfire amplified my voice so that it shattered glass and cracked wood, and sent shards of glass flying into the room. The challenge alone knocked him off the bed and across the floor. Alexis scampered across in front of me to gather her pants and top, then found an out of the way corner to hide in. I stepped through the shattered window and flung my hands forward, screaming the release phrase for the spell at the top of my lungs. "*MITTERRE* !"

Infernal flame flew across the room in a solid column of sickly blue and black, leaving a dull *boom* in its wake. King almost got a strong enough defense up, but not quite. The purple miasma of his shield bowed in for half a heartbeat before the hellish flames, then it buckled. The blast hit him mid-chest and flung him across the lodge. As in: through the wall, across the main room, and out through the other wall. I crossed the bedroom to the smoking ruin of the inner wall, sparing a moment to give Alexis a glance and a nod as she scrambled into her clothes.

Brad and the boys cowered back when I stepped into the main room, caught between me in my adolescent wrath, and their master's twisted spell over them. Their half-naked master clambered back in through the hole I had sent him out through, looking stunned and worried.

"Who the hell are you?" he blustered.

"Chance Fortunato, asshole!" I yelled back at him as I pulled the TK wand from my pocket and the paintball gun from its holster on my left leg. Without stopping, I sent a blast from the TK wand screaming across the room at him and flung him back out through the same hole.

He came back in barely a second or two later, and I had to hand it to him for sheer balls. Not many people could handle a blast of Hellfire, much less survive a telekinetic blast as a chaser. I suppose that should have been my first clue as to how deep in it I really was. When he moved again, it was an impossibly fast leap into the room. I barely got a TK blast off before he was right in front of me, and I was sliding across the floor on my back. It was only after I stopped moving that I felt the pain in my chest from where he'd stiff-armed me. My arms were heavy as I tried to get the wand back up, but I found myself staring at empty hands. Then, he was in front of me again, with his fist drawn back and a savage snarl on his face. I barely had time to think "Not again!" before it came crashing down across my face and the world went black for the second time that night.

Chapter 14

~ Never assume anyone you've broken will stay that way. ~ Infernal provern.

I woke up to a new ringing in my ears and the sound of flesh on flesh. The whole left side of my face felt like it was on fire and my arms were pinned behind me by something firm, but kinda fuzzy. There was another slap across my left cheek, and my head was rocked to the side.

"Wake up, boy," King growled. My eyes grated open, though the left one only came up about part way. "Time to scream."

"You," I rasped, "hit like a girl." That earned me another slap, and maybe a few more minutes of semi-consciousness. When my focus cleared again, King was still there, with his index and middle finger of his right hand pressed against my forehead.

"Who's with you?" he demanded. The reverb in his voice and the pressure in my head were demanding an answer. It felt like it would be so much better to tell him what he wanted to know, what he deserved to know, so I could be good and he would reward me. The compulsion hit my mental wards like a bug on a windshield. "Who brought you here?"

Another compulsion broke against my defenses. I knew I could hold him off pretty much indefinitely, but eventually, he'd figure that out. I had no idea how long I'd been out, but hopefully, Lucas and Wanda had called the police by now. Still, I needed to give them as much time to get as far away as they could, and wait for the cops to get here.

"I...I came..." I whispered, willing him to lean in closer. He did, and I drew my head back and smashed it into his nose. There was a sickening crack and I felt cartilage give against my forehead before I saw King staggering back with his hand over his nose and blood streaming over his scraggly beard. "I came alone!" I said defiantly.

King howled in pain for a moment, then straightened and started pressing against his nose with his fingertips. My stomach lurched as I heard a grating sound, then he pulled his hands away. No more blood flowed from his nostrils, and his nose looked close to straight.

"Werewolf, dumbass," he chided me. "I can heal from most anything. He's not alone, boys."

"He hangs out with some Goth bitch named Wanda, and that loser, Lucas Kale," Brad offered.

"Good thinkin'," King said with narrowed eyes. "Pete, take a couple of the boys and head for the road. Check by the gate."

I cursed silently. How had he figured out I was stalling? Had his mind control worked somehow? "What makes you think I'd drag anyone else along?"

"If you came alone, you'd want me to think you didn't." He gave me a smug grin as I thought about what he'd said. He was right, if I'd been alone, I'd be trying to make him think the cavalry was coming when it wasn't, so he wouldn't want to hurt me for fear of being found out. In trying to buy my friends some time, I'd admitted to doing something stupid instead.

"You're not as dumb as you look," I admitted. He just gestured to Brad in response, and suddenly, I was hoisted over his shoulder. He carried me into another room and dumped me on the floor. My head bounced off what felt like concrete or stone, and I saw stars for a moment. When my vision cleared, the lights were on, and I could see that I was in a kitchen. Everything was done in industrial steel and institutional white except for the red stone floor against my face.

"You son of a bitch!" Brad hissed, and my inspection of the floor was interrupted by his boot in my stomach. "Who was that bastard with you at school? Who shot Rick?" Each question earned me another boot to the body. With my hands tied behind me, I couldn't protect myself very well, even curled up into the smallest ball I could manage. He kicked me one more time, and I spewed lunch across his shoes. With a curse, he danced away from me.

While he was wiping his shoes clean, Alexis slipped in and closed the door. Her eyes zeroed in on me as I lay there gasping and retching, and a frown flickered across her face. Brad started for me again, but she stopped him with a hand on his shoulder.

"Brad, please," she said softly.

"Don't tell me you feel sorry for this punk," he sneered.

She shook her head and closed her eyes before turning them on him full force. "No, it's not him. You know I hate it when he makes me go with him like that," she said softly. "I need your touch, Brad." She melted into his arms for a moment, then his hand went to the nape of her neck. He pulled her head back by her hair and nuzzled at her neck before he covered her mouth with a deep kiss. His other hand reached around and groped at her ass while he held her against his body.

ᴜr.

"Too bad. Learn quick, boy. Better him than you!"

"The third guy's a cop!" someone called out.

"What?" King bellowed. "Son of a bitch! You idiots took a cop?" More thumps and cries of pain followed.

"We didn't know!" one of the guys cried out. "He wasn't in a cop car, and he didn't have a uniform on!"

"He prolly told someone where he was going," King growled. "Pigs don't go nowhere alone."

"What do we do, sir?" Brad asked with a tremble of desperation in his voice.

"I'm thinking! We gotta get rid of them somehow…leave no trail back to us," King replied. The rest was cut off as Alexis pushed the door closed. She stepped out of sight, and I heard water running, then she was kneeling beside me with a rag in her hand. For a moment, she seemed undecided about something as she cocked her head at some muffled sound from the front room. Then she slipped her hand in her right front pocket and pulled something out.

"We have to get your friends out of here," she whispered as she reached behind me. I heard the click and scrape of handcuffs being unlocked; suddenly, my wrists were free, and Alexis was tucking a pair of handcuffs lined with pink fur into her back pocket.

"Yours?" I had to ask. She just nodded and blushed. Monkey brain expressed its approval, and I slapped it back down before it could conjure up any visuals to distract me. As I was wrestling my hormones, she reached down and snapped the rope around my ankles. I sat up and she pressed the wet rag into my hands. While I wiped my face off, Alexis went back to the door to keep an eye on things. I knew she was a victim here as much as anything, but I still wasn't sure how far I could trust her. At the moment, though, I didn't have much of a choice. She was our only shot at getting out of here alive.

My knife, wallet and a couple of my cinnamon candies were on the counter's smooth surface, next to a leather shoulder holster and another wallet. Once the knife and my wallet were back in my pockets, and one of the cinnamon candies was burning my tongue, I flipped the wallet open to see a badge and ID. Officer Demetrius Collins' stern face stared back at me from the card. Lucas' keys and Wanda's cell phone were under the holster, and I stifled a curse. How in the hell was I going to get all three of them out of there?

As my brain wrestled with the problem, I went to the end of the counter and flipped my knife open. Lucas and Wanda were just tied up, and the ropes were easy enough to cut through. Collins' feet were tied, but he was handcuffed like I had been…only without the cute fur. It was a good bet his key was in someone's pocket in the front room.

"Inside my right shoe," I heard Collins say softly. His eyes were open, but glazed with pain. My jaw empathized with him. I tucked my fingers inside the top of his loafer, and found the key duct-taped in the lining on the inside of his ankle. A few seconds later, his hands were free. Lucas moaned as he tried to sit up, then his bleary eyes found me.

"You brought the cops at least," I told him by way of greeting.

"Told you sidekicks never listen," he shot back, wincing as he rubbed the back of his head. He turned when Wanda stirred, and went to her side, murmuring softly to her as she came to.

"What in the Hell are you mixed up in, Fortunato?" Collins asked, as I handed him his gun.

"A bunch of stuff I'll explain *after* we leave, officer. For the moment…you're going to have to trust me a little."

"I have to get you kids out of here is what I gotta do," he argued. Stupid grownup.

"Good idea. You got a plan to get us out of here without anyone knowing?"

"Through the storeroom," Alexis answered from behind me. I hadn't heard her even move. Collins nodded, and I breathed a silent sigh of relief. I hated to leave my wand and Dr. C's paintball gun behind, but I wasn't about to risk my friends for a couple of replaceable toys. I grabbed Lucas and Wanda's stuff and handed it over, then followed Alexis to the door to the store room.

"The delivery door leads to the back of the lodge," she explained as she pointed to the double doors not twenty feet away. "Go to your right once you're outside, that'll keep you downwind of the pack. You should be able to see the road from there." Collins took the lead as I nodded and gestured for Lucas and Wanda to go in front of me.

Alexis touched my arm as I turned for the door. "The pack's territory ends at the edge of the camp. If you can make it to the road, you might be able to claim safe passage from there. The boys won't like it, but they'll deal with it if you're out of bounds."

"What about King?"

"He...I don't know, Chance," she answered after a moment. "The only rule he follows is the Law of the Wolf."

"I'll make do," I told her. She nodded and stepped back as the door closed, and I was on my own. Collins waited at the outer door with his hand on the knob. I gave him a nod, and he pushed the door open. There was a dry groan of metal on metal as rusty hinges grated against what had to be years of disuse. Collins winced as he pushed the door open hard and sprinted to his right. Lucas pushed Wanda ahead of him as we followed. When he got to the corner of the building, Collins stopped and peered around the edge before he waved us forward. The open field of the parking lot beckoned to us, awash in the orange glow of a sodium security light. My friends started forward, and Collins followed as soon as I passed him, his right hand tucked beneath his left arm, on the butt of his pistol.

We made it only a few steps into the lot, where we were nice and exposed and yards from any cover, when the first yells erupted from inside the lodge. Our jog had barely turned into a sprint when four black-clad forms streaked out of the front of the lodge. They blurred around in front of us, and I heard more feet on turf as the rest bounded up behind us. Collins' gun came out, held with the barrel pointed at the ground between the jocks and us. His eyes flicked toward me when I put a hand on his shoulder.

"You'll only piss them off if you shoot them with that," I explained. Truth was, the only weapons that would even slow them down were somewhere in the lodge, and without them, we were wolf chow. Collins didn't look like he believed me, but he didn't try to shoot the Weres, either. The boys circled us, standing with their fists clenched and eyes glowing.

"Well, well, well," King sneered as he came into the light from the front of the lodge. "You're a tricky bunch." Collins' gun came up, and a red dot appeared on King's chest as he spoke.

"Stand down!" Collins ordered, but King ignored him, instead glaring at me.

"A tragic animal attack is about to claim the lives of three stupid kids and a New Essex police officer."

"Aren't you just a criminal genius," I remarked.

"Old tricks are old tricks because they still work, punk," he said. I felt the wave of warped energy sweep out from him and slam into the pack. In a heartbeat, they all *changed*. Smooth skin split and sprouted fur, and their bodies changed shape like wax melting off a mold, revealing half human, half wolf shapes laying curled up on the ground in steaming, wet heaps. They growled in unison as they straightened and rose, baring sharp fangs and red eyes. Crap.

"What the hell?" Collins asked. I held up a hand to shush him, and to my surprise, he shut up. There was hope for the grownup yet.

"So, you're gonna hide behind your pack like a bitch," I taunted, playing a hunch. "You ain't got the balls to take me. And they're gonna see that." My words sank home, not only with Dominic, but with the rest of the pack, too. The growls stopped, and wolfish eyes went to Dominic. My hunch had paid off, and I had a few more seconds. The wolves shuffled back half a step, unsure of what to do, until Dominic opened his mouth again.

"You wanna insult me, you do it to my face, boy, and you insult *me*," he sneered, "but, no, you come here, smash up our den, and insult the whole *pack*. I don't gotta face you."

"You've never given a damn about the pack unless there was something in it for you," Alexis said from behind me.

It was an even match between Dominic and me, as to which one of us had the more surprised look on his face. His spell had forced eight Weres to change, but Alexis didn't look like she'd gone even a little furry. Either she wasn't a werewolf, or she had some serious mojo going on. As surprised as King was, I was betting on the mojo. The rest of the pack went to King's side, as if taking some sort of strength in being close to him. Knowing how King worked, it was probably the other way around.

"How the…" King muttered in disbelief as Alexis stepped up beside me and handed me the paintball gun in its holster and my red TK wand. I buckled the holster around my hips quickly. As I was doing that, King gestured at her, and the same energy he'd used earlier flooded over her, driving her to one knee, but she stayed human.

"Chance, what the hell's going on?" Wanda asked in a tiny voice.

"A little macho posturing, followed by a lot of running and screaming," I replied, hoping I sounded more confident than I felt as I buckled the second strap around my left leg. When I looked back at Alexis again, though, the tide of the contest of wills between her and King had turned. She was slowly straightening, fists at her sides, her head bowed as she fought to stand.

"Get back down on your knees, you little bitch!" King barked. It was the wrong thing for him to say. She let out a feral snarl as her head snapped up and she leaped at him. He barely had enough time to react before she planted her hands on his chest in a stiff armed shove that knocked him on his back.

"Never again," she spat. The pack eyed Alexis as she turned her back on her former leader and walked away. She walked among them, head held high, moving slowly, like some wounded goddess. As she came toward us, she laid a hand on each half-changed wolf. In her wake, each of them calmed a little, no longer trembling in the eagerness for the hunt, and where her hands had been, there was a little more intelligence in their eyes. It was only a few moments before she had laid her gentling touch on each of them, except the biggest of them: the huge gray one I figured was Brad. Her hand went to his massive jaw and slid up behind one ear. He closed his eyes and tilted his head into her palm, rubbing his jaw forward into her touch. Her touch lingered on him for just a moment, then she turned to face me with a sadness in her eyes that made my gut go tight in understanding. Her look told me what no words could. She was leaving the pack, and I could see that it hurt her deep.

She took one long look over her shoulder at Brad and stepped up to me, then reached out and laid her hand on my cheek. Her touch was warm, soft, and electrifying. My skin tingled beneath her fingertips as she leaned in toward me. I thought she was going to say something to me, right up to the moment her eyes fluttered closed and her perfect, red lips touched mine.

If her touch was electrifying, her kiss was like being struck by lightning. My knees felt like they were melting, but my back went ramrod straight, as well as a couple of other things, and I almost dropped the paintball gun and my TK wand. My lips were telling me that hers were soft, wet, warm, smooth, and–damn it!– they were gone! Every other part of my body agreed with my mouth that the whole thing had ended way too soon. Her hand left my face and fluttered to her own mouth, and I could see her tongue flicking over her lips. Then, a single tear slid down her cheek, contrasting to the tiny smile that pulled on the corner of her mouth.

"Wow!" I gasped. "But…why?"

"Because I didn't *have* to." Her words hit hard. This was probably the first time in who knew how long that she wasn't being forced to be someone's plaything. It was her first kiss by choice, and she was giving it to me in front of Brad and Dominic. Stunned silence fell as I stared at her and fought the urge to kiss her again.

"I'll give you as much of a head start as I can," she whispered, "if you'll do one thing for me." She only wanted one thing? Just then, I would have done a hundred things for her.

I raised an eyebrow. "Name it."

"Wait for me."

"Until the sun never rises," I said, quoting an old oath.

She turned back to face King and I stepped back until I was beside Collins.

"So much for the macho posturing," I muttered.

"Cue the running and screaming?" Wanda asked.

"Like a pack of werewolves is after you."

"Yeah, because that's pretty much the case," Lucas added. He grabbed Wanda's hand and pulled her into a sprint for the road. Collins looked at me for a second, then we took off after them. The faint starlight gave us enough light to follow the road as it turned to the right around a sharp ridge, then back to the left again. We sprinted up the road for what felt like only a few seconds before I heard the howl of the pack lifting into the night sky behind us.

"We're so screwed!" Lucas moaned, but they kept running.

I heard the half-human yelps and barks as the pack found our scent, then the distant crashing and snapping of wood as they took to the woods after us, not bothering with the turns in the road. I turned when I heard twigs and branches snapping above me and to my right, and caught the outline of a quasi-human shape cresting a boulder on top of the ridge. I pointed the TK rod in its general direction and called out "*Ictus latior!*"

Magick coursed from my center and down my right arm, and there was a louder snapping of tree limbs and tree trunks as I sent a broad wave of force crashing through the woods, figuring if I didn't catch him with the force itself, maybe one of the chunks of terrain I was throwing around might hit him, or at least scare him as it went by. I was rewarded with the yelp of a werewolf moving away from us, hopefully not under his own power.

I kept on running, and felt a surge of hope as I saw the flashing hazard lights of the *Falcon* a couple of hundred yards ahead. It died in my chest when I heard the triumphant howl erupt from the woods, not twenty yards behind us.

"Oh, Goddess!" Wanda cried. "We can't outrun those things!"

"You don't have to outrun *them*," I growled as I caught up to them and shoved her forward. "You just have to be a little faster than *me*."

Lucas grabbed her hand and put his head down, almost dragging her along as he picked up his own pace. Collins struggled along behind them with his gun probing in front of him. A rush of adrenaline surged through me as I turned back to face the oncoming pack. I started walking backwards as fast as I could, wand and paintball gun sweeping back and forth, searching with my eyes and ears for a target. When it came, it was from an unexpected direction.

I heard Wanda shriek from behind me, and turned in time to see her and Lucas stumble to one side as one of the Weres leaped out at them from the brush on the side of the road. This topped the list of bad plans it could have chosen. I pointed the wand at him and started to release a spell, but Collins opened fire before I could. He put three rounds into the half-wolf in a split second and knocked it out of the air. As he pushed Wanda and Lucas forward, he fired three more rounds into the yelping Were as he passed. From what I knew about Weres, I figured he'd live, but he wouldn't be happy about it for a while.

A short growl was all the warning I had before another one leaped at me from the side of the road. I threw myself to the ground and rolled in time to avoid a nifty new set of scars, but my jacket was probably going to turn furry with the next full moon. When the Were landed on my left, I pointed the wand at him across my body, and he crouched to leap, probably thinking I couldn't get the words off before he was either on me or out of the way. I knew that, too. I pulled the trigger on the paintball gun three times instead, and he went down with a yelp.

A ton of fur landed on me then, and I found the air knocked out of me while one of the Weres growled at me from three inches away. It grabbed my left wrist in a grip like iron, closing his hand around mine and squeezing. He grabbed my right hand as I yelled in pain, and I felt the bones of both hands grind together. The TK rod fell from my fingers, and I did the only thing I had the leverage and presence of mind to do: I brought my knee up. Werewolf, human, it didn't matter; if you were male, that would *always* hurt. His grip on my hand and wrist went slack and he slumped with a gasping *yipe!* I brought my knee up again, this time hard enough to pitch him over my head in an ungainly flip. He hit with a *whoof* of air. I grabbed the TK wand with aching fingers, then added insult to injury by doing a backwards somersault onto his chest. It wasn't neat or slick looking, but it forced more air out of his lungs, and gave me a few more seconds to get to my feet and start backpedaling.

This time, I heard the snapping of twigs to my left and pulled the trigger as fast as I could without even looking. The Were's graceful leap at me turned into a stumbling sprawl as the gun clicked empty after the fourth shot, but I had hit him with at least one of them: enough to put him out of the fight for a couple of minutes.

I backed up as I put the TK wand between my teeth and pulled the release for the hopper. I dropped the hopper and fumbled another one blindly into place, not knowing what I'd grabbed. The release rod *clicked* back into place, and I remembered to press the safety button just in time to see another half-wolf come charging out of the brush at me. I thrust the gun at him and pulled the trigger twice, hoping for knockout balls.

Fur flew from his nose and forehead as he took what had to have been two wolfsbane and silver pellets right in the face, and I knew a brief moment of elation. I had hit him on the fly with both shots. Of course, the range I was shooting at, I could hardly miss, but I was still impressed with me.

His yelp of pain turned into a human cry as the wolfsbane and silver temporarily suppressed the transformation and reverted at least part of him back to human. He rubbed at his eyes, and I knew a moment's pity for him, but it was a short moment. I backed up another few steps while I grabbed the TK wand again and saw the half-wolf that was curled up in the middle of the road start to get up. A quick TK bolt sent him sprawling still further back. A few more steps, and I was almost stepping in bloody wolf chunks, and I looked to my left to see the half-wolf Collins had shot still writhing on the road.

Behind me, I heard car doors slamming, and a heartbeat later, the sound of the *Falcon's* engine turning over. I turned and ran for the gate, now only a hundred yards or so away: twenty seconds or less from making it to freedom. That, of course, was when Brad and the last of his cohort leaped out in front of me. Both arms came up as I did the last thing they expected me to do.

I charged them.

"*Ictus!*" I cried as I pulled the trigger. I sent two paintballs at Brad, but I only heard one hit him. His buddy took the TK blast in the chest, though, and went skidding along the roadway, leaving a trail of fur and blood.

I almost ducked past Brad's punch and pulled the trigger three more times, this time catching him in the face with two more of the balls while my left cheek exploded with pain. He doubled over, and I finished the hopper on him while I staggered backwards, then threw a telekinetic shot at his partner that caught him a glancing blow and sent him spinning. My right arm was aching from all the magick I was using, and the shot I had hit him with was nowhere near as strong as the first one I had thrown. I backed up until I felt the iron beam of the gate hit me across the back of the legs; I did a clumsy flip over it, managing to land on my back and only lose *most* of my dignity.

A black-clad Alexis leaped over me a second later, her red hair streaming behind her. She landed gracefully and turned to face the road, her eyes ablaze. I scrambled up as Lucas turned on the *Falcon's* headlights. Dominic strode out of the darkness that pressed in at the edge of the cone of light, flanked by two naked Weres in human form. Behind me, I heard the *Falcon's* doors open, and I heard shoes scrape on the gravel to my right, and Collins stepped up beside me, his gun up and pointed at King in a two-handed grip. I brought the paintball gun up and copied his stance. The hopper was empty, but I was betting King didn't know that.

"Stop right there," Collins ordered as King got to the gate. It worked about as well as it did the first time.

"So, the bitch shows her true colors," King smirked as he got to the edge of the gate. I stepped forward, ready to shove those words down his throat, but Alexis stopped me with a hand on my shoulder. I lowered the gun a little and looked over my shoulder at her.

"Fuck you, old man," she snarled. "You had this coming." Her shoulders were straight and pulled back, but I could feel her hand trembling on my shoulder.

214

"You backstabbing little *bitch!*" he snarled as he stepped forward. I brought the paintball gun back up to eye level, and he stopped in his tracks. His eyes darted back to Brad, who was still writhing on the ground in his half-turned state, as his body tried to decide whether it was wolf or human.

"We're outside your territory, King. You hold no sway beyond that gate." Were or human, he had an ego a mile wide, and he wasn't going to stand for losing face in front of anyone.

"I'm in charge wherever I am, boy," he said, "especially with this bunch. I was making werewolves before your mother was spreading her legs for the locals."

"Did he just go *straight* to insulting your Mom, Chance? Because that's like, the ass end of lame," Lucas asked from behind me. His voice was high and shaky, but the insult was a lot better than anything I could come up with.

"Shut your mouth, boy!" King bellowed. He put his hand on the paintball gun, but stopped as he heard the hammer click back on Collin's pistol. Behind me, I heard Lucas gulp, but he stood his ground, and so did Wanda.

"Careful, Fido, they're on *my* turf now. And the kid's right, you did go straight to 'Yo Mama,'" Collins remarked, as he stepped up beside me.

"I go where I want, pig. I *take* what I want. Borders, rules, they're for the weak." He snarled in my face. As if to make his point, he held his hand up and let me see his fingernails grow into claws as his hand deformed. I could smell his breath, stale beer, and something that smelled like a mix of rotted onions and rancid meat.

"You're still outnumbered and outgunned," I said, trying to keep my voice steady as I reached up and pulled his hand away from the gun. I backed up a step, and Collins followed suit. "So, right now, no, you don't. Right now, you're the weak one. Obey, or suffer. So…stay…good dog."

As I talked, I'd been backing up, and by the time I threw the last insult out, Alexis and I were standing next to Lucas. He had his seat angled forward, and we piled into the passenger side as fast as we could. I could see the dome light in a blue Neon click on as Collins got into it, then I heard the *Falcon's* engine rev as Lucas backed away and did a quick turnaround in the middle of the road.

"Are we clear?" Lucas asked from the front seat.

"For now. He'll have to go back and get his bike. But he can find me, no matter where I am. Look, um…" she faltered and touched Lucas' shoulder.

"Lucas. That's Wanda."

"Thanks, you guys. My friends…call me Shade," she told him hesitantly, and robbed him of the ability to speak for the rest of his high school career, short of divine intervention.

"Come on, Chewie," Wanda said. "Geez, always thinking with your hormones." I didn't get the reference, but evidently Lucas did. He shook his head, then made a low trilling sound deep in his throat as he headed for the highway. I reached in to my book bag and pulled out the baggie holding the sliver of claw and the strand of what I now knew was werewolf hair, and dropped the three hairs I had plucked from the back of Dominic King's hand in with them. I had a hunch I wanted to play, and I'd need something personal of King's to play it.

"Dude, that was…wow," Lucas said softly over his shoulder.

"You so saved our asses," Wanda added.

"I told you guys I was the most dangerous thing out there."

"You were right," Alexis said from beside me. I smiled at the compliment, and took a quick stock of myself. I hurt…a lot. My right arm was trying to cramp up, my left wrist felt like it was on fire, and my ribs felt like they'd been kicked by a horse, not to mention the shiner I was working on. Top all that off with the monster of a headache that was forming behind my eyes from overdoing the magick end of things, and getting punched in the face so many times, and I was going to feel like three different levels of Hell by morning. On the plus side, both of my friends were okay, and I'd been kissed by Alexis Cooper, the hottest girl in school. It didn't hurt that she thought I was the most dangerous thing out here, when she had a cop and a whole pack of werewolves to choose from, including herself.

I curled up against the passenger side of the car and tried to ignore the pain my body was in. My right arm refused to do anything other than lay against my side, and my left really, really wanted to join it. My face was on fire, and my head was pounding.

Shade's hand on my cheek was a pleasant surprise, but her kiss was even better. Like the first time, it was like having a million volts of electricity shoot through me, and this time, it held the promise of a whole lot more. Her lips were hot on mine, but soft, and there was a passion to the kiss that the first one hadn't had, nice as it was. My left arm went around her as we melted into it, and I felt her tongue touch my lips as she drew back a little to look up at me in the darkness. Lucas was just pulling onto the highway as we stared at each other: I in surprise, and she with an intensity that made my soul want to open up to her. But, after seeing what being in my head had done to Dr. C, I wasn't going to let that happen.

"What was that one for?" I whispered to her.

"Because I *wanted* to," she whispered back. Her left hand slid inside my jacket and she laid her head in the hollow of my left shoulder as she pulled herself closer to me. She squirmed around a little to get comfortable, then rubbed her cheek against my chest for a second before she settled it back where she had started. I heard a soft sigh escape her, and felt her breath through my shirt, a warmth that slowly spread to other places. She felt good next to my body, and I didn't mind things the way they were.

We were safe for the moment. The regular pattern of light and dark from the streetlights, the hum of the *Falcon's* motor and the sound of her tires on pavement all made for a temporary haven of peace as we drove. I was in the company of friends, with the memory of a beautiful girl's kiss still tingling on my lips, and her warm, soft curves pressed up against me. It was enough to help me forget, for a few minutes, how deeply screwed my life was just then.

I didn't think I could say the same for Lucas and Wanda. They were quiet in the front seat, and I knew their lives had been completely changed by what they'd seen tonight. To their credit, they'd handled it pretty well, seeing werewolves for the first time and surviving the experience. They'd also been faced with another revelation: their new friend was a warlock. They got to see me at my worst, handing out pain and destruction like candy. I might have saved their lives, but they had still seen what I was not only capable of, but *willing* to do. For now, them not freaking out was good. I just wondered if they'd do so well if they knew the rest.

We took the exit for the Pittsburgh/Joplin area, and slipped back into regular life. Fast food restaurants, convenience stores, strip malls, and office buildings surrounded us, and I saw Lucas' hands relax on the steering wheel. He took the longer-but-brighter path back to the school, and parked under one of the light poles in the parking lot.

Shade stirred as we stopped, and my left side felt suddenly cold as she sat up and moved away from me. One hand went to move a loose strand of hair from her face, and she looked at me with a sheepish smile. We crawled out after Lucas and Wanda and stood in an awkward group for a couple of seconds before I broke the silence.

"Shade, you'd better come with us to talk to Dr. C. He'll know what to do." I winced as her eyes went wide.

"We can't tell a teacher about this!"

"Why not?" Lucas asked, as Collins pulled in behind us. "We already told a cop."

"Dr C's a wizard," I explained. Lucas and Wanda traded a wide-eyed look.

"I *really* can't tell him, then! Wizards *kill* Weres!" Shade was backing away, toward the darkness.

Collins appeared next to her, looking concerned. "You planning on letting me know what this is all about, Chance?"

"You gonna arrest me?"

"For what? Kid, no one's gonna believe me if I try to tell 'em about this. Hell, I saw it with my own eyes, and I don't want to believe it!"

"Look, I can explain, but we need to get inside, okay? Just…trust me on this. Inside, good: opposite of out here, bad."

"But…a Conclave wizard, Chance," Shade protested. She backed to the edge of the circle of light.

"He's pretty cool. Believe me, he had every right to turn me over to the Conclave earlier, and he didn't. He'll hear you out. He'll hear *me* out."

"How can you be so sure?" Shade asked from the edge of the light. Her eyes flicked to Collins, then back to me.

"I looked into his mind tonight, and…I know him. He's not about absolutes or rules. He's more into doing what's right. And he gives a damn."

She took a couple of steps closer, and I held out my hand. As soon as she took it, I headed for the door.

"You read Dr. Corwin's mind?" Wanda asked in a voice that was just above a whisper. Her eyes were wide, with a familiar gleam to them.

"No, we looked into each other's minds. It's a lot different than simple mind reading. You walk around in their head; they walk around in yours.

You see everything about the other person while they look at your life like an open book. It's...disturbing."

"But you can..."

"Yes."

"Could you..."

"No."

"You didn't even hear the question!" she said hotly as we headed up the steps.

I pulled the door open and stepped inside. "You wanted me to show you how to do it," I told her. I narrowed my eyes at her, daring her to lie to me. "Everyone asks that."

"Why wouldn't you show someone how to do it?" Lucas asked.

"It's invasive. And, I think it's against one of the magi's rules."

"But you've done it before," Shade said softly.

"Lots of times. It...used to be part of my job...before. Look, let's go talk to Dr. C. I'll explain everything then." I got four nods, and started down the hall, moving stiffly.

"What the hell did you used to do?" Collins asked.

"I'll tell you in a minute." My arms were stiffening up, and my legs were still burning from sprinting half a mile uphill. The stairs were a new challenge now, but I finally made it to the top with the tops of my thighs feeling like they were on fire, and we started our weary way down the hall to the science lab.

Dr. C was waiting for us, still looking a little messed up, but that was mostly the haunted look around his eyes. He took in the bruises forming on my face and the dirt on my clothes, then his eyes flicked to Wanda and Lucas, who were covered with dots of Were blood. I tried not to make a face, but Dr. C saw the grimace that scrunched up my nose. I hadn't been able to see the blood on them in the weak light out at the camp.

"What did you get them into?" he asked me seriously. He frowned when he saw Collins come in behind me. "And how did the police get involved?"

"The jocks' hang-out turned out to be a Were den," I explained.

"He told us to stay in the car, Dr. Corwin!" Wanda added quickly.

"I followed them out," Collins explained. "Fortunato's a person of interest in a murder investigation."

"Which almost explains why you're here. And where do you come in,

Alexis?" Dr. C asked patiently.

"I'm...I *was*...one of the werewolves," she answered quietly, "or...I was part of the pack until tonight. I didn't want to be, but..." She sat down, and tears began to course down her face. "Dominic turned me...for Brad...when we were in eighth grade. He'd already turned Brad and the rest of the guys, and they were the big football stars, even in middle school. Brad told me it meant..." she paused for a moment and wiped her eyes. "He said no one else could go out with me. That I would kill my date if I ever went out with anyone but him...or that he would. It was supposed to be perfect."

"But?" Dr. C prompted her after a few seconds of silence. I gave him a dark look, and he held up one finger to silence me.

"Our freshman year, Dominic started having us...do things. Beat people up or rob them. I stole things, too, but he had me do the solo jobs. The quiet ones. We didn't want to at first, but Dominic said it was time to pay him back for what he gave us. That's when we started to learn about the Law of the Wolf. One of the boys, Jesse, tried to leave last year. Dominic...killed him. Slowly. After that, none of us dared to challenge him. Then I found out that I wasn't just Brad's girl any more. Dominic started 'borrowing' me. His right as pack alpha, he said. And when I tried to say no, he..." She couldn't continue.

I came up to her and knelt in front of her, not knowing what to do, just wanting to do *something*. She looked down at me, then pulled me to my feet, took my hand in hers and laid her face against my knuckles. When she rubbed her cheek against the back of my hand, her face went slack and relaxed. I looked over my shoulder to Dr. C with a confused look on my face, but he only smiled and shook his head. I moved so I was standing beside her, and laid my hand on her shoulder. She leaned her head over to lay her cheek on my hand for a second, then straightened and took a deep breath.

"Brad and the boys enjoy taking runs," she said softly. "I started to do my own jobs for him, if they were going to steal things from people who could afford it. But even if we didn't want to, Dominic could make us do it. He'd get in our heads, and we'd be doing what he wanted us to do. It was like he was there, pulling our strings or something. But tonight, when Chance hit him with whatever it was he did...he couldn't make me turn anymore, like he used to. I mean, I felt the call, but I...I didn't."

"She saved our asses, Dr. C," I offered.

"She made all the other werewolves calm down long enough for us to get out of there!" Lucas chimed in.

"Yeah, she's cool, Dr. Corwin," Wanda said. Shade looked from one face to another as we vouched for her, and I saw her eyes go all misty again.

"I don't doubt that she is, guys. Don't worry, I'm not going to do anything to her. Alexis, did you calm the other wolves, like Lucas said?"

"I've always been like the pack's mother. Since Dominic never helped us out, I was sort of the one to keep the peace when the boys got a little high strung. They may be jerks sometimes, sir, but they're still my friends."

"Alexis..."

"Shade," she corrected him. "It's my pack name. When I turn, my fur is black."

"Okay, Shade," Dr. C continued, "from what all of you just told me, I'd have to say you're probably an alpha. Specifically, the alpha female of the pack, or *an* alpha female, depending on your desires."

"Doc, you aren't making a lot of sense," Lucas prompted him.

"Sorry, it's hard to concentrate tonight. Shade, you're a bigger threat to Dominic than you know, simply because you may be his equal as a werewolf. Alphas are rare, and even the weakest alpha can still be very potent. The Conclave isn't sure of their full range of abilities. However, we believe that they're not only able to induce the change on other werewolves, but they can sometimes prevent it, as well. And, they're reputed to be able to call on the power of the pack to make themselves more powerful in battle. If he knows you're an alpha, he's going to go to great lengths to get control over you again. Which is an abomination in and of itself, to say nothing of the way he ran the pack."

"Dominic's big on blind obedience. The Law Of the Wolf: the strong rule, and the weak obey, or suffer. He always made it seem like he was the only alpha, and that was that."

"Well, I'm sure that's not the true Law of the Wolf. So, why did he let you go?"

"He didn't. I walked on my own. I left the pack." The pain in her voice mirrored what I'd seen in her eyes after she had touched Brad. Her wolf instincts needed them, I guessed, and stepping out of that circle must have been hard to do.

"He didn't challenge you then and there?"

"No, I waited to see who my rebellious little bitch was gonna run to," came a voice from the back of the room. We all turned to see Dominic King crouched in the empty window frame.

Chapter 15

~ Even a demon will keep his word when his pride is on the line. ~
Johann Faust 15ᵗʰ century mage

Wanda let out a little yelp, and Lucas didn't quite stifle a curse. Dr. C, Collins, and I all drew weapons. Mine wasn't loaded, but I was betting King didn't know that. Shade's shoulder went tense under my right hand, and I felt as much as heard the low growl she let out. King just looked at us and gave a satisfied grin. Smug bastard.

"You're on neutral ground, King," Dr. C said calmly.

"Yeah, the flagpoles out front are kinda hard to miss," King said. "Ain't gonna stop me from killing the boy for trespassing on my pack's turf." He hopped down from the windowsill and walked halfway across the room.

"Careful, King," Dr. C said in a chilly voice. "The boy is my apprentice. If you're accusing him of wrongdoing, you'll face me in challenge, not him."

"I ain't gonna challenge him, mage. I got the right to just kill him. Besides, the Council won't give a damn what happens to a warlock anyways." His words must have hit a nerve with Dr. C, because a bright red dot appeared on his chest, and I heard Dr. C take a sharp breath. King turned and started for the gaping window. "Hell, I could kill his family, and the Conclave would prolly give me a damn medal or something."

My heart started pounding in my chest as I felt my world start to crumble around me. This was my fault. My mother's and sister's death would be on my hands.

"Dr. Corwin, you have to *do* something!" Wanda cried.

The red dot disappeared, and I saw Dr. C's gun drop. "I can't," he said softly. King started laughing, and I felt a line of ice slide down my spine.

"Challenge!" I called out, the words hard on the heels of a half-formed thought. The silence that fell was thick, and I felt every eye in the room turn to me.

"What?" King chuckled as he turned to face me again.

"Chance, what the hell are you doing?" Dr. C demanded.

My thoughts tumbled around in my head as I asked myself the same thing. "Dominic King, I accuse you of the murder of Sidney Chomsky," I heard myself say.

"Who the hell are you to challenge me?" King demanded with a sneer.

"I am Chance Fortunato," I said, and for the first time in years, I stood straight and tall. Anger coursed through my body like fire. "Mr. Chomsky was my Master…and he was my friend. As his apprentice, I challenge you to trial by combat." The word Master barely tripped me up, but where Mr. Chomsky was concerned, I could use that word without getting too messed up.

King laughed and turned his back on me. "Fuck you, warlock," he said over his shoulder. "I don't gotta accept no challenge from you."

"Coward!" The word hit him like a brick. I turned to Shade as she continued, "You're too scared to face him. I'll make sure the rest of the pack knows you ran from a challenge."

"Shut up, bitch," King snarled. "Only Pack members got the right to challenge. He's just a dumbass human who insulted my honor."

"What honor?" Alexis snapped. "You turned us and use magick to slap us down when we act like the wolves you made us into. You hide behind us when it suits you, but now it's *your* honor that's all insulted? I *am* Pack, Dominic King," she said as she stood up beside me, "and I say you're weak. I say you're afraid to face a normal human."

"He ain't normal, bitch," King replied. He turned to face me. "You wanna challenge me boy? Okay, I'll take that challenge. And after I kill you, I'm gonna find your family, and I'll kill them, too." He crossed the room as he spoke, and ended up right in front of me. "You think you can handle the price for losing to me?" he planted his finger in the middle of my chest.

I raised my hand and let the hatred flow. I mouthed the activation word, and black fire flickered to life around my fingers. "Touch me again, and

I'll rip your arm out of its socket. Threaten my family again, and I will incinerate you."

He snarled at me, but his finger came off my chest, at least. "Big words," he said. "We'll see if you can back 'em up. Tomorrow night, midnight. At the camp. The bitch knows where it'll happen." He turned and walked to the window, then slipped through it into the darkness.

"And don't call her a bitch!" I called after him.

"What the hell was that all about?" Collins lowered his pistol.

"Chance just backed King into a corner, and very likely ensured that he is going to have the shortest apprenticeship ever," Dr. Corwin said in exasperation. "However, he does have a fighting chance, this way. A very slim one, but better than if he'd let him walk out of here."

"Is he gonna have to fight this guy?" Collins sounded unsure of himself. Everything he'd just seen went against the way things were supposed to go in the *cowan* world. Kids weren't supposed to have to fight grownups. Werewolves were supposed to stay safely on the TV screen or in scary books, not chase you through the woods at night.

"Yes, Officer Collins, he is. To the death, most likely, in a codified, sanctioned duel." He turned to me, and his eyes turned hard. "You'd better be right about your accusation, Chance. Unless you have some kind of proof, King can refute your challenge. If he does that...no one can help you."

"I've got proof, Dr. C," I said slowly. I pulled the baggie with the hair and claw sliver in it out of my satchel. "All it'll take is a quick poppet spell to prove that it was either King, or one of his pack."

"You're betting your life on this, Chance. You'd better be right," he countered as he took the baggie from me.

"I'm betting my mom and my sister's life on it, sir. I'm really right. I'm sure of it."

"Then we have a lot of work to do. From what I've seen, you're not much more than a cookbook sorcerer."

"Hey!" I protested. "I can cast spells without a focus or a circle…well, a couple, anyway."

"You can't be serious about letting him do this!" Collins interjected. "I got King dead to rights on assault at least, and I know I can make a case for a lot more with Miss Cooper's testimony."

"After what you saw tonight, do you actually think you could bring him in?" Dr. C asked flatly.

Collins face went tight and his hands balled up into fists, but he didn't have an answer other than that.

"Can I kind of ask a question here?" Wanda said quietly, reminding us that there were still people in the room who weren't mages, cops, or werewolves.

"You kind of just did," Dr. C pointed out with a wry smile.

"Then I'm going to ask a few more. Why does this Conclave want to kill Chance; what do you mean, warlock; and just who or what the hell are *you*, Dr. Corwin?"

"I'm afraid you two already know too much, Wanda. If I answer your question, you'll only be drawn into this even further. You should probably go home now, and forget everything you just saw tonight. Convince yourself that none of what you saw was true, and that there's a rational explanation for all of this. If you know what's good for you, you'll walk away now, and never look back," Dr. Corwin said. As much as I hated to, I had to agree with him.

"Screw that!" Lucas said vehemently. "This guy knows who we are, and I smarted off to him. We're as ass-deep in alligators as anyone else in this room. We deserve to know the whole truth!"

I raised an eyebrow at Dr. C; Lucas had a point.

"Some of it…isn't my secret to reveal. Chance, it's up to you if you want to tell them the whole story."

"The whole story would take too long. My father sold me to a demon named Dulka when I was seven, as part of their agreement. Dulka did his bidding, kept him rich, laid and powerful, and I did Dulka's dirty work for him so that the Conclave couldn't come after him for anything. Nothing got traced to a demon, since it was me doing the work, technically by choice. He also made me recruit souls for him. I made him more powerful, and I learned a lot of black sorcery while I did it."

"How did you helping him…recruit…make him so powerful?" Lucas asked.

"Even a part of a mortal soul is very potent, since it's supposed to be infinite. If he got a person to the point where they had given too much of themselves to him, they'd do anything for him. After a while, when you've lost too much of your soul, you don't care about right and wrong, and you can't really feel anything good. You'll do anything for a little happiness, or even something that seems like it. Once I had enough of their soul stripped from them, I would point them to Dulka, and they'd offer him anything he wanted. Then, he could make a deal, and their soul was his."

"But, if a soul is infinite, how do you get 'enough' of one?" Wanda asked me.

"What's lost from a person's soul can heal, but it takes time. I kept them giving it up too fast for it to restore itself."

I stopped then and waited for their reactions. Wanda looked like she had a thousand more questions for me, and I could see the wheels spinning behind Lucas' eyes. I looked to Shade, and saw a kinship in her eyes. We'd both been used, and we'd both been scarred by it. We understood each other. I looked over to Dr C, but he'd already seen this through my memories.

"Last Friday night, I escaped." Such a simple thing to say, and it didn't really cover how big a deal that was. "I blew up part of a school in the process."

"Truman High School…you really did that?" Wanda asked.

"I can't believe what I'm hearing!" Collins exclaimed.

"No familiar has ever escaped from his master before. Chance, what you did was unprecedented, and supposedly impossible," Dr. C said after a moment. "I'm afraid the Council will take a somewhat less…compassionate view of your plight. If you were truly unwilling, in their eyes, you would rather have died than do his bidding. So we're on our own in dealing with this."

"Nothing new," I said with a bitter smile. "Not for me, anyway."

"What about your scars, dude?" Lucas asked quietly.

"Mostly Dulka's work."

"That's…that's…*evil!*" Wanda blurted.

"Demon. Go figure!" I said sarcastically.

"Neither one of you should have had to suffer like that!" Wanda finally sobbed. Lucas took her in his arms and let her sob into his shoulder.

"She's right, you know," he said to us, over her head. "And this Conclave? They *suck* if they think you're a bad guy, Chance. What about you, Doc? What's your story?"

"The Conclave sent me here to look for Sydney's killer and act as his replacement. He was also looking into reports of a warlock who had been released by his master. But Sydney and I are part of the Conclave that *doesn't* suck. Neither one of us agreed with the High Council's decision to execute all warlocks."

"Oh. Well, that was kinda normal and boring compared to Shade and Chance," Lucas said skeptically. "Listen to me! You're a wizard, and *that's* normal and boring compared to the tale of woe my friends just told me. How screwed up did my life just get?" Wanda gave a hiccup of a laugh from his shoulder and turned to face us, her eyes damp, red, and puffy.

"Sir, you called Chance a warlock, but you said you were a wizard. What's the difference?" Shade asked.

"A warlock is generally someone who uses dark forms of magick, like the Infernal magick that Chance was taught by Dulka, or certain kinds of necromancy, among others. It's also a term the Conclave uses for people who break the Laws. As for me, a wizard is a ranking among magi. Like a Jedi Master is to a Jedi Knight."

"So, you're like, one step from the top of the heap?" Lucas asked.

"Two, actually, but that's a conversation for another time. Right now, we have a very serious problem on our hands. In case you've all forgotten, Chance has a challenge to deal with tomorrow night, and you can bet that Dominic is going to do everything he can to stack the deck in his favor. Which means we have to do the same thing, only honorably."

"If he's gonna cheat, why can't we?" Lucas asked.

"One thing you have to learn about true magick, Lucas, is that breaking rules can have serious consequences. Your word has to be good. You can't cheat, and you can't break your promises. It's part of the price of a wizard's power. When you work magick, the universe listens to you. If your words and your actions match, it keeps listening. So, you have to behave honorably and keep your promises, Chance. That doesn't mean you can't be clever, but you have to avoid lying if you can."

"Do I have to tell the whole truth?"

"There is a subtle difference between telling the truth and not lying. It's a good bet he's going to try to limit you in what you can do, but keep as many of his own advantages as he can. We're limited in what we know about a challenge among Weres. I need some time to do some research and check some references, and you kids are probably expected home soon. Can you make it back here tomorrow?" He looked at us, *all* of us, expectantly.

Wanda and Lucas blinked in shock for a few seconds, and both nodded.

Collins' face didn't change, but he nodded. "I can't believe I'm even thinking about doing this," he growled.

"It's the only way you can stop him, Officer Collins. I think that's important to you."

"I want this guy brought to justice. I'll be here."

"My parents are gone most weekends anyway," Shade said softly. "I just have to be there early to get ready for the game."

Dr. C looked to me.

"My mom has some market thing she wants to go to tomorrow morning. I can come after that."

"The Farmer's Market," Wanda said. "This is the last weekend they're holding it until spring. My mom's going, too. Lucas and I can meet you there and give you a ride."

"All right, then. You four go home, and I'll see you here tomorrow," Dr. C dismissed us. We all got up, even Collins, but Dr. C stopped me on the way out.

"We still need to talk a little, Chance."

"What about?" I asked, as Lucas pulled the door shut behind him. Dr. C came up and put his thumb on my chin. With a gentle pressure, he nudged my chin to the right a little and examined the left side of my face. My cheek felt swollen and hot, and it was probably turning a really ugly color by now.

"First off, we need to take care of this. I'm no healer, but I can lay a glamour on it to hide it." He made a little gesture with his other hand, and I felt the gentle tingle of magick slide over my skin. "Second, I just need to make things official. As far as I am concerned, you are my apprentice, Chance. I will do my best by you, to teach you and guide you on your new path. Will you accept me as your teacher?" He hesitated for a half a heartbeat before he said the last word, and I knew he was avoiding using the word 'master' for my sake. I couldn't say it or hear it without feeling like I was back on my knees in front of Dulka, and there was no way I could deal with that.

"Yes, sir. I'd like that." I thought for a second before I spoke again, "You're defying the Conclave for me, sir. That could get you killed right along with me."

"I'm willing to take that risk."

"You've seen inside my head. You know they're not too far off the mark."

"They're farther off than you think, Chance," he said cryptically. "Go home. Be fifteen for a few hours. Come back tomorrow, we'll deal with the big life and death things then."

Chapter 16

~ Chance favors only the prepared mind. ~ Louis Pasteur, 19th century alchemist

Morning came all too soon, as far as my body was concerned. A night spent on the floor made all of the bumps and bruises I'd collected the day before ache even harder, and my muscles had stiffened up overnight. Between the "football tryout" during the day, the werewolf attack after school, the heavy duty spell-slinging, and the second close encounter with the pack that night, I felt like a mile of bad road. By the time we got to the Farmer's Market, I felt kinda human, but I wasn't going to win any beauty contests.

The Westside Farmer's Market was a collection of colored awnings over the back ends of trucks and vans, set up in the parking lot of an old factory on the western edge of the city. Even though we were here just to kill some time, I decided to do some shopping. As I passed one of the tables, I caught a glimpse of a pair of eyes gazing out from beneath the bumper of the truck backed up to the awning. I kept my gaze moving and tried not to start in surprise, but I was almost certain that it was a brownie. Some farms had them, and some of them even knew about them. Even if they did, though, they never mentioned them to strangers.

I moved on, checking out the stalls as I went along, looking now to see if anyone else had been accompanied by their hearth helpers or garden fae. Once I started looking, I could see dozens of fairies and pixies going by. A couple of the stalls had groups of pixies flying overhead, either chasing off the more mischievous fairies or doing business with other pixies, since the fae didn't care about the market's time table. If you were there late, you just had to catch up. I knew that domestic fae tended to regard any garden or field they lived in as much theirs as the humans who tended it with them, so in their eyes, anything harvested from it was as much theirs to trade with as it was the humans'.

It wasn't long before I found a promising-looking stall. Even from halfway across the market, I could see the glow of pixie wings hovering over it. The hand-painted sign over the front of the green awning read "Dandry's Herbs & Sundries" in cheerful, bright green letters, with plants and flowers sprouting through the words. The table itself was covered with small baskets filled with herbs, all neatly labeled, in nice, straight rows.

The little guy behind the table hummed happily to himself as he set out the baskets, his round face creased with a contented smile. He looked up at me with bright blue eyes and included me in his happy smile for a moment.

I felt the pull of his eyes: the pull only a mage would have. We both looked away, then I saw his gaze slide back to me, his eyes taking on the slightly unfocused look that meant he was aura-gazing me. After a moment, his chubby little face went pasty white, and a fine sheen of sweat broke out on his forehead. In one quick motion, he ran his hand through his thinning brown hair and stood up straight, though it looked more like he was cringing from me, somehow. It was times like this that I hated being me.

"I don't want any trouble," he stammered.

"Me, either," I sighed. "I was interested in buying a mortar and pestle."

"B-b-b-b-buying?" he stuttered, sounding like a motorboat.

"Yes, sir, buying." If I had floored the little guy by not threatening him, then I just about gave him a stroke when I was polite.

His jaw fell open, then shut, and his eyes went wide. "I...I don't understand," he finally managed. "You're not...you look like a..."

"A warlock, I know. It's a long story, but really, I'm just here to buy some stuff, okay?"

"Um, sure. But can you wait until the market opens? It's only a couple more minutes, and if you'll just let me know which one you'd like, I'll put it back for you!"

"That's fine, I can wait." I smiled and stepped back, and he just stared at me, like he wasn't sure he could believe what he was hearing.

"It's too damn early to be awake on a Saturday," Lucas said, as he and Wanda came up beside me and started eying the little stall. It didn't take a genius to see him making the mental list of things he wanted to buy. Wanda's eyes wandered over the growing array of stuff that Dandry was carefully setting out, too. She had on what looked like a pair of overalls that turned into a ragged skirt. Her only other concession to practicality was the wedge heels on her platform ankle boots, with a pair of black and red striped socks that came up to her knees. Under the overall bib, she had on an artfully slashed Love 'N Chains t-shirt. It was the pigtails that made me do a double take.

Lucas wore his denim coat and jeans, with a t-shirt that read, "Morning comes too early in the day to be *good!*"

When a fourth shadow fell across the table, I saw Dandry go ashen again, and his smile faded. I looked to my right to see a skinny man in a black western shirt, black pants, and black cowboy boots, standing beside Wanda. His greasy black hair was laid back along his skull in lank strands, leaving his narrow, pallid face exposed in all its pockmarked glory. The only favor he did the world was in growing a thin, scraggly mustache that hid about a square inch of pasty-faced ugly; okay, so he wasn't doing the world a *big* favor. His hands twitched at his sides, and he watched Dandry like a cat about to pounce on a slow, fat mouse.

My eyes narrowed as I caught the scent of mold and dirt from him, and my mystic senses recoiled in recognition as soon as I sent them his way. This was the warlock Brad had been dealing with Tuesday night. I hadn't been close enough to catch the signs of necromancy off of him that night, though. Most dead-bangers showed some sign of decay, like this guy's disease-riddled face, and the scent of grave dirt coming off of him. Plus, some part of my mystical senses caught the aura of death around him. Most people would feel a sense of wrongness about this guy, and they would avoid him without knowing exactly why.

"Mitchell," the round little mage said with a gulp.

The necromancer smiled and stepped up to the edge of the table. "That's no way to treat a customer, Roland," he said. He reached out and flipped one of the little boxes on the table at Dandry, sending bits of green flying. Dandry let out a little cry of dismay, but he didn't seem to want to attract attention to himself. He looked left and right with worried glances, as if he was afraid anyone might notice his predicament.

Of course, it was too late for that. I already had, and my brain had gone to that cold, calculating place where it went when I wanted to hurt someone. I took a step back and moved behind Lucas and Wanda, trying not to make any noise as I stalked up behind Mitchell. Moving over asphalt, it wasn't really that hard.

"You're not a customer of mine," Dandry stammered, trying to sound defiant. "What do you want?"

"I want what everyone wants, Roland. To be on the winning side in what's coming. It's out in the open now, and my master is going to have it." Mitchell walked around to the side of the stall, out of easy view, and farther away from me. His right hand dipped into his front pocket, and came out with what looked like a pair of slim pieces of wood capped at either end with brass. The metallic half-moon at one end gave it away as a *balisong*: the infamous Filipino butterfly knife.

"I…I don't know who had it, Mitchell, and I wouldn't know where it is right now. I'm just a minor mage," Dandry said quietly. I could hear the desperation in his voice, and my jaw clenched. Dandry seemed like a decent little guy who just wanted to sell his herbs and gardening stuff, and who took a lot of pleasure in the simple, pleasant life he'd made. He didn't want a lot of power or glory; he just wanted to have his table nice and neat. Mitchell had chosen him because he thought he was an easy mark. I saw a lot of my mom in this pudgy little mage, and seeing Mitchell prey on him really pissed me off.

"Well, I'm a full-fledged necromancer, fat boy, so you'd better come up with something I can use if you know what's good for you. You're too small for the Conclave to give a rat's ass about."

I wish I could say I saw red, or lost control, or that I just exploded. I didn't. I knew exactly what I was doing when I picked up the heavy marble mortar and pestle on the edge of Dandry's table. The mortar went into my right hand, and the pestle was wrapped in my left fist. Dandry saw the movement, but the necromancer didn't, and I thought about taking advantage of it for a second, but, I didn't want tall, dark, and loathsome to be able to say I hit him when he wasn't looking. I *really* wanted him to see this coming.

"Hey, corpse-humper," I growled.

Mitchell turned toward me with narrowed eyes. "Go away, worm," he sneered, and I felt the edge of a compulsion in the command. I'd been keeping a demon lord out of my head for years, though, and no two-bit necromancer was going to lay a charm on me.

"No, you carcass-banging loser." I smiled when his eyes went wide. Finally, he got that I knew what he was.

"You really should've minded your own business, boy," he hissed.

He started a complex set of moves to open the *balisong*, and I laid the mortar across his left temple. He took a staggering sidestep into the stall before his knees gave out and he went down on his butt. As soon as his ass met the pavement, I stepped up and swung with my marble-weighted left fist. The punch hit him across the jaw and laid him out flat on the asphalt. The knife fell from limp fingers, clattering a few inches away from his hand. I put the mortar and pestle back on the table and scooped up the knife before Dandry could do more than gasp in shock.

"Wanda, keep an eye out for anyone coming our way, Lucas, help me get this guy out of sight before whatever he was using to cover himself wears off," I ordered.

They stared at me for a few seconds, then shook their heads and moved into action. Lucas and I dragged the limp Mitchell back into the shadowed space between Dandry's brown van and the white panel van next to it. Around us, no one seemed to notice that I'd just slugged a guy and dragged him out of sight. Wanda and Lucas' lack of reaction told me that dead-boy had some sort of *neglenom* charm on him to make people ignore what he did unless he let them see him. It made sense, since I didn't feel him until he was actually beside me. Odds were, it wasn't a spell he'd cast on himself, since more complex and delicate enchantments like that were beyond most necromancers. Charms and enchantments didn't cast well with the energy most necromancers put off, and most of them didn't bother to study them anyway.

I propped him up against the side of Dandry's van and ran my hands along the side of his neck, hoping to find an amulet, and sure enough, I found the black leather cord. My fingers tingled when they touched it, and I let it be. For the moment, it was doing us as much good as it was him.

Dandry followed us, making worried noises with each step. "What have you done?" he asked, his voice rising near panic. "He's going to be mad when he wakes up, and he'll take it out on me, I know it!"

"Not if I have anything to say about it," I told him. "Can you wake him up?"

He nodded, then stretched his arm as far as he could and touched a fingertip to Mitchell's shoulder for a half a second. The spell fell from his lips in a rush, and he leaped back as soon as the words left his mouth.

Mitchell flailed his arms weakly for a second, then his eyes focused on me, and his face curled into a sneer. "Who are you?" he demanded.

"The guy asking the questions, Mitch. Who do you work for?"

"I don't have to tell you, boy. If you run away now, you might not ever find out, and believe me, you really *don't* want to know who my Master is." His voice carried a casual contempt for anyone who wasn't him. I slapped him, and a little of that contempt slipped.

"Okay, I tried asking nicely," I said as he shook his head. "Let me speak a language you can understand a little better." I shifted mental gears, and asked the next question in Infernal patois.

"Whose bitch are you? Whose hairy ass do you kiss, hoof-licker?" It was about as pleasant as Infernal got. Behind me, Dandry gasped, and I could feel Lucas stare at me. Infernal patois is a harsh-sounding language, even at its best.

"How…how can you…" Mitchell asked incoherently. "You can't act against another servant!"

"I'm not a servant. Now, who do you serve? Who owns your sorry ass?" I slapped him again, this time adding a backhand as well.

His eyes went wide as he struggled to understand what I was saying. "Synrhodi'ir!" he snarled back at me. The haughty look in his eyes told me he thought I should be really scared by hearing that name. I'd heard of Synrhodi'ir, and knew he was lower in the ranks of Hell than Dulka. Where Dulka was a noble among demons, Synrhodi'ir was more like a clerk in Hell's Hall of Records.

"What does he want?" I asked.

"Your ass on a platter!" he sneered.

I grinned as I opened the *balisong* slowly and put the point under his right eye. "Okay. Question and answer time's done," I said cheerfully as I pushed the point against the thin skin of his cheek until blood flowed, and he cried out in pain.

"What are you doing?" Dandry asked fearfully.

"He's not going to cooperate," I answered, sounding bored and resigned. I turned to Dandry and pulled the bloody point of the knife just far enough away from Mitchell's face that it was right where the necromancer could see it. "At least, I *hope* he's not. He's useless to me now, so I'm just going to take his eyes. I've got a neat new spell that calls for the eye of a necromancer. I just can't remember if it's the left or right eye, so I figure, why take chances? I'll just take 'em both, and keep the other one to hex this poor bastard with later. After all, the eyes are the window to the soul, right?"

As I finished, I winked at Dandry with the eye farthest from Mitchell. Either he didn't catch it, or he was such a gentle soul that he couldn't stomach even the threat of torture. I gave him the benefit of the doubt, and assumed he was a gentle soul. Either way, he didn't look too reassured.

236

Lucas, on the other hand, was trying to hide a smile, which I didn't get until I looked back to Mitchell and saw the fear-stricken look in his eyes. He was shaking like a leaf, and his mouth was working, but no sound was coming out.

"Aw, crap! He's trying to talk. Okay, what's out in the open now? What does your master want?" I kept my tone bored and added some irritated.

"The...the...the *Maxilla!*" he finally stammered. "It's a sword; the wizards have it! It was under some sort of concealment spell, but it was broken a few days ago. Now everyone wants to find it before war breaks out! That's all I know!"

"Well, *that* was disappointing. Maybe I should still take one eye, though, you know, just to make a point. Besides, I've still got a fifty-fifty chance of getting the right one!" I gave him a chilling smile as I leaned in and he squealed in terror. I put the point under his right eye again.

"No! Please! I don't know anything else!" He sounded so scared, I almost felt a little pity for him. Almost.

"What did you sell Brad Duncan the other night?" I demanded.

"Who?"

"The jock you were making a deal with at Dante's."

"That? That was nothing, just a couple of charms," he said in disbelief. I pushed the point against his cheek until a bright drop of blood welled up around it. "Just a negator hex, and he asked me to make him a love spell! That's all!" I felt a growl start deep in my throat, but I managed to choke it off. That made his eyes go wide, and he started to whimper.

"Damn. That's two pieces of information you've given me: one for each eye. You don't happen to know any other necromancers that you're not too fond of, do you? No? Well, here's how it is, then. I'm going to keep your blade, because it's kinda cool and I like it. You get to keep both eyes, and you never, *ever* come near Dandry again. No harm, no bad luck, not even an unkind word about his mother. If I hear that you, your master, or anyone who even knows your *name* has given him a hard time, you're going to get your knife back, and I'm going to get the eyes I need. Plus whatever other body parts I want at the time."

"You can't dictate what my master will do!" he managed to spit, finally getting back some of his courage.

"I laid a beat down on a Count of Hell; don't think that I can't do the same to an ass-lick chancellor like Synrhodi'ir." That got his attention.

"You're…you're…*him!*" necro-boy managed to stammer. He went pale and slumped against the van as his eyes rolled back in his skull and fluttered shut.

Beside me, Lucas stood up from where he'd knelt beside me and shook his head. "Man, I think you literally scared the crap out of him!" he said in disbelief. I raised my eyebrows in surprise. It certainly explained the smell.

"You're the one who escaped?" Dandry asked. His voice had lost most of its fear, but the look in his eyes was far from friendly.

"You know who I am?" I asked. Dr. Corwin had said that the wizards were looking for a rogue warlock, but I didn't figure they had a lot of details.

"You're…just a boy," Dandry said in disbelief.

"Yeah, just a boy," I snorted as I pulled the concealment charm over the necromancer's head and tucked it into my messenger bag. I felt like I needed to wash my hands after being so close to him. "Tell that to the demon."

"Chance," Wanda said quietly from the opening between the two stalls, "Is he going to be okay?" She looked a little pale, and I could see the worry on her face. Wanda wasn't a violent girl, and her Wiccan teaching probably made her very aware of karma and the Law of Return.

"I guess so. He woke up pretty quick, and I didn't hit him that hard."
"You're not what I expected," Dandry continued. "I mean, for a warlock. The stories make you seem…older."

"Older, huh? I was kinda hoping I didn't come off as evil as you'd heard."

"You did just scare the crap out of a necromancer, dude. Not really seeing the warm and fuzzy in that," Lucas observed. Wanda shrugged and nodded.

"So, what will you demand from me?" the plump little mage asked me nervously.

"What?" I asked, displaying my keen grasp of the situation.

"You extended your protection. There's always a price."

"No price. He was being a dick to you."

"Are you serious?"

"Of course I'm serious! It's not like you *asked* me to help you out or anything. He was being an asshole, so I beat him down. I just didn't want you to have to deal with any crap because of me, that's all."

"I don't understand. Where is the profit in this for you?" Dandry asked, genuinely confused.

"I'm not looking for a profit, Mr. Dandry. I just want to buy some stuff. He was making that kinda hard, you know?" He looked at me like I was speaking gibberish. "It wouldn't hurt if it made me look good, though. If anyone asks about me, I'd appreciate a little good publicity with the Conclave."

He nodded enthusiastically, making his round little face jiggle like a bowl of my mom's pudding. "Of course! You're very powerful, not a, um…person to be trifled with, obviously!"

"Could we just go with how I'm not so evil? That's all I'm looking for."

He nodded again, his head bobbing up and down so fast I thought it might pop off and go bouncing. "Well, yes, I could do that." He sounded uncertain, and I decided to take it at that and go on. Someone's watch beeped on the hour, and he looked around. Money was changing hands, and it was time to do business.

"You really don't do the whole negotiation thing very well," Lucas commented as I started looking over Dandry's wares again.

"I used to do it all the time for my old boss," I said darkly. "I'm trying to get out of that business." In the end, I walked away with a mortar & pestle, a set of knives, and some essential oils for mixing spells and potions, along with a laundry list of herbs: two bundles apiece of sage and cedar, a jar of bay leaves, and packets of cinquefoil, arnica, and St. John's wort.

"You know, you're going to have to deal with some pretty serious karma for what happened back there," Wanda said, with a worried tone in her voice, as we headed to the next stall.

"I already have a ton of bad karma to deal with, what's a little more?" I asked. It took me a few steps to realize that she'd stopped in her tracks. I turned to face her, and she caught up to me. "What?" I asked when I saw her confused look.

"People usually dodge that issue," she said quietly. "They try to justify what they're doing, or claim that they're agents of karma or something like that. You just...accept it, like it's no big deal."

"Well, I have a problem with karma. It's not perfect. I didn't do anything to deserve being Dulka's bitch for eight years. If you think I'm going to get back violence three times as bad for what I did today, then let me tell you something. I have enough scars that I ought to have a little credit on the books. But if not, then fine, I can handle it. I'm used to it by now. What I *can't* handle is a system that kicks me around for doing something good for someone, even if I have to get a little bloody to do it, just because someone says violence is always bad." I stopped as Wanda took a half step back, and felt like an ass when I saw the shocked look on her face.

"I...I never thought about it...I mean, where your situation was concerned..." she stammered for a few seconds.

"Hey, it's okay," I reassured her. "Sorry I jumped your ass about it."

"Still, I gotta wonder," Lucas mused, "if Chance really *wasn't* acting as karma for that necromancer guy, Wanda. And if the good he did outweighed the violence."

"Don't tell me you're an agnostic Pagan," Wanda said, exasperated.

"Nah, I'm just thinking that Chance did pretty much get hosed, karma-wise. And we don't know what this necromancer dude's done. He might have gotten off light."

"Who knows?" Wanda shrugged. "But we're wasting good shopping time with this. All I know, Chance, is that if you do good things, you get good stuff back."

"I hope you're right," I said to her back as I followed her into the throng. The powers knew I needed something good to happen.

Chapter 17
~ Plan in broad strokes. Everything changes on the battlefield. ~
Unknown.

We pulled into the school parking lot around noon. Shade was already waiting for us when we got to Dr. Corwin's lab. She looked nervous as we came in. Hot as hell, but nervous. She'd ditched the usual preppy-girl look, but she hadn't gone all the way to black leather, either. She wore a pair of low-slung black jeans and a pink shirt that had the bottom half ripped off, so that the edge curled up at the bottom to show an expanse of soft skin that ran a few inches below her navel. The word "Bitch" arced over her breasts in cute black letters. She pulled her feet up to rest her white sneakers on the rung of her lab stool and offered us a smile as we came in. I smiled back, partly in greeting, and partly because she was sitting in her usual spot in the room during class, halfway back on the left side from the door. I headed for her side. Lucas and Wanda perched on the table closest to the door, evidently not creatures of habit.

"You doing okay?" I asked, when I got closer.

"Yeah, kinda. Spent the night tossing and turning, wanting to go hunt," she replied. Her eyes went wide for a moment. I smiled as I sat down beside her. "How about you? Your face looks a lot better than it did last night."

"I've gotten better looking since last night? Damn, that whole beauty sleep thing works," I joked. She swatted my shoulder, making me wince.

"Sorry!" she said quickly. "I didn't mean to hit you too hard!"

"No, pretty much everything hurts after yesterday. I got hit a lot."

"Well, you looked good doing it," she confided as she leaned closer. She didn't lean back after she stopped. Instead, she laid her head against my right shoulder and wrapped her arm around my biceps.

"Thanks," I said, more than a little confused. I looked down at her, and she gave me a guileless smile in return, looking up at me through her eyelashes with soulful green eyes. I tried not to squirm with her so close to me. Yeah, part of me really loved the attention, but I wasn't used to it, so it also made me pretty uncomfortable. Of course, for the last eight years, the only time anyone had tried to touch me was when they were either beating the crap out of me, or trying to molest me. She rubbed her cheek against my shoulder a couple of times before she settled her head back against me.

The cinnamon scent of her hit my nose about the time Dr. C walked in. Shade straightened as his eyes swept over us, then stiffened as another man followed him in a step behind.

"What the hell is this? The Conclave's version of Sesame Street?" the man asked in a raspy voice as he looked around the room. Dr. C gave him a dark look.

"Kids, this cheery soul is Sinbad, the alpha of the Springfield pack," Dr. C said, as he set his briefcase down on his desk, then slid a backpack off his shoulder and set it alongside the briefcase. "Sinbad, this is Lucas Kale and Wanda Romanov, and the rather disreputable young man over there is Chance Fortunato. The young lady with him is Alexis Cooper…Shade, the alpha I told you about."

Sinbad wore a beat-up brown leather jacket; a black t-shirt; worn, almost-white jeans; and a pair of heavy black boots. He wore his white hair down to his shoulders, and a white Van Dyke beard, cropped close. Three Futhark runes were tattooed on each temple. Somehow, he pulled off a weathered look without coming off as old. Gray eyes bored into me for a moment, then fixed on Shade. He crossed the room in almost total silence and offered Shade a hand. I felt Shade's hand tighten around my arm, and her own hand stayed in her lap. His eyes narrowed before he lowered his hand.

"I can smell the fear coming off you, girl," he said softly. "That ain't right for an alpha. You were right, TJ," he said over his shoulder. "She needs my help. Girl's plenty screwed up."

"Chance is the one fighting," Shade said. "He's the one who needs the help."

"TJ will help your *gothi* get ready to *fight* your alpha. I'm here to give you the help you'll need if he *wins*," Sinbad said with a feral gleam in his eyes.

"What's a *gothi*?" I asked. Sinbad's attention fell on me almost like a physical thing.

"The Norse priests, the keepers of their lore, and their rune-masters. An alpha's adviser: the one he trusts most to have his back. My *gothi* is one of my pack, but that ain't always how it is. It's an honor that has to be earned, warlock. For now, it's enough that she trusts you." He turned back to Shade, and I felt the weight of his focus slide off of me. "You and I have a lot to do, Shade," he said.

She turned to me, and I gave her a nod. Dr. Corwin didn't trust people without a good reason. She pulled herself away from me, leaving a cold feeling down my left side, and followed the older alpha out of the room. I could hear Sinbad's voice fade as they walked down the hall.

"Okay, first things first," Dr. C said after the door closed. "We need to figure out how to keep you *alive* in a hand-to-hand fight with a werewolf. Then, we have to figure out how to make sure you *win*."

"You make it sound so easy when you put it like that," Lucas quipped.

"It's not easy: just simple. Two different things," Dr. C told him. "We have to figure that King is going to try to weight the fight as far in his favor as he can from the start…and then, he's going to cheat."

"Paranoid much?" Wanda snorted.
"It's only paranoia if you're wrong."

"What is it if you're right?" Lucas asked, worry in his voice.

"Good planning. Now, what does King know about you?"

"He knows about the TK spell, and he's seen Hellfire up close and personal, too. I figure he's gotta know about the augment charm I had if he's talked to the guys at all since last night."

"He saw the paintball gun at work, too," Wanda added.
"And you said that he used sorcery of his own, without a focus. So, he's probably going to try to play to his own strengths and limit yours. He's seen you use a focus, so he knows you're a cookbook mage."

"What *is* that?" Lucas demanded. "You said that last night."
"It's one of the most basic methods of using magick without a circle. It's someone who has to use tools and trigger words to cast spells. Half of the work is done by the tool, half by the person wielding it. That's a vast oversimplification, but it's the basic way it works. The mage provides the power and the intent, and the focus channels the spell. At the next level, the mage's mind becomes the transmitter and his body becomes the focus, or it creates it through gestures. It takes a lot of discipline and practice to cast a spell with only words and gestures. That's about as far as most mages get."

"And King is at least there with the mind control he uses on the pack," I said, thinking along the lines where Dr. C was pointing me.

"Or he might be using a trigger implanted in the spell itself, like a post-hypnotic command. Gods, I hope that's the case. It would sure make all this less scary if it was. However, we'll win this thing by assuming it isn't.""

"So, safe bet is that King is gonna say no to foci, but yes to magick. That'll give him a huge advantage."

"What about the augment charm you mentioned?" Dr. C asked.

"It crapped out after school yesterday, when Brad and the rest of the pack jumped me the first time. Right before someone shot me with a knockout round."

"Well, I think I already paid for *that* little faux pas in spades. Can you recast it?" He had a point, but I wasn't going to admit it yet.

I rummaged in my bag and pulled out my notebooks, tossing them on the table. "Yeah, if I have the right ingredients and supplies, I can bake that cake. And a few more." He flipped through my notes for a few moments, then looked at me with one eyebrow raised. Lucas picked one up and flipped it open.

"You managed to keep all of these from Dulka?" Dr. C asked.

"No, I've been writing things down in those since I got away, before I forget anything."

"You wrote *all* of this down from memory?" Lucas asked as his head popped up from the notebook he was looking through.

I nodded.

"Wow," Wanda whispered. "So, like, pop quizzes don't scare you at all, do they?"

"Not really."

"You have a very good memory," Dr. C said as he flipped through the notebooks. "Not surprising, given the conditions you had to learn under. So, let's see here… love spell, love spell, another love spell, curse, hex, curse, curse. Boy, you must have been a real hit at parties."

"I was. All the other demons were jealous," I answered as I flipped through the first notebook, looking for the physical augment charm. A moment of dead silence answered, and I looked up to see a trio of shocked faces. Everyone looked like I'd just told a Jewish joke at a bar mitzvah. "What? I can't joke about it?"

"I'm sorry, Chance, I should never have…" Dr. C started to say, but I held up a hand and cut him off.

"Yes, you should, sir. The less of a deal you make of it, the easier I can forget how bad it sucked. Laughing at it makes it…suck less. So, yeah, I have a lot of fun tricks in my spell book, mostly charms, but they're all based on foci: amulets, rings, potions. All things King will try to say I can't use."

"Yes, he will. I have an idea. First, we have to recast the augment. Lucas, Wanda, I need you two to leave while we do the preparations. Technically, I'm not supposed to even acknowledge the Conclave exists to outsiders. I'm not about to show you the nuts and bolts of magick unless you're my students, which you aren't. So, away with you until we're finished."

"Party pooper," Lucas said, as he herded Wanda toward the door. "C'mon, we'll go hang out at the bookstore until Dr. Jekyll and Mr. Hyde here finish playing mad scientist."

"When can we come back?" Wanda asked at the door.

"After the game. Chance, give them your jacket," he said. He tucked a little charm into the jacket pocket. "It suggests the presence of a person. People's minds will fill in the blanks."

"You were pretty harsh with them," I said, as the door closed on their dejected looks.

"I was honest. There's a difference." He went back into the store room and began setting up a Bunsen burner and a distillation system. "If I didn't

246

trust them, I would have tried to sugar-coat it, or give them some kind of bogus errand to run, or a meaningless task to do. They're both too smart for that, Chance. I may have offended them, but I didn't lie to them, or insult their intelligence. Remember what I told you about lying. It weakens you, distorts your magick. You can't afford that, especially not now." The sound of glass and metal against each other was familiar, and almost comforting.

"I think it was King who killed Mr. Chomsky," I said a few minutes later. From behind me, silence fell.

"Why?" Dr. C asked a moment later.

"It's a bunch of things, really. First, the person who killed Mr. Chomsky had claws, and I sensed dark sorcery in the room. King's a werewolf and a sorcerer, so he fits that bill. Duncan also told King that the pack had never killed anyone before, so that eliminates them."

"Are you sure he was telling the truth about that?"

"He didn't have a reason to lie. King was pretty pissed off about them taking so long to get that stupid case anyway, and it would have been easier to just keep his mouth shut."

"Case?" Dr. C was suddenly at my side. "What did it look like?"

"It was black, with red symbols on it. About four feet long, a foot wide, and about six inches deep, maybe less."

"Did you see any of the symbols?"

"Not up close. They were across the room, and I was looking at an angle, through a dirty window. It was kinda hard to make out details. So this case…it was from Mr. Chomsky's house or something?"

Dr. C nodded and gave me a sad look. "It's the why of Sydney's death. I knew someone was going to be after it, I just didn't expect it to be a two-bit werewolf thug. It was missing when I got home last night."

"What's in it that's so damn important?" I asked. A sudden heat washed through my blood as I thought of Mr. Chomsky being killed over some stupid trinket or something.

"It's an ancient artifact, and it's very powerful. That's all I can tell you. Sydney was charged with its care almost thirty years ago, and when he died, that burden passed to me. He reported an attempted break-in last Sunday, and on Tuesday, he found the person who'd set off his wards and called Draeden at the Conclave to report it. It was your girl Shade; the wards left a mark on her aura. He wrote that in his journal, even though he never got a chance to tell Draeden that. I figure King sent Shade in to find it and take it if she could. She set off the wards and left. King came here Tuesday night and killed Sydney to weaken the wards, since a lot of them were tied to him, then sent his boys in afterwards to get the...artifact. Last night was the first night I wasn't in the house until after dark."

"Sir, I know you can't tell me what he was guarding, but I think I know. We ran into a necromancer today who was looking for a sword called the *Maxilla*. He said the spells concealing it had failed a few days ago. The case I saw would be about big enough to hold a sword."

"Good guess, Chance. The Maxilla is very powerful, and in the wrong hands, it can do a lot of damage. And believe me, Chance, it's been in the wrong hands more than once."

"King still has what he wanted, though, and Mr. Chomsky died for nothing, unless I beat that son of a bitch, and take it back."

"Sydney didn't die in vain," he told me with a wicked smile. "Though kicking King's ass is still on the agenda."

We worked in silence for a couple of hours to redo the augment charm. Instead of using an amulet, though, Dr. C had me take my shirt off, and he painted a series of glyphs between my shoulder blades in a black, smelly ink.

"Do I have to be a dick to my friends if I'm going to be a mage?" I asked as he drew the glyphs.

"No. There are going to be a lot of things you can't tell anyone else, though. Concealing information is a way of life for a mage. Don't think that being direct with them is more insulting than not trusting them." He paused for a moment and I heard the clink of wood against glass.

"How do you get away with not lying to people?" It had been bothering me since he'd told me about the problems it caused, since I hated not telling my mom the truth about what happened to me.

"By being mysterious and cryptic." I could hear the smile in his voice. "That's the first spell done."

The sun set as we worked on the spells, and in the distance, I heard the band start playing the school fight song. Cheers and brassy music drifted our way from time to time, and I found myself resenting Brad and the rest of the Wolf Pack for being out on the football field and getting all the glory, while I was stuck in the lab getting ready to fight their alpha.

Once the spell glyphs were done, I hopped up on one of the lab tables and watched Dr. C cast his circle. He etched it into the linoleum with a *boline,* a single-edged working knife, then worked through the incense for fire and air, and covered every inch of the edge with salted water to represent earth and water. With all four earthly elements in place, he used an empty glass bowl as his Void, then he added two pieces that I had never seen before: a bone talisman and a bowl of nightshade leaves. Once those were in place, he began placing the candles in their positions just like I'd been taught, going clockwise, or as he referred to it, *deosil*, the direction of increase and growth. As he placed the candles, he intoned a single word for each one. I started to feel like my hard-won education under Dulka was really, really incomplete.

Finally, he stood in the center with his *athame*, a double-edged ritual blade, and pointed at the yellow eastern candle. The circle's power hit my senses like a solid wall as he turned clockwise, growing like a tide of static in my head. When he closed the circle, the static buzz turned into a clear, beautiful tone in my head, almost bringing me to tears with its simple beauty and clarity. My magick had never felt like this, had never felt so…pure. Dr. C went to the edge of the circle and used his *athame* to create an open place in the circle.

"You are invited to enter this circle in peace, apprentice," he said.

I hopped down and stepped across the boundary. He led me to the center of the circle, and I sat down and crossed my legs. The next two hours was a blur of magick and chanting as Dr. C retraced each spell across my back, and charged the glyphs. The charms tingled across my back by the time he was done.

Finally, he laid his hand on my left shoulder. "What was here?"

"Dulka's mark," I said softly.

"Did you know it was gone?"

I looked over my left shoulder at the blank patch of skin that used to hold Dulka's symbol, three red lines through a half circle. "Cool. I don't know how, but I'm glad it's gone. He left plenty of other marks, though."

"You get to choose if they're the wounds you bear as a victim, or the marks of a hammer, left in the forging of a weapon."

"Dulka isn't some kind of blacksmith. Don't try to make what he did right, somehow," I growled.

"No, he was just the hammer, the tool. You are the one who forged yourself, Chance. Even your pain can be a weapon. I can help you put the edge on that blade, too."

"We only have a few hours."

"What I can teach you will take a lifetime to master, but you've already had your feet set upon that path. The real question becomes if you want to continue to walk it or not."

"I'm not sure I have much of a choice," I said, unable to look at him.

"There are always choices, Chance," he said with a smile. "People tend to make decisions based on consequences, though."

"Not a lot of those that I like."

"I guess there aren't. Well, it's not as altruistic a reason as I would prefer, but you're right. You don't have many options open to you right now. Maybe...I can open some doors for you. Starting tonight."

"Yeah, seeing tomorrow morning would be good."

"You can see an aura, right?" he asked.

"Yeah. Dulka made me learn that way early."

"Good. I'm going to teach you how to use that to your advantage." He started by having me open my aura sight, and watching him as he went through a training kata. As he began each movement, he had me watch his hand or his foot. I could see his aura begin to move just a little in the direction he was going to move it in right before he started moving. It wasn't much, but it could give me a split second's warning before someone was going to throw a punch or make a kick. I told him I could see it, and he stopped.

"Good. Now, I'm going to teach you the baby steps of how to extend that to an attack. A person's aura is affected by his thoughts. Aggression usually shows red. When it's aimed at you, there is a connection that you can exploit. Watch closely."

He stood there for a moment, and then a red wave of his aura flowed toward me. I moved my hand instinctively, and caught the punch on my forearm.

"Perfect. Again!"

Another wave moved toward me, and I caught the other hand on my other arm. Suddenly, several red tendrils began to arc out at me, and I found myself trying to see which one was the real thing.

"Hey!" I cried out, confused.

"That's what it looks like when someone is considering several attacks. Now, watch as I decide on one." The red lines began to fade, leaving one or two still bright. Then only one was left, and I barely managed to get my arm in front of the punch in time.

"Crap, that's going to make things hard if he makes up his mind real fast."

"Actually, it can work to your advantage if you realize that he's not concentrating on defense while he's weighing his options to attack. If you relax, you'll also learn, in time, how to take your opponent's attack and make the energy he put into it flow back to him. But, that takes more time and practice than we have."

His eyebrows creased together and he shook his head. "I'm still not sure this is going to do it. A werewolf still has too many physical advantages over a normal person, or a mage without access to his magick. What we've done tonight will help, but I don't know if it will be enough to handle an experienced Were like King."

I reached into my front pocket and pulled out the baggie with the hair and claw sliver in it. "I think I might have something that can help with that."

Lucas and Wanda made it back a little after eleven, with a reluctant-looking Collins in tow. He had on jeans, high tops, and a blue jacket over a dark blue t-shirt, and, tucked under one arm, he had a thick folder with New Essex Police Department markings on it.

"I hit the jackpot on King," he told us as he laid the folder down on the desk. "Spent a couple of hours this morning with a sketch artist, and I went through the mug shots. Our boy Dominic's got himself a record you could choke a damn horse on. Arson, robbery, drugs, you name it."

"Murder?" I asked.

"Two counts, acquitted both times," Collins scowled. "Damnedest thing. Witnesses kept on dying."

"How convenient," Dr C added dryly.

"Yeah. I handed pictures of him out during the game, and he's got a couple of warrants out on him, so we're golden there. But, I still don't like letting the kid go up against this guy. You're supposed to be some kind of big shot, why aren't you doing it?"

"Because Chance made the challenge. Otherwise, I *would* be gearing up to step into that arena. There's nothing I'd like better than to go in his place, believe me."

"What if he doesn't walk outta there?" Collins demanded.

"I'll kill the bastard myself," Dr. C said.

"That makes me feel better," I snapped.

"Sorry, Chance. I just wish I could fight in your place tonight."

"Well, you can't, so we work with the plan we have, okay?" Collins and Dr. C looked at each other for a moment before they nodded. Somehow, that wasn't any more comforting than knowing Dr. C would kill King if I didn't survive the night.

"Unfortunately, we don't have any other choices. But, as far as the plan we have goes, I have something for you, Collins. I hate the thought of being the only back up Chance has. This should help even the odds a little," Dr C. said as he pulled out another bundle from his desk drawer and unwrapped handful of bullets tipped in silver. "Did you ever watch *The Wolf Man?*"

As Dr. C told Collins about the silver rounds, I saw Shade poke her head in the door and crook her finger at me. She didn't need to ask me twice. As soon as I was out the door, she stepped up to me and wrapped her arms around me. She'd changed into her pink sweats and "Bitch" t-shirt again.

"I spent the whole game worrying about you." Her voice was soft as she bent her forehead to touch mine.

"I was a little worried about you, too," I said into the narrow space between us. *Lame, lame, LAME*, I scolded myself. "I didn't know if King was going to try something before we went out tonight."

"He's not above it,"

"I was with Dr. C. He would've mopped the floor with King if he tried anything."

"He'd be doing the world a favor if he killed him," she growled. Her eyes flashed gold, and I could feel the depth of her hatred for him in her voice. I never wanted to be on the receiving end of that.

"No, I want my shot at him first." The anger I had been keeping under wraps all afternoon threatened to boil over. I clamped down on it, tucked it back into the dark little place I had buried it to let it ferment until I faced him tonight.

"You and me both," Shade answered with a ferocity to match mine. "Sinbad needs to talk to you about the challenge tonight. We may both get our shot at him."

"He killed Mr. Chomsky, Shade. There's no way he's walking away from the challenge alive. No way."

"Just talk to Sinbad, and listen to him. I need you, Chance…not just for this. Promise me you'll do what he tells you to do?" She lifted her eyes to meet mine, and I knew I would promise her anything she wanted.

"I promise. I'll listen to him, and I'll do what he tells me." I felt the familiar warm rush wash over me, and upped my quota of promises allowed in one week by another notch.

"Thanks." She looked at me for a moment like she wanted to say something else, but Sinbad's voice cut her off.

"Okay, you two, enough with the kissy-face crap," he growled. Shade straightened in my arms, and turned to face him. They stared at each other for a moment, and Sinbad leaned in toward her. She backed up a step, then looked down and turned her head to one side. He gestured for her to go, and she slid into the lab.

"What did you want to talk to me about?" I asked him. If I wasn't exactly respectful, he could bite me.

"The Kin have all kinds of rules and traditions surrounding a challenge. You're an outsider, so you're gonna have to follow them even better than King does."

"Like he's gonna play by the rules," I sneered.

"That's why you gotta do it. King doesn't know I'm gonna be there, but you can bet he was already planning on using the rules to his advantage. What you gotta do, kid, is turn that around on him. Whatever he asks you to do, you do it, and you smile about it, like you're humoring him. Offer to do a little more, so that he looks weak no matter what happens."

"How literal are your rules?"

He gave me a slow smile. "Very."

Chapter 18

~ Among honorable men, be twice the gentleman; among outlaws, be twice the bastard. ~

Klaus Von Bismarck, 19th century wizard

"No one said anything about a cop," Sinbad snarled when Collins came out the front door with Dr. C and my friends. "We don't bring in the *cowan* authorities, Corwin, you know that!"

"He followed us last night," I said. The alpha looked down at me. Shade stepped up beside me, and I felt the sleeve of her black jacket brush against my arm as she took my hand.

"And you told him what was going on, didn't you, wizard?"

"We need an ally; *Chance* needs an ally," Dr. C said, "and Collins is worth more to us knowing about the other side of the Veil than he is wallowing in continued ignorance."

"You can't convince me of that, wizard," the Were barked.

"He's the only person who can legally kill Dominic King," he said flatly.

That stopped Sinbad short. "I was wrong about you, Corwin," he said after a few moments of silence. "You're a harder man than I thought."

"I'm a wizard," Dr. C's tone dropped the temperature a few degrees, "I'm as hard as I need to be to keep Chance alive. Okay, kids. Let's load up and move out."

I piled into the *Falcon* with Wanda and Lucas, while Dr. C opened the driver's side door of a beat-up old green Land Rover and climbed in. Sinbad straddled a heavy-looking vintage chopper and kick-started it, while Shade slipped her black helmet on and got on a sleek black and red sport bike. She led us out of the parking lot, followed by Dr. C and Sinbad, with the *Falcon* playing tail-end Charlie.

We were quiet on the ride out. What do you talk about when you're about to jump into an arena with an alpha werewolf? When we pulled up to the gate of the Boy Scout camp, King was waiting for us astride a big chopper, with the boys behind him on their sport bikes, pointing their headlights at us. Shade rode around to park her bike between our vehicles and the gate, and pulled her helmet off while the rest of us got out.

"I knew you weren't man enough to face me alone," King called as we peered at him through the glaring lights. His glance went to Sinbad sitting silently astride his bike, and I could see a frown start to crease his forehead.

"But nine-to-one in *your* favor makes you all studly and cool?" I shot back, gesturing at the collected pack behind him. "Or did you already forget what I did on my own last night?" I could see that strike a nerve even against the lights.

Without bothering to respond, he started up his bike and gunned it. He twisted the bike around, spraying us with gravel in a show of contempt before he took off down the road. The rest of the pack followed, leaving us with only the light of our own headlights on the heavy wooden gate and the sounds of their retreating bikes. We all scrambled back into our vehicles as Shade pushed the gate open and rode in first, waiting for us to follow her back down the winding road.

"It doesn't seem as long when you're not being chased by werewolves," Lucas joked nervously as we drove into the lot in front of the shattered lodge. Off to one side of the lodge, floodlights illuminated a sunken area bordered in concrete, and King and the rest of the pack waited on the raised lip. A wooden sign labeled it "The Pit." Boy, were they creative or what?

We got out, and the feeling of dread that I had been fending off all night started to creep into my stomach. I felt like I had swallowed a lump of lead as I got out of the car. A grim-looking Dr. C and Sinbad joined us, and Dr. C pressed two holstered guns into my hands. One was the paintball gun, huge and heavy in its rig. The other was the one that scared me. It was a real gun, the same one he'd shot one of the wolves with the night before.

"What…" I stammered.

"Just one more thing he'll have to demand you take off," he explained as he helped me belt the two weapons on my hips. "But, just in case, there's a full magazine in it, and a round in the chamber. The safety is off, so if it comes down to it, all you have to do is put the red dot on your target and pull the trigger."

"Isn't this kind of dangerous?" I adjusted the holsters along my legs. "Giving a fifteen-year-old kid a loaded gun?"

"Not quite as dangerous as letting you walk into a duel with a full-grown werewolf."

"Nothing like a little perspective to cheer a guy up," I muttered, pulling a few of the green paintballs from one of the spare hoppers and slipping them into my pocket. "Where's Collins?" Collins was a key part of the plan, and I was didn't like not knowing when he was going to show.

"He'll be responding to an anonymous tip soon," Dr. C answered.

I finished with the holster, then straightened. Guns settled, I turned to face King, and everyone fell in behind me. I felt like a gunfighter in the Old West, with two guns strapped to my ass, facing the outlaw at high noon, only it was high midnight. Dr. C was behind my left shoulder, Sinbad on the right, with Lucas and Wanda behind them, and Shade on my right side, her slender hand in mine. I walked forward with my heart pounding like a trip hammer in my chest, my stomach clenched into one huge knot, and my palms sweating. King stepped in front of me as I got to the edge of what turned out to be an old, battered amphitheatre.

"Did you change your mind?" I asked, as he put out a hand to stop me.

"This is between you and me. They got no business here," he said as he gestured at everyone behind me.

"This was never just between you and me," I growled. "So shut the fuck up and quit stalling." That made the rest of the pack look at King with feral eyes. They sensed weakness, even if it was only implied. He had to answer it, and there was almost no good way for him to do that. If he let me into the amphitheatre, I was the one who had forced it. If he stuck to his guns, he risked showing fear, whether there was any or not.

I pushed past him and took a few steps into the Pit, then turned back and looked up at him. "Come down here and face me." I jumped the last few steps and landed on the broad expanse at the bottom. King glared at me and leaped the entire distance, landing with a heavy *thump* in front of me. As entrances went, it beat mine hands down.

"I'm the one who got wronged, here. I set the terms. No gun. No wands or any other focuses. No help from the peanut gallery." He strutted back and forth as he ticked off each demand on his fingertips.

I remembered Sinbad's advice and nodded like I'd expected this all along. "Do you need me to do anything else to handicap myself for you?" I taunted. "Maybe tie one hand behind my back, or wear a blindfold?"

"Shut up, boy! Do what I say, or die right now!" I could smell the foul stench of his breath as the sound of his voice buffeted me.

"So, you're afraid of me with the guns and the wand. Fine: no guns, no wand. Dr. C, no help from you, okay? So, are you feeling tough enough to face me now?" I unbuckled the holsters and tossed them on one of the amphitheater seats, then laid the TK wand down on top of them.

"None of that Infernum crap from you, either," King smiled. His eyes went to Sinbad at the top of the Pit. I sensed a trap, and weighed my next words carefully, trying to avoid falling into it. If Sinbad hadn't warned me, I would have fallen into it like an idiot.

"Oh, so we can't use spells? I can still tie one hand behind my back, if you're that worried." From above me, I could hear the chuckles of the pack as they sensed the balance of the fight already starting to shift. "Do you need someone else to come fight for you, too?"

"Fine, keep your damn spells, brat. It'll make it last longer." He took a step back, so I did, too. We both shucked our jackets off and stood facing each other in jeans and black t-shirts. He had a good six inches of height on me, and well over fifty pounds of weight. Even if not much of it was muscle, he was still a werewolf. He could pulp my bones with one hand if he wanted to, and I was pretty sure he did.

"Whenever you're ready, punk," he said from across the makeshift arena.

This was it. I centered myself, and let my aura sight overlay my vision, so I could see where he was going to move. I'd faced a major demon and kicked its ass only a week ago, and here I was, worrying about a fight with a werewolf. I told the little voice in my head that was trying to remind me that I'd spent three years preparing to fight Dulka to shut up, and dropped into a decent imitation of a fighting stance I'd picked up from one of Dr. C's memories, then looked up at King.

"Let's do this."

He took me at my word and jumped, crossing the distance between us in one flailing leap. Time seemed to crawl as I watched him fly at me, and my aura sight showed me where he intended to swipe at me. I stepped forward to catch him at the hips, and planted my right shoulder into his side. The impact made me stumble, but it threw him to the ground in a tumbling heap. I turned to face him as he rolled to his feet and brushed a hand across his jaw. He bounced on the balls of his feet and floated at me with his fists up. A line of red flowed out toward me from his right hand, and I ducked to my left, outside of his punch, and shot my left hand into an uppercut into his ribs. I hit him again before he threw a backhand that connected. Knowing where he was going to hit only worked if I could move out of the way. Even pumped up like I was, he was still faster than me, and a lot stronger. The back of his right hand slammed into my jaw, and I saw stars. The shot spun me around and sent me sprawling to the concrete floor. I hit and rolled to one side, and barely missed being crushed under King's boots as he landed where I had been a heartbeat before. I rolled again, but not fast enough. His boot caught me in the gut and flung me into the air. I managed to right myself in midair, thankful for the enhanced reflexes of my augmentation spell, and stumbled as I hit the ground, on my feet now, no matter how clumsy I'd been about doing it.

When I got my feet under me, though, King was almost on me in a lineman's rush. I couldn't get out of the way in time, so I dropped beneath him, kicked my feet up into his crotch and sent him sailing over my head. I did a kick-up, enjoying the surge of strength and turned to face him. I hurt, but I still felt strong. King struggled to his feet and looked across at me, and I saw the blur of multiple attacks being considered, each red line fading as he dismissed it in favor of another, then another, until only a few lines radiated out from him. We were both balls-to-the-wall brawlers; we relied on the power of an attack to make up for any lack of skill. Against any other kind of fighter, we would have been more effective. Against each other…it was gonna be a hell of a fight.

Suddenly, King's aura shifted to a single, broad red line, an attack of sheer strength and speed I couldn't hope to block and that was supposed to be so fast I couldn't dodge it. He rushed at me with his right fist drawn back to his ear, and I stepped forward and to my right. My left arm rocketed out and caught him in a clothesline, sending him flying with his feet in the air. He landed on his shoulders, hitting so hard that the toes of his boots rebounded off the concrete next to his head. I took a page out of his book of fighting tactics and rushed him while he was down, trying to ignore the wash of hot pain that shot up my left arm and across my back.

It was a mistake. His foot came out of nowhere and knocked me spinning. As I tried to clear my head, I felt a mule kick me in the ribs, and I went flying again. No fancy landing this time. I hit the ground like a side of beef, with the wind knocked out of me. As my diaphragm tried to re-learn how to do its job, King picked me up by the throat and held me suspended in front of him.

"Gotcha," he snarled triumphantly. He slowly started to squeeze, and my windpipe began to constrict under his grip, just as my lungs started to work right again. I struggled against him, trying to tear his hand free from my throat, but he casually slapped my hands away. As my vision began to go gray, and little black dots started to float in front of my eyes, I reached into my front pocket and pulled out the green paintballs. I squeezed with the last of my strength, and they burst, sending essence of wolfsbane and concentrated silver nitrate into his face and eyes.

Suddenly, I could breathe again, though my poor throat wasn't as happy about that as the rest of my body was. I fell to my knees, gasping and coughing as King staggered away. I heard him cursing and gagging while I panted for breath, and my vision slowly cleared. When I could lift my head, he was pulling himself up over the far edge of the arena's floor, soaking wet, his face and eyes red and swollen, but otherwise fine. I looked out into the darkness behind him and saw the glimmer of moonlight on water. Crap. The arena was on the lake; he'd washed the wolfsbane off. Still, I'd bought myself a few precious seconds to get my wind back.

"I said no guns," King growled.

"Didn't say anything about the ammo," I croaked back at him as I got back to my feet and into a fighting stance.

He chuckled as we started to circle each other, more wary now that we had each other's measure. "Slick. You got some lawyer in you?" he asked with a feral grin.

"Used to negotiate for a demon."

"Almost as bad. Be a shame to kill you. Give it up, and I'll let you live. You can even have the bitch sometimes."

"Can't do that," I said hoarsely. "You killed my favorite teacher."

"Prove it, boy," he scoffed.

"Okay." I tugged at the leather thong around my neck, pulling out the small pouch on the end of it. "*Capillus canis, homo ut lupinum,*" I incanted harshly as I slid my hand down around the pouch. Inside the pouch, the hairs and claw sliver grew hot and began to smoke, searing my palm

262

through the thin leather. I tightened my grip and gritted my teeth against the pain and focused my will on the spell. King arched his back and cried out in pain as the transformation to wolf was started against his will. Fur sprouted from his jaw and forehead, and I could see it rippling along his arms.

"Tribuo suus viris ut meas!" I roared, and a wave of energy swept from him to cover both of us. I fell to my knees again as my body began to sprout fur as well, and my muscles and bones began to reshape themselves, nails stretching, elongating into keen edged talons. I felt my eyes begin to burn, and my gums were suddenly on fire as my eye teeth pushed themselves out, becoming razor sharp fangs.

I tried to scream my pain out, but instead, I uttered an ululating howl. As the echoes of it died out over the lake, I heard an answering howl from the rim of the arena, and looked to its source to see Shade in her hybrid form, standing upright on the edge of the Pit.

"What did you do to me?" King cried out. I looked over at him in his half-transformed state, staring at his hands, then at me in horror. In my singed hand, the pouch had been reduced to ash as the binding components of the spell were consumed in the transformation that split the essence of his lycanthropy and transferred half of it to me temporarily. At least, I *hoped* it was temporary.

"I took what you left lying around," I growled at him as my eyes adjusted to their new grayed vision. Colors were muted, but everything seemed brighter, sharper, and I could hear and smell everything around me. Suddenly, the Pit smelled like a charnel house of blood and death. The smell of old fires tinged the whole thing, touching an animal's fear of the bright bane of darkness. But, carrying over everything on the damp breeze off the lake was the sweet smell of fear. I rose to my feet and began pacing around my prey. He was scared, disoriented and hurting. Pain lanced through me as well, but it was a distant sensation that paled before the thrill of the hunt, and it was fading fast. He was an old gray-hair, but he was all the more dangerous for it.

"You left a strand of hair and a piece of one of your claws outside the lab the night you killed Chomsky," I explained as I circled closer. My voice was a rumbling growl as I gloated over him. "More than I needed to take part of your power for myself. Everything came from the same being…if it didn't, this spell wouldn't work. You killed Sydney Chomsky, and I hold your power as proof of that."

"I said no focuses!" he growled triumphantly. He pointed to Sinbad and howled, "You heard him agree!"

"He said no guns and no wand, and you agreed, dumbass!" Sinbad called down at him. King turned to me and snarled.

It was exhilarating to be this strong, this powerful, and not have to answer to anyone weaker than I was. I could see how Brad had fallen prey to the temptation it carried. The spell had split King's wolf essence between us, so I only had half of it to wrestle with. I wondered how Shade kept a lid on the beast inside all the time, if this was just a part of what she had to deal with.

King surged to his feet and shook his head with a growl. He was throwing off the initial shock, and getting himself back under control. While that should have worried me, I only felt a sense of elation. Now we were going to get down to some *real* fighting.

We leapt at each other at the same time, snarling, slashing, and punching. We hit midair in an explosion of fur and teeth, each punching the other several times before we hit the ground and sprang apart. We came together again, both throwing and blocking punches in a lightning exchange, even faster than our own human minds were able to comprehend, but our animal instincts were able to follow it with chilling clarity. When we sprang apart moments later, the air between us was filled with slowly falling bits of fur. Neither of us had scored a single blow on the other in an exchange of more than a dozen blows. We danced around each other, slow grins spreading across our faces as we contemplated new tactics.

I blinked slowly and tried to bring the aura sight back; it slid back into place with ease. The web of potential blows was a haze in front of King as he contemplated even more new attacks. Then, he moved at me, and I was dodging and striking, this time using knees and elbows as well as fists, but King was a step ahead of me, and I sprang back as he scored a long slash across my chest. I cried out in pain as blood flew across the arena's floor, but King wasn't giving me any room to recover. He leapt at me once more, and I barely managed to duck beneath his sweeping left-handed slash at my throat. He sank the claws of his right hand into my back, and I turned my head to sink my teeth into the soft flesh under his right arm. He let me go as I dug my claws into his stomach and shook my head with savage abandon.

We came apart with blood on both of us. I spat out a gobbet of meat and cloth and flexed my shoulders, feeling torn muscles burn with the movement. I could feel my body straining to heal itself, but it wouldn't have time. King circled opposite me and flexed his right arm as blood spread down his side. I could feel the warm flow of my own blood seeping down my back and chest. We sprang together again, my aura sight and speed giving me just enough of an edge to keep from getting shredded in the whirlwind of attacks that we threw at each other in a handful of seconds. We pushed away from each other in a flurry of fur and claws, and stood panting, sizing each other up. His experience in wolf form had been enough of an advantage to get a few shots in, and I'd managed to score a few gouges in return, but now, we were too evenly matched for either of us to get the upper hand.

"The spell was a good touch," King said as we stood facing each other across the blood-splattered floor. His voice was rough with fatigue, and I nodded my acknowledgment. Muscles were slowly starting to knit, and skin was beginning to scab over as we stood there.

"It evened the odds a little," I admitted.

"Guess it's time to kick it up a notch, huh?" With a growl, he uttered a familiar syllable, and I felt a surge of noisome energy wash through me, bringing me to my knees. Agony lanced through me, and I uttered a lupine whimper as I hunched over my rebelling body.

"You idiot!" he crowed, as he stalked towards me. "You didn't think I couldn't control you the same way I controlled those pathetic little pups for three years?" He backhanded me and sent me sprawling. "You may be tough, but you're no alpha. You're no match for my power over the wolf!" He gestured with one hand, and a new surge of pain slammed into me. I felt my limbs thrash and convulse as he played with me like a puppet. He laughed as he stood over me, taunting me as I lay there in uncomprehending pain, unable to think, unable to speak, unable to do anything but suffer and hope for a moment's relief.

When relief came, it wasn't from King. Instead, I heard a clear, beautiful howl as a she-wolf lifted her voice into the night, and brought with it the sweet wash of warm, soothing aid. Other voices lifted into that howl, until the night rang with the chorus of their joined song, and I felt the tide of King's will swept away by the combined force of their presence. I turned my head to see eight wolves sitting atop the rim of the arena, muzzles turned up as they followed the lead of the black female in the middle. Only Brad stood as a human, and his eyes were filled with hate as he stared down at me.

Their voices ceased as I struggled to my feet, and the wolf that Shade had become looked down at me with her golden, mysterious eyes. *Champion,* I felt from that look. Deep in my head, I could feel the presence of the pack, giving me their own strength to fight for them, their voices speaking separately, each saying the same thing. They were free of King's control, proud wolves, warriors all. Their hearts were with Shade now, and hers was with me. She had broken King's control over the Pack while he was distracted with me. With his power halved, it must have been even easier.

We all fought as one now; their combined strength was mine, and their joined will was focused through me. King couldn't touch me, couldn't stand against all of them, all of *us.* I raised my head to face him and saw him take a step back, fear plain on his face. I advanced slowly on him,

266

feeling my wounds knit as the pack nurtured me. I knew from the shared memory of the pack that he hadn't shown Shade how to channel the pack's strength into one warrior. We didn't think he knew how, because if he did, he would have forced his way into our bond and disrupted it.

He leaped at me, and I backhanded him to the ground. With a snarl, he rolled to a crouch, and then launched himself at me again in a low, flat leap. We went down in a snarling heap, claws and teeth latched onto tender flesh. I finally managed to kick him free, and we both surged to our feet to face each other. King's right side was coated in red, and he hunched over as he limped away from me. The few gouges he'd managed to score healed even as I watched. I roared at him, confident, defiant, and furious.

"Guess it was a good thing that you didn't agree to no spells," he said as I took a step toward him. My feet stopped, and the fading human part of me warned me that he was up to something. He growled something in a harsh-sounding tongue, and I sensed another presence enter the arena. Newfound lupine senses perceived it without even trying, and my human experience told me it was Infernal.

My eyes narrowed and I gathered myself for a leap. The wolf in me knew only one solution to a threat: rip its throat out. My legs tensed, and I sailed through the air, the leap perfect, jaws open, eager to feel the hot spray of King's blood on my tongue. His hands came up wreathed in greenish-black flame, and I realized he'd expected that. This was going to hurt.

I hit the ground an agonizing eternity later with the stench of Hellfire and burnt fur in my nostrils. My back stung from sliding on it across the arena floor, and my head was ringing, probably from bouncing it off the pavement when I landed. I managed to get my right elbow under me and propped myself up.

King was on his feet on the other side of the arena, his right fist still enveloped in green-tinged black flames as he limped toward me. He hunched over as he made each painful step, and he held his left hand against his right side. A circle of black about the size of a man's fist flickered under the fur on the right side of his chest, then a green flash seared the hair away and left a demonic symbol visible.

"Gedeon," I whispered in recognition. It explained how King could use magick so well in his wolf form. My heart beat madly in my chest, and I had to fight down a surge of terror. Gedeon was a Prince in the Nine Hells, and a general of six legions. There was no way I could beat him like I had Dulka. My feet scrabbled against the concrete as I tried to crawl away from King in near panic.

"Your old owner wants you back, but my employer wants you dead," King said. "I get your mother and your sister as a bonus, and I'm still gonna kill your friends. I'm gonna do it slow. Then I'm gonna put my little bitch back in her place." He threw a blast of black flame at me, and I barely rolled away from it in time.

The sound of King laughing ignited a familiar burn in me, and the fear turned into a fire in my chest that went beyond rage, and into the cold place that had figured out how to beat Dulka. I reached down into that place and tried to tap into the well of hatred that fueled my own Hellfire. The hate and anger were there, but the Infernal power seemed to be just out of my reach.

"*Ignus Infernum!*" I growled. My hands glowed black, then the glow faded. I stared at my treacherous hands for a split second, before another blast caught me in the chest and sent me sprawling. This time, I rolled to my feet just in time to dodge another blast.

King threw his head back and laughed again. "Look at you! Running like a scared pup!"

We circled each other again.

"Look at your champion now, bitch! He can't use his magick because he's got the spirit of the Wolf in him. He's just a punk-ass little bitch now!" He looked toward the top of the Pit.

My brain raced while he taunted Shade and the rest of the Pack. Without magick at my command, I had to fight him up close, and I knew he wasn't going to let me do that. Of course, even if I could get him up close, I was no match for him in a fight. About the only thing I could do better than him was take a beating. Dr. Corwin's words came back to me. Even my pain could be a weapon.

268

The next bolt of Hellfire barely clipped my left shoulder and spun me around so that the one right after it hit my right side full-on and knocked me staggering. A chorus of yelps sounded from the top of the arena as the pain spread itself liberally among the pack.

"Come on, boy! Show me how tough you are!" King hit me with another burst.

I heard someone howling in pain, and it took a moment to realize it was me. It had been only a week since I'd hurt this bad, and I'd already forgotten how my screams sounded. I dodged the next black ball of Hell fire, but another one slammed into my shoulder and spun me again. Two more hit my back less than a heartbeat apart and drove me to my knees. I caught myself on the first concrete step, and caught a third blast in the small of my back. I screamed in agony.

"Chance!" Shade howled from above me.

I looked up to see her in her half-wolf form. Sinbad stood with his back to me, the corded muscle of his left arm showing the strain as he held her back. I reached into my mind and found the place where the pack was pouring their support into me. For a moment, I let myself enjoy the feel of Shade's fierce affection, and reveled in the possibility that it might become something else before I shut myself off from it. Shade let out a tortured wail and slumped into Sinbad's grip, and I felt King grab me by the scruff of the neck and toss me back to the middle of the half-circle of concrete.

His foot came impossibly fast, and my arms came up just a little too slow to catch all of the impact. The kick sent me rolling, and I heard heavy footfalls as he came at me again. He caught me in the side, and I felt ribs crack. Before I stopped rolling, he kicked me again, and this time I got a little air under me before I hit the ground like a sack of wet cement. I managed to stagger to my feet and backpedal before he could get another kick in, and ducked under his punch more by luck than skill. His other fist slammed into my stomach and knocked the wind out of me. I doubled over and retched, but there was nothing left in my stomach.

He grabbed me by the back of my hair and dragged me toward the center of the Pit. All I could do was stumble behind him until he pulled me back upright. I staggered, eyes half closed, barely holding on to consciousness.

"This is the law of my pack!" he yelled. "The strong rule, and the weak obey, or suffer! This boy is weak, and he must be punished for challenging me. No one challenges Dominic King and lives! NO ONE!"

As I swayed on my feet, I let my third eye open again. Even though my eyes were closed, I could See the auras of everyone around me. King's had a puke green color to it that hadn't been there before.

He grabbed me by the shoulders, and I saw the flow of aggressive red flow from it toward my throat. "Sucks to be you, boy," he said.

The red touched my aura, and my left hand shot forward as I felt him lunge toward me. I felt coarse, brittle fur under my hand as the shock ran up my arm, and I heard a choked gurgle as my hand convulsed around his neck.

"You have no idea," I whispered into the silence between us as my head came up.

I opened my eyes.

This close, there was no way to prevent a Horus Gaze. If King thought he was strong, I was going to give him a walk around in my memories, and see how he handled eight years of Hell on Earth. We passed through each other, and suddenly I was in a dark place, experiencing all the horrible things he did to Shade from his perspective. Humiliation and shame when he had been kicked out of Sinbad's pack for raping a Gamma female. Growing up with a father who hit him, and who did terrible things to him in the dark. The moment when he had found his father's gun, and pulled the trigger. Reveling in the power of violence, and later, corrupting the power of the Wolf.

In the back of my thoughts, I could feel King experiencing my father's moment of betrayal, every beating, every broken bone, every humiliating moment of my childhood. If his life had screwed him up this bad, what was going through mine going to do to him? I struggled to break the gaze, to get back into my own mind, and get out of King's. I felt the pull break, and I started the long fall back into my own head, grateful to be back in my own mind. As our awareness brushed on our way back into our own heads, I heard a long, pitiful wail. I hoped it wasn't coming from me.

Suddenly, I was standing in front of Dominic King, with my hand wrapped around his throat. The wail I had heard was coming from him. I let him go, and we staggered back a step as I tried to remember what I had just been doing. Fighting, my brain tried to tell me. But that had been a lifetime ago right? No. Only a few seconds had gone by.

King fell to his knees in front of me, and I remember that I had to kill him. Or…I had to prove that I could kill him. Someone…Sinbad, yes that was the guy…had told me I could just put my teeth to his neck to claim a win. I staggered forward and punched King in the face with a wild swing. He fell backward, and I dropped to my knees beside him, grabbed him by the back of the neck, then pulled him to me so I could put my teeth to his throat.

"Mercy," I managed to grunt, then I fell into the welcome darkness of oblivion.

Chapter 19

~ There is a curious strength to be found in those who dedicate themselves to something outside their own interests. Beware the man who would sacrifice himself for something or someone other than himself. Every now and again, such men are hard to kill. ~ Shaitan, High Prince of Hell

Being dead hurt. No surprise there, all nine Hells were supposed to be one long torture-fest, and the way I felt seemed like a good warm up to infinite suffering. In the distance, I heard the wailing and gibbering of some other lost soul, and I could make out the voices of other beings talking. Probably planning my first torment. Still, the darkness was a little comfort, and it almost felt good to lay still. The pain even seemed to be fading a little. I decided to take my sweet time about moving. I had eternity to endure this; I might as well milk the moment for all I could.

A wet spot of warmth fell on my cheek, and I opened my eyes. It wasn't supposed to rain in Hell. I couldn't remember whether it was supposed to be hot or cold, but rain was definitely not in the Infernal forecast. The sight that greeted me when my eyes could focus was just as confusing; there weren't supposed to be angels in Hell, either. Not redheaded ones with halos and green, green eyes and lips I wanted to kiss. Of course, I didn't know if angels could cry, either. I blinked, and the blurry edges of everything sort of sharpened, and the angel's face turned into Shade's. The halo became the lights from the amphitheatre shining through her hair, and she *was* crying. Another teardrop hit my face as she sniffled and looked down at me.

"Shade," I managed to croak out, then her lips were covering mine, and I couldn't remember what I wanted to say. I lost myself in her kiss, enjoying it and trying to tune out any other distractions like pain and the smell of burnt skin. She finally came up for air with my name on her lips, then she crushed me to her in a rib-creaking hug.

"Shade," I gasped, "Can't…breathe!"

She let go and laid me back down. "Sorry." With a gentle gesture, she brushed a strand of hair from my eyes and stroked my cheek. "I thought...I thought...you were..."

"He's too strong for that," came another voice. "Or maybe it's just pure stubbornness, to match the deep well of stupidity." Dr. C knelt down beside me, with Lucas and Wanda on either side of him.

"I'm glad I'm still alive, too, sir," I told him with a weak smile. "Not sure how, but I'm glad I am."

"King's lycanthropy is still trying to heal the physical damage he did to you with the Hellfire," Dr. Corwin said. "Shade re-established the pack bond with you after you and King dropped, so that's helping too. I'm not saying it wasn't a near thing, nor that you're not going to hurt for the next few days, but you should make it through this relatively intact."

"Until my mom gets hold of me," I groaned, not liking the repercussions of that conversation.

"Better grounded and on your mother's bad side for a couple of weeks than dead, I think," Dr. C countered. He was right.

"What about King?" I asked.

"Still gibbering like an idiot," Lucas supplied after a quick glance over his shoulder.

"What did you do to him?" Sinbad asked.

"We got to know each other a little better," I said with a wolfish smile.

"You know, when I said your pain was a weapon, I meant that metaphorically," Dr. C said.

I shrugged and closed my eyes, basking in Shade's attention instead of worrying about later. I felt other presences closing in on us, and opened my eyes to see the rest of the pack surround our little group. Dr. C stood up and turned to face them with Lucas and Wanda at his side. Shade stayed beside me until I grunted and tried to get to my feet. She slipped an arm under my shoulder and effortlessly brought me to my feet to face Brad and the boys. Sinbad stepped back, with a narrow smile on his face.

"He beat our leader," Brad said accusingly. "How can you sit there and cry over him? How could you *help* him? We owe Dominic everything!"

"We don't owe him a damn thing," Shade growled. I pulled my arm from around her shoulders and stood swaying as she advanced on Brad. "For two years, he's feasted on our efforts, and fed us the scraps of our own kills. He's forced us to live like his lap dogs, sitting at his feet like domesticated animals instead of running free like the wolves we are. He killed one of our pack, and he forced me into his bed like his personal sex-toy. He wasn't our leader, Brad; he was our Master. If you want to go back to being his pet, then you go. I'm free, and I am going to *stay* that way."

"None of us beat him," Brad argued. "You know the Law of the Wolf! The strong rule! The weak obey, or suffer. I'm not going to be ruled by a human! I challenge you, Chance Fortunato! Right here and now!" The rest of the pack turned to me, and I stepped forward. Doubt clouded his expression for a split second. He'd probably expected me to back down.

"Retract your challenge, boy," Sinbad growled. Brad turned and snarled at him.

"Take it back, Brad, or face me," Shade hissed.

"Why?" Brad asked. I heard confusion and pain in his voice, something I'd never heard before. "Why are you defending him? Why are you choosing him over the pack...over me?"

"Because you waited until you thought he couldn't beat you. You're weak, just like King. When you had the chance to help us beat him, you held yourself back from the pack bond. The pack helped Chance win. He's my *gothi*, Brad, my adviser and champion. He's one of *my* pack. If you want to challenge him, you challenge me first!" She stepped forward and faced off with him, fists clenched at her side.

Off to the side, I heard Sinbad chuckle.

"*I'm* King's second," Brad said belligerently. "If King is down, I run this pack. If you want to do this, then it's my way or the highway. And I say this punk goes, or he takes my challenge. You're my girl, Shade. No one moves in on my woman."

"I'm not *your* girl," Shade snarled. "I'm my own woman."

"Wolves mate for life," Brad argued, "so it's not like you have much of a choice."

Shade gave me a quick glance, then her eyes narrowed and slid back to Brad. "You were never my mate, Brad. What you did to me was rape. And you let King do it to me, too. Chance stays, and the pack chooses its own path. You either deal with that, or you face me." Shade stepped between Brad and me, and the rest of the pack came around to stand behind her.

One of them, the guy Dr. C had shot, stepped out and extended a hand to Brad. "Come on, Brad. We've been through too much together. Stay with us."

"Screw you, Tyler. Screw all of you. This isn't a pack any more. It's a...*herd!* He spun on his heel and bounded up the rows to the top of the amphitheater. Shade shook her head sadly as he went. He stopped and looked down at us in disgust before he ran into the darkness.

A moment later, Collins stepped into view at the top of the concrete semi-circle. He drew his badge as he came down the steps, and had his hand on the gun holstered at his hip.

"Dominic King, you're under arrest for assaulting a minor and attempted murder," Collins said as he took the last step down onto the amphitheater's floor. King managed to focus on him as Collins pocketed his badge and pulled a pair of handcuffs from his belt.

As he rolled King over and ratcheted the cuffs onto his wrists, I caught Shade's eye and gestured at her to go. She gave me a warm smile and a kiss on the cheek before she led the rest of the pack up the steps. Dr. C was heading up the steps, gesturing for Lucas and Wanda to come with him as he went, and they weren't wasting time about doing it.

While Collins finished cuffing King, I went to the pile of gear that I'd dropped before the fight had started. The TK wand went into my pocket, and I grabbed the pistol belt.

"I'da thought you'd learned your lesson last night, pig. You can't stop me," King said as Collins pulled him to his feet.

"I figure you haven't learned anything," Collins replied calmly. "I got a wizard for back up and a mag full of silver rounds. What you've got is the right to remain silent. If you give up that right, anything you say can be used against you in a court of law. You have the right to an attorney present during questioning."

"You can't touch me and you can't take me in, cop. So shut the hell up. I got people to go kill," King sneered as he pulled his arm free of Collins grip. He flexed his shoulders and I heard metal snap as he broke free of the cuffs. Before I could move, he was across the arena and digging in his jacket.

"Hands where I can see them!" Collins ordered, as he pulled his gun.

On the top of the amphitheater, Dr. C began a spell, and King made his move. His hand came out of the jacket with a pistol. He shot Collins three times, then aimed over my head and squeezed off three more shots before Collins hit the ground.

Along with the clatter of Collins' gun on the cement, I heard Dr. C grunt, and turned to see rounds bouncing off of a hastily erected shield. Wanda and Lucas crouched beside him, trying to stay behind the barrier. But maintaining a shield that big without a focus was taking a lot out of him.

With superhuman speed, King turned the gun on me, and I had to dive to the side, praying my still-enhanced reflexes would help me dodge the bullets. I tried to pull the TK wand from my pocket as I fumbled one of the pistols from its holster. Rounds hissed by me amid the roar of the gun, and I hit the ground and slid to a stop a few feet from Collins. Before I stopped moving, King had reloaded the gun, and was firing at Dr. C, who staggered back with one hand to his head, and the other raised to focus his warding spell.

As fast as King was moving, we would be lucky to keep him on the defensive even if we were at our best. As it was, we were barely holding our own. I spared a brief thought for what Mr. Chomsky must have faced, as I got to my feet and moved toward Collins. I finally managed to get the wand free of my pocket as King turned toward me.

"*Ictus!*" I yelled as I ran.

King ducked the blast of force and fired at me at the same time, but his aim was off, and he blew a chunk out of the concrete, instead of my ass. As I dove to the ground behind Collins, King turned and fired at Dr. C again, then there was a quick moment when the night was silent except for the echo of the slide locking back on his pistol and the hollow sound of brass casings bouncing on concrete. Dr. C stumbled and caught himself against one of the light poles, and I felt the weak shimmer of his hastily cast shield fade from my mystic senses. Beside me, Collins moaned, and I saw King's gaze focus on him.

Time stopped for a second as I met King's eyes. I only had as long as it took for him to reload to stop him or someone was going to die, and he was going to get away. I didn't know if I could beat him home, or if I could get Mom and Dee out in time. Collins was between us, and Dr. C was effectively helpless. The cruel gleam in his eye told me what no words could; he wanted to make me choose who was going to die. He gave me a slow grin as he turned his right hand and worked a catch on the side of his pistol. Time crawled slowly into gear again, and I was hyperaware of everything happening in microsecond snapshots in my head.

The magazine slipped free of the butt of his pistol, and his left hand dropped to his side. I dropped the TK rod and grabbed Collins by the belt with my now-empty right hand, then rolled using my amplified strength, drawing him across the top of my body, so that for a part of a second, we were face to face. Collins' eyes were wide as I flung him over my body and onto the first step. From the other side, I heard the full magazine slide home into the pistol, and the empty hit the floor with a loud clatter. While my face was full on to the floor, I heard the tiny, almost imperceptible *snap* of the catch on the side of the pistol being worked, and I heard the slide click home. My left hand felt like it weighed a ton as I came to my feet, facing King, for the first time realizing I had grabbed the pistol instead of the paintball gun. Our gazes met, and his smile faded. A little red dot appeared on his chest. From somewhere, I heard a single *click* as things seemed to pause again for heartbeat. An explosion hammered my ears, and I flinched as my left hand told me it had been kicked hard.

My eyes opened to see the red dot on King's chest replaced by a hole in his shirt, and a widening circle of red around it. A thin wisp of acrid smoke drifted up from the barrel of the gun in my hand like a silent accusation. I blinked in shock as King staggered and put his empty hand to the wound in his chest, then looked back at me when it came away shaking and covered with his blood. He took a couple of unsteady steps backward, then his legs just gave out, and he ended up on his butt. The gun in his right hand fell to the ground, and he just sat there with a blank look on his face. He stared at me for a few seconds, then he blinked, and his expression went flat. Whatever spark of life was left in his eyes faded, and he slumped to the side. Off in the distance, the echo of the gunshot rolled across the black water of the lake.

I set the gun down gently. I had just shot a man and watched him die. There had been no dignity in his death, no glory in killing him, no snappy one-liner on my lips to punctuate the moment. There was fear and anger, but no happiness that he was dead. The only comfort I found was that Dr. C and Officer Collins were still alive, and that Mom and Dee were safe.

"Chance?" Dr. C said gently, suddenly at my side. "Are you okay?"

Collins came up beside me, his face drawn tight with pain.

"You were right about me, Dr. C," I whispered. "Dulka turned me into a weapon."

Collins reached down and picked up the pistol, then wiped it off with his sleeve. He hefted it and gave me long, searching look before he spoke. "Corwin, get the kid outta here before my backup gets here. I got this." He grimaced as he pulled his shirt free of the Kevlar vest that had saved him, then went to King.

I let Dr. C lead me up the steps, still numb from what I'd just done. Shade and the pack were staring down at me from the edge of the arena, and Lucas and Wanda were peeking up over the edge. What did they think of me now?

"Hey, kid," Collins called from the bottom. I turned to look at him. "I owe you, big time."

It took me a moment to find my voice. "No. You don't."

Epilogue

~ You can't judge someone for killing a person. It's how they react afterward where you see their true character. ~ Thaddeus Bonewitz, Right Hand of Death

I'd killed a man. How was I supposed to end that day? What kind of person did that make me? My thoughts circled as Shade and I huddled together in the camp's beat-up chapel, watching the world deal with what I'd done. Further down the hill, we could see the flashing blue and red lights of police cars and ambulances. Dr. C had left with Lucas and Wanda, and the rest of the pack had scattered into the night. Collins was probably lying through his teeth to cover for me with the cops, and my friends had to avoid me so Dr. C could cover for me with the Conclave. I had no idea where Sinbad was, or even when he'd left.

I turned away from the window and walked across the open floor of the chapel. The black case I'd seen the other night was laying open on the ground, with a crumpled piece of paper on the ground next to it. I crouched next to it and picked up the paper. In the moonlight, I could see writing in a flowing, neat hand.

The contents have been relocated for security reasons. Sorry for the inconvenience,

Sydney Chomsky, Wizard

A tarot card lay under the note, and my fingertips tingled as I flipped it over. The Page of Swords looked up at me with blade in hand. A grim smile spread across my face. Mr. Chomsky hadn't died for nothing. In the end, he'd beaten King by being smarter. I folded the note and slipped it and the tarot card into my back pocket. Shade stepped in close and put her arms around me.

"King didn't give you much of a choice, Chance," she whispered in my ear. She snuggled up closer to me and I felt her lips brush my cheek. "You didn't go in there intending to kill anyone."

"Right. I had good intentions," I said. "I know what the road to Hell is paved with. What I did tonight…was more of the same. I just wish I knew the way back. I don't even know what that road to redemption looks like."

She planted a long, slow kiss on me. After we came up for air, she stepped back and gave me a slow smile. Then, she reached down and pulled her shirt over her head, revealing a white satin bra and perfect skin that seemed to glow in the moonlight. With a smile, she reached behind her back for the bra clasp, and I heard the snap of it coming undone.

"Shade, what are you doing?"

She slipped one of the straps off her shoulder. Her eyes slid to me, and I could feel the heat in her gaze. "Saying thank you," she whispered. She leaned in and kissed me.

Much to my monkey brain's disappointment, I put my hand on her shoulder and pushed her back. Where she had been pressed against me, warmth was replaced with cold night air. "No, Shade."

"Why? What's wrong?" Confusion was plain in her voice. "Don't you...want me?" Her tone dropped to a seductive purr.

"Hell, yeah! But right now, you think it's something you owe me." I slid the strap of her bra back onto her shoulder. She tilted her head to one side as I kissed her gently. "If you're gonna be with me, it should be because you *want* to, not because you think you *have* to."

For a long moment, she was silent, and I could feel her body trembling. "No one ever let me say 'no' before," she finally said in a quavering voice. She leaned into me, and I felt hot tears on my skin through my borrowed t-shirt.

As she cried on my shoulder, I realized I *did* know what the road to redemption was paved with: hard choices. We stood there and held onto each other as the shadows made their slow way across the chapel floor, until her tears and silent sobs stopped. Without a word, she looked up at me and gave me a soft, slow kiss.

"Thank you, Chance," she whispered. I felt my face get hot, and she turned away. She looked over her shoulder at me as she reached behind her back and refastened her bra. In one smooth motion, she bent down and scooped up her top and slipped it on, then headed for the door.

"They're gone," she said after a quick look down the hill. I followed her out, and she tossed her helmet to me, then straddled her bike and thumbed the starter.

She took an overgrown maintenance road out to the highway, and as we rode toward town, I found my thoughts going back to the note in the case, and all the things that meant. The Maxilla was still out there, somewhere…wherever Mr. Chomsky had hidden it. The Conclave would think it had been stolen, and Gedeon would think that the Conclave had tricked him. And I was the only person who knew that neither side had it. If it was as powerful and important as Dr. C had said it was, it didn't take much to imagine how far either side would go if they thought it was still up for grabs.

I sighed and uttered a soft, but heartfelt, curse. All I'd wanted when I got away from Dulka was to have my own life. And when my Mom had walked through the door in the police station, I thought I would get to have something like a normal life.

Normal. Me. I rolled that thought around in my head for a few seconds and tossed it out as a lie. I was a fifteen-year-old warlock, a demon's runaway slave, a fugitive from the wizard's Conclave, and I had a man's life-blood on my hands. I owed a demon lawyer a debt of honor. Oh, yeah: the girl I had the hots for was a werewolf. I barely shared the same *planet* as "normal."

As we turned down my street, I remembered that I was very late, and my mom would be REALLY pissed. Shade left a gentle kiss on my cheek before she rode off, and I headed for the door, and the inevitable ass-chewing that awaited me. Compared to the last eight days, though, being grounded for a month was almost a blessing. I'd barely survived my first week of freedom, and I could hardly imagine what the next three years were going to be like. I had thought that when I escaped from the demon, my life would be easier. Now I knew that Hell had nothing on high school.

The Demon's Apprentice

Dear Reader,

Thanks for picking up The Demon's Apprentice. This book has always been close to my heart because it was my first completed novel. The Demon's Apprentice was originally published by a small press in 2010, but I recently regained the rights to it. If this is your first time reading this, I hope you enjoyed your first foray into Chance's world. It can be a dark place sometimes, but it's never boring. Even I'm surprised by some of the things I find there.

Like any author, my success is in the hands of my readers, and I'm glad you're along for the ride. I always appreciate honest reviews, and I'd love to hear what you thought of the book. Your feedback is vital to the process of my improvement as a storyteller, and I always want to write better books for you. You can leave a review here.

Chance will return in Page of Swords in February. I'm very excited to have this series out once more, and I hope you'll join me once again as I return to New Essex and Chance's adventures. Turn the page to see what awaits in Page of Swords!

Sincerely,
Ben Reeder

Page of Swords

Chapter 1

By eight on Friday night, my weekend was already dying an ugly death. My favorite moping place, the back booth at Dante's, gave me a great view of the dance floor and the stage. It was perfect for those nights when I showed up to Dante's without Shade. For the fourth week in a row. Suicidal Jester seemed to hover over the crowd as they played one of their own songs, "Maddened Heart," and Mike Destine was moaning the lyrics into the microphone:

> *Where are you now? In the middle of the dark,*
> *In my mind's fevered eye, I see you laid down,*
> *In grace pale and stark. My maddened heart watches over you,*
> *And you can't know, you don't know to care, but I don't care!*

His voice rose on the last word, and the lead guitar matched him as it launched into a screaming solo. In the crowd, I could see a familiar mane of flame red hair as I found Shade. She had her arms up in the air as her hips writhed like a snake, dancing with her eyes closed to a rhythm it seemed like only she could hear. Shiny black boots flowed up over her knees and clung to her thighs, leaving a few inches of pale white skin showing before a painted-on black leather miniskirt wrapped itself tight around her hips. The top of her skirt disappeared under a black satin corset that was laced up the back; the only color in the outfit came from criss-crossing lines of blood red ribbon cinching her into it. Even though she was dancing by herself, I knew she hadn't come alone, and that twisted the knife in my weekend a little more.

"Dude!" Lucas yelled from across the table. I could barely hear him over the music. "Maybe she brought him here for some kind of Pack business or something!"

He'd taken off his denim trenchcoat, showing off his black t-shirt that read, "I have epiphanies." Strands of black hair brushed his eyebrows and the tops of his new glasses, narrow-lensed with half rims. He'd gotten titanium frames and high impact lenses after his old pair had been broken for the second time around Yule.

Beside him, Wanda was in a red top with black hearts all over it, wearing a red choker trimmed in black lace and red lace fingerless gloves that hugged her elbows. Her new pentacle, a silver star flanked by crescent moons, rode over her shirt. Her mom had given it to her when she'd started her year-and-a-day training as a Wiccan dedicant, and it never came off, no matter how much crap she caught about it at school. Below the table, she had on a red and black plaid skirt and red lace stockings that matched the gloves. One of her heavy wedge-heeled boots was on the seat beside me, black with red flames coming up off the soles.

"What kind of *business* is she doing in a *mini-skirt?*" I yelled back.

"But Chance, she's so into you!" Wanda said.

She tried to give me a reassuring smile as she brushed a few bright red strands of hair away from her cheek. The red framed her faltering smile and the rest of her hair, cut in a black line that ran just below her ears, swung as she nodded. Always the optimist, Wanda never thought Shade would date anyone else.

But my thoughts always went back to the last kiss Shade and I had shared at Imbolc last month. One of the problems with trying to date a werewolf is the danger of having your face eaten while you're making out, and that had come damn close to happening when we'd tried to move past kissing. But the memory of just kissing Shade made my lips tingle, and reminded me of what I couldn't have. She'd told me after that she needed an alpha. Something I wasn't, and short of a werewolf bite, I never would be.

"She's here with another guy, and she's dressed to thrill. I'm pretty damn sure she's not here on business, and it looks like she really not that into me. So stop trying to cheer me up, okay? Besides, it's better this way." I said the last quietly.

I tried to want her to be happy, but it hurt like all the Nine Hells just to see her. I wanted her to be happy with *me*, but that didn't seem like it could happen. So, I figured the best thing to do was avoid her. Made it easier to keep my hands to myself that way. And, it made it easier for her to find what she needed.

"Yeah," I lied to myself a little more. "It's better this way." It was Friday . . . yay. I tried to let the music wash over me and forget everything else.

"Are you the guy who does magick?" a girl asked as I was losing myself in the music. She'd almost had to yell to make herself heard over the pulsing beat of the band.

I tried not to grimace and looked down from the stage show to look her over. She was kinda pretty, I guessed, but I could only see the right side of her face. The left side was covered with a curtain of brown hair streaked with black. Half of an oval face peered at me, the one visible brown eye giving me the same once over I was giving her. I figured she was fifteen, the same age as me, maybe sixteen, probably a sophomore. A faded peace symbol was stretched across the front of her dark blue t-shirt, tight enough that I could see she had at least one piercing her parents weren't supposed to know about. Her dark gray hoodie hid most of the other side, so I couldn't tell if she had a matched set or not. A pair of tight black jeans rode low on her hips. All this girl lacked to make her a complete Emo chick was the dark eye make up. Her black-tipped fingernails tapped against the tab of her hoodie's zipper as she waited for me to answer.

"What?" I yelled back.

I gave Lucas and Wanda a quick glance across the table in our booth, and caught a nod from Lucas. He seemed to know the girl.

"You're Chance Fortunato, right?" she leaned forward. "You're the guy who does magick!"

The song ended just as she yelled it out, and people around us turned and stared at her while the rest of the crowd cheered. I gave her a glare as Dante's filled with sound. The girl pulled an empty chair up to the end of the table and sat down.

"Do I have a sign over my head that says 'I do magic tricks!' or something?" I asked as the band picked up with cover of Linkin Park's *Shadow of the Day*.

Nobody covered Linkin Park like Jester, and it was one of my favorite songs, which just pissed me off even more. More than the fact that she was right. I did know magick. Lots of it was black sorcery, but I was learning some new stuff. Her being right didn't piss me off as much as the fact that she was yelling it out in public. I wasn't exactly on the Conclave's good side these days. They didn't care why I'd worked for a demon, just that I had. My demon master had called me his apprentice; I called me his slave. Guess who the guys in white robes believed? Go figure.

"My friend Robbie told me you broke a love spell some psycho bitch cast on him a couple of months ago. You gotta help me out."

Her story fit, the name was right, and the time was pretty close. I leaned back in the seat and crossed my arms so I could favor her with a glare that should have peeled a couple of layers of skin off her face. As she matched my look, I remembered Dr. Corwyn telling me after the fact that I shouldn't have told the guy I'd broken the spell. It sucked when he was right, especially since that was most of the damned time. My weekend wasn't going to end well.

"And?"

"I need your help. I think . . . someone put a spell on my girlfriend."

Ben Reeder was born in Honolulu, Hawai'I and grew up in Corpus Christi, Texas, reading Asimov, Tolkien and Robert E. Howard, among other authors. Even as a boy, he loved telling his own stories and he always dreamed of being a writer. He has served in the US Air Force and worked a variety of jobs. He's been a member of the SCA, done live-action role-playing and acquired a skill set that would make his characters proud.

The Demon's Apprentice was his first book, and since it was first released, he has also authored the Zompoc Survivor series. You can keep up with him on his website www.chancefortunato.com.

Made in the USA
San Bernardino, CA
19 September 2015